BLOOD FALLS

BLOODFALLS

BLOOD FALLS

Tom Bale

WINDSOR
PARAGON

First published 2011
by Preface
This Large Print edition published 2012
by AudioGO Ltd
by arrangement with
The Random House Group Ltd

Hardcover   ISBN: 978 1 4713 1076 8
Softcover   ISBN: 978 1 4713 1077 5

British Library Cataloguing in Publication Data available

Printed and bound in Great Britain by
MPG Books Group Limited

For my son, James

CHAPTER ONE

They set a trap for him, and it nearly worked. Despite all his precautions, years of living like a hunted animal, he didn't see it coming.

He was a needle in a haystack. That was what he'd allowed himself to believe. They would never find him, because they didn't have the organisation, or the dedication. Because they weren't clever enough.

But he was wrong. What he'd overlooked was that they didn't need to be particularly clever. All they needed was patience, determination and a little bit of luck. Spend long enough combing through the haystack and eventually that needle was going to tumble into their grasp.

Whether it landed flat, or stabbed them in the process, was another matter . . .

*   *   *

It was the corner that saved him. The corner, the high scaffolding, and his own generous measure of luck.

Five minutes earlier he'd been at ground level, drinking a coffee that the householder had brought out. As he mounted the ladder to get back to work, Ryan had said, 'Knock off for lunch in ten.'

'Really?'

'Yeahhh, why not?' Even Ryan sounded slightly taken aback by his own generosity: he often worked all day without a break. 'We've been grafting since half-seven.'

1

Fair point, and Joe spent the next few minutes in pleasant anticipation of a hot pub lasagne and a refreshing pint of lager.

The two men came round the corner from Sion Hill, just twenty or thirty feet away. They were on foot, and the acute angle between the pavement and the top level of the scaffolding meant that Joe wasn't visible from below. Had they been in a car, or approached from further along the street, they'd have spotted him at once.

And they were talking. Nothing he could distinguish clearly, but Joe tuned into the coarse estuary accents—voices that always put him on guard. He crouched down, choosing that moment to refresh the paint on his brush. One of the men called out: 'Oy, mate?'

The shout made Joe's stomach tighten. He stayed low as the men closed in. Heard a tiny metallic clink as someone's watch or ring made contact with a scaffolding pole.

Joe leaned over, just enough to catch a glimpse of the two men standing beneath him. One of the faces he didn't recognise at all, but the other was grimly familiar.

It was the face of a man he had killed.

*   *   *

Twenty to twelve on a cool overcast Tuesday in early October—an autumn of heavy rain, with more expected in the coming days. Ryan felt that this week represented their best opportunity for outside work. So far he'd been right, although all morning the clouds had been massing over the Avon gorge.

Ryan's practice was to use ladders wherever

possible; failing that, a lightweight mobile scaffolding tower. But the property they were renovating was a substantial Georgian town house, three storeys high. Nothing less than fixed scaffolding would suffice.

Unlike most of the other houses in the street, which wore a fine stippled render, this one was clad in a thick pebble-dash. Joe had assumed they'd spray it, but Ryan told him that would be a waste of time.

'To get the paint into the gaps you have to spray really slowly. Then it starts dripping everywhere, so you keep stopping to mop up. Easier just to use a brush in the first place.'

Easier was a relative concept, Joe soon discovered, for a process that involved prodding the brush into crevices an inch deep, then working it round to ensure that the paint coated the entire surface area.

And there was the mess to contend with: not much less than a spray would have caused. In addition to full-length overalls, Joe was wearing gloves, goggles and a woolly hat. As the brush jabbed at the render it threw back a fine mist of droplets that through the course of the day would coat his body with little dots of plasticised paint.

But right now he had only gratitude for the arduous nature of the task. A smooth render would have had him perched on a ladder, helplessly exposed.

Careful not to make a sound, he eased the goggles off and set them down. Removed his hat and mopped the sweat from his face. Half his attention was on the conversation below; the other half weighing up the options available to him.

3

The man he didn't recognise spoke first. 'We're looking for this bloke. You seen him anywhere?'

A pause. Joe risked another peek over the edge. The man had grey hair, slicked back and thinning to nothing at the crown. He wore jeans and a battered old brown leather jacket. He was showing Ryan a photo.

Joe couldn't see it clearly, but he didn't need to. He knew exactly who they were hunting.

*   *   *

Ryan sniffed. 'Nope.'

'Only he's supposed to be working round here.'

'Casual stuff,' the other man cut in. 'Cash in hand, probably.'

This was Danny Morton, a slight, twitchy man with narrow shoulders and long bony fingers. Short-cropped brown hair that stuck out at all angles, and a thin face with a pink puckered scar, the size of a pea, in the centre of his left cheek.

'I steer clear of all that,' Ryan told him. 'Not worth the aggro to fiddle it these days. For all I know, you could be Customs and Revenue.'

'Do I look like the fucking taxman?' Danny growled.

Ryan ignored the question. 'Who is he, anyway?'

'His name's Joe Clayton,' the other man said. 'Sure you haven't seen him?'

'He might have changed since this was taken,' Danny added. 'Different hairstyle. A few years older.'

'Still don't know him. Sorry.'

Joe thought Ryan sounded convincing enough, but he wanted the conversation over. The longer it

4

went on, the more chance that Ryan would slip up.

A shuffling sound as Leather Jacket withdrew the photo and maybe even started to move away, but Joe could sense a lingering tension. He imagined Ryan's mind processing what he'd been told and understood the young man's dilemma. There was one question that a person with nothing to hide would be compelled to ask.

'What d'you want him for, then?'

It was Danny Morton who replied. 'He murdered my brother.'

CHAPTER TWO

Joe didn't dare move. Given what Ryan had just heard, even a tiny unconscious glance upwards could give him away.

His options for self-defence were limited, to say the least. Perhaps wait until Danny or his sidekick reached the top of the ladder, then swing a can of paint at them . . .

Except that they wouldn't need to mount an assault on the scaffolding. Joe knew that Danny routinely carried a gun—and he was deranged enough to use it.

That meant flight was the better alternative. Smash a bedroom window, get out through the backyard and across the rear of the neighbouring property. He should gain twenty or thirty seconds' head start on them: it might just be enough.

He hoped that neither course of action would be necessary. It all depended on Ryan now. Whether he would stay loyal or whether he would crack.

'Jesus,' Ryan said. 'So he's on the run?'

'Four years.'

'And is he, like, dangerous? You know how the police always say you're not to approach—'

'We know he's round here somewhere, and we want him.' Danny sounded impatient, as well he might. Ryan's inquisitive nature had driven Joe mad at times over the past few weeks; right now it was a tactical masterstroke.

'I'll keep my eye out,' Ryan promised. 'I assume the cops are on the hunt for him as well?'

From Danny, only a grunt. His colleague must have offered a card or a note.

'You see him, call us on that number. There'll be a drink in it.'

'Unless you don't want cash in hand?' Danny muttered scornfully.

'Yeah, no, that's great. I'm happy to help. I mean, no one wants a murderer on the loose.'

Don't overdo it, Joe thought. Fortunately Ryan's interrogators had tired of him and were moving away. The bad news was that they continued along Princess Victoria Street, where the pavement ascended on a gentle but—for Joe—potentially fatal gradient.

He lowered himself down, wincing as the scaffolding boards shifted and groaned on the transoms. Lying flat on his belly, head turned to the side, he felt like a butterfly pinned under glass. He prayed that the toeboard would be high enough to conceal him from view.

Ryan was back at work, whistling furiously as he

painted. Joe took that to be a signal of sorts: *Stay where you are.*

Sure enough, after a couple of minutes he heard Ryan put down his brush and tap on one of the uprights.

'They've gone.'

'You sure?'

'Yeah. Do you wanna come down and tell me what the hell is going on?'

*   *   *

Ryan Whittaker was short on stature but big on character, a successful entrepreneur at twenty-four. As well as the building and decorating business, he was also a key investor in his older sister's chain of hairdressing salons and had recently set up a website selling, of all things, designer baby clothes and maternity wear.

He'd agreed to employ Joe on a trial basis, carefully monitoring his skill and diligence for several days before pronouncing him acceptable. Contrary to what he'd told Danny Morton, he was perfectly willing to pay cash in hand. The only source of tension had been Joe's vagueness about his past, but Ryan had accepted that it was information he could do without. He was simply glad to have found someone willing to work as hard as he did himself.

'And it's not like you're all that young, either,' he'd added with sublime tactlessness.

'Pretty ancient, compared to you,' Joe had said.

'Well, yeah. But you know how to graft, don't you? Not like lads my age, pissing away their wages and then calling in sick 'cause they've slept till

7

bloody lunchtime. What kind of attitude is that?'

In a gruff military tone, Joe had declared: 'Bring back national service!'

'Bring back . . .?'

'Doesn't matter.'

A slow grin from Ryan. 'No, I get you. I sound like a miserable old sod, slagging off the youth of today.'

'They're not all bad, are they? You aren't. Your sister isn't.'

'I s'pose not,' Ryan had conceded. 'Becoming an employer, it changes your view of the world. So bloody frustrating to see people choosing *not* to do what's best for them.' He'd sighed. 'Though we're all guilty of that at times, aren't we? We're all a bit fucked-up.'

'Yep, we are,'. Joe had agreed. 'But trying our best not to be.'

*   *   *

As soon as his feet hit the ground, Joe pulled off his gloves and started undoing his paint-splattered overalls.

'I'm sorry. I owe you more of an explanation than I can give you right now.'

'Is it true you killed that guy's brother?'

'There's more to it than that, but yes.'

'And you're wanted by the law?'

'No. I was a police officer when I did it.'

'Ahhh.' Visibly relieved, Ryan's hand drifted towards his cheek. 'What's with his scar?'

'A screwdriver. That happened when he tried to kill me.'

'Bloody hell. So how did they track you down?'

8

'That's what I need to find out. Once I'm well away from here.'

Joe stepped out of the overalls but kept his trainers on. Underneath he was wearing jeans and a black T-shirt. He bundled up the overalls and stowed them on the lowest deck of scaffolding, next to their empty coffee cups.

'Any idea where you'll—' Ryan gave a twitch of a smile. 'No, you can't tell me, can you?'

'Best not.'

'Fair enough. But I'm sorry to see you go.'

As they shook hands, Joe's gaze was drawn back to the overalls. There was something troubling him. Something he'd missed . . .

The coffee cups.

Maybe he'd been lucky, he thought. Maybe they hadn't noticed the cups at all, or had seen them but had failed to make the connection: that Ryan wasn't working alone.

'What's up?' Ryan said.

Joe didn't reply. He was listening. There was a lot of traffic noise from the streets around them, but one engine sounded louder, more urgent than the rest.

He turned, saw a car roaring towards them. It was a beaten-up old Ford Granada: just what he'd expect them to use. Probably legally acquired but unregistered, set to be junked when the assignment was complete.

There were two men inside, their faces still indistinct at this distance. But the driver wore a brown leather jacket.

CHAPTER THREE

The car picked up speed. From the passenger side Danny Morton leaned out of the window, his left arm stretching towards Joe. It didn't make much sense until Joe realised that there was something in Danny's hand.

'Gun!' Joe shoved Ryan away from him and leapt in the other direction. Both men hit the ground as a shot rang out, the noise a shocking boom in the stillness of the residential street. The bullet struck the front of the house, gouging out a chunk of pebble-dash and spraying them with fragments. The Granada was weaving in the road, the driver flapping his arm at Danny, suggesting a disagreement over tactics.

Even with Morton firing wild, Joe knew that a ricochet could be just as deadly: the lattice of scaffolding poles offered no real protection. He got to his feet.

'I'll draw them away,' he told Ryan, who was lying face down on the pavement and seemed too shocked to respond.

Running for the corner, Joe stayed low, using a row of parked cars for cover. He was a little surprised by Danny's loss of control. He'd always imagined that the Morton family would prefer to capture him alive. Danny in particular had a grisly aptitude for torture, but his old man, Doug, and even Valerie, his ferocious hard-as-nails mother, were almost as bloodthirsty.

But there was no time to dwell on it. He had to focus on an escape route. Turning into Sion Hill, with the grand Georgian facade of the Avon Gorge hotel directly opposite, Joe sprinted up the hill towards the east tower of the Clifton suspension bridge. A trick of the perspective made the thick supporting chains seem as delicate as a spider's web.

Perhaps he should try to cross the bridge, he thought, then get hold of a car. Steal one. Hijack one, if he had to. Whatever it took to survive.

*   *   *

No. The bridge was a bad idea. Far too exposed, and there were lots of people around. Lots of cameras, too. Joe needed a route that would be difficult to follow in a car.

Cutting right at the next junction, he crossed the road and leapt up onto a grass bank. Then into Sion Lane, a narrow street of quaint cottages and slightly dilapidated workshops. It was clogged with parked cars. Better still, about halfway up it veered left, so he'd be out of sight within seconds.

Just before the bend he risked a look back, and his heart sank. Danny Morton was pursuing him on foot. The only consolation was that he no longer had the gun in his hand.

Joe put on a burst of speed. He had no idea where the Granada had gone, whether the driver would have been smart or lucky enough to intercept him at the top of Sion Hill. Bracing himself for an ambush, he emerged from the lane, the bridge now away to his left, and checked the traffic. No sign of the Granada.

He dashed across the road, narrowly avoiding a collision with a pickup truck. Its horn blared as Joe

11

made it to the opposite verge. Now he was on the edge of Clifton Down, an area of parkland with plenty of mature trees to give him cover, just in case Danny still felt inclined to take another shot at him.

It was a steep ascent. Although Joe had been working hard for Ryan, he'd neglected his normal exercise regime for several weeks and he was punished for that lack of fitness now: his lungs burning, his knees jarring on the uneven ground. But he knew he was running for his life, and that meant enduring any amount of pain.

He negotiated a diagonal path across the Down, heading broadly in the direction of Christ Church. Several times he glanced over his shoulder and saw he was extending his lead, but there was no mistaking the fury, the determination on Morton's face. Having got this close to Joe, he wasn't about to give up now.

Then Joe heard him yelling: 'Here! Fucking here, you twat!'

He looked round. Danny was facing Gloucester Row, gesturing frantically. He was mightily pissed off, and Joe could see why. Having gone the wrong way, the Granada was caught in a line of traffic heading for the bridge.

Then a quick double-beep caught his attention. Not from the Granada, but off to Joe's left, near the church.

Danny reacted to it as well. Joe saw the triumphant smile on his face as he nodded and made a broad sweeping motion with his arm. Its meaning was clear: *Cut around and head him off.*

For Joe, it was like a punch in the gut. They had a second car.

It was an old Vauxhall Astra. Like the Granada, it had seen better days, but it was more than adequate for its purpose. There seemed to be only one occupant. He was quick to respond to Danny's command, racing along Clifton Down Road, no more than sixty or seventy yards away from Joe.

Crossing into Canynge Road, Joe heard the distant screech of tyres and a chorus of angry car horns—no doubt in response to some kind of illegal manoeuvre on the part of the Granada's driver. Soon he would be back in the chase.

Thankfully Joe was now heading downhill. Running flat out, he calculated that he had no more than ten or fifteen seconds before the Astra caught up with him. He needed to vanish.

The opportunity presented itself halfway along the street. He passed an office block on his right, then a narrow car park. The parking spaces backed on to a row of half a dozen tiny terraced gardens, bordered by a brick wall about five feet high. Perfect.

A quick look back: no one in sight. Joe raced through the car park and dropped to his knees behind a red minibus. A moment later he heard the Astra roaring past. As soon as it had gone, he hauled himself up onto the final section of wall. From here he was able to leap across a narrow alley and clamber up onto a flat-roofed building.

In a crouching run he crossed to the far corner and lowered himself onto another flat-roofed structure that faced along the next street. Breathing hard, he caught a faint tang of chlorine in the air.

It was only when he dropped to the pavement

that Joe found he'd been climbing over the premises of Clifton High School's swimming pool and gym. As he hit the ground, a woman locking her car turned and gaped at him. He straightened up, gave her a polite smile and was on the move again, his ankles protesting at every step.

At the bottom of Clifton Park Road he went left, checking in both directions for Morton or the cars. Still nothing. He crossed the road and turned right. Now he was into the home straight: College Fields.

It was a beautiful place to live, a wide, quiet street with the school's playing fields on one side and a succession of large detached properties on the other. Big square bay-fronted villas, faced with pale Bath stone. Some had been converted to flats, but others remained as single dwellings.

Joe's landlord was Lindsey Bevan, a retired professor of philology. After several decades of renting rooms to students he'd become tired of the aggravation and now ran something of a cross between a modern B&B and an old-fashioned boarding house. There were two long-term residents, Audrey and William, both retired academics and contemporaries of Lindsey's. All three tended to be effusively nice to Joe even while they bickered like children among themselves.

Arriving in late August, Joe had negotiated an attractive deal by paying for the first two months in advance. Lindsey had been more than amenable to Joe's offer to carry out maintenance on the property in return for use of the washing machine and other appliances.

It wasn't home—nowhere was home any more—but it was the best accommodation Joe had had in well over a year.

As he approached the house, there was no traffic in sight except for a refuse lorry passing the junction on Percival Road. The playing fields were deserted. He could see nothing untoward, nothing out of the ordinary, and yet he felt a tingling as the hairs rose on the back of his neck.

He slowed his pace. Directly ahead, a middle-aged woman emerged from her garden gate, a small dog scuttling beside her. She registered Joe's presence with a sniff of disapproval, then cut across the road to avoid him. That was when he spotted the girl.

She was standing in the road beside an ancient Peugeot hatchback, parked at the opposite kerb, almost parallel to Lindsey Bevan's home. Probably in her late teens or early twenties, she was short but bulky, wrapped in a pink fluffy cardigan over a tight denim skirt. Spiky blonde hair with dark roots and lots of big, cheap jewellery.

Her back was to Joe as she gazed over the roof of the car at the sports field. There was a phone at her ear, and it struck him that she was listening with an unusual intensity.

Joe reached the boundary of Lindsey's property. The house looked peaceful enough. Lindsey's Volvo estate was parked on the drive, next to a brand new Seat which belonged to a German family—some distant cousin of Audrey's who was staying for two nights.

Before he stepped through the gates Joe took another look at the girl. At the same time she glanced round, saw him and flinched, then turned away, speaking quietly but emphatically into the phone. Joe couldn't make out the words but the urgency, the tension in her body language, worked

15

like semaphore: *He's here. The man you're hunting is here.*

CHAPTER FOUR

Joe didn't want to believe it, but in his gut he felt certain. They hadn't just traced him to Bristol. They had found out where he was staying.

If he was right, the girl must be calling them in now, which meant he wouldn't have time to retrieve his belongings.

He'd become accustomed to travelling light, with no more than a rucksack needed for his clothes and toiletries. He had two fake identities and kept one of them on him at all times, together with a couple of hundred pounds in cash. The other ID and the rest of his savings were inside his lodgings, as were the only personal items that meant anything to him: photographs of his daughters.

As a natural precaution in a house he shared with strangers, Joe had made sure his valuables were well hidden. He'd stashed them in a far corner of the loft, beneath a layer of rock wool, having offered to lay fresh insulation for Lindsey. It should ensure they were safe from discovery, but that didn't make the prospect of leaving them any easier to bear.

He stayed on the pavement until he was level with the girl, then abruptly cut across the road. Once again she turned, instantly read the determination in his face and took a step backwards, bumping against her car.

'Give me that.' Joe grabbed her right hand,

16

squeezing the phone from her grasp.

She cried out and struck at him with her free hand, but he blocked it, keeping his arm raised to ward off further attack. As he brought the phone to his ear he heard Morton's voice: 'Stacey? You there? Stace?'

Joe disconnected the call and lobbed the phone over the high chain link fence onto the school field. The girl launched herself at him, clawing at his face and shrieking: 'You fucking bastard!'

He fought off her blows, not wanting to retaliate but aware that time was running out. Grabbing her shoulders, he spun her round and trapped her against the car. Pinned her arms against her sides and clamped one hand over her mouth. She made a muffled screeching noise in her throat.

'Be quiet, Stacey, or I'll have no choice but to hurt you. Nod if you understand.'

She bucked and writhed, trying to open her mouth enough to bite him. He tightened his grip until her resistance subsided. Finally, a nod.

'I'm also taking your car,' he said. As he moved his hand away from her mouth, she spat on his palm.

'It's my boyfriend's. He'll kill me—'

'Then you shouldn't have got involved.' Joe eased her round until she was facing the opposite kerb, then propelled her away from the car. She sprang back to confront him.

'Danny's gonna catch you. I hope he fucking rips you to pieces.'

Ignoring her, Joe opened the driver's door and got in. Fortunately, the key was in the ignition. He started the engine while fumbling for the lever to move the seat back. He caught movement in the wing mirror. The Astra had turned into College Fields and was coming up behind him.

* * *

Joe put the Peugeot into first gear and released the handbrake. His foot was on the accelerator, itching to get moving, but then he had a better idea. He stayed where he was.

Stacey was positioned in the middle of the road, gleefully beckoning the Astra and jabbing a finger at Joe: *Here he is*.

In the wing mirror Joe watched the Astra closing in: fifty yards, forty, thirty. Slowing down, but not too much. A situation like this, he guessed the driver wouldn't hit the brakes till the last minute, pulling up close to box him in.

Stacey grasped that Joe wasn't going anywhere and darted towards the car, her face contorted with hate.

'Fucking dead now, you are!'

That was when Joe put his foot down. The Peugeot lurched away from the kerb just as the Astra was about to draw alongside. Stacey was sandwiched between the two cars.

In other circumstances Joe might have been concerned for her well-being. Right now he couldn't care less. As he moved diagonally into the road she leapt back, straight into the Astra's path. The driver reacted on pure instinct, swerving right to avoid her. He was already braking hard, and the violence of the turn sent him skidding across the road. The Astra mounted the kerb and struck a stone pillar that marked the entrance to Lindsey Bevan's driveway.

The impact was like a bomb going off. The Astra's bonnet crumpled, a burst of steam escaping from the punctured radiator. Both front tyres had deflated, and that was good enough for Joe. It meant the Astra was out of the game.

Reaching the junction with Cecil Road, he looked left and saw the Granada speeding towards him. Danny Morton was back in the passenger seat, howling at the driver as he spotted his quarry.

Joe went right and accelerated as best he could. There were deep grinding noises as he moved through the gears, and the Peugeot's engine didn't sound too healthy. He willed it not to give up the ghost on him in the next few minutes.

From a tactical standpoint he knew it made little sense to keep the car. It was no match for the Granada's speed or power. Right now that advantage was negated by the terrain: short residential streets with frequent junctions. But if Joe tried to find a route out of the city in the Peugeot he would soon be outrun.

He took the next right, College Road, then left into Guthrie Road. The suspension groaned. He felt the tyres struggling to gain traction. The noise and the speed attracted anxious looks from a group of women pushing buggies along the pavement. He was skirting the grounds of Bristol Zoo, which meant these streets had a much higher concentration of pedestrians: a lot of scope for tragedy should either car lose control.

But he was committed now. There was no option but to keep going.

The Granada missed Joe's turn. It had to brake and reverse, while Joe raced past the zoo and took another quick right, slamming his own brakes on

19

at the last second when he saw a motor scooter approaching. The back wheel of the scooter had barely cleared his path when Joe sped forward. The Granada was closing in fast.

A left into All Saints Road, and Joe almost rammed a car that was double-parked on the corner. He managed to swerve round it, but in straightening up the Peugeot fishtailed and the offside rear scraped against a skip, making a noise like fingernails on a blackboard. A couple of builders ran into the road and watched, slack-jawed, as he accelerated away. In his rear-view mirror Joe saw the Granada looming up behind them and he winced, bracing himself for a terrible impact.

If Danny Morton had been at the wheel he probably would have ploughed into the builders, but his driver was slightly more merciful, leaning on the horn until the two men jumped out of the way. The Granada slowed, giving Joe a few more precious seconds. Now he had to make that time count.

*   *   *

All Saints Road was another quiet, leafy residential street. It ran straight for a couple of hundred yards, then gently curved to the right. By the time he reached the bend Joe had managed to coax the ailing Peugeot up to sixty miles an hour: an insanely reckless speed.

Thankfully the road was clear. The junction with St John's Road was coming up fast. Tall trees and a four-storey building obscured his view before the turn, but he knew he would have to take a calculated risk.

He worked the brake, slowing to fifty, then forty, then he changed down to second gear and went back to the accelerator, the engine screaming as the Peugeot lurched onto the wrong side of the road. St John's Road was now dead ahead. A car passed from left to right, but there was nothing coming in the other direction.

Praying it stayed that way, Joe steered a wide arc to take the junction without reducing his speed. The Peugeot slithered and squealed its way around the corner. Joe was glad of the noise— the 'calculated' part of the risk being that anyone travelling along St John's Road would hear him coming and take avoiding action.

The only traffic heading north was a cyclist, a young man wearing thick glasses and a lime-green helmet, wobbling to a halt just a few feet short of the junction. Joe raised a hand, not in thanks, but gesturing towards All Saints Road in warning: *There's another one coming.*

In a concession to the rules of the road, Joe flicked on the right indicator, kept the car in second gear and braked a little more before his next turn: into the car park for Clifton Down railway station. As he turned he checked the mirror and saw the Granada nosing out of All Saints Road, the bewildered cyclist mercifully still intact just beyond it.

The car park was long and narrow, on a steep downward slope, with parking bays on the right-hand side and the entrance to the station at the bottom of the hill. Joe threw the Peugeot into the first vacant space and jumped out, leaving the key in the ignition.

He sprinted down the hill, attracting odd looks

from a group of students loitering outside the Roo Bar. Once past the pub he veered left, staying close to the boundary wall. He was now in another car park, this one reserved for the university; more importantly, he was out of sight of anyone in the public car park.

Breathless, he couldn't help but slow his pace as he ran up the slope. At the top he glanced back and saw the Granada parked behind the Peugeot. Leather Jacket was standing between the cars, hands on hips. There was no sign of Danny Morton.

Joe emerged into Whiteladies Road, hoping he could lose himself in the lunchtime crowds around the Clifton Down shopping centre. There were lots of people about but they all gave him a wide berth. Catching his reflection in a shop window, he immediately saw why.

He was hot and dishevelled, the grimy T-shirt clinging to his skin, his face flushed and dotted with white paint. At just under six feet tall, with broad shoulders and a muscular physique, he looked like a sweaty, rampaging thug.

Time for Plan B, he thought, as the ideal solution rumbled to a halt on the other side of the road. Joe darted between the traffic, took one more look to make sure Morton hadn't caught up, then dug in his pocket for some change.

*   *   *

The bus had pulled up at the stop opposite the railway station. Joe didn't know exactly where it was heading, except that south on Whiteladies Road would carry him towards the city centre. Good enough for now.

The cool, damp weather had caused the windows to steam up. Joe took a seat halfway back, on the driver's side, cleared a patch of condensation with his index finger and peered through the glass.

Danny was standing at the entrance to the university car park, thumping his leg in frustration as he gazed up and down the street. In Danny Morton's world, buses were strictly for the poor and the weak. It wouldn't occur to him that Joe might escape on something so slow and inefficient.

As the bus nosed out into the traffic, Joe's last glimpse of Danny saw him stalking towards the railway station, one fist rubbing angrily at the scar on his cheek. Joe let out a long sigh and shut his eyes for a moment. *Too close for comfort.*

Then he made a call on his mobile. Ryan answered, his voice subdued: 'You're all right, then?'

'Just about, but they won't be happy. It occurred to me that they might pay you another visit.'

'Yeah, same thing crossed my mind. I've rescheduled a couple of inside jobs for this week. And I just recruited my cousin Dex to help out.'

'The bouncer?'

'Cage fighter, he is now.' A short laugh. 'He's a crap decorator, but he'll watch my back.'

'Ryan, I'm sorry I dragged you into this mess.'

'Not your fault, really. I just hope you manage to find a way out of it. I mean, you can't live all your life on the run, can you?'

The comment provoked a rueful smile from Joe. 'Actually, I thought I could. More fool me.'

23

CHAPTER FIVE

She woke to a headache like nothing she'd ever experienced. Her first waking breath was a gasp of pain. She longed to be unconscious again, but it seemed like a hopeless ambition.

Her eyes fluttered, and might have opened, but no light came in. She shut them tightly, kept her breathing as shallow as possible, her whole body tensed and utterly still, as if immobility would lessen the pounding in her skull. It made no difference.

Some time passed, and maybe she did drift off. Not sleep, but a kind of disassociation. She stepped away from the pain, moved to a state where she could assess it with some objectivity.

A blow to the head, perhaps. But surely that would be more localised? This was a sensation that seemed to fill her skull to bursting point; it went rolling down her spine, it leaked from her eyes like tears, or blood.

Blood. She lifted a hand to her face, touching the skin reluctantly, as though it belonged to someone else. It felt hot and puffy, damp in places and slightly sticky. But she didn't think it was blood; more like sweat and grime.

Beneath her head, then? She couldn't lift it, not when her skull was filled with molten lead, but she could turn it, she could feel the dry scrunch of her hair as she moved. It felt normal, without the tight, gloopy sensation that she associated with lying in a pool of blood.

She wasn't bleeding. She wasn't stuck, or

restrained. So why . . .?

She drifted off again. Her brain was clogged up, as though submerged in oil. Every thought came out tarred, contaminated by the greasy after-images of a nightmare: dirty jokes and dirty hands; street lights sliding beneath the roof of a car.

If she wasn't injured, had this been self-inflicted? God, she'd had hangovers before, dreadful ones, but nothing like this. She imagined her parents, offering their usual caution about drinking to excess: 'Now then, ———, we know—'

The memory came to a grinding halt.

Her name was missing.

What was her name?

*   *   *

She might have laughed, if she hadn't been so afraid. She had forgotten her own name, the way you sometimes forget the name of an actor on TV. Her mum was always doing that: *Isn't he the one who was in that thing with what's-his-name, the detective? In real life he's married to the woman from those silly adverts, you know the one I mean. She's got long hair and a really irritating voice . . . .*

Okay. Start with Mum and Dad. They worried about her overdoing the booze. She worked to produce a picture of them in her mind, but all she could summon was a generic middle-aged couple: grey hair, no distinguishing features. Who were they?

The absence was so disturbing that she let the question sink back into the tar. Another stray thought bobbed to the surface, like an air bubble.

Party.

There had been a party—no, *talk* of a party. She'd been in a pub, or perhaps a café, and the idea had been to move on.

Dirty jokes and dirty hands; streetlights sliding above her as she sank across the seat . . .

Somewhere better than this, he had said. In another town, not too far away. 'Come on, Jenny. You won't get a better offer than this.'

Jenny. She was Jenny.

*   *   *

Sweet relief. She had a name. An identity.

And maybe, just maybe, the pain in her head was easing slightly. She stopped trying to think and instead she focused on breathing better: slow and deep, not fast and shallow. More time passed, the pain receding like an outgoing tide, and when she felt calm and relatively clear-headed she opened her eyes to find—

Nothing.

She blinked, felt the tickle of her lashes. There was nothing over her eyes, nothing impeding her vision. She was in absolute darkness.

She lifted her arm in front of her face, only inches away, and couldn't see a thing. The panic squeezed her heart. She could be in a cavern or a coffin.

Not a coffin. Please, not that . . .

Tentatively, she raised her arm again, stretching, waving, and met no resistance. The air she stirred was cool and vaguely damp. Musty. There was no echo from the sound of her breathing. She wasn't in a coffin, at least. Probably a room of some sort. An underground room.

A cell.

And she was warm: a fever heat. She placed her hands on her face. Her cheeks were burning, her palms much cooler, almost cold. She patted her neck, her chest, and gasped. Her hands quickly moved down, confirming what she'd already feared.

She was naked. She had been stripped.

Gently, she slid her hand between her legs, provoking a fresh wave of pain so sharp that it made her retch. There was something sticky on her thighs, which dried as she rubbed it with her fingertips. *This* was blood.

She must have trusted him. But she wasn't a fool. How could she have been so careless?

Come on, Jenny. You won't get a better offer than this.

He'd taken her somewhere. She had to find the name. It started with T. Tre ... Treb ... Tren ...

No. Trel ... The first letters were T.R.E.L.

Concentrate, for God's sake. Find the name.

That was Jenny's brave voice, the one that made her strive for independence. But there was always a competing voice, lazy and cynical, that said: Why? What difference does it make?

It means I can think clearly. And if I can think clearly, I have a chance ...

She nearly had it. The name of the town floated above her like a banner towed by an aircraft, just a little too high to read. But she remembered him telling her where it was. Along the coast from Port Isaac, not far from that place where the famous chef lived.

Padstow. The chef was in Padstow.

And Jenny, Jenny was in ...

CHAPTER SIX

Trelennan.

The name had eluded Joe at first. It eventually came to him on the bus to Weston-super-Mare. Later, in WHSmith's, he looked it up in a road atlas and plotted his route to the north coast of Cornwall.

In Bristol he'd been wary of boarding a train at Temple Meads. Too much chance that Morton and his men would be prowling the stations. Instead he took another bus. It was an hour's journey to Weston, which gave him time to think about where he should go next.

The cash he carried with him wouldn't last long. He needed someone who could offer him sanctuary. Not family or friends: too dangerous. It had to be a connection that pre-dated his involvement with the Mortons.

One name popped into his head: Diana Bamber.

*   *   *

Before leaving Bristol, other precautions had been necessary. In Marks and Spencer he'd used the toilet to clean up, scrubbing flecks of paint from his face, and in the menswear department he had bought a zip-up beige jacket and a flat cap.

Together with a sandwich, some chocolate and a bottle of water, the bill had come to just over sixty pounds. A lot of money in the circumstances, but the clothes represented a simple but effective disguise. By stooping, and walking more slowly,

28

Joe could make himself appear a good twenty years older. From now on he wanted to avoid being recognised by anyone—and that included on CCTV.

Once in Weston he made a final call on his mobile phone. Lindsey Bevan sounded far less agitated than Joe had expected. The Astra had been abandoned outside his property, but because there were no reported injuries and the only other damage was to the gatepost, the police hadn't shown a lot of interest.

'They're sending someone along, but goodness knows when,' Lindsey told him. 'Is this connected to the men who were looking for you earlier?'

'Could be,' Joe admitted. 'What did they say?'

'They claimed a relative of yours had passed away. Apparently they've been searching for you for months in order to make sure you receive a substantial legacy.' He snorted. 'I was extremely suspicious, not least because of their manner and appearance. A pack of lies, is it?'

'Yes.'

'I'm sorry. They showed me a photograph. My instinct was to deny knowing you, but alas Audrey happened to walk past.' Lindsey tutted. 'Honestly, that woman. No attempt to gauge the mood. She just pipes up, at the top of her voice: "Oh, that's our Joe, isn't it?"'

Joe sighed. 'It's not her fault. I brought this on myself.' He told Lindsey that he'd have to relinquish the room and wasn't sure when he'd be able to collect his clothes. He made no mention of the valuables hidden in the loft. What Lindsey didn't know, he couldn't let on to anybody.

He also promised that he would one day pay for

29

the damage to the wall. Lindsey wouldn't hear of it.

'I have more than adequate insurance. You just take care, Joe. If you need anything, you know where I am.'

After the call Joe ditched the phone and bought a replacement for thirty pounds, which included ten pounds' airtime. Then to the railway station, where the cost and the convoluted nature of the journey nearly forced a change of plan—except he knew that he had no real alternative.

Trelennan it was. Another forty pounds from his rapidly dwindling funds.

And when he got there, if he couldn't find Diana—if she'd moved away, or was on holiday— then he knew he might end up sleeping on the streets tonight.

*   *   *

It took him more than six hours to reach the town. Three trains: starting with Weston to Taunton, then on to Plymouth, on a fast modern service that had come all the way from Dundee. Racing through the drab autumnal landscape, Joe quickly found himself dozing, his head lolling on his chest.

When he woke it was raining hard and already growing dark, the low cloud hastening the dusk. The sleep hadn't done much to refresh him. He felt tired and thick-headed, his body rimed in sweat.

Reaching Plymouth at a quarter to six and boarding a local train to Bodmin, he envied the returning commuters the mundane certainty of their evening plans: warm homes, welcoming families. Food and drink and mindless television. *Oh, to be comfortably numb . . .*

30

It was a close-run scrape with self-pity. Joe deflected it by concentrating on the question that was uppermost in his mind; the question he was almost afraid to ask.

How had they found him?

*   *   *

He must have made a mistake somewhere. Either that or he had been very, very unlucky. The third possibility, the one he was loath to contemplate, was that he had been betrayed.

No one in Bristol knew his true identity. He was simply Joe Carter, an itinerant manual worker. And no one else, no one from his past life, knew where he was.

There was only one former colleague he trusted enough to keep in touch with: Maz Milani. Even then, they mostly communicated via email, Joe preferring to use various Internet cafés in Bristol rather than his landlord's computer.

During Joe's period in exile, Maz had represented the only link to his past life. Two weeks ago, at Maz's instigation, Joe had contacted his brother Peter, who had sombre news. Their mother Ruth, now aged seventy-four, had been diagnosed with stomach cancer. It was in the early stages, and the prognosis was good, but Pete had urged him to get in touch. *It would be just the tonic she needs. If there's any way you can do it, please call her.*

So he had. From a phone box in Newport, a location he'd selected at random and reckoned was far enough away from Bristol to be safe.

She had been delighted to hear from him, although it had taken Joe the best part of ten minutes to reassure her that he was all right. Whenever he tried to discuss her condition she brushed his concerns aside, insisting that it was *his* well-being that mattered most.

Growing tearful, she'd said, 'I haven't given up, you know.'

'Good. Pete said the treatment has a high success rate.'

'Not that. I mean you and Helen, and the girls. I'm still praying that one day I'll see you all living as a family again.'

'So am I, Mum,' he'd said. 'So am I.'

It wasn't a lie, exactly, but it had felt to Joe that his voice lacked conviction. To hear his dream articulated by someone else served only to emphasise how unlikely it was ever to be realised.

That night, back in Bristol, he had drunk himself into oblivion at the knowledge that his entire family had been fractured by his stupidity and stubbornness, condemned to live in miserable isolation from each other. And rather than diminish over time, with each passing year, each month, each week, the pain of that isolation seemed to grow more intense.

Now Joe had to face the likelihood that the Mortons had tracked him down through the people he cherished the most.

CHAPTER SEVEN

From Bodmin he caught a bus to Wadebridge, where he discovered that the services to the coast had finished for the day. He was given the number of a local taxi firm and negotiated a price: fifteen pounds to take him to Trelennan.

The taxi arrived five minutes later. The driver was in his fifties, shaven-headed and overweight, rolls of fat wrapped around obsolete muscle. His thick forearms were a mass of crude tattoos and he wore a heavy gold crucifix round his neck. When he demanded the money up front, Joe didn't argue.

They chatted agreeably for the first few miles, until the conversation veered on to the subject of immigration. Within seconds the taxi driver was virtually foaming at the mouth, ranting about 'subhuman scum, bleeding us dry' and bemoaning the weakness of politicians who lacked the will to 'just round 'em up and send 'em back where they fucking came from.'

'And what if they come from here?' Joe asked.

'I don't give a toss what they try to claim—'

'You'd send them back, anyway?' As the driver nodded enthusiastically, still assuming he was talking to a like-minded individual, Joe added: 'Any of your family fight in World War II?'

'Uh? Yeah, my grandad and his brother. What about it?'

'Just strikes me as ironic, that's all. They fought a war against genocide and racism, and here you are talking about immigrants the same way the Nazis talked about Jews.'

The driver said nothing. The remainder of the journey was completed in a tense, glowering silence. The only illumination came from the taxi's headlights, their beams catching individual raindrops in glints of silver. The hedgerows lining the road were high and close, obscuring any sense of the landscape around them. It was like driving

33

through a long, bleak tunnel.

Its engine straining, the car laboured up a gradual but punishing slope. As they crested the hill the lights of a pub blinked into view. The road widened enough to acquire a centre line. Here and there they passed driveways, the entrances to farms and country cottages.

'Where d'you want dropping?' the driver asked, in a tone that suggested the answer ought to be: *Off a steep cliff*.

'Town centre's fine.'

The driver grunted. 'Tell you what, this'll do.' He braked hard, pulling over to the side of the road. 'You said Trelennan. Here it is.' He raised his left arm to point, his elbow almost jabbing Joe in the face. 'Centre's that way.'

He was clearly spoiling for a fight, but Joe had nothing to gain and much to lose if he rose to the bait. Climbing out, Joe muttered, 'Safe journey back.'

With matching insincerity, the driver cackled, 'You're gonna fucking love it here, you are.'

*   *   *

Joe watched the taxi driver execute a messy three-point turn and roar away. The night was chilly, with a brisk wind, but at least the rain was light enough to endure. He was already cold and tired and hungry: a bit of damp couldn't make it worse.

As far as he could tell, the town was laid out on a steep hillside, curving around a narrow bay. The road he was on appeared to follow a winding course down the hill, and he assumed it would lead

34

eventually to the seafront. That seemed like the best place to begin his search.

He passed a development of relatively modern bungalows, then the road narrowed as it descended through an older part of town: an attractively chaotic jumble of stone cottages, mostly well-maintained, adorned with hanging baskets and a variety of wall plaques. Lots of parked cars, slotted into every available space, but no passing traffic, no pedestrians. Barely eight p.m. and the town was asleep.

The severe slope put a strain on his ankles and shins. Joe found himself leaning back so as not to break into a run. Glimpsing the lights of distant properties to his left and right, his impression was of a bowl-shaped settlement, hidden away from the rest of the world. Directly ahead, the horizon was blotted out by cloud and rain. Somewhere below it the sea lay dark and forbidding: an absence of land rather than a presence in its own right.

He took a left turn into a wider street that looked to be a more direct route to the front. The homes along here were bigger, mostly rendered and painted white, with brick chimneys and roofs of slate or tile. For the first time there were pavements, and grass verges, and even a little passing traffic. Joe found himself watching every car closely, his muscles tensed for flight.

Ten minutes later he was on the seafront. A coast road ran parallel to a wide promenade, with a small harbour at roughly the midpoint. Joe crossed the road to get a better view of the buildings that faced out to sea.

The promenade was an attractive space, with ornamental granite benches positioned at regular intervals between clusters of palm trees in large stone planters. Illumination was provided by Victorian-style street lamps, throwing a weak light into the drizzle. Once again, there wasn't a soul to be seen.

Turning to face the town, Joe made out half a dozen signs for guest houses and B&Bs. He crossed back and headed to the nearest one. Tregary House was a plain square building, three storeys high and painted pink. As he reached the driveway he saw the sign in the downstairs window: CLOSED FOR WINTER.

He carried on in the direction of the harbour, passing several large Edwardian properties that had been converted into flats. The next B&B was called Britannia Place. A Union Jack hung wetly from a flagpole jutting from above the ground-floor window. There were three cars parked on the drive.

No sign to indicate whether they had vacancies, but at least it appeared to be open for business. Joe walked up to the front door and tried the handle. It was locked. There was a doorbell set in a brass surround in the shape of a rosette, and below it a sticker that said: NO HAWKERS, NO JUNK MAIL, NO FREE NEWSPAPERS.

He rang the bell. After half a minute the door was wrenched open by a man of about sixty, with suspiciously dark hair Brylcreemed into a razor-sharp side parting. There were two boil plasters on his neck, just below his left ear.

'Yes?' Not outwardly aggressive, but not friendly, either.

'I wonder if you can help me. I'm looking for Diana Bamber.'

The man's eyes narrowed. 'Who?'

36

'Roy and Diana Bamber? They ran a B&B down here. Roy died a few years back.'

'Nope. Can't help you.'

'All right. Supposing I wanted a room here, how much for one—?'

'We're full.'

'At this time of year?'

The man seemed furious that Joe was doubting his word. 'A couple of rooms are out of action. While we paint 'em.'

He was lying, and Joe held the man's gaze for a moment, to communicate that he knew. 'Can you tell me where I might find a place to stay?'

The man sucked air between his teeth. 'Bit late now.'

'It's twenty past eight.'

'Late,' the man repeated, '*and* it's late in the year. You want a room, you'd best get the bus out to Wadebridge.'

'There aren't any more buses.'

The man shrugged: *not my problem.* Without another word, he slammed the door.

Joe turned away, his neck tingling as his departure was tracked from one of the ground-floor windows. Despite his earlier efforts to smarten up, he wondered if he still looked too unsavoury. If so, he was unlikely to find anybody willing to give him accommodation tonight.

But the man hadn't just lied about not having a room available. Joe felt sure he'd seen a glimmer of recognition at the mention of Roy and Diana. The hotelier *did* know who Diana was, but had chosen not to say so.

CHAPTER EIGHT

The rain intensified as Joe continued towards the town centre. Even with his collar pulled tight he could feel it trickling down his neck. The spectre of a night in a bus shelter loomed large.

Across the road from the harbour there was a junction with what turned out to be the High Street. A pub on the corner, the Harbour Lights, had opaque windows, so Joe couldn't tell if it was doing a roaring trade or was completely empty. Probably the latter, judging by the lack of sound from within: no raised voices or muffled thump of music.

But there was a definite pounding noise coming from somewhere else. He realised it was beneath his feet.

He crossed the coast road and peered over the harbour wall. Water was churning and foaming as it gushed from a culvert that ran under the road. Several small boats moored close by rocked vigorously in the swirling current. This must be from a stream running down the hill. Parallel to the High Street, maybe.

He headed in that direction, climbing the steep slope, and again he was struck by the lack of activity. Where were the bored teenagers, clustered in doorways, or the older kids racing up and down on mopeds? Where was the *nightlife*, for Christ's sake?

As if in answer, a faint burst of laughter reached his ears. Coming from a pub, tucked away in a little plaza that also contained the library, an Italian restaurant and a barber shop. The restaurant was open but only one or two tables were occupied, whereas the pub was thriving. Through the patterned glass windows Joe could see a mass of silhouetted drinkers.

Somebody in there might know Diana, but an innate caution made him reluctant to venture inside. Did he really want to advertise his presence to the entire town?

While he hesitated, the pub's double doors clattered open. Joe took cover in the doorway of a bank and watched as three men crossed the plaza.

The middle one was very tall, perhaps six foot four, wearing a long black overcoat and a top hat. Joe glimpsed a strong profile with a Roman nose, a face in late middle age but with skin that was unusually pink and smooth, as though it had been highly polished. There was no hair peeking from beneath the hat, and Joe guessed he was completely bald.

The men who flanked him were younger and shorter, but dressed in similar formal attire. They had the demeanour of lackeys, nodding heartily at everything the tall man said.

Once they were out of sight, Joe entered the plaza and found a woman hurrying towards him, head down as she struggled to unfurl an umbrella. It opened with a pop and she looked up, saw Joe and gave a cry of surprise.

He raised his hands: the universal gesture of placation. 'Sorry. Can you help me? I'm trying to find someone.'

'Oh yes?' The woman's tone was dry, but not necessarily hostile. She was wrapped in a thick wool coat. Thirtyish, he would have said, with dark hair and big, dark eyes lively with intelligence.

'Do you know a Diana Bamber?'

Frowning, the woman took half a step back. She looked Joe up and down as if rethinking her first impression. 'Diana Bamber?'

'She ran a B&B with her husband Roy, but he—'

'I know who you mean. Diana Walters, she is now. She reverted to her maiden name.'

'Ah. Can you tell me where she lives?'

The woman motioned toward the seafront with her free hand. 'Left at the bottom of the High Street, follow the coast road along to Potters Lane. The B&B's called the Dolphin. It's about halfway up, on the right.'

'Thanks.'

'My pleasure,' she said, as though it was anything but.

*   *   *

Brooding on another charming encounter, Joe retraced his steps and turned along the seafront. There was a white van approaching, headlights splashing yellow light on the road. It slowed as it drew alongside, and Joe felt the driver's gaze. A young man, in a uniform of some kind, giving him a good hard stare of the sort Joe had often employed during his own days in uniform: *I've clocked you, sunshine.*

There was a logo on the side of the van, too dark to see clearly. After it had turned into the High Street Joe glanced back a couple of times, half expecting the driver to reappear and check him out again.

Potters Lane turned out to be only seventy or eighty yards from Britannia Place. The junction was little wider than a domestic driveway, squeezed between two low slate walls constructed in a distinctive herringbone pattern.

The hill was even steeper than the High Street, and lined with attractive white stone villas, marred only by the presence of an electricity substation. In a concession to the gradient the gardens were mostly paved and set out in a series of terraces. The driveways contained BMWs and Mercedes and Audis. In one, a road-legal Yamaha quad bike worth at least five grand was parked, unsecured, just inside the open gates. Joe felt sure it would be stolen by morning if the owner didn't come out to secure it.

Then the road curved sharply to the right, and finally the Dolphin came into view. It was an imposing Victorian property, possibly once a rectory or even a manor house, built of traditional Cornish stone and bay-fronted at each end, with a pair of hipped dormers in the roof. Joe guessed it must have at least six or seven bedrooms. Roy and Diana had done well for themselves, Joe thought.

The property was enclosed by a wall of matching Cornish stone. Mature trees and plants grew along the boundary, but much of the front garden had been paved over, with half a dozen parking bays marked out in white lines. Only one was occupied, by a newish Mazda MX-5. Not the sort of car he'd have pictured Diana driving.

Three wide steps led up to a recessed porch with a tiled floor. There were narrow frosted-glass windows either side of the front door. The door itself was made of dark oak, with iron fittings. Next to an old-fashioned bell pull there was a sign that read: *The Dolphin Bed and Breakfast, open 1 May till 30 September*. That explained the solitary car out front.

Joe checked the time: just after nine. Late for a surprise call, but not excessively so. He hoped she would understand.

* * *

He rang the bell. The door opened almost immediately. He hadn't seen Diana for over seven years, and at first he was taken aback. Was this the right house, the right woman?

She was wearing a pink knee-length dress with a white pashmina shawl over it, the dress tight-fitting and rather low-cut. She had never been seriously overweight, but now she was positively slim and shapely. She wore some subtle make-up, and her hair was shorter and probably coloured: it had a reddish tint. She looked, bizarrely, younger than he remembered her from nearly a decade ago.

Diana had opened the door without a hint of caution, a friendly smile on her face. Now Joe watched the smile fade, along with the colour in her cheeks. Her knuckles tightened on the door, as though preparing to slam it shut, and it occurred to him that she'd hurried to answer the bell because she was expecting someone else.

He said, 'Diana, it's me. Joe Clayton. Roy's old colleague.'

She gave a sombre nod. When she spoke, there was a hopelessness in her voice; she might have been deflating before his eyes.

'I know who you are, Joe. But why did you have to come here?'

42

CHAPTER NINE

It wasn't the reaction he'd been hoping for. Then again, he could hardly blame her.

'I'm sorry. I need your help.'

A long hesitation, while the door trembled in her hand, betraying her deliberations: let him in, or shut him out. Finally she said, 'This isn't a good time for me.'

'You're not in any trouble?' Joe asked.

'No, it's nothing like that . . .' She tailed off again, clearly unwilling to explain.

'All right. I'm sorry to have disturbed you.' Joe couldn't bring himself to beg or plead. He had no right to do so. He stepped off the porch into the fine pelting rain, heard a creak as the door moved behind him.

'Wait.'

He turned back, conscious of the rain dribbling down his face and neck, and wondered, if it had been a dry evening, would she have relented at all?

'Sorry,' Diana said. 'I don't know what I was thinking. Come in.'

'Are you sure?'

'Yes. I was just . . . shocked, I suppose. It's been so long.'

'It has,' he agreed. 'And I'm largely to blame for that.'

*　　　*　　　*

Joe stepped into a wide hallway, took off his jacket and his trainers. As he went to hang his cap

43

on a coat hook, Diana said, 'That's not a style I'd associate with you.'

'Me, neither. That was the point.'

She looked at him quizzically. 'A disguise?'

'Pretty much.'

'Where have you come from? Do you have a car?'

He shook his head. 'Trains and buses, all the way from Bristol.'

'Bristol?' She leaned towards him, studying his face. 'You're exhausted. Have you eaten lately?'

'Not really. I'd kill for some coffee.'

'That's easily solved. Follow me.'

Diana led him along the hall, through a formal dining room with half a dozen small tables, and on into a spacious kitchen, which had been extended to encompass a breakfast room. The table in here was larger, with a pile of glossy magazines on it. There was a local newspaper open at the property pages, a clean ashtray and a used teacup and saucer.

'Take a seat,' she said, filling a jug of water for the coffee maker. 'I could rustle up some food if you're hungry.'

'No, that's imposing on you.'

'I'm not offering a three-course meal. How about hot buttered toast?'

Joe laughed. 'My mouth's watering now. I'd better accept.'

With Diana busy, he took a moment to examine his surroundings. The kitchen was warm and homely and slightly cluttered: exactly the sort of place he imagined she would inhabit.

'You're closed for the season, then?'

'Yes. Things tailed off as soon as the kids went back to school. Some would say they barely got

44

started, what with all the rain we've had. August was a total washout.'

'I assume there's quite a rivalry down here. The proprietor of Britannia Place said he'd never heard of you.'

'Oh, that's Vincent Hocking. He's an awkward so-and-so. Takes a dislike to virtually everyone he meets.'

'Trelennan's own Basil Fawlty?'

'Exactly. Every town should have one.'

She brought him a plate with four slices of thick toasted bread, together with butter and a pot of raspberry jam. He inhaled deeply. 'Glorious. Just what I need.'

As she went to fetch their drinks, he added: 'Luckily I asked someone else, who told me you'd reverted to your maiden name.'

For a second, Diana froze. Then she nodded. 'Yes, I'm Diana Walters again now. I never really liked "Diana Bamber". It's got an odd rhythm, hasn't it?'

She turned, as if interested in his reaction, but at the same time he sensed that further discussion would be unwelcome. He shrugged, said nothing.

Taking the seat opposite, she held her coffee mug in both hands and let the steam warm her face. There was a moment when Joe might have reached out and touched her arm, but he couldn't be certain that he was reading her correctly.

'Are you sure there isn't something wrong?' he said.

'Quite sure. Why?' She took a sip, but she slurped it nervously, spilling a few drops on her chin.

To spare her embarrassment, Joe said, 'Don't

45

you hate it when that happens? I'm always pouring beer down my front.'

'In my case it's senility, I think.' She tutted, but these admissions of fallibility seemed to steady them both, and it was in the tone of the old, familiar Diana Bamber that she declared: 'Now, Joe Clayton, rolling up on my doorstep after all these years. You'd better tell me where you've been and what it is you want.'

'The second part's straightforward. I need somewhere to stay for a few days.'

Diana nodded, but it seemed more an acknowledgement of his request than the granting of it.

'Don't you have a suitcase, or a bag?'

'Just what I'm wearing. It'll be a while before I can retrieve my stuff.'

Tight-lipped, she gave him a glance. 'Oh?'

'Look,' Joe said, 'this isn't easy to explain. First of all I have to ask you something. Have you seen Helen, or heard from her at all?'

*　　　*　　　*

It was a moment or two before Diana answered. 'Not for a long time. Why?'

'Anything in the past four or five years?'

'I don't think so. We used to exchange Christmas cards, but that seemed to tail off after we moved down here.' There was a hint of reproach in her voice.

'I'm sorry. I felt terrible that I couldn't get in touch when Roy died.'

Diana looked up at the ceiling as she searched her memory. 'Helen phoned me to explain.

46

Actually, that might have been the last time I spoke to her. The funeral was in December 2005, the week before Christmas.' A flash of pain in her eyes. 'She said you were involved in a very sensitive case. I assume that meant undercover work?'

'Yes. Lasting nearly a year. But I hated missing the funeral. Roy was a great friend and mentor to me.'

Diana frowned. 'Wait a second. Why are you asking about Helen? You make it sound like you're not together any more.'

'We're not,' Joe said. 'I haven't seen her for four years.'

'But if you're only in Bristol . . .'

He shook his head. 'It's a lot more complicated than that.'

*   *   *

He'd told the full story only once before, more than a year ago, to a woman for whom he'd worked as a bodyguard—and only then because he was poised to depart from that job and knew he would never see her again. In that sense, his secrets had been safe with her: Cassie had had no idea who he really was, or where he was going next. Nothing he told her could feasibly harm either of them.

This time it was very different. Diana was a friend from his old life. From the days when he had been only Joe Clayton, and no one else. What he told her now would be carried into her future, and into his, and might have grave implications for them both.

And yet he saw little choice but to level with her. There was too much that couldn't be explained

47

away without resorting to some fairly outrageous lies, and she'd been a policeman's wife for too long to be taken for a fool.

'The undercover work destroyed our marriage,' he said. 'Specifically, the same case that prevented me from attending Roy's funeral.'

'I'm not surprised, if it lasted a year. Helen must have been going out of her mind.'

'She was, even though she didn't know the full details at the time.'

Joe paused. Astutely, Diana said, 'I quite understand if there are parts you can't tell me.'

'Okay. I had to infiltrate a gang who were planning a massive gold-bullion raid. The trouble was, by the time I was admitted into the inner sanctum they were getting seriously paranoid. I had to break off virtually all contact with my bosses and the backup team.'

Diana looked pained. 'Helen always said you were addicted to risk. She told me once that she had a recurring dream where you were killed in the line of duty. But I expect you just laughed that off, the way Roy did when I used to worry about him?'

Ruefully, Joe nodded. 'I've had a lot of time to regret it since, believe me.'

He continued with the story: how the lack of contact meant he was unable to contribute vital intelligence to the team responsible for foiling the robbery. As a result, the operation ended in disaster.

'One police officer killed, two more badly wounded. Four of the gang died, including the son of the gang's leader.'

He paused again. Diana said, 'It's all right. You don't have to say who they are.'

48

'No, but I think I should. The gang was led by Doug Morton.'

CHAPTER TEN

Until the moment he uttered Morton's name, Joe hadn't been completely sure if he was going to tell her. Once he had told her, he wasn't completely sure if it had been the right thing to do.

Diana put a hand over her mouth. 'Oh my God. I remember it on the news. And Roy knew of him, from way back. Said he was a monster . . .'

'The whole family are monsters. Doug Morton went to prison but made it known there was a price on my head. I was offered a new identity, then languished in a safe house for months while they carried out an internal investigation. Finally they told me I wouldn't face prosecution, but I was no longer welcome to remain in the police service.'

'Oh, Joe.' Diana stared at him, unable to take it in. 'Helen must have been devastated. I wish I'd known. There might have been some way I could have helped . . .'

'Helen really withdrew into herself at that point. Because I'd killed Doug Morton's son, it was fair to assume that our own kids might be a target.'

'But they're safe, aren't they?'

'As far as I know.'

Now she looked puzzled. From the hallway, a phone began to ring. Diana flinched, but her attention remained with Joe.

'What do you mean?'

'Helen was also given a new identity. She and

49

the girls moved away to set up a brand-new life. I wasn't part of the deal.'

'What? Was that your choice?'

'Not exactly.'

The phone went on ringing. 'I'll let it go to answerphone,' Diana said, shaking her head. 'Your beautiful little girls. How on earth could you live without them?'

The question stung Joe more deeply than he would have thought possible. He sat back in his chair, clearing his throat into a sudden heavy silence as the phone stopped ringing.

'Helen insisted that I wasn't to know where they were going. After putting their lives in danger, I couldn't blame her.'

'And you've seen nothing of them for four years?' Diana winced. 'I must admit, I was hurt when you both seemed to break off contact. With Helen, I wondered if it was . . . well, if maybe she'd heard rumours or something . . .' Blushing, she stared at her lap.

'I don't think so. It was one kiss at a party. And no one saw us.'

'No, you're right.' A brisk nod: eager to move on. 'But you must feel such bitterness, knowing your daughters are growing up without you?'

'Sometimes,' Joe agreed. 'Bitterness. Anger. Self-pity. You name it, there's not a negative emotion I haven't felt. But for all that, I still think it was the right thing for Helen to do. And after what happened today,' he added heavily, 'I believe that more than ever.'

*   *   *

50

There was a buzzing sound from one of the kitchen units. A mobile phone skittered across the polished worktop.

'Somebody's keen to reach you.'

Diana looked fretful. 'I'd better take it. Sorry.'

Joe waved away her apology and took a gulp of coffee. It was lukewarm. 'Do you mind if I get us another?' he asked.

'I'm fine, but help yourself.'

He followed her across the room. Diana picked up her mobile, checked the display and gave an audible sigh. She answered with a soft 'Hello' and wandered out to the dining room. A tiny click as the door was discreetly shut.

Joe tipped the dregs of the coffee into the sink, rinsed his mug and poured a fresh cup from the jug on the hotplate. He added milk and sugar and then, instead of returning to the table, he crept over to the dining-room door and listened. Gradually the murmur of Diana's voice coalesced into words he could understand.

'No, it's fine,' she was saying, quietly insistent. 'Ancient history.'

She laughed, and Joe frowned, not wanting to jump to conclusions. There was a longer pause, then: 'That's silly, there's no need. Yes, I'll see you tomorrow . . .' Another laugh. 'You too. Now bog off.'

Joe just made it back to the table as Diana came in. 'Sorry about that.'

'Don't apologise. I'm the one who's come here and disrupted your life.'

'It's not that bad.' Then she registered his grave expression. 'What?'

'There's another reason why I felt I had to

51

confide in you.'

'Oh.' She was a policeman's widow: it didn't take her long to guess. 'Doug Morton?'

'As I said, he wants vengeance for the death of his son, Gary. Doug's still in prison, but he has another son, Danny. Gary was like his dad, vicious but relatively straightforward. Danny Morton is a stone-cold psychopath.'

'And he's coming after you?'

'He tracked me down today, in Bristol. I only just got away.'

'But he didn't follow you here?' There was concern in Diana's voice, but not panic.

'No, I'm certain of that. Nobody else knows I'm in Trelennan, either, and I intend to keep it that way. But it's only fair that I tell you. If you want me to leave, just say so.'

Joe didn't think she would turn him away, although there was a moment when she seemed to consider it, perhaps for reasons that had nothing to do with Danny Morton. He thought about the call he'd eavesdropped on; the way she'd blushed while referring to that foolish lapse at Roy's retirement party.

Then she smiled and said, 'Of course I'm not going to chuck you out. After a sob story like that?'

'Thanks. By the way, I'm Joe Carter now, not Joe Clayton. That's very important.'

'Of course.' Diana slapped her palms on the table and stood up. 'All right, Mr Carter. I expect you'd like to clean up?'

*   *   *

She gave him a room on the top floor, where the

52

roof space had been converted into three additional bedrooms. Joe's was at the northern corner of the house, a cosy attic room with sloping ceilings and a single dormer window, covered by a Roman blind.

'It's nice and private for you up here. The bathroom's not en suite, but it's right next door.'

'Believe me, this is the height of luxury compared with some of the places I've stayed.'

After showing him the bathroom, she fetched fresh towels and flannels from a cupboard at the end of the narrow landing. He told her he'd probably take a long bath and then go to bed.

'Diana, I can't thank you enough for this. And I really hope it hasn't caused you any problems.'

It was the closest he dared get to the subject, but Diana blithely dismissed his concerns. 'Oh, I was just being silly earlier. I think it was the shock of seeing you.'

'Maybe, but I don't want to be a nuisance. If there's anything I can do to help you during my stay, you only have to ask.'

'Thank you. I will.'

*   *   *

Lying in a bath of almost scalding water, the reality of his new predicament enveloped Joe like steam. He knew nothing with certainty: how they had found him, who they had spoken to; whether other people had suffered as a result of their search.

Most alarming of all, he had no idea whether Helen and the girls were safe.

That thought nagged at him like a toothache. He knew it wouldn't go away until he'd found the answer. But he was taking a risk every time he talked to Maz, and now that risk itself had to be reappraised.

He chased his concerns in pointless circles while the water grew cold and began to settle like slime against his skin. It wasn't until his chin slipped beneath the surface and he jerked upright that Joe realised he'd begun to doze.

He pulled the plug, wrenched himself to his feet and ran the shower for thirty seconds to rinse off. He wrapped up in a towel and opened the bathroom door to find a dressing gown and a pair of old-fashioned pyjamas, folded neatly on the floor. On top of them lay a toothbrush, toothpaste and a unisex deodorant.

In the bedroom, Diana had left him a pair of jogging pants and a couple of plain white T-shirts: medium size, which might be tight across the shoulders, but they would do for now. He'd rinsed out his underwear in the bathroom sink and hung it to dry on the radiator. Tomorrow he'd have to sort out some new clothes.

After turning off the light, he stood at the window and lifted the blind. He could faintly distinguish the shape of the buildings that sat below him on the hill. As before, he had a sense of the sea as no more than a brooding space beneath the sky. A void.

The rain was coursing down the glass, but he wanted fresh air. He opened the window an inch or so, waiting a moment to make sure it wouldn't let too much water in.

As he climbed into bed, an image of Danny Morton came to him: the fury and disbelief on his face as Joe had slipped from his grasp.

He won't give up, Joe thought. *After today he'll be*

54

even more determined to get his revenge.

But, for now, he was safe. Joe shut his eyes and told himself he'd been lucky today and he would be lucky again: that the next time he and Danny Morton came face to face, it would be on Joe's terms.

CHAPTER ELEVEN

A phone call at midnight. Diana was in bed, the mobile gently gripped in her hand, knowing that he would ring. She had nothing to say, but better this than have him come hammering on the door.

'You in bed?'

'Mmm.' Her voice sleepy, hoping this would keep the conversation brief.

'Alone?'

'Very funny.'

'He's good-looking, that's what I hear.' And when she didn't rise to it: 'But not as good-looking as me?'

'Exactly.'

'He's staying over?'

'Just a couple of days.'

'Even a couple isn't great, Di. Not right now.'

'It won't make any difference.'

'Who's to say? It's my livelihood at stake.'

'It was my decision to take him in. Do you think Leon's going to hold it against you?'

Silence. So that meant the answer was probably *yes*.

'Come on, love, I don't want to take the chance. If he hears about this and I'm not up to speed . . .

well, you know how it'll look.'

'I can't throw him out now, Glenn. And I won't do it just to keep Leon sweet.'

A soft tutting in her ear. 'You know, you should be more careful what you say.'

'Glenn, it's late and I'm tired.' Diana could hear the breathlessness of panic in her voice. 'Can we discuss this tomorrow?'

'Oh, we're going to. I want to know everything about him.'

'I told you, it's been years since Joe left the force.'

'He'll still have a cop's instincts. In Leon's eyes, that makes him trouble. Just like your Roy, eh?'

'Stop it. You don't have to say that.'

'Sometimes you need reminding. Without me, you're only a copper's widow. And in this town that's not a good thing to be, is it?'

Alone in the dark, Diana shook her head. 'No,' she said. 'I'm sorry.'

'I know you are, sweetheart. And I am, too. I don't mean to sound so harsh.'

She heard him blow a kiss and she blew one in return, trying not to feel ridiculous. Then she put the phone down and lay back on the pillow, and only then did she realise there were tears in her eyes.

'I'm sorry,' she whispered again, to the silent room. 'I'm so sorry, Roy.'

CHAPTER TWELVE

The cry of seagulls woke him, dissolving a dream that left no clear images. For a moment Joe was a child again, waking on the first morning of a holiday at the seaside: Paignton, or Weymouth, or Cromer. That sound represented optimism and joy: swimming and sandcastles and ice cream and, for one glorious week, his parents saying *yes* more often than they said *no*.

He opened his eyes, blinked a few times, took in his surroundings and reconsidered the optimism and joy. He was thirty-eight, living under a false identity and on the run from people who wanted to kill him. No one's idea of a holiday.

And yet, somehow, that knowledge didn't feel quite as oppressive as it had last night. Perhaps it was the tang of salt in the air, wafting through the open window. Just knowing he was by the coast seemed to lift his spirits.

Opening the blind, Joe was greeted by a fine view of sea and sky, framed by a patchwork quilt of rooftops and chimneys in rain-washed reds and greys. He opened the window wide and leaned out. The air was cool and delicious. He could hear the slow drip of water in gutters, the distant wash of the sea against the shore. The sky was streaked with blue and grey cloud, glowing softly as if lit from below. The departing rain was no more than a yellowy haze on the horizon.

He thought about Ryan, how he'd have welcomed the dry weather to finish the house in Clifton Village. Joe realised how much he was going to miss working with the young entrepreneur.

On the subject of work, and the lack of it, he counted his money. Just over fifty-five pounds left. That wasn't going to last him long.

He used the bathroom, and was glad to find his underwear had dried on the radiator. He dressed in his own jeans and one of the T-shirts that Diana had loaned him, then went out on the landing. It was seven-thirty: not too early to get up.

As he descended the stairs he heard activity from below. A conversation between a man and a woman.

Last night Diana had briefly described the accommodation on the first floor. There were four guest bedrooms, two of them en suite. Diana's own bedroom and bathroom were at the end of the corridor, separated by a glazed partition and a door marked 'Private'.

A window on the landing looked out over the front garden. When Joe checked it he found a dark blue Toyota Hilux on the drive, slewed across three parking bays. Just beyond it, a young man in jeans and a hooded sweatshirt was idly kicking at a clump of pampas grass while he smoked a cigarette.

After a few seconds he turned and squinted at the house. His face was thin and surly, instinctively hostile. The man made eye contact with Joe, then turned and spat ostentatiously into the flower bed. Joe had no doubt it was done for his benefit.

A moment later a door closed somewhere downstairs, and Diana's early-morning visitor strode into view from the side of the house. He was a good twenty years older than his associate: early forties, tall and stocky with a hard, chiselled face. He wore a well-cut grey suit, collarless shirt

58

and brown leather shoes. His thick black hair was slightly unkempt, and just long enough to give him a somewhat bohemian air.

Reaching the Toyota, he opened the driver's door and paused as the younger man tossed his cigarette away and said something, nodding towards the house. Both turned to the landing window just as Joe stepped out of sight.

He thought of Roy Bamber as he heard the car doors slam and the big Toyota roared away. As a sergeant with eighteen years in, Roy had taken the rookie Joe under his wing. At that stage Joe still held firmly to the view that snap judgements about people were often unfair, sometimes bigoted and prone to all kinds of lazy assumptions. What he'd quickly learned was that, in Roy's case, those initial assessments tended to be spot on.

Not the sort of people you'd welcome into the house, Roy might have said about these two. Or to sum them up in one word: *Trouble*.

*   *   *

Diana was in the kitchen, putting a plate and a coffee mug into the dishwasher. In the hall Joe had found a *Daily Mail* on the mat. Now he offered it to Diana as she turned to greet him. She smiled, only vaguely flustered.

'Morning! Oh, you can read that. I barely look at it.'

'Don't blame you. Isn't it a permanent cry of "The world's gone to hell in a hand basket"?'

'Probably. I only keep it for the TV pages and the showbiz gossip.'

Joe crossed to the table, where Diana had set out

59

a jug of orange juice and a couple of glasses. He considered asking after her visitor but didn't want her to feel he was spying on her. Better to see if she volunteered the information.

'Cooked breakfast?' she said.

He hesitated. 'This seems more and more like I'm imposing.'

'You don't know what rate I'm charging you yet,' she shot back. 'Are you hungry?'

'Starving.'

'Full Cornish it is, then.'

*   *   *

Over his enormous breakfast—while Diana nibbled on a wafer-thin slice of wholemeal toast—they reminisced without venturing too close to the night of the party, preferring instead to speculate upon the fate of various dimly remembered colleagues and their spouses.

When the conversation moved on to the trials of running a business in the recession, Joe saw his chance. 'What is your daily rate, by the way?'

'What?'

'I intend to pay you. This is a B&B, after all.'

'But you're staying here as my guest. In any case, what are you doing for funds?'

'I have money. I just can't lay my hands on it straight away.' He decided to test the water. 'Usually, wherever I land up I'm able to find myself some casual work.'

'Really?' If the idea of him sticking around worried Diana, she hid it well. 'Do people still get away with working for cash?'

'More than ever when times are hard.' Joe gave

her a flavour of his experiences over the past year: backbreaking farm work in Norfolk, Lincolnshire and Humberside, a few months as an assistant in a hardware store, which fortunately coincided with the harshest spell of a bitterly cold winter, and then, prior to Bristol, the thankless task of kitchen porter in an exclusive Manchester hotel.

'If you keep on the move, how did Danny Morton manage to trace you?'

'I don't know. But I'm certain he couldn't have tracked me here. You don't need to worry on that score.'

Diana smiled, but it was the sort of brave smile you feel obliged to give when you're humouring a friend. Refusing the offer of more coffee and toast, Joe said he'd get out from under her feet.

'You're welcome to borrow my car if you need it.'

'Not at the moment, but thanks for the offer.' At the kitchen door he paused. 'Anything I should know about Trelennan before I go out and explore?'

'I don't think so.'

'But it's a nice place to live? You like it here?'

Diana nodded. But she seemed uncertain, as though he might have been teasing her.

Or maybe, Joe realised later, it was because he'd asked two distinct questions, and each one had a different answer.

CHAPTER THIRTEEN

Joe didn't go looking for trouble, but sometimes trouble found him. Something in his character seemed to attract it.

He'd exchanged mobile numbers with Diana, although she warned him that the coverage was patchy at best. From a display of tourist brochures in the hall, she selected a leaflet that included a street map. She also gave him a spare door key, which led him to comment on the lack of a burglar alarm.

She chuckled. 'This isn't London, Joe. It's very safe down here.'

Sure enough, when he descended the hill the quad bike he'd noticed last night was sitting undisturbed just inside the open gates. Even more noteworthy was that only a handful of properties appeared to have alarm systems. Those that did had identical diamond-shaped boxes, navy blue, bearing the letters *LRS*.

The logo seemed vaguely familiar. After puzzling over it for a minute, Joe realised it might have been on the van that had scoped him out.

*　　　*　　　*

It was a little after nine o'clock when he reached the seafront. Beneath the veil of grey cloud the town looked muted, still half-asleep. The air was cool, with a blustery wind that made him grateful for his unfashionable beige jacket. Apart from the occasional passing vehicle, it was very quiet: none of the bustle and activity of Bristol.

He unfolded the map and compared it with the sight before him. On the western side of the harbour, where he was standing, the promenade ran for about half a mile and terminated at the point where the land rose sharply away from the shore. To the east, beyond the harbour, lay a wide expanse of untamed sandy beach: no breakwaters, no promenade or sea wall.

Looming above the beach was an almost sheer granite cliff, and above that a steep hillside which put Joe in mind of the German alps, the slopes thickly wooded with patches of dark rock gleaming wetly through gaps in the trees. Here and there he glimpsed imposing-looking homes or hotels, some of traditional Cornish stone and slate; others were in a Victorian Gothic style, with towers and spires and high narrow gables.

He decided to head west, away from the harbour, and see if he could circumnavigate the town in the space of a few hours. The sea air tasted exhilarating, and his muscles yearned for a chance to burn off that magnificent breakfast.

At the spot where the promenade ended with a pay-and-display car park there were signs advertising a coastal path around the headland and into the neighbouring bay. Walkers were cautioned that sections of the path were treacherous at high tide. An exploration for another day, Joe decided.

He turned inland, into Crabtree Lane. The road commenced on a gentle incline, with a series of modest bungalows on his left and agricultural land to his right. The fields were enclosed by low-slung electric fences; water troughs and feeders indicated that some sort of livestock was kept here.

The road began to twist and turn as the gradient steepened abruptly. Joe judged that he had climbed for nearly a mile before it began to level off. The farmland gave way to a golf course, laid out over the hilltop and dotted with dark, mysterious copses, the trees deformed by the westerly winds.

Nearer to the summit, the houses became increasingly more imposing, new-builds intended to look like traditional Cornish dwellings, albeit three or four times the size. Some advertised holiday lets; many had shutters on the windows. Almost every one had a security system: the blue diamond boxes of LRS.

A successful local firm, he guessed. And then he turned the corner and found trouble waiting.

*   *   *

Joe took in the scene in an instant. A Daimler hearse was parked on the road outside the gates of a large modern home. The engine was running, white smoke pumping from the exhaust and being sucked away by the wind.

There was a man in the driver's seat, his head turned towards the pavement where two figures grappled in an uneven conflict. One was the very tall, pink-skinned man that Joe had seen emerging from the pub with his acolytes. Now the formal attire made sense: he was a funeral director.

Battering ineffectually at him was a young woman, not much more than five feet tall, with a body that was compact rather than slim. She wore black jeans and a denim jacket. Her shoulder-length hair was straight and dark with reddish highlights. Her face might have been pretty, had it

64

not been contorted with painful emotions.

'You lie to me,' she cried. 'You have seen her, I know it.' Her accent was Eastern European. Joe had heard plenty during his stint in the Manchester hotel; he thought she might be from one of the Baltic states.

Instinct almost propelled him forward to break up the fight, before a sense of self-preservation took over. Stepping into a recess at the entrance to the neighbouring property, he concealed himself from view at the precise moment when the funeral director's patience ran out.

One huge hand grabbed the woman by the throat, and he rammed her back against the Daimler. She tried to speak, but could make only a harsh gurgling sound.

'I've told you, I don't know anything.' He leaned closer, snarling a threat in a voice too low for Joe to hear.

He must have loosened his grip slightly, for the woman was able to gasp. 'Mr Cadwell, please. I beg you . . .'

'I'm sick of hearing it. I have no interest in the silly bitch—'

'Kamila. Her name is Kamila. Please . . .'

Joe took a step forward, then paused. He didn't need to get involved. He was no more than thirty feet away: close enough to act if he felt the woman was in serious danger.

The conversation was halted by the sound of a vehicle approaching. A van whipped past Joe and screeched to a halt beside the Daimler. It was a Ford Transit, bearing a familiar logo: the letters LRS in white on the background of a blue diamond.

The funeral director, Cadwell, released the woman and she twisted away from him, clutching the roof of the hearse for support as she coughed and retched. Cadwell took a step back and smoothed down his suit. A thin, complacent smile formed as he prepared to greet the new arrivals.

Two men climbed out of the Transit. One was about thirty, stocky, with close-cropped greying hair, the other younger and thinner, with dark curly hair. They wore generic security uniforms: navy blouson jackets and grey trousers with heavy utility belts. Both nodded greetings to Cadwell, who reserved his attention for the stocky guard.

'Morning, Reece. Good to see you.'

'What's she done this time?' Reece asked. Unlike Cadwell, he had a thick local accent.

'More ridiculous accusations,' the funeral director said. Then he murmured something else, which elicited a disgusted response.

By now the girl had sunk to her knees, one hand over her face as she sobbed quietly. The curly-haired guard knelt down and took the girl's arm. Joe assumed he was concerned for her welfare, but he tightened his grip and wrenched her to her feet. She screamed.

Joe couldn't watch any more. His body made the decision for him, launching him onto the pavement before his mind had caught up.

'Leave her alone!'

Cadwell and both guards turned to stare at him. The woman also looked round, seeming more confused than grateful.

'This man just assaulted her,' Joe said, pointing

at the funeral director.

Reece's chin came out. 'You what?'

'I witnessed an assault. He had her by the throat.'

Reece nodded in a way that suggested this was of no interest to him whatsoever. He turned to Cadwell, who said, 'She was lying in wait for me when I left the house. Going on and on about that damn girl—'

'She's my sister!' the woman cried. Her face was puffy, with inky smudges of mascara on her cheeks.

'I have a right to walk the streets unmolested,' Cadwell declared. In daylight his skin looked even more unnaturally smooth and pink. His eyes were large and pale, almost colourless.

Reece exchanged a glance with his colleague, then propelled the woman away from them.

'Get lost,' he told her. 'Don't let us catch you round here again.'

Head down, the woman seemed to size up the situation before sniffing loudly, as if instead of some choice parting insult, and marching away.

'You can piss off, too,' Reece said to Joe.

'What?'

'Before I change my mind.'

'You have powers of arrest, do you?'

'Yeah. Citizen's arrest.' He took a step towards Joe. 'Want us to prove it?'

*　　　*　　　*

Joe shrugged. The voice of common sense told him to be contrite, to extricate himself from this situation as tactfully as possible, while he was still anonymous. No real harm done.

Good advice, but he heard himself say: 'Go

67

ahead and try.'

Reece looked at his colleague, who wore an eager smirk, and then at Cadwell. The funeral director shook his head, but Reece appeared not to notice.

'Who the hell are you, then?'

'My name's Joe. Who are you?'

'You don't live in Trelennan.'

'Well done, Einstein. I'm a visitor.'

'Yeah? Well, you might want to end your visit pretty soon. 'Cause if I run into you again, you're going to regret it, and that's a fact.'

A moment's stand-off. Then Cadwell gave a growl of impatience and said, 'I have work to do. Let's put this little incident behind us, shall we?'

Reece unclipped his phone. 'You want me to report back?'

Cadwell said, 'If you wish. I'll be speaking to him later.'

'Right you are.' With a final malevolent glance at Joe, Reece returned to the van. The hearse pulled away first, and the Transit followed, the driver watching Joe in his mirrors until the curve of the road obscured him from view.

Joe turned to look down the hill, but the woman was already out of sight. He considered going after her, then decided that would be taking his involvement further than was wise.

CHAPTER FOURTEEN

The reports came in quick succession, disrupting Leon's state of mind on what should have been a

68

morning of unblemished delight. Glenn's was first: a brief, one-sided phone call. Leon couldn't ask questions or issue commands, except in code, and although Glenn was one of the brighter men on his team he still wasn't *that* bright.

'She swears he's not a problem, but I dunno. I got the feeling she might be keeping something back.'

'How do you mean?'

'The way he's turned up out of the blue like this. No phone call or nothing. And no family with him, though Di says he's married with two kids. She was a bit funny about that, too. According to Vince Hocking, the guy was on foot and he didn't have any bags. Just the clothes he stood up in.'

'That does sound interesting.'

'Yeah. I got to thinking, there's really only one thing it can mean . . .'

'Go on.'

'He's gotta be in trouble of some kind. On the run, maybe?'

'That's a possibility, I agree.'

'I pushed her on what he does for a living. She swears he left the force years ago, just does painting and stuff these days. But you know what they say. Once a cop, always a cop. What do you reckon, Leon?'

'Oh, I'm taking a relaxed view, long-term.' This was a lie, of course, and Glenn should have known better than to keep asking questions that Leon couldn't answer openly.

In a bright, upbeat tone, Leon ended the call with: 'Thanks for keeping me in the picture, Glenn.' Which meant: *You lousy useless fucker, I'm gonna tear you a new arsehole*.

Nothing else he could do right now. Leon was in the back of his E-class Mercedes, travelling to Exeter for an important photo op. He'd chosen the Merc because it was classy without being too flash, and he'd chosen Warren to drive because he scrubbed up smarter than most of his employees.

In honour of the occasion Leon had even made an effort to look the part of a respectable and prosperous businessman, which was exactly what he was. He'd got himself a new suit for the occasion, a sober dark grey Ted Baker job. It came with a waistcoat, but that would have been taking things too far.

Day to day, Leon was a lot more comfortable schlepping round in polyester tracksuits, living up to the image people had of him as a rough and ready chancer: a bit of chav scum that had got lucky. He encouraged people to think like that, because it was all the more satisfying when he made them eat their words. Today was going to be a grade-A example of that.

While he indulged in a little daydreaming about it, the stumbling block to free speech was sitting beside him on the back seat, pretending to admire the passing countryside while sneaking glances at Leon whenever he thought it was safe.

His name was Giles Quinton-Price. He was in his mid-fifties, a lank-haired wet-lipped twat with a strange honking voice that managed to sound both deep and squeaky at the same time. It was driving Leon spare, but he couldn't block it out or shut him up. Couldn't smack him in the mouth and dump him on the hard shoulder.

Because Giles was a journalist on a national newspaper, writing a feature article about Leon and Trelennan. He and Giles had been joined at the hip for two days already, with at least one more day to go. Leon didn't know how much longer he could handle it, that weird grating laugh and his stupid fucking questions.

Like this: 'Got yourself a few personnel problems?'

'Something like that.'

'People! The bane of your existence, I dare say?'

Leon nodded, thinking: *Pricks like you are.*

'Still,' Giles said, 'a day like today makes it all worthwhile, does it not?'

'You bet it does.' Leon tried not to sound sarcastic, then realised he wasn't being sarcastic. It *did* make it worthwhile, getting his picture taken with the chief constable. A big two-fingers to all the lowlifes back on the Trelawny estate who'd written him off from the start. Even more so to all the filth who'd tried to bring him down over the years. Shaking hands with their boss, making it clear that he and Leon were on equal terms—that was going to taste really fucking sweet.

And a boost for the business, too. Good publicity meant more money rolling in. Nice clean spendable money. Money you could flaunt, if you wanted.

All very different from the old days.

*   *   *

The second call was from Derek Cadwell. Not an employee as such, but quicker on the uptake than Glenn. A man who knew where his best interests

71

lay.

'That foreign bitch was outside the house again.'

'You talked to her?'

'I tried. She refuses to listen.'

'Same here. Sometimes it takes a bit longer for the message to sink in.'

Derek's voice lowered. 'You can't speak freely? Oh—the journalist's with you.'

'Exactly.'

'Bugger. We need a proper discussion about this. She virtually attacked me.'

'Get hold of Clive. Arrange a meeting for late afternoon.'

'Thank you.' There was a pause: more bad news to follow. 'During our confrontation, somebody else got involved. A stranger. He looked pretty unsavoury. Said his name was Joe.'

'Did he?' Leon said, aware that Giles was straining to hear the other end of the conversation.

'One of your patrols was on hand. Reece and that other lad. I have to say, this Joe didn't seem particularly intimidated by them.'

'I wouldn't worry. Already on my agenda.'

'Really? You know who he is?'

'Like I said, go through Clive. We'll catch up this afternoon.'

Leon put his phone away. He knew he couldn't dwell on it now, but something had to be done with the girl. Nobody else in Trelennan would say a bad word about him, but she was a head case, shooting her mouth off to anyone who'd listen. A sap like Giles wouldn't necessarily know it was crazy talk.

And then there was this feller. It had to be the same one Glenn had described. An ex-cop, pitching up at Diana's with no car, no luggage. Could be on

72

the run, in which case Leon needed to find out why. Leon could sniff out an opportunity better than anybody.

But Glenn was right about something else. *Once a cop, always a cop.* In which case this guy wasn't an opportunity at all, but a nuisance. A threat.

Forgetting for a moment the image he was trying to project, Leon let out a long heartfelt sigh. In response, Giles tutted sadly.

'The price of greatness is responsibility,' he declared in a grand voice, like he was quoting from a play or a speech.

'Too right,' Leon said. With a pointed look at the journalist, he added, 'Especially when I'm surrounded by fuckwits.'

CHAPTER FIFTEEN

Joe tried to put the incident with the security men out of his mind. He explored a series of narrow lanes on the town's southern perimeter. Beyond the crest of the hill, and thus robbed of the stunning sea views, he discovered a large council estate, dating back to the 1950s or '60s, the houses constructed of prefabricated concrete panels. There were a few unkempt gardens with the usual broken bikes and discarded mattresses, but for the most part the properties were well kept. Plenty of pot plants and satellite dishes that had escaped the attention of the local vandals.

Or maybe there weren't any vandals. Joe passed a couple of empty houses, their doors and windows boarded over, but even these had no graffiti, no sign of fires or attempts at forced entry. Trelennan might have its own slice of poverty to accompany the affluence, but its inhabitants seemed remarkably well behaved.

And no burglar alarms here, he noted. No sign of the LRS logo at all.

Beyond the estate, the town's boundary resumed along the top of the hill. Here, on the south-eastern corner, the incline was much steeper than on the western side. This was the wooded area that Joe had seen from the seafront: the Alpine district, with a scattering of large, secluded homes and one or two exclusive hotels dotted among the trees.

Joe smiled ruefully. He was firmly back in LRS territory. Their alarm boxes were everywhere; then one of their vans came drifting along a parallel street, slowing at the junction while the driver checked him out. Not Reece or his buddy, but it could have been the man he'd seen last night.

He carried on walking. The road was arranged in a series of switchbacks, with stone retaining walls to hold back the banks of bracken and gorse. Signs urged drivers to remain in a low gear. There was no pavement for pedestrians, and Joe had to press himself against the wall every time a car came past.

The sound of rushing water alerted him to a fast-moving stream. Joe peered over the wall and watched the clear, bubbling water flowing beneath the road. After that, he was sure he could hear its progress as a distant, almost subliminal noise as he descended into the town.

As he emerged from the tree cover, the blustery wind hit him full in the face: an effect that the locals probably described as 'bracing'. But the clouds were slowly breaking up, allowing a hint of sunshine to

74

peek through, and Joe felt his mood lifting.

At the top of the High Street he paused by a large office building with a religious bookshop on the ground floor. The front of the block was shielded by a cloister. Joe stepped behind one of the brick columns for shelter and privacy, made sure his phone had a signal, then checked the time: just after eleven o'clock.

Perfect.

*　　　*　　　*

It was Joe's new phone, so the number wouldn't be familiar, but he was calling a mobile that Maz reserved only for him. Just as he'd expected, his friend was eating when he answered.

'Anything nice?'

'Cream doughnut,' Maz said, all but purring.

'Lovely. I wouldn't normally interrupt your elevenses, except that I ran into a face from the past.'

'You're kidding.' There was a sudden bout of coughing.

'Jesus, Maz. Don't choke on your doughnut.'

'Too late.' More coughing. 'What happened?'

Joe gave him a brief update: Danny Morton, the chase through Bristol and Joe's escape. Nothing about where he'd gone afterwards.

'How the hell did he find you?'

'I don't know. You got any ideas on that score?'

A beat of silence. Then: 'Christ, you don't think that I . . . ?'

'No. What I meant was, you're the only direct contact I've had.'

'But you never told me where you were.' Maz's

75

voice was indignant. 'You just said the south-west, not Bristol.'

'I know—'

'And I told you about your mum. Weren't you going to get in touch with her?'

'Yes. I phoned her from a call box in Wales. She's doing pretty well. I also emailed my brother. I'm not blaming you for a second, Maz. But something's going on here.'

'What do you mean?'

'You remember last time, the reason my cover was blown?' Joe didn't want to spell it out—that he'd been betrayed by a police officer on Doug Morton's payroll—and Maz understood his need for caution.

'Uh-huh.'

'I wonder if something similar has happened again. Perhaps they picked up "south-west", used that as their starting point and then got lucky.'

'But that means someone close by.' Maz groaned. 'I'm bloody careful, Joe.'

'Then maybe they tracked the emails, but that would take some serious outside help. The Mortons aren't exactly technical wizards.'

'Either way, it's not good.'

'Don't I know it?' Joe was gazing idly at a selection of religious tracts in the shop window. The one that caught his eye was called *Praying for a Miracle?*

'Are you safe for the time being, while I try and work out what happened?'

'I think so, but that's not my main concern. What if they've managed to trace Helen and the girls?'

Maz swore softly. 'I'd have heard something. I'm sure they're fine.'

'You don't have any idea where they are?'

'No. Whatever else might be leaking round here, that secret is still locked up tight.'

'I hope so. I never thought I'd say this, Maz, but it's almost a relief that you haven't found them.'

*   *   *

Afterwards, Joe felt bad that he might have offended his friend, and yet a tiny disloyal voice in his head refused to be silenced. Had Maz said or done something, however inadvertently, that had drawn Danny Morton to Bristol?

Brooding again, he continued down the hill. The High Street was busy, but the demographics were markedly different to the part of Bristol where he'd been living. The streets of Clifton were full of affluent, trendy young mothers, as well as lots of students. In Trelennan the residents might still be well-off by national standards, but they were older—and less concerned with fashion.

That was putting it kindly, Joe thought, as he realised how well his zip-up jacket allowed him to blend in. There were very few students—hardly anyone in their teens or twenties, in fact. Some harassed-looking mums with babies and toddlers and a sprinkling of tourists, again mostly elderly. There was no real ethnic variety, but that probably wasn't too unusual for a small West Country town. Even so, something about the mix nagged at him.

One refreshing difference was the individuality of the shops themselves. Aside from a Co-op and a Boots, there were hardly any of the generic chain stores that rendered most towns indistinguishable from one another.

77

Having made this observation, Joe felt like a hypocrite when he realised that Boots was actually the one shop he needed.

He picked up a toothbrush, deodorant, shaving gel and a pack of cheap disposable razors. There were two checkouts open, both staffed by young women. One was serving a customer, while the other chatted and giggled with a man in a security guard's uniform.

When her attention wavered the guard looked round, and Joe saw it was Reece's partner, the man with the curly hair. He puffed out his chest and sent Joe an intimidating glare. Quite untroubled, Joe held his gaze, and after a few seconds it was the guard who turned away.

Joe paid for the toiletries and left, trying to push aside the feeling that he'd unwittingly embarked on a route towards a confrontation he could do without.

His next stop was the plaza, and specifically the library—if it was open. He'd come to rely heavily on libraries over the past couple of years, and he was dismayed by the constant threats to the service.

According to the sign outside, this one closed two days a week but was open today. Joe pushed through the doors, the doubts already setting in. After what he'd said to Maz, should he risk going online while he was here?

Then he approached the counter and saw who was behind it. But by then it was too late to turn and leave without it looking like a personal snub. She had spotted him, too.

78

CHAPTER SIXTEEN

It was the woman who'd given him directions the previous evening. She seemed as reluctant as Joe to renew their acquaintance, greeting him with a brittle smile.

'Hello again,' Joe said. 'Is it safe to ask you another question?'

The smile turned wry, but warmed up a fraction. 'Depends what it is.'

'I'd like to use one of the computers.'

'It's three pounds sixty an hour—unless you're a member of the library?'

'Uh, not here. I only need it for ten minutes.'

'Well, the first half-hour is free of charge for members.' Theatrically checking there was nobody within earshot, she said, 'I suppose I might be able to bend the rules. Since it's you.'

'Thanks.'

She was smaller than Joe remembered, perhaps because last night she'd been bundled up in a thick coat. In a tight-fitting purple tunic over a thin black sweater, she looked slim and petite. Her face was framed by very dark hair, cut in a pageboy style. Her features were finely drawn and symmetrical, and she had a pale complexion that made it easy to see the laughter lines around her eyes and mouth.

Joe reassessed her age upwards by a few years: mid-thirties, he'd say. A lot of experience in those big dark eyes, to go with the intelligence and the sardonic humour. The eyes of a woman who might be about to kiss you or slap your face, and you wouldn't know which until she'd done it.

'I still need you to fill in the form,' she said, and while she hunted for it Joe turned away, aware that he'd been scrutinising her rather too closely.

The library was in a modern building that could have done with a fresh coat of paint, though the utilitarian metal shelves were well stocked and the books themselves looked to be in good condition. Joe could see several people browsing, and in the children's section a woman was reading a picture book to a pair of toddlers. He guessed that no one was going to criticise the decor when the entire service was under threat.

Supplied with the form, he filled it in, giving his name as Joe Carter. A phone rang on the desk below the counter.

'Trelennan library, Ellie Kipling speaking.'

Passing the form back, Joe waited out the call by examining a rack of tourist leaflets. He picked up one for a place called 'The Shell Cavern' just as Ellie said, 'Yes, it came back in this morning. I've put it aside for you.'

She put the phone down and told him: 'That's amazing. You must go and visit.'

'Where is it?'

'Top of the town. Only twenty minutes' walk.'

'Okay. I'll check it out some time.'

She seemed gratified by his interest. 'Here for a while, then?'

'A few days.'

'I expect Diana was delighted to see you?'

Joe nodded, unsure whether the note of sarcasm was specific to the question, or whether it was merely her natural tone of voice.

'We're friends from years back.'

'Really? Must be a long way back.' When Joe

80

frowned, she added: 'Because you didn't know where she lived.'

'Oh, I see. No. We sort of lost touch.'

'Evidently. So you'll have noticed the difference in her appearance?'

Joe had a feeling he was being lured into a trap. 'Quite a transformation.'

'Isn't it? I think she looks fabulous—for her age.' A flash of humour in her eyes served to lessen any malice. Joe couldn't find it in him to take offence on Diana's behalf.

He offered his hand. 'Pleased to meet you, Ellie. I'm Joe.'

'I know. It says on the form.' She surprised him by looking slightly abashed. 'Sorry if I was a bit brusque last night.'

'Brusque? I'd say downright hostile. Though that seems par for the course.'

His tone was light-hearted, but Ellie took the comment seriously. 'What do you mean?'

Joe described the confrontation he'd witnessed. At the mention of the funeral director Ellie blew out her cheeks, as if suppressing the urge to vomit.

'Derek Cadwell isn't the most charming of men.'

'The girl seemed convinced that he knew something about her missing sister.'

'Mm. Alise is a sad case. She spends hours in here, searching through the missing-persons websites. Either that or she's killing time in the harbour café.'

'And what about her sister?'

'Vanished without trace, apparently. Whether she was ever here or not, I don't know. Alise isn't doing herself any favours, throwing accusations at people when she's got no proof.'

81

'And would anybody help her, do you think, if they could?'

Ellie pursed her lips. 'What a strange question to ask. Why?'

'Well, from my experiences so far it isn't all that friendly round here.'

For a moment Joe thought she might bridle at the suggestion and leap to the defence of her home town, but she simply gazed at him and then nodded, sadly.

'No. It's an odd place, I suppose.'

*   *   *

She came out from behind the counter, light on her feet like a dancer. Joe followed her to the computer terminals, clutching his shopping in one hand and the tourist leaflet in the other. He could hardly discard it now that she'd recommended it to him.

There were six PCs set up in the centre of the room, presumably to discourage the browsing of unsavoury sites. Only one was in use. A man in his sixties with ruddy cheeks and a misshapen purple-veined nose was tapping away with surprising dexterity, punctuating his typing with little grunts and sighs. Although the room was warm, he wore a navy greatcoat and a trilby. He tutted as Ellie directed Joe to a seat on the opposite side.

'I really do have to concentrate, you know,' he said, huffing.

Ellie gave him short shrift. 'These are public computers, Mr Bastian, available for anyone who wants to use them.'

Joe sat down. Ellie crouched over the desk, using

82

the PC monitor to hide her from the man's view.

'I wouldn't mind,' she whispered, 'but he comes in to write complaint letters to the council, and half of them are about the library service.'

After making sure that Joe was set up, she lingered for a second, and he took the opportunity to say casually, 'Another thing I've noticed is a logo with "LRS" on it. They seem to have vans and security guards everywhere. I assume it's a local business?'

'Oh yes.' Ellie was still whispering. 'Leon Race. This is Leon's town.'

CHAPTER SEVENTEEN

Even when said quietly, it was a bold statement. Before Joe could ask what she meant, a sharp rapping noise made them both jump. There was a man at the counter, plump and prosperous, with a leather document wallet under one arm.

'Major troublemaker number two,' Ellie muttered, a sly delight in her voice. 'With any luck they'll cancel each other out.'

The man registered Ellie's presence and beckoned her towards him. A moment later he spotted the complainer, Bastian, and seemed to recoil.

'Councillor Rawle!' Ellie called. At the sound of the name Bastian jerked to life; half out of his chair, he stared at the councillor with a ferocious intent. Then the unfinished letter dragged him back down and he started typing frantically.

While Ellie and Rawle conversed in low voices,

Joe noted the man's stiff, self-important manner; from his body language it was clear that he didn't regard Ellie as sufficiently deferential. Either that or he was uncomfortable in the presence of an attractive woman.

Joe turned to the PC and opened a couple of Internet pages. In one he searched for the Shell Cavern's website, and in the other he called up Hotmail and logged into his account.

There was a single new message—from his brother—sent two days ago. Their mother had completed the first session of chemotherapy and was bearing up well. Making jokes about wig-shopping, should that be necessary.

Joe wanted to reply. He was almost certain it was safe, that his email could not be traced; that his brother's computer had not been compromised. Ninety-nine per cent certain.

But not a hundred per cent.

So he didn't send the email. He gazed at the screen and wondered if he would ever again live in a normal world of uncomplicated relationships and open communication.

*   *   *

There was a clunk as Bastian pushed back his chair and stood up. Not content with the hat and coat, he now wrapped a scarf around his neck. Joe caught the foul, meaty waft of body odour as the man swept past, honing in on Ellie and Rawle and all but vibrating with the need to interject. Within seconds Ellie stepped back, allowing Bastian to slip into the gap, his opening remarks loud enough for the whole library to hear.

'Councillor Rawle, the minutes of the, ah, finance committee meeting. I wonder if you would kindly elucidate certain . . .'

As Ellie headed towards him, Joe casually swapped the page on screen from Hotmail to the Shell Cavern. Ellie gave him a wicked grin.

'Rawle's the man who will wield the axe, and enjoy doing it. Let him explain himself to one of our most dedicated users.' She noticed the website. 'Don't you trust the leaflet?'

'It sounds fascinating, but . . .' Joe shrugged. 'I have a bit of a claustrophobic thing.'

'Oh, it's quite spacious down there. And well lit.'

'Yeah, but it's underground. Stick me in a wardrobe, or an aeroplane toilet—even a large suitcase—and I can deal with it. But underground . . .' He shook his head.

'Well, if you need somebody to hold your hand . . .'

'I'll bear that in mind.' He waited a beat. 'What did you mean about Leon Race?'

'Nothing, really.' She took a step sideways, checking behind her. 'He's the owner of LRS, that's all.'

'But he's pretty important?'

Ellie nodded. Glanced round again. Rawle was still being buttonholed by his constituent, his horror written all over his face as he backed towards the exit.

'Like a dog with a bone, your Mr Bastian,' Joe observed.

'Yes. He prides himself on holding our elected officials to account.'

'Someone has to,' Joe said. 'But it's Leon Race who has the real power, then?'

85

'Look, I'd rather not say any more.' A quick, nervous laugh. 'For all I know you might be one of his spies.'

'Does he have spies?'

'I'm joking,' Ellie said. 'But this is a small town. People love to gossip. You can bet there'll be tongues wagging about you and Diana. Having an old flame turn up on her doorstep . . .'

'Old *friend*,' Joe corrected her. 'Anyway, she's got a new man in her life, hasn't she?'

Ellie's face coloured. 'What?'

'Diana. I got the impression she has a . . . boyfriend.'

'Hasn't she told you?'

'Not yet,' Joe said. 'And I didn't like to pry.'

'In that case, it's not for me to divulge.'

'Okay. But with all this gossiping you mentioned, I thought you'd—'

'Ahem!' Rawle having made his escape, Bastian was at the counter, glaring in Ellie's direction. A middle-aged couple were behind him, clutching several books each.

'Sorry,' Ellie said. 'If you're curious about Diana's love life, you really should ask her to explain.'

* * *

Ellie was still busy when Joe left the library. He raised a hand to wave, but she didn't look up.

Outside there was a welcome surprise: bright sunshine and even a hint of autumnal warmth. All at once the town seemed more colourful, more attractive. Benign, if not exactly friendly.

At the bottom of the hill, directly opposite the

86

harbour wall, Joe found the café that Ellie had mentioned. When he stopped to read the menu in the window, he could hear the water gushing from the stream that ran under the road. A couple of teenagers were leaning over the wall, spitting and dropping leaves into the harbour. It was the closest thing to rebellion Joe had seen so far; in a strange way it was reassuring.

Less pleasant was the fact that he had to study the menu and weigh up the price of a coffee and a scone. Peering through the window, he saw the girl, Alise, inside. That swayed his decision; that and a desire to avoid getting under Diana's feet for another hour or two.

A bell rang as he opened the door. The café was small and quaint, fewer than a dozen tables crammed into a modest space. Lots of pictures on the walls, mostly with a nautical theme, all with little price stickers on them. The tables were covered in floral cloths, with laminated menus propped between salt and pepper pots, a china bowl full of sugar lumps and a vase of dried flowers.

Two other tables were occupied: a young couple in bikers' leathers at one and two elderly women at another. Alise was in the corner, reading a local newspaper. Joe moved alongside her and indicated the chair opposite.

'It's Alise, isn't it? Do you mind if I sit down?'

She looked up, then stared at the empty table next to her, as if wondering whether Joe was blind, or stupid.

He said, 'I was there this morning, when you were arguing with the undertaker.'

Her eyes narrowed. Joe felt a stab of guilt, recalling the moment when Cadwell had grabbed

87

her by the throat.

'I wish I could have been of more help.'

She shrugged. Muttered something he didn't quite catch. He decided to make one last try.

'I heard you asking Cadwell about your sister.'

She leapt on the comment, instantly energised. 'Did you know Kamila? Do you know where she is now?'

Her desperation provoked a shudder of recognition in Joe. This was precisely how he had felt last night, asking Diana if she'd heard from Helen.

Once again he ignored his best instincts, pulled out a chair and sat down.

'I'm afraid not,' he said. 'But I'd like to hear what happened.'

CHAPTER EIGHTEEN

Few things in life can sap your strength as much as the fruitless search for a loved one. Joe understood that, dispassionately, from his time as a police officer, but he appreciated it even more viscerally from personal experience. With every false lead, every dead end, a little more energy seeps away, leaving you exhausted, dispirited and even bitter. He knew it was possible to end up resenting the object of your search, blaming them for your misery and failure.

Joe saw all of that in Alise. He saw it in the set of her body, and the lines in her face; in the difficulty she had putting any real light into her smile. He saw it most of all in the long pause; the process of evaluation while she decided how much to reveal. Telling the story of her sister's disappearance would consume precious emotional energy; having been through this routine many times, she'd be anxious to conserve that energy.

During her deliberations, a waitress approached: a sturdy woman in her fifties with short hair, tightly permed and inexplicably tinted bright orange. Joe ordered coffee and a scone, and Alise asked for another pot of tea. Then, her decision made, she described the situation in a series of verbal bullet points.

'Kamila is twenty, three years younger than me. We are from Latvia. I have been in England four years. In London. Kamila came to London last summer. In Latvia she studies to be accountant. I help her find job in hotel. Very long hours. Bad pay. Some kind people but also rude nasty people.'

Joe nodded. He could attest to that himself.

'But this is good way to learn English. She stay a few months, then home to Latvia. At Christmas she works a few weeks, then home to study. Easter, same thing. Then, in June, she meets a man at hotel. He pays for her to take holiday. He is much older. A rich man.'

Alise pulled a face, as though the very idea was distasteful. The waitress brought their order, and Alise resumed her account.

'They go to a place with beautiful countryside, a village in . . . the *Cots-wolds*?' She phrased the word as though it sounded absurd—which, in a way, Joe realised, it did.

'We speak on the phone, and she is so happy. She will not return to Latvia at end of holiday. But the next week I talk to her and everything is changed.

89

She has broken with this man, but she refuses to tell me why. Just that they are not together.'

'But she didn't go back to London? Or Latvia?'

Alise shook her head. 'She says she has money to see more of England. This is what she will do, then study next year.' Alise hesitated, sniffed a couple of times.

'In this conversation, she scare me. If she has this money, it could help much more in Latvia. Always we work hard, save everything we can. For our future,' Alise added, choking up as she emphasised the final word.

'And she came to Trelennan?' Joe asked, feeling like he was back in an interview room, coaxing information from a traumatised witness.

Alise said, 'Other places, first. Cardiff. Bristol. Every day I send texts. Sometimes I get reply. Sometimes nothing.' A juddering sigh. 'Then she goes to furthest place . . . the End something?' She frowned, trying to recall the name.

'Land's End?'

'Yes. Then Newquay. She likes it. Lot of surfers, lot of nice guys. She says she might stay, find job in hotel. I am so pleased. This sound more like normal Kamila.' She clamped her hands over her heart in a gesture of relief. 'Then I hear she has met someone new. With him she is going to Trelennan. I ask her, will you find job there?'

Her voice was thickening again. The bikers were staring at Joe with a vague disdain.

'Kamila says there is no need for a job. This man is very powerful. This man will pay for everything.'

'Sounds too good to be true.'

Alise nodded vigorously. 'I say this. I tell her, be careful. Kamila is not a child, but she is . . . not

90

experienced. Not wise?' She tapped her forehead, rooting for a better word.

'Naive. Innocent.'

'Innocent, yes. With me, I am hard person. With everyone, I learn to ask: What do you *really* want? But Kamila is not like this.' She leaned over, pulled a tissue from her bag and blew her nose. 'After that, no more phone calls. No texts. Silence.'

Joe sighed. 'What did she tell you about this man?'

'Nothing. Because I am older sister, I maybe get too . . . too much control, you know?' A regretful smile. 'She calls me witch. It was August twenty-eighth, the last time I speak to her, and we say horrible things. We fight like we hate each other, and now I just want to find her and tell her how much I love her, my little sister.'

Alise had tears streaming down her cheeks. Joe gave her time to compose herself while he pondered on what he'd heard, knowing that he shouldn't even think of getting involved but at the same time wanting to offer her a glimmer of hope; something to focus her search.

'She never said anything that could help you identify him?'

'Oh yes,' Alise said, and he realised she had been holding this in reserve. 'She tell me his name by mistake. "You should see Leon's car," she said.'

'"Leon's car",' Joe echoed.

'Leon Race. It was Leon Race who took my sister.'

*   *   *

The allegation hung in the air like smoke: visible,

91

toxic, dangerous. Joe took a look around. The bikers were holding hands across the table, absorbed with each other. The elderly women were talking in loud voices. Joe tuned in for a second: they were discussing a friend's golfing holiday in Portugal, a marriage in trouble. They seemed engrossed, but Joe sensed that one of the women had ten per cent of her attention elsewhere; periodically sweeping the room for something more interesting.

Joe remembered Ellie's comment, quickly retracted, about Leon's spies. Lowering his voice, he said: 'You're certain about this? It was definitely Trelennan?'

'Definitely Trelennan. And definitely Leon.'

'But you have no evidence?'

Looking scornful, Alise clicked her fingers as though performing magic. 'Where do I find evidence?'

'But you went to the police?'

'Oh yes. At first they don't want to hear. Said she is grown woman, able to decide for herself. I say I will go to newspapers, to BBC. So they make enquiries, but in Newquay . . .'

'Because that's where she was last seen.' Joe saw her scowling, and added, 'Which is reasonable enough. It's the best place to start.'

'Maybe. But they find nothing there. Because she has come to Trelennan.'

'Is that where she was, the last time you talked to her?'

Alise hesitated, and Joe knew she was contemplating a lie. 'No. Just before she left, she makes a call to me without Leon knowing. Because of all the messages I leave for her.'

'Didn't you think that was odd, that she should

92

need to phone you in secret?'

'Of course. I say I am scared for her. But, to her, I am the interfering witch. She says I am jealous . . . because she is so pretty, and I am plain.'

Joe groaned in sympathy. 'I used to have arguments like that with my brother. It doesn't mean anything. And you're not plain,' he added, perhaps a touch too hastily.

Alise grinned and said, without false modesty, 'Compared to her, I am plain.'

She rummaged in her bag and produced a battered 6×4 photograph. Taken on a beach somewhere, it showed a willowy doe-eyed girl with long dark hair, beaming at the camera. She was stunning.

Joe studied the picture. 'So what did the police do next? Did they come here?'

'Finally, yes. They say they speak to Leon, and he knows nothing. Has not been to Newquay. Has never met Kamila.'

'He had an alibi for that last night, the night you spoke to her?'

'Yes. Says he is here in Trelennan, with many people. Mostly the men who work for him, but also Derek Cadwell. And a politician, Rawle. All of them say this for him.'

Joe sighed. With that level of alibi, the police would have no cause to dig any deeper.

'They tell me she will be recorded as missing, but I can see they do not care. Maybe she has gone back to her own country, they say, and in their eyes they are wanting her to be gone. Wanting me to be gone, too.'

'Is there no chance that she's returned home?'

'And not told me? Or our mother, our cousins?

93

No. This could not happen.'

'All right. But she might be elsewhere in the UK.'

'Her phone is dead. The police say switched off. No more signal after Newquay.'

'Perhaps it broke, and she bought a new one. Perhaps she hasn't got in touch because she's angry with you?'

'Then she would speak with someone else. Other family, her friends in Latvia.'

'Did she have a bank account over here?'

'Yes, but it is almost empty. The police say no one used it since August.'

'Okay. That's a strong indicator that something has happened. But you still don't know for sure that Leon brought her here. She might have changed her mind. Or maybe the relationship ended, like the one before it.'

Alise folded her arms tightly, as if warding him off. 'You don't want to believe me. You look for reasons to call me a liar, a fool.'

She'd raised her voice, and now the bikers were staring at Joe again. So were the elderly women.

'I'm trying to be thorough,' he said. 'You have to examine every possibility at the outset, otherwise you go running off on a wild-goose chase.'

'Huh. Don't you think I pray every night for a good reason for her to be missing? Don't you think I hope she is somewhere else, safe and happy? So I can leave this terrible place and go back to my home, and my job, and my life?'

Weeping again, she found the tissue she had previously discarded, folded it until it was impossibly small and yet managed to blow her nose on it.

94

Chastened, Joe reached out and grasped her shoulder briefly. 'I'm sorry. It's not that I don't believe you.'

Alise let out a sigh. 'You must ask these questions. I know.'

'Where do you work?'

'For insurance company, in the City. I am an actuary.'

Joe must have made a bad job of concealing his surprise, for she eyed him with a glint of humour. 'You think I would be cleaning the toilets?'

'No. But I'm surprised you're able to get time off to do this.'

'I use all my holiday for the year, plus some compassionate leave. Plus a warning that they will fire me if I am not back one week from now. I am good at my job, but their patience is nearly at the end. I need to find Kamila very soon. Even if she is dead . . .'

Alise tailed off, giving a simple shrug. The tears had stopped. In their place was a calm, quiet pragmatism that chilled Joe, even though on another level he understood it perfectly.

'If she is dead, I want the body to bury.'

CHAPTER NINETEEN

In general, like most people, Leon thought sunshine was a good thing. Good for business, in a town reliant on tourism. Good for the mood—hence expressions like 'a sunny smile' and 'a sunny disposition'. And good for photographs, taken outside, of a group of important but not particularly

95

attractive middle-aged men, all keen to project an aura of power and prosperity.

So, for the latter reason at least, Leon was glad when the weather changed for the better. It allowed a bright, optimistic light to shine on the little group of dignitaries as they stood, chests puffed out, trading phoney smiles and frozen handshakes for the cameras.

Leon was confident that he looked every bit as powerful and prosperous as anybody else— and almost as respectable. A job well done, with all kinds of future benefits in terms of reputation and prestige. Plus, very sweet timing that Giles Haw-hee-haw was there to see it and include it in his article.

But on the journey home the sunshine wasn't so kind. During the buffet, while listening to some arse-licker from the chamber of commerce, he'd had a sense that a migraine was developing. A couple of times his vision had distorted, like glancing into a funhouse mirror. There was a vague not-quite-nausea swelling in his throat.

He'd ignored the signs. Sometimes, if he stayed mellow enough, he could pretty much wish it away. But that meant not thinking about Alise-fucking-Briedis, or this new feller in town.

On the way back the pain came creeping up on him, intensified by the sunlight lancing through the screens. The Merc's tinted windows didn't help; neither did his two-hundred-quid Oakley sunglasses.

As the car pulled into the wide gravel driveway, Leon reached forward, gripped the passenger headrest and overcame the urge to vomit by the sheer force of his will.

Giles swallowed loudly. 'Leon . . .?'

Warren, from the driver's seat, said, 'The boss gets terrible headaches.'

'Migraines,' Leon said. If there was one upside, it was that he didn't have to fake a reason to ditch the journalist.

When the nausea receded, he got out of the car, keeping his back to the sun. He spotted Glenn in the doorway, his whole posture screaming crisis. Leon tipped his head sideways, discreetly motioning for Glenn to go back indoors. Then he gave Giles some guff about checking out the amusement arcade.

'Used to be a tip. I snapped it up, put Glenn in charge of the renovations. Added a snack bar. A bigger car park. Persuaded the council to stick a skate park and basketball court next door. We even took on some young kids, a couple of the . . . what do you have to call 'em? "Special needs"?'

Giles pulled a face. 'Alas, we do, now the PC brigade have us in their Stalinist grip.'

'Yeah. Soft in the head, we used to say. They do a decent job, though. No fuss about minimum wage. Could pay 'em in jelly beans and they'd be grateful.'

With the journalist dispatched, Leon hurried inside. Saw Pam, his housekeeper, and tapped his head. Then Glenn started up; Leon silenced him with a raised hand, and cut into the toilet just off the hall. Turned out the need to vomit had only been postponed.

After throwing up, he rinsed his mouth with cold water. Splashed his face. Pam brought the box of Maxalt and a glass. He popped a 10mg tablet from its blister pack, told it to work fast or else.

That was one pain confronted. Now for the

other.

*   *   *

'Fuck were you playing at?'

'I thought you'd want to know.'

'Yeah, but how could I answer with Giles practically parked in my lap? Engage your fucking brain in future.'

'Sorry, Leon.' With a morose sigh, Glenn followed Leon across the wide hall, the sound of their footsteps on the stone floor jarring Leon's brain. He glanced in one of the living rooms and spotted Kestle, pimply and ginger, glued to his Nintendo DS.

'Why aren't you in Truro?'

Kestle, panicked, said: 'That's Marc's route today. I just got off my shift.'

'Yeah? Well, rustle up some drinks, would you? I'll have my usual, and get Pam to do me a cheese sandwich and some crisps. Lots of crisps.'

'Didn't they have a spread laid on at the council?' Glenn asked.

'Only some finger food. Vol-au-vents and shit like that.' Leon snorted. 'Still, paid for by our taxes, so I'd have been pissed off if it had been caviar and steak.'

'I bet they keep that back for themselves,' Glenn said darkly.

'Yeah. Whatever.' Leon didn't rise to it; he knew Glenn was sucking up to him. 'Makes no difference, seeing as how I just dumped most of it down the bog.'

Although there was a small private study upstairs, Leon's main office was on the ground

98

floor: a vast room that contained a desk, a couple of sofas and a conference table spacious enough for a dozen people.

Derek Cadwell was sitting on one of the sofas like a lumbering white zombie, a cup and saucer balanced primly on his knee. Clive Fenton was behind the desk, a stack of paperwork under one elbow, two laptops up and running in front of him. Fenton was another big man, not as tall or freaky as Cadwell but massively overweight. Hair like a baby duckling's, teased and brushed to look thicker than it was.

Fenton was Leon's right-hand man—although Glenn, in his own head, probably thought he occupied that position. But Fenton had real brains, as well as solid experience in the world of law and accountancy. Proper legitimate skills and a great head for figures, albeit not as good as Leon himself. Nobody could touch Leon on arithmetic.

Both men greeted him warmly. Both spotted that something was wrong.

'Migraine coming on,' he said.

'Maybe you should have a lie down,' Glenn suggested.

Leon took a chair at the conference table. 'In a minute. First I want to hear exactly what we've got going on.' He saw Glenn opening his mouth, so he said, 'You first, Derek.'

*   *   *

As it turned out, neither of them had much new information. Leon wasn't happy to hear that.

Kestle came in with tea and coffee, plus cranberry juice for Leon, who didn't care for hot

99

drinks. He took a careful sip, his stomach lurching and queasy and yet craving food, as often seemed to happen with the migraines.

'I wanna know more about this Joe Carter,' he said, stabbing a finger at Glenn. 'You think Diana's holding back on you?'

Glenn shrugged, his cheeks bright red. 'I bloody hope not—'

'Me neither. So find out. I don't expect you to slap her around, but you can get more than this. Tell her to search his room, or you do it. I want to know what's in his wallet, what's on his phone. Gotta be something there.'

Glenn nodded, but without much enthusiasm. Pam delivered his sandwich and a selection of crisps: salt-and-vinegar, cheese-and-onion, as well as Quavers, his favourite. Leon grabbed a bag, tore it open and inhaled the contents.

'So what about this damn girl?' Cadwell said. 'I can't go on like this, soaking up the heat on your behalf.'

'I know that,' Leon snapped. 'But I got this journalist on me like a second skin.'

'Of course, long-term his article could exacerbate the situation,' Fenton cut in. 'If it raises your profile, she might be encouraged to shout all the louder.'

Leon prised the debris of the crisps from his molars while he translated Fenton's words into English. Eventually he signalled his agreement with a grunt. 'Good point.'

'Then she has to be removed,' Cadwell said. 'It's that simple.'

'Hardly simple,' Glenn said, indignant on Leon's behalf.

100

Cadwell shrugged, like it was beneath him to respond to anything Glenn said. He addressed Leon: 'Your friends on the force can turn a blind eye, can't they?'

Something about his tone got Leon's hackles up. 'They won't have to, if we're smart about it.' He opened a bag of salt-and-vinegar and stuffed a handful of crisps in his mouth. Aware that Cadwell was wincing at the noise, he crunched as loudly as he could, mouth wide open, spraying fragments into the air. 'If we do it, we need to move fast.'

'Agreed,' Fenton said. The others nodded.

'Tonight.' Leon swallowed, smacked his lips together. 'And I wanna talk to her first.'

CHAPTER TWENTY

Over a fresh round of tea and coffee, Joe asked more about Alise's life. Did she have any kind of support network in London?

'Only my boyfriend,' she said, with a derisive snort. 'He works for same company, in IT development. We had been two years together, we talked of marriage. Then Kamila goes missing and Jason is not worried. He thinks Kamila is spoilt bitch.'

'What was her opinion of him?'

'Huh. She always tell me I can get a better man. She is right. When police are here, talking to Leon, I call him, and Jason is like . . .' She mimed a yawn while making a *yak yak* motion with her fingers. 'So I dump him.'

'I'm sorry to hear that.'

101

'Better to find out now he is a prick, instead of marrying him first.'

The bluntness of her response made Joe laugh; after half a second Alise joined in.

'And you?' she said. 'You are new to this town?'

'I'm staying with a friend. She runs the Dolphin B&B.'

Alise grimaced. 'When they find out why I'm here, none of these places would give me a room. They know I am blaming Leon. In their eyes I am his enemy, so they want nothing to do with me.'

This is Leon's town. Although Ellie had subsequently downplayed the statement, Joe was inclined to believe it had been a truthful response, before she'd thought to worry about speaking out of turn.

He surveyed the café again. The two women had just departed, the nosier one treating Joe to a haughty glare on the way out. The bikers remained engrossed in one another. The waitress was behind the counter, wrapping a cake in cling film.

'Not everybody's like that, surely?'

Alise waved dismissively at the window. 'Some days it can look beautiful, but this is not a nice town. No one cares. No one will help.'

Then a long, calculated pause. Joe knew what was coming. He couldn't stop it. Couldn't blame her for saying it.

'But you care. Will you help me?'

*   *   *

He knew he should refuse outright, but it shamed him that he had stood and watched while Cadwell grabbed her by the throat. Now, during this

102

conversation, he'd shifted into professional mode, assembling the raw material of the case as if preparing to investigate it. That was no doubt how it would seem to Alise—raising expectations that he couldn't fulfil.

So, for now, he avoided giving an answer, diverting her with another question.

'What do you know about the first man your sister met? The one who took her to the Cotswolds?'

'I know his name, but nothing more. You think we should talk to him?'

'Was he interviewed by the police?'

'No, I . . . did not mention him.' She blushed, suddenly haunted by guilt. 'Did I get this wrong?'

'Not at all. I'm sure he isn't involved, but it's a place to start. Did you say he met Kamila at the hotel where she worked?'

'Yes. Palace Garden hotel, in Piccadilly.'

'Any friends of Kamila's there? Anyone who could look up the records and find his address or a phone number?'

Alise was starting to read his thought processes; smiling and nodding even before Joe finished the question.

'Yes. There is one man. He liked Kamila, also. He is worried for her.' She beamed at him. 'This is good. I never think of this. Thank you.'

Joe shrugged, a little rueful because he was still backing himself into a corner. The worst thing was, part of him didn't particularly mind.

'I will call him this afternoon,' Alise went on. 'Let me take your mobile number, yes?'

He gave her the number, reassuring himself that it couldn't really hurt. Another thought struck him.

'Do you know where Leon lives?'

Alise looked taken aback. 'It is on the hill above the town. There is a cave, for tourists. Follow the sign to the cave. Leon's house is just before this place.' She studied him for a moment, her eyes misting over. 'All this time it is my dream to have someone who listens.'

Joe felt unworthy of the praise. The voice of caution reminded him that Ellie Kipling, whilst appearing to be no great fan of Leon's, had nevertheless been scornful of the allegations that Alise was making. Joe wondered if he was susceptible to a sob story like this because, in their own way, his own wife and children were missing.

'What about Derek Cadwell?' he said, remembering that Ellie had at least shared Alise's loathing of the undertaker.

'Cadwell and Leon work together on many things.' Alise crossed her fingers to illustrate the point. 'You should speak to a man named Patrick Davy. He owns a gallery along from here. Ask him if Derek Cadwell is a—'

She broke off as the bell over the door jangled and a man entered the café. He was young and smartly dressed. Joe had a feeling he was one of the men he'd seen last night, leaving the pub with Cadwell.

He didn't pay Joe much attention, but when he saw Alise he flinched as if he'd been slapped. After ordering three coffees and a hot chocolate to take away, he glared at them both, then began tapping out a message on his phone.

Alise picked up her handbag and took out her purse. 'I must leave now.'

There was a good-natured dispute over the bill. Alise wanted to settle it in full, because she'd eaten lunch prior to Joe's arrival. They agreed to go halves, and Joe tried to ignore the wrench of pain as another tenner disappeared. He now had roughly forty pounds left.

Once outside, Alise said, 'That is Ben. He works for Cadwell.'

'I thought so.' Joe followed Alise along the pavement, both of them squinting in the bright sunlight. Alise indicated a large building on the corner of the block.

'The gallery. But it is shut this afternoon.' She went up on tiptoe, peering over Joe's shoulder. 'Ben is leaving,' she whispered.

Joe turned, saw the young man crossing the road, carrying his drinks in a tray made of paper pulp. He got into a Vauxhall Astra that had been parked on double yellow lines next to the harbour wall.

'You said Cadwell was one of the people who gave Leon an alibi?'

'Yes. But there is more than that. Much more.'

Alise's tone seemed unnecessarily dramatic. Joe wondered if she was embellishing certain aspects of the story in order to secure his help.

'The job he does,' she said quietly, almost hissing at him.

Joe nodded. A gruesome idea had been floating at the back of his mind for the past few minutes. If Kamila had been murdered—which was surely the unspoken assumption—then a man in Cadwell's line of work could be very useful when it came to disposing of the body.

'If you mean what I think you mean, that's quite an accusation.'

'He would help Leon do anything,' Alise said, fearfully looking around. The street was quiet, a handful of tourists drifting along the promenade. 'He has no choice. Leon knows his secrets.'

'What kind of secrets?'

Alise watched Joe closely, perhaps anticipating a sceptical response. 'Things he does . . . with the dead.'

'What?'

'Leon hid a camera in the funeral home. So now Cadwell must do anything for him.'

Joe gave her the reaction she must have expected. 'If that was true, he'd lose all his business overnight. No one would go near him.'

'They are careful with this secret. Very few people know.'

'Then how did you find out?'

She'd been expecting this question as well, forlornly shaking her head. 'I cannot tell you.'

'You're asking me to take a lot on trust here.'

'Please, Joe. I cannot tell you,' she said again. 'But I know it is true. I swear it.'

CHAPTER TWENTY-ONE

Jenny Foster.

She had a name, an identity and a raging thirst.

She had a full recollection of who she was but not—thankfully—of what had been done to her.

The wound between her legs was healing. She knew that because her captor had told her so. But

106

while it healed, it stung and burned and throbbed. When it was touched she felt as though she'd been set on fire.

She knew that because he'd touched her again. He had tried to rape her, but the screams had put him off. Even when he stuffed a rag in her mouth, the scream emerged through her whole body: it vibrated along her bones and poured from her skin like sweat.

'Couple of days,' he'd said after he climbed off, giving her a bad-tempered kick while he zipped up. 'Then you'll be good as new.'

* * *

He had visited her twice. The first time, the attempted rape, he brought with him a battery-operated torch. Its illumination was weak but had an incredible effect on her. She was almost willing to suffer the pain he inflicted, if only because he had rescued her from the darkness.

She had practically no sense of time. His visit might have been hours after she first recovered consciousness, but she thought it was probably longer: a day or so. When he left, he took the light with him. She was bereft.

The second visit, by contrast, seemed much sooner: only hours after the first. Her mind was clearer, despite the rhythmic bass-drum-and-cymbal clash of a dehydration headache. She knew who she was. She understood, at least partially, what had happened to her.

This time, as well as the light, he brought water in a bucket, a towel, and some food.

'All right?' he growled. Unhappy about

107

something.

Jenny realised she was making noises: sobbing, whimpering. She forced them to stop, and he grunted and put the bucket down at her side, slopping water over the rim. The cold splash of it on her skin caused her to gasp and turn towards him. He kicked her savagely, and she screamed, her mouth wide open but making no sound.

She wasn't to look at him. She had learned that on the first visit.

'You stupid bitch,' he said. 'Drink some of this, then clean yourself up. Afterwards, use it for a toilet.' She felt him crouching, bending over her, his breath hot on her face. 'And wash the blood off your tits. Haven't you got any self-respect?'

He opened the door and she sensed the dim light bobbing in the darkness, moving away from her.

'Leave me the torch.'

'Fuck off.'

'So I can see, to clean myself. Please.'

In his hesitation, she understood what this represented: the chance to open a tiny chink in his armour. A small but significant repositioning in the balance of power between them.

He set the torch down, strode out and slammed the door behind him.

Jenny waited a few seconds, then wept with joy at the scale of her victory.

CHAPTER TWENTY-TWO

Joe walked back through the town and then followed a different route from the one he'd taken that morning, winding his way up the hillside. He hadn't actually committed himself to helping Alise. This was purely a way of killing time, he told himself. No harm in it.

Eventually he reached level ground and found a sign urging him to sample the thrill of the Shell Cavern, a hundred yards further on. He was back in the wealthy neighbourhood, but Alise's description wasn't precise enough for him to distinguish Leon's property from the other large homes, all shielded by high walls and dense foliage.

For lack of a better idea, he wandered towards the tourist attraction. The site was on a small plot of untended grass, thick with nettles, bordered by a chain-link fence. No car park, but there were several cars and a minibus parked on the street outside.

The visitor centre was housed in a ramshackle windowless building, possibly an old cattle shed, made of weathered stone and with a moss-encrusted roof. Joe pushed through the double glass doors into a room about thirty feet square, with poster-sized photographs and display units, and a gift area with tables selling the usual tourist fare: pottery and ceramics, exotic stones and crystals, mugs and postcards and overpriced confectionery.

The room's only occupant was a member of staff, a tall, rangy man in his fifties with greying blond hair tied back in a ponytail. He gave Joe a cautious appraisal before nodding a greeting.

Next to the counter, an open doorway beckoned. Joe eased his way over and peered in. A set of stone steps dropped twenty feet or so, then curved out of sight, lit by a series of weak bulbs strung along the

109

roof of the cave.

Joe shuddered. Not his thing at all.

'I guarantee you'll be awed,' the man told him. He spoke with the deep, calm gravitas of a counsellor or clergyman. 'For some, it's a life-changing experience.'

Joe smiled, but shook his head. 'Another day, thanks.'

He made his exit, feeling slightly foolish. What had Ellie said about holding his hand?

Hmm. She was a prickly woman, unlikeable in many ways, and decidedly catty where Diana was concerned, and yet . . .

She had definitely stirred something in him. Something that had lain dormant for a long time.

He sucked air between his teeth and carried on walking. *And yet* was dangerous, he thought. *And yet* could get him into trouble.

*   *   *

Joe soon discovered that the road led nowhere. It ended in a bulbous turning circle, beyond which lay a thick copse of trees and unwelcoming thickets of brambles and blackthorn.

Retracing his steps and passing the Shell Cavern once again, he noticed a narrow footpath that he'd missed the first time. It was overgrown with weeds but Joe eased his way through them. A noise grew in volume as he followed the path through several twists and turns: the roar of rushing water.

The bushes on either side towered over him, blocking his view until a final abrupt turn brought him out in a small clearing. A steel fence, eight feet high, had been erected across the path. It bore a plethora of warning signs: NO ENTRY and PRIVATE and DANGER: LANDSLIP.

The path appeared to continue beyond the fence, dropping away steeply as it weaved through the rocky, tree-covered hillside. Joe guessed it might lead to the sandy beaches east of the town. If so, the views during the descent would be spectacular.

He stepped close to the fence and looked through. To his right he caught glimpses of the shore and a slice of tranquil sea. Directly ahead there appeared to be a deep but narrow cleft in the hillside, which was almost certainly the location of the pounding water.

Then he caught a flash of light: sunlight reflecting on glass. A house was poised on the edge on the gully, with a veranda running along the rear and a timber deck on one corner, jutting out to form a viewing platform. Joe could see steel supports angled into the rock face beneath the platform.

There was a man on the decking, wearing what might have been the uniform of an LRS guard. He lifted a pair of binoculars and directed them at Joe, who waved, somewhat sarcastically, then made a point of admiring the view for a minute or so before slowly turning away.

Back at the road, Joe was grudgingly impressed to find an LRS van waiting for him.

*   *   *

The driver was a heavyset man in his thirties. Shaved head, goatee beard and the needlessly aggressive bearing of a nightclub bouncer. He was standing on the pavement, arms folded across a barrel chest.

111

'Path's closed,' he said.

'I gathered that.'

'And it's private property.'

'Not where I was.'

'You were intent on trespassing.'

Joe shrugged. He saw no sense in arguing with someone who was intent on a fight. Better just to fight and have done with it.

The man jerked his head towards the van. 'Get in.'

'What?'

'The owner of the property wants to see you.'

'Why?'

'He'll tell you that himself.' He took a step back, opened the passenger door and jerked his head again: *Get in*.

'Who's the owner of the property?'

The man scowled, making it clear that he ought to be beating Joe's face to a pulp rather than answering his questions.

'Leon Race.'

CHAPTER TWENTY-THREE

The journey to Leon's home took less than two minutes, and most of that was spent turning the van round.

Joe could have refused to go, but he guessed that might cause more problems in the long run. If what he'd heard so far was true, it seemed likely that he would show up on Leon's radar at some point during his stay. Despite the van driver's thuggish demeanour, Joe didn't regard himself as in any

112

particular danger, and his instincts for these things were generally reliable.

The entrance to the property was marked by a set of steel gates. A wide gravel drive cut between leaf-strewn lawns. Mature trees ran along the high perimeter wall, which was constructed of a weathered yellow stone.

The house itself, built from the same pale stone, was a solid, symmetrical Georgian mansion, with a dark slate roof and thick chimneys at each end. The ivy that crept towards the upper windows gave the sense of a building that was long rooted in the landscape and might one day be consumed by it.

To the right of the house another high stone wall enclosed a kitchen garden. A modern ugly car port had been erected against the wall, with several cars and vans parked beneath it. Joe's immediate reaction was to wonder how the owner had managed to obtain permission to build such an eyesore—and then he remembered who the owner was.

*   *   *

The van rolled to a halt behind an E-class Mercedes, and Joe climbed out. Another guard was waiting for him in the doorway. He looked about nineteen, thin and pimply, with dark red hair and a ferocious shaving rash on his neck.

'Leon Race?'

The man gawped, until it registered that Joe was taking the piss. 'I'm Kestle.'

Joe shrugged: *As if I care.* Stepping into a large entrance hall, he was instructed to leave his bag and remove his jacket.

113

'I have to pat you down,' Kestle said.

'You're joking.'

'That's the rules.' The guard turned his head, as if seeking reinforcements. With perfect timing, an obese middle-aged man came waddling towards them, dress shoes clopping on the flagstones. He wore pinstriped trousers and a pink shirt, his neck bulging over the collar like a cake spilling from its mould.

'Just a small courtesy to Mr Race,' he said. He had a soft local accent, and a voice that sounded like his sinuses were blocked. 'I'm Clive Fenton.'

They shook hands, then Joe allowed Kestle to perform a quick, ineffective search. He missed several places where Joe could have concealed a weapon.

Fenton led him across the hall and into what Joe guessed was a secondary living room. It had a polished wood floor with several Turkish rugs, a collection of sofas and armchairs, a mid-sized plasma TV, but little sign that it saw much use. There was a coffee table with a stack of newspapers, mostly tabloids, and a large metal tambour cupboard that looked more like it belonged in an office. No pictures on the walls, no ornaments or personal belongings.

Fenton shut the door behind them. The room's other occupant was standing at the window, watching a gardener trudge across the grass, sucking up leaves with a hand-held vacuum.

'If he worked any slower he'd fucking rust.' He turned his unhappy gaze upon Joe. 'I'm Leon Race. And you are . . . ?'

'Joe Carter.'

'Hello, Joe Carter, I'd like to hear why you were

114

spying on me.'

*   *   *

Leon didn't really correspond to the image that Joe had formed in his head. In a few aspects, certainly: the coldness in his voice, the steely glint in his eyes. But physically Leon Race was disconcerting. Maybe an inch or two over six foot, he had to weigh at least sixteen stone; and somehow he managed to look both blubbery and strong.

He had a round face with chubby features, soft white skin, blue eyes and fine silky hair the colour of straw. He wore an olive-green T-shirt and blue polyester jogging pants. His huge feet were encased in gleaming white trainers, which perhaps explained the spring in his step. Even standing in one spot he kept bobbing up and down on his toes.

His hands were also large and expressive, constantly on the move. Chunky platinum rings on both forefingers.

'I wasn't spying,' Joe said. 'I didn't even notice this place until I saw your guy with the binoculars.'

'You were trying to find a way onto my property.' Leon sounded stern rather than aggressive. Joe had the impression that this was a game; a test of some kind.

'I'd been to the Shell Cavern,' he said, pulling the crumpled leaflet from his pocket. 'I spotted the path and decided to check out the view, but your fence put paid to that.'

Leon waited for more, but Joe knew that game well. He said nothing.

Then Leon abruptly jerked his head back and laughed, as though he and Joe had been friends all along.

'You wouldn't believe all the grief I got over that fence. Bloody ramblers or whatever they are.' He winked. 'In the end we had to stage a landslide to help the council prove it wasn't safe. That saw 'em off, eh, Clive?'

Fenton addressed his response to Joe. 'It is genuinely hazardous, of course.'

Leon tapped the side of his nose with his forefinger. 'Very clever man, my Mr Fenton. D'you want to see it?' he added, so swiftly that Joe was baffled.

'See what?'

'What d'you think? The fucking view.'

*   *   *

Leon strode out of the room, through the hall and into another, larger room that was being used as an office. Joe followed in his wake, with Fenton bringing up the rear, puffing from the effort of matching his boss's pace.

Behind the desk, full-length louvre blinds covered a set of double doors. Leon pulled the blinds aside and threw open the doors, letting in dazzling sunshine and the sound of water pummelling rock. They stepped onto the veranda that Joe had seen from the other side of the gorge. It ran along two sides of the building, and at several points there were steps down to a lower level of hardwood decking.

Leon marched across to the viewing platform in the far corner. It was enclosed by a high rail and boasted a set of wrought-iron furniture. Red-faced and panting, Fenton grabbed one of the chairs and

116

sat down, sighing gratefully.

The view was every bit as spectacular as Joe had anticipated. He took in the grand sweep of the bay, the town laid out on the hillside to his left, and the rocky tree-studded slopes to his right. The motor boats in the harbour looked like toys. The sea was such a deep, sparkling blue that its gentle waves might have been lapping against a Caribbean shore.

Leon beckoned him forward. 'Come here.'

Joining him at the rail, Joe peered over. A narrow ravine ran beside the property, carving up the lower section of the terraced gardens. The stream widened into a deep, churning pool, then spilled over a rocky ledge, forming a waterfall about twenty feet high that disappeared into the trees on the hillside beneath them.

Joe found himself calculating his chance of survival should Leon suddenly pitch him over the edge. He didn't think it was going to happen, but he gripped the rail tightly just the same.

'Is this the stream that runs into town?' he asked.

'Kind of. At the top of the hill it splits into two. A couple of centuries back this channel was dug out to support a mill that used to be just down there. At the bottom of the hill it runs underground and joins the main flow that comes out in the harbour.'

'It's stunning,' Joe said.

Leon nodded, but the air of convivial host was absent once again. He turned and scrutinised the hillside, pointing out the spot where Joe had been standing.

'Are you gonna tell me why you were watching my house?'

'I wasn't. I had no idea who lived here.'

'But you've heard of me. You know who I am?'

Joe shrugged. 'Your name's been mentioned.'

Leon exchanged a glance with Fenton, then snorted. 'I bet it has.'

*   *   *

Joe decided that a dignified silence was his best response. He leaned his back against the rail so he could look directly at Fenton but also monitor Leon in his peripheral vision. Just in case.

'What are you really doing here, Mr Carter?' Fenton said.

'In Trelennan, you mean? Visiting an old friend.'

'Diana Walters,' Leon said, and ignored Joe's surprise, as though vaguely insulted that Joe hadn't expected him to know. 'So what's she to you?'

'Like I said, she's an old friend.'

'What about her husband? Was he an "old friend" as well?'

'He was, yes.'

'And a fellow officer of the law, maybe?'

Joe pushed himself off the rail and stood upright, facing Leon. Trying to project a calmness he didn't entirely feel, he stared into Leon's eyes and said, 'That's none of your business. Why the hell do you care who I am or what I'm doing here? Unless you've got something to hide.'

He waited a beat, savouring the shocked, incredulous reaction from both men.

'Well?' he said. '*Do* you have something to hide?'

118

CHAPTER TWENTY-FOUR

As she sent the text, Alise felt a thrill run through her. After so long on her own, it was wonderful to have an ally, someone willing to fight alongside her.

Not that Joe had actually said as much. She shouldn't get overexcited. Experience had taught her that too much hope could be a destabilising force, especially when the promised results failed to materialise.

But Joe seemed genuinely interested in her plight. There was a quiet strength to him that had impressed her. The sort of man who wouldn't boast or shout about his capabilities; he would just get on and do it.

And he had a hardness, a flinty, stubborn streak that was as dangerous as it was useful. She had seen it in men she had known back home. One had been in the Military Police; the other was a notorious drug smuggler in Riga who'd been shot dead by his Russian supplier. Joe had the same look in his eyes: that even *he* might not know what he was capable of until it was too late.

But nice eyes, also, she thought, blushing inside. Warm eyes.

Then again, her judgement could be wrong. Once Joe understood what he was facing he might decide he wanted nothing more to do with it.

Getting too negative . . . She gave herself a mental slap on the face. *Stop it.*

For the past hour she'd been sitting on the promenade, but the air was rapidly cooling. She stood up and crossed the road. Walking was the best way to keep warm.

She was lodging unofficially in a building where the landlord, a mean and suspicious man, lived on the ground floor. Her flatmate, Karen, finished work at five. By then the landlord was normally at the pub. Alise would hide around the corner until it was safe to sneak inside.

An odd way to live, on top of everything else. Afternoons were the worst, finding somewhere to wait out the endless hours. Maybe it was a good thing that her employers had run out of patience. Perhaps, after one more week without progress, she should return to London . . .

She started up Crabtree Lane, vaguely intent on wandering past the undertaker's home. Too preoccupied to notice the van rolling to the kerb behind her. She didn't hear the soft clicks as first the passenger door opened, then one of the rear doors.

The van was plain white, no livery, the registration plates obscured by dirt and grease. Three men ghosted onto the pavement, dressed all in black and wearing sunglasses and baseball caps. One of them carried a knife. He didn't expect to use it, but if he had to, he would.

Finally Alise sensed their approach, but too late. All she knew was a sudden muffled darkness, some kind of hood or blanket thrown over her head, a hand clamped on her mouth, strong arms dragging her backwards. Her heel bumped against the kerb and she felt one of her shoes loosening, falling away. A man said, 'The shoe,' and another said, 'Got it,' and she realised there were two of them at least, probably more: it was a team.

A team had been sent to get her, to snatch her

120

off the street in broad daylight. That could mean only one thing.

It was over. She had failed Kamila, and now she would suffer the same fate.

* * *

Leon stared at Joe, a feral look in his eyes. Bouncing on his heels as if preparing to attack. Then he turned and hammered out a primitive drum roll on the rail with his fists. The noise reverberated through the decking, competing with the roar of the waterfall. When he turned back, he was calmer.

'That's a brave question to ask,' he said in a sober voice. 'Fucking cheeky, too.'

'I don't understand your curiosity about me.'

'You've been speaking to people. Ellie Kipling. And that Russian nutjob.'

'Alise?' Joe queried. 'Why should you think we were discussing you?'

'Because that's the only thing she ever talks about. That and her bloody sister.'

Joe shrugged. 'She believes the two subjects are linked.'

'Yeah, but that's because she's got a screw loose. Did she tell you she even got the police down here? Interviewing me. Bothering my friends and associates. Fucking embarrassing, and a total waste of everybody's time. I've never set eyes on her sister, and I doubt if the poor cow ever set foot in this town.'

'She doesn't accept that.'

'No. And what do you call a person who won't accept reality? A lunatic.'

'She seemed perfectly sane to me.'

121

'We'll agree to disagree, then.' Leon dragged a couple of chairs out, sat on one and pointed at the other. 'Tell me, Joe, what do you do for a living?'

Joe pulled the chair another foot or so away from Leon before he sat down. 'Various things. Painting and decorating, most recently.'

Leon nodded thoughtfully. 'How long are you planning to stay here?'

'I haven't decided yet.' Joe wondered if he was going to get his marching orders. *Leave town by sunset or face the consequences . . .*

'Well, if you're sticking round for a week or two I might have some work available.'

Wrong-footed, Joe stared at Leon for a moment, waiting for the catch. Leon could see it; he looked grimly amused.

'Has anybody explained what I do?'

'Not really. Though I've seen the security business in operation.'

Joe's ironic tone was lost on Leon, who said proudly: 'Started that up from nothing, ten years ago. Now we have forty guys doing patrols in half a dozen local towns. More than eight hundred homes signed up to our personal-response service. Thousands of others with alarm systems. Thanks to me, crime in Trelennan is non-existent.'

'Very impressive.'

This time Leon detected the hint of sarcasm. His mouth tightened. 'That's the core business. I also provide security for pubs, clubs, concerts, sporting events. I've got a few pubs of my own, plus a taxi firm and the amusement arcade here in Trelennan, and a vending-machine business with customers all over the South-West.'

'What about the funeral director's?'

122

'That's not mine, though the proprietor, Derek, is a friend.' Leon paused, irritated by the break in his momentum. 'The fact is, I always need people available at short notice, willing to work irregular hours. Cash in hand all right for you?'

Joe nodded, as non-committally as he could manage. 'It can be.'

'It'd be mostly driving, deliveries. Ferrying people and stuff from A to B. Cornwall's a nice place to live, but the public transport is shit.' He grunted. 'What do you say?'

'I'll definitely think it over. Thanks for the offer.'

Leon looked like he was going to take offence. He glanced at Fenton, whose face remained impassive.

'Right. You do that.' Leon stood up, signalling that the meeting was concluded.

As they turned to go inside, Joe caught movement from an upstairs window, as though somebody had quickly backed out of sight. The after-image left in Joe's mind seemed familiar.

A phone rang as they were passing through the office. Fenton picked up a cordless handset and passed it to Leon.

'Reece?' Leon said. 'So what's up?' Reaching the hall, he put on some speed, extending the distance between him and Joe. He listened for a while. 'No, I get you.' Listened some more. Consulted his watch. 'Not yet. Make it, say, around eight.'

He finished the call. Tossed the phone to Fenton, who fumbled and dropped it.

'Don't ever play cricket, lardy,' Leon muttered.

*　　　*　　　*

123

At the front door, the red-haired guard was welcoming another visitor: a man in his late forties, slim and well groomed, slightly effete, with a distinct air of superiority about him. Joe heard Leon give a quiet groan, at odds with the hearty greeting that followed.

'Giles! You're back early. Hope you got the full tour?'

'I believe so.'

'Fantastic. Hey, say hello to Joe . . .' He gripped Joe's shoulder. '. . . *Carter*, isn't it?'

Joe nodded. He doubted very much that Leon had forgotten his surname.

Leon went on: 'Joe's maybe gonna be the latest addition to the team.'

'Congratulations.' Giles sounded enthusiastic, but there was boredom in his eyes. He shook hands limply but didn't bother to introduce himself.

'Be with you in a minute,' Leon said.

'You're feeling better now, I hope?' Giles enquired.

'Not too bad.'

'Have you been ill?' Joe asked as Fenton led Giles away.

'Migraine. But I fought the bastard off.' He spotted Joe's bag of shopping, picked it up and peered inside before handing it to him. Smirking, he said, 'Let us know when you've decided, yeah?'

'I will.'

Joe walked out and crossed the drive, resisting the urge to turn and see if he was being watched. All he could think was: *What the hell just happened?*

He took the quickest route back into town. His phone buzzed as he reached the High Street: a text from Alise. She'd spoken to someone at the hotel

124

in Piccadilly and identified the man that her sister had befriended. His name was Jamie Pearse, with a phone number and an address, not in the Cotswolds but in Poundbury, Dorset.

Joe sent a brief reply: **Thanks, Alise. This is a good start. Speak soon.**

He carried on walking, feeling strangely exhilarated. Almost tempted to whistle, but not quite. And still thinking: *What the hell just happened?*

CHAPTER TWENTY-FIVE

The first room off the hall was a boot room. When he'd seen it in the estate agent's brochure, Leon had been astonished by the idea that some people felt they needed an entire room for their shoes and their coats. Madness.

Once the house was his, the room had rapidly undergone a change of function. It was just large enough for a single L-shaped desk with half a dozen monitors, pulling in the feed from his network of cameras. A perfect command centre.

Trusting Fenton to keep the journalist occupied, Leon started to open the door but met resistance. There was a muffled cry and Glenn stepped back, one hand cupped over his nose.

'Clumsy arsehole,' Leon said, without malice.

'I was coming to get you.' Glenn sniffed, examining his palm for signs of blood.

'You're fine.' Leon looked at Derek Cadwell, loitering in the far corner like a sinister hatstand. 'They've got her.'

'Already?'

'They saw an opportunity and took it. But they'll have to keep her till tonight. Can't bring her here with Giles around.'

Cadwell nodded, deep in thought. Glenn filled the silence with a question: 'Is that right, you've offered Di's friend a job?'

'Yeah.' Leon kept a steady eye on Glenn. 'Any problem with that?'

'No, but . . . It's risky, isn't it?'

'Why? We can control where he goes and what he does. And it's the best way to keep an eye on him. Perfect, really.'

Stepping past Glenn, he rubbed his hands together and addressed the fourth man in the room. 'Show me the pictures.'

*   *   *

The man at the desk was Phil Venning, a thin, morose Welshman. He had unusually tiny ears, of a completely different colour and texture to the rest of his skin, as though they'd been taken from a child and transplanted onto his head.

'Got some lovely coverage,' he said. He brought up footage of Joe walking towards the front door. Hit a button and showed him in the hall with Fenton. Then out on the deck, leaning casually against the rail.

'The stills are even better,' Glenn said, patting a Nikon DSLR camera that was linked to the computer by a USB cable.

Venning opened a folder on another monitor. Leon crouched down and peered at the thumbnails, then selected the slide-show view.

A head shot of Joe Carter filled the screen, captured with a long lens when he'd first been spotted on the path. Then came several taken from an upstairs window as Joe climbed out of the van. Lastly, a couple of him on the decking, again taken from an upper window.

Leon tapped an image of Joe by the van. 'This is the best one. Get it cropped and printed. I want all our people to have a copy. And email it to everyone we deal with, tell them to spread it round their networks. Somebody's got to know who "Joe Carter" is.'

'Do you reckon that's his real name?' Cadwell asked.

'I doubt it.' A pointed look at Glenn. 'That's your job to find out.'

Glenn nodded. 'I still think he's on the run.'

'Maybe,' Leon said. 'I saw the stuff he'd bought in town. Shaving gear, deodorant. He definitely left somewhere in a hurry.'

'The question is, what's he running from?' Cadwell said.

'Nah, the question is *who*.' Leon grinned, sucking air between his teeth. 'We find out who's after him, and he's ours.'

*   *   *

The way Joe saw it, Leon's proposal made no sense. If he suspected Joe of taking Alise's side, why would he offer him work? Was it to sow confusion, or to force Joe's hand?

Either way, it suggested that Leon had nothing to hide—or nothing that he thought Joe could find. Joe should also take caution from the

127

demonstration of Leon's power: the fact that he already knew Joe had been speaking to Ellie and Alise.

Joe would be mad even to consider the offer. So why hadn't he turned it down flat?

The answer was thrown into focus when he browsed a couple of charity shops in the High Street. Even most of their clothes were beyond his budget. He needed money.

At the B&B there was no sign of Diana's car. Joe let himself in, feeling like an intruder at first, made uneasy by the unfamiliar creaks and groans of the house at rest.

He put the coffee maker on and had just sat down with the newspaper when he heard the front door open. Diana called out a greeting and trooped into the kitchen, laden with shopping. She put the groceries on the counter, then handed Joe a carrier bag from a menswear store.

'Hope it all fits. I had to guess.'

In the bag he found a tailored jacket, jeans, a couple of shirts and some underwear. It had to be a couple of hundred pounds' worth of clothes. He looked through them, touched by her generosity but also sick and furious with what he'd made himself: a charity case.

'I'm going to pay you for these.'

'No. They're a gift. My way of saying sorry for how I reacted last night.'

'You have nothing to apologise for.'

'I do.' Diana poured herself a coffee and joined him at the table. 'The thing is, a lot has changed since I last saw you. Not just losing Roy.' She laced her hands together, nervously twisting her fingers. 'God, I hate how this sounds, but I've moved on. I

128

had to.'

'Of course.' Joe smiled. 'I think I spotted your young man leaving the house this morning.'

She looked mortified. 'He hadn't stayed over. He just called in while I was making breakfast—'

'Di, it's all right. You're perfectly entitled to see whoever you want.'

'Mmm.' She unclasped her hands, examined them sadly, then shrugged. 'Sorry. I'm not used to discussing relationships. It feels all the more awkward with you.'

'Because I was friends with Roy?'

'Partly that. But also . . .' She reddened. 'Oh, I know it was just a silly, drunken mistake. I regretted it straight away. I'm sure you did, too. But . . .' She turned her face away from him, took a deep breath. 'Part of me *didn't* regret it. Part of me wished it had been more than it was.'

Joe let the words sink in, aware that it would seem crass if he rushed his reply.

'Actually, that's pretty much how I felt about it, too.'

Another significant pause. Then she laughed. 'Oh dear, this is so embarrassing.'

'Shall we change the subject? As it happens, I had quite an eventful day.'

*   *   *

First he described the confrontation between Alise and Derek Cadwell, then his conversation with Alise. He was debating how to phrase a couple of awkward questions when Diana volunteered an answer to one of them.

'She came here a few weeks ago, wanting to

129

know if I'd had any guests who fitted her sister's description. She showed me a photo of the girl, but I wasn't able to help.'

Joe nodded. Now came the really awkward one. 'Did she ask you for a room?'

'Not that I recall. Why?'

'She told me she'd met some resistance locally. An unwillingness to give her accommodation.'

'That's awful. Of course, it might have been when I was full. I did have a busy spell in early September.' Her voice wavered slightly; she cleared her throat.

'You know she's alleging that someone in Trelennan is responsible? A man called Leon Race.'

'I had heard rumours, yes.' She seemed about to elaborate, but clamped her lips together.

Joe said, 'Alise believes there's a conspiracy at work, involving Leon and Derek Cadwell.'

As a diversion, Diana had taken a sip of coffee. The cup shook in her hand as she set it down.

'Leon Race is no saint. By all accounts he was a right tearaway in his youth, and he doesn't mind who knows it. And Derek, what with the line of work he's in, and his unfortunate appearance . . .' She shook her head. 'But they're both very successful. I can't see why they'd be involved in anything so dreadful. If this girl . . .'

'Alise.'

'If Alise had any evidence, the police would be all over it, surely? And if she doesn't, harsh as it is, you have to wonder if she's barking up the wrong tree.'

'That's a strong possibility,' Joe agreed. 'In a way, I hope it's true. Because I also had an interesting

130

encounter with Leon Race.' He explained how he'd been intercepted by a security patrol, and had decided it was an opportunity to form his own opinion of the man.

'And what did you think?'

'He's obviously very bright. Streetsmart rather than classically educated. Strong. Charismatic. And not somebody you'd want to cross. I was chatting to a woman in the library—Ellie Kipling. She made it sound as though Leon rules the roost down here.'

Diana had gone pale. It happened so abruptly that Joe had to force himself not to stare.

'I know Ellie,' she said, her voice stilted, almost robotic. 'She's a woman with a vivid imagination.'

'All those books?' Joe said, trying to make light of it. But Diana didn't smile. Unnerved by the look in her eyes, he pressed on. 'Leon offered me a job.'

Another shock. Diana responded quickly: 'You're not going to take it?'

'Don't you think I should?'

'I thought this was a place to hide. Isn't the idea to steer clear of . . .?' She shrugged, leaving him wondering what it was she couldn't bring herself to voice. *Trouble? Danger?*

'I know. Maybe it isn't the most sensible thing to do. But I'm Joe Carter here. No one but you has any idea of my real identity. As long as it stays that way, I should be fine.'

He waited for her objections. She was wrestling with something, but wouldn't come out and say it.

'It's a question of priorities,' he went on. 'The safest thing for me is to leave it a while before I get my stuff from Bristol. In the meantime, I'm determined not to be a drain on your finances. I have to earn some money.'

131

'Joe, how many times do I need to say it? You're here as a friend.'

'Even so, I don't want to take advantage. Or make things awkward for you, especially with your new boyfriend.'

Diana snorted. 'That word sounds ridiculous. I'm fifty-one, for goodness' sake. How can I have a "boyfriend" at my age?'

'Because you're never too old for a relationship.' He smiled as he saw her relax, some of the colour returning to her cheeks. 'Are you going to tell me about him?'

Shyly, she said, 'His name's Glenn. He's quite a bit younger than me, actually. Forty-three. He was a builder originally, but he had a change of career.' She looked embarrassed but also, Joe thought, faintly amused.

'Don't tell me he became a cop?' Joe said. Even as the words left his mouth, he realised the true answer was going to be very different.

'No,' said Diana. 'Glenn works for Leon Race.'

CHAPTER TWENTY-SIX

Leon didn't deliberately set out to lose his temper with Alise. He must have foreseen the possibility, though, because he chose to interview her in a room with bare oak floorboards. He had the sofas dragged aside, and a thick polythene sheet spread out beneath the plain kitchen chair on which she would sit.

The journalist had been softened up with whisky, bullshitted until his eyes glazed over and despatched to his hotel for the night. Leon took another Maxalt and stole a quick nap. He woke when they were five minutes out, his head clear and steady. Stepping into the shower to freshen up, he realised he was getting hard just thinking about Alise tied to the chair, helpless.

After the shower, he smeared hydrocortisone on a patch of dry skin around his groin. The cream felt deliciously cold, turning him on even more. He dressed in a T-shirt and a fresh pair of jogging pants, but stayed barefoot. He liked the tactile sensation of walking on different surfaces: carpet, wood, stone. Polythene.

By the time he got downstairs they'd unloaded and set her up. She was conscious, her hair and clothes a mess, her face deathly pale, eyes large and bright with dark bags beneath them. Not a pretty girl, in Leon's view. Her features were too large, too chunky. Not a face to earn a second glance, or linger in anyone's memory.

Her feet had been bound to the legs of the chair, her hands tied behind her back. Her mouth was covered with packing tape. She saw him in the doorway and reacted with horror, then a quick flash of something else: a desperate plea, directed not at Leon but at the man who'd appeared at his shoulder.

It was Glenn, looking anxious. One hand shoved in his pocket, playing musical balls.

'I'm getting off, then,' he said.

'You not gonna stick around, watch the fun?'

'I've agreed to see Di.'

'You're well under the thumb.'

Glenn scowled. 'You want more information from Diana, don't you?'

133

'Why, are you gonna tie her to a chair as well? I'll be there for that.'

'Leave it out.' Glenn backed away as Fenton waddled over, eager to take his seat in the front row.

'Go on, run along to your little woman.' Feigning concern, Leon checked the time. 'In fact, you'd best get a move on.'

'Why?'

'Well, she's bound to be screwing Joe by now, isn't she?'

Fenton chipped in: 'With any luck you'll catch them red-handed.'

'Red-dicked, more like,' Leon cackled.

They watched Glenn slope away, like the only kid with a curfew. Fenton rubbed his palms together, his hungry eyes glittering, and said, 'Are we all set?'

'Derek's not here yet. We'll start without him.'

They entered the living room. Alise was being guarded by a couple of the team who had grabbed her, Reece and Todd. Leon signalled to Reece while Fenton settled on a sofa, shuffling his enormous buttocks until he was comfortable.

The girl made an angry noise in her throat, which turned into a shriek as the tape was ripped away from her mouth.

'You can stop that fucking noise,' Leon warned her. He knelt down on the polythene sheet, bringing his face level with hers. She flinched. The chair creaked and rocked, and he thought she was going to tip it over. From this close he could smell the terror on her. Could see her fighting to keep it in check.

'You're here because you keep spreading lies about me.'

'It is not lies,' she yelled. Then she spat at him: a gesture so defiant, so pointless, that it took him completely by surprise.

It landed on his nose, his cheek; Leon could feel it cooling on his skin. The fury rose up like a sickness, overwhelming him. He drew back his fist and punched her full in the face.

*   *   *

Roy Bamber's retirement party had been held in the function room of a pub in Westminster. It was a night of wild and drunken revelry: precisely what you'd expect when a group of mostly old-time coppers gathered to celebrate the departure of one of their own.

Midway through the evening, to howls of lecherous delight, a couple of strippers had materialised. The surprise had been arranged by a small band of Roy's colleagues, notorious for their practical jokes. Needless to say, Diana and some of the other wives had been rather less impressed.

Despite a vow to pace himself, Joe had ended up throwing shots down his throat. This was 2003, when his daughters were still toddlers and any kind of night out was a rare treat, easily taken to extremes. A last minute foul-up with babysitters meant that he'd come alone—although that, he thought later, was no excuse for what he'd done.

It had happened shortly after Roy's sentimental but touching farewell speech, during which he'd made it plain how glad he was to be leaving the force and embarking on a new life in Cornwall. Unfortunately he'd barely mentioned Diana: no reference to the support she'd given throughout his

135

career, or the part she would play in this exciting new venture.

The effects of the alcohol hit Joe suddenly. Seeking fresh air, he'd stepped outside and found Diana in tears. Joe couldn't recall much of what they discussed, but one line had stayed with him through the years: 'It's his future, Joe, not mine.'

He had put his arms around her. Looking back on it, he was sure he'd intended no more than a hug, an innocent show of support. But the hug was followed by a kiss, and then another: long and deep and passionate, until they broke apart, shocked, panting, reality like ice-cold water thrown over them.

Afterwards, the guilt had lingered for a long time, vying with a half-acknowledged desire to do it again. But Joe was happily married, with a young family, and not about to betray either Helen or Roy. He told himself it was a regrettable lapse, blamed it on the booze and thanked God that no one had seen them.

Nothing like it had happened since and, in truth, Joe hadn't given it a thought in recent years. But it was certainly on his mind now, as they sat and ate together. Diana had insisted on providing him with a meal, a spicy chicken risotto.

'This is a treat,' he told her, 'I've not had much home cooking for a while.'

'Don't,' Diana said. 'It breaks my heart to think of you and Helen being stranded from each other.'

They talked about the situation for a minute or two—as long as Joe could bear—and then he suggested they wander along to the pub after dinner. 'I can just about afford to buy us a drink.'

She laughed. 'That's a nice offer, but Glenn's

coming round later.'

'Ah.' He felt oddly rejected. 'I might grab a pint, though.'

'Glenn and I will probably have a bottle of wine and watch the telly. Not the most thrilling way to spend an evening, but you're welcome to join us.'

Joe politely declined, and Diana didn't push it. 'So how come you and Glenn don't live together?' he asked.

'There's no good answer to that. He has his own place up the road. I don't really want to give up the B&B. We just prefer it this way.'

'As long as you're happy . . .'

'Isn't happiness a bit of a myth?' Diana's voice had a tinge of bitterness to it. 'At my age, anyway. You have to settle for whatever you can get.'

*   *   *

The night was cold, with a fresh wind and clouds scudding across the sky, suggesting that today's dry spell would be short-lived. Joe decided to try the Harbour Lights, at the foot of the High Street, on the basis that he'd walked up and down enough hills today.

He pushed through the doors and found himself in a genuine old-fashioned pub. Lots of wood and leather and brass, but all of it weathered and comfortable, not newly installed to fit some designer's view of an olde-worlde inn.

It was quiet, but not entirely deserted. Maybe a dozen customers in all, of varying ages. There was background music: something light and classical, pleasantly unobtrusive. A couple of fruit machines, but nobody playing them, and no arcade games. A basic menu written out on a blackboard, and a good selection of real ales.

The barman was short and plump and vaguely piratical in appearance, squeezed into a tight black waistcoat over a frilly white shirt, though he greeted Joe in a broad Midlands accent that couldn't have been further removed from the swashbuckling Spanish Main.

As Joe ordered a pint of Tribute, he sensed that he'd caught the attention of the solitary drinker at the bar: a man whose bony middle-aged frame didn't quite do justice to his Calvin Klein jeans and exquisitely tailored jacket.

When he glanced round, Joe saw it was the man he'd met in the hallway at Leon's. His eyes were filmy and struggling to focus, though from his posture he appeared perfectly sober. A finely honed talent for concealment, Joe guessed.

'Met you today, didn't I?' the man said, with barely a slur to his voice. 'Jim-somebody?'

'Joe. Can I get you a drink?'

'God, yes. Thought you'd never ask.'

CHAPTER TWENTY-SEVEN

The force of the punch sent the chair tumbling over. Alise screamed as her head hit the floor. Leon made no move to help her.

'You're going to talk to me,' he told her. 'Don't make me hit you again.'

Reece and Todd set her upright. There was blood pouring from her nose, running over her lips and dripping from her chin. With her hands tied, she couldn't wipe it away. Instead, she kept dribbling it out of her mouth, her face twitching in a desperate reaction to her helplessness.

Leon knew it was going to drive him mad, so he got Todd to clean her up. For good measure, he stuffed thick wads of tissue up her nostrils. They all had a laugh at that.

'Fucking hell, you're a sight,' Leon said.

'Ought to get it on YouTube,' Todd muttered.

Leon gave him a withering look. 'That's how half those arseholes end up in jail. Twat.'

There was a knock on the door. Cadwell eased into the room, nodded at Leon and took a seat next to Fenton. He studied Alise, a satisfied smile creeping onto his face. 'Have I missed anything?'

'Only the warm-up,' Leon said.

Infuriated by the way Alise continued to glare at him, Leon faked another blow, making her jump so violently that the chair actually moved an inch or two. More laughter.

'Her shirt's covered in blood,' Cadwell observed, the comment weighted with meaning.

'Yeah?'

'Well . . . shouldn't we remove it?'

'Plenty of time for that.' Leon snickered, his gaze never leaving Alise's. 'You were in the café today, pouring out your heart to some feller. What did you tell him?'

She shrugged.

'You *are* going to talk to me,' he said quietly.

'It was . . . same thing as to others. About Kamila.'

'That wasn't very wise, was it? I told you to stop badmouthing me. Derek here told you to stop. We asked you nicely, and you ignored us. Now we can't

139

be nice any more, and it's your fault.'

He hit her without warning, a slap this time, fast and strong but not so powerful that it knocked her over. Her scream set his teeth on edge, which earned her another slap, and then he just lost it: laying into her with both hands, hungrily, jubilantly, building a rhythm, loving the sound it made, drowning out her cries. He had no idea how many times he hit her before the others waded in and pulled him away; his only concern was to draw up his legs, curling his body so that they wouldn't see how aroused he was.

Cadwell stepped past him, walking gingerly around the polythene, and observed the girl from a safe distance. She lay in a twisted heap, the chair clinging to her back like prototype wings. Leon realised the plastic sheet was running with blood.

'Dear me, she's a mess,' Cadwell said. Unspoken was the accusation: *You've gone too far.*

Leon's response was a grunt: *Fuck it.*

Behind him, Fenton said, 'You might want to see this.' He passed Leon a pink Nokia phone. 'The text she sent today.'

Leon read the message. Something about a man called Pearse, who lived in Poundbury. A phrase caught his eye: *K's friend.*

K for Kamila.

'Look who it was sent to,' Fenton said.

The number had been programmed into the memory with a single name: Joe. And there was a reply from him: Thanks, Alise. This is a good start. Speak soon.

'Joe,' Leon murmured. Alise was conscious again, her breathing harsh and ragged, her face swollen almost beyond recognition. Even Leon was a bit shocked by the sight of her. Had he really done all that?

'What's with this text you sent Joe?'

Her head rose, then dropped back to the floor. No fight left in her, thank Christ. She tried to speak, dry lips smacking together.

'I asked . . . I asked him to help me.'

'Yeah? Well, that's too bad. Because you're way beyond help now.'

*   *   *

Jenny had been sleeping—or what passed for sleeping in the not-real world of her cell. With no sense of day or night, no energy or desire to move, her existence was reduced to a state of permanent semi-consciousness. She drifted, sometimes dreaming even while she could feel her hands around the torch her captor had left her.

It was a nightmare that shocked her awake. The images, the details, faded immediately. What lingered and would not be repressed was the soundtrack: a distant but piercing scream.

She sat up, carefully placing the torch between her feet, and rubbed her face with both hands, reassuring herself that she was intact. Then she wrapped her arms around herself. It was usually too warm in the cell, but now she felt cold.

The batteries in the torch had begun to fail. Jenny spent most of her time in darkness, reserving a few moments of weak, flickering illumination for when she needed to use the bucket. It seemed as though her captor hadn't visited for a long time. When he did, she would beg him for fresh batteries.

And she knew she would offer him anything in

141

return.

Now, though, the darkness aided her concentration. She strained to hear above the trip-hammering of her heart. In all her time in the cell, there had been no external noise, no evidence of an outside world at all—

She heard it again. A scream. A woman: terrified, in pain. Not a nightmare, not an aural hallucination, but real. Happening somewhere beyond the cell. Somewhere close by.

The thought gave her a rush of confidence, for a second, at least—and then the reality of the situation came crashing down on her.

It meant there was another victim. Someone else was suffering in the way that she had suffered.

Jenny wept for her, even while she felt a terrible, shameful sense of relief.

Because it also meant that she wasn't alone.

*   *   *

The man who'd introduced himself as Giles Quinton-Price sipped the whisky that Joe had bought him and said, 'So, you're taking up employment with the mighty King of the Chavs?'

'I haven't decided yet. Do you work for Leon?'

'Lord, no. I'm a journalist, writing a feature article on Trelennan.'

'A travel piece?'

'Lifestyle, with a strong political slant. For our readers, this place is the embodiment of their wildest dreams.' He spread his hands as if displaying a banner. '"The town that puts the rest of Britain to shame." And it's all down to your chap Leon.'

142

Joe shrugged. 'I hardly know him.'

'No? Then beware. To look at him you'd conclude that he was little more than a drug-addled dollop of benefit-scrounging, housing-estate scum, destined for prison and a pauper's grave.' He laughed, then realised the barman was loitering close by, possibly within earshot.

Slightly abashed, he hurriedly added: 'The fact is, what he's achieved here is nothing less than a miracle. To all intents and purposes, *there is no crime*. Women can walk the streets at night. People leave their doors unlocked, their valuables lying around. Not only that, but there's no vandalism, no antisocial behaviour. And it's *clean*.'

'I had noticed that,' Joe admitted. 'There's hardly any litter.'

Giles lifted his eyebrows, as if to impart some extra meaning that should have been obvious to Joe. 'It's "clean" in more ways than that. Put it this way, there's a notable lack of variety, shall we say, as regards *ethnicity*.'

Joe played dumb. 'What?'

'Between you and me, doesn't it make a refreshing change from London these days, where there's barely a white face or an English accent to be found? And I don't just mean the less salubrious parts of town. Kensington and Chelsea, you can't move for the bloody Arabs, the Russians and God knows who else.' With a disgusted sigh, he lifted his glass and gulped the whisky down.

Joe took a deep breath. 'So Trelennan represents an ideal world, in your view? An "England for the English"?'

Giles gave him a cautionary frown. 'I'm rather too discreet to use a phrase like that, but yes.

143

Certainly that's how our readers see it. Poor old Mr and Mrs Middle-Aged Average—from the vantage point of their little white bungalow in Surrey the world is a dark and dangerous place, teeming with hostile foreigners.'

'Isn't that only because the newspapers tell them so?'

Giles chuckled, as though accepting a compliment. 'Quite. Absolutely. Whereas Trelennan, as portrayed by *moi*, will seem like Shangri-La. Of course, you and I know it has its downsides. Atrocious food. No theatres or museums, no bloody nightlife at all. That's why I'm slumming it in this . . . in here.'

'But you don't you think that, beneath the surface, Trelennan has exactly the same problems and inequalities as anywhere else?'

'Not part of my brief. This is about one strong individual providing something that's proved to be beyond the wit of the public sector. Precisely what our readers want to hear.' He grunted. 'And, rather more importantly, what our *proprietor* wants our readers to hear.'

Joe smiled. 'Sounds like the story was already written before you came here.'

Giles stared at him for a long time, as though he was deciding whether to take offence. Finally he nodded. 'Truth is, it could have been, but I don't look a gift horse in the mouth. Three days on full expenses. Besides, I'm on the lookout for a holiday home. Just sold a place in Italy and quite fancy a bolt-hole down this way.'

CHAPTER TWENTY-EIGHT

Joe woke the next morning to the sound of heavy rain drumming on the roof. He listened to it as he thought about Diana and her new boyfriend, Leon Race and Derek Cadwell, Ellie Kipling and Alise and her missing sister. It had been an eventful first day; not at all what he'd have wished for.

So leave right now. He could do it. Retrace his route to Bristol, maybe hitching rides to save on rail fare. Scope out Lindsey Bevan's home to make sure it wasn't under observation, then retrieve his belongings and get out of there. He could go anywhere. Forget all about Trelennan, Diana, Ellie, Alise . . .

His idle speculation ceased when he realised he was smiling. *Who am I kidding?*

He had no intention of leaving. It simply wasn't in his nature to walk away from a challenge. He knew he possessed the skills to help Alise with her search, and it wasn't just guilt that compelled him to offer his services. For his own sake, he wanted to find out what had happened to Kamila.

And then there was Diana, and the impression he had that she was concealing something from him. Something that made her profoundly unhappy. Something that frightened her.

*　　　*　　　*

Last night Joe had endured Giles's company while he gulped down another pint, and then only because he wanted the journalist to buy a round. When he

145

got up to leave, Giles looked bereft.

'Don't say you're baling out on me . . .'

'Sorry,' Joe said, though he wasn't. 'See you later.'

'You won't, actually. I'm leaving tomorrow.'

'Oh. Good.' The response was automatic, and earned a baffled stare from Giles.

Joe had returned to the B&B, feeling as apprehensive as a teenager who fears he'll stumble upon his parents having sex. It was a huge relief to discover that Glenn and Diana had gone out.

He'd been asleep by ten and hadn't heard Diana come in. Now, slipping from his bed at seven o'clock, he wondered if he still had the house to himself.

He showered, dressed in the clothes she had bought him, and went downstairs. The kitchen was deserted, but Diana's handbag was sitting on the counter.

He started up the coffee maker and ate a bowl of cereal. He was slotting bread into the toaster when Diana padded in, sleepy-eyed and wrapped up in a thick robe. She gazed at the rain streaming down the glass and tutted. 'This weather.'

'I know. I considered a run and quickly changed my mind. Coffee?'

'Please. How was the pub?'

'Not bad.' He told her about Giles Quinton-Price and the article he was writing.

'Glenn mentioned that. He says Leon's delighted by it.'

'Really?' Joe remembered Giles's less than flattering description of Leon. 'What does he hope it'll achieve?'

'A better public profile, I suppose. He grew up

on the Trelawny estate, on the way into town. It's nowhere near as bad now, but twenty, thirty years ago it was a hellhole, apparently. Huge problems with crime, drug abuse, kids running amok. He's done well to get out, and he wants everybody to know it.'

'Fair enough. Uh, I thought I would accept his offer,' Joe said. 'Give it a week or so. If you're okay with that?'

She sighed. 'Is that wise?'

'I don't honestly know,' he admitted. 'A calculated risk.'

'Mmm.' Diana nodded, looking pensive, but he knew she wasn't going to voice her objections. The silence that followed was comfortable enough for Joe to take a bold step.

'What did Roy think of Leon Race?'

The question made Diana flinch. She got up and walked across the room, one hand up over her face.

'They didn't have a lot to do with each other.' She opened the fridge, took out a pot of yogurt and turned back to him, having regained her composure. 'Hardly anything, in fact.'

'And what about Glenn?'

Diana pondered the question while peeling the foil lid off the pot. 'We don't tend to discuss his work. I suppose Glenn looks up to him. Say what you like about Leon, you can't dispute that he's made a success of himself.'

'And he's a big fish in a small pond.'

'Yes. I hadn't thought of it in that way.'

As she opened the cutlery drawer to get a spoon, Joe was sure he heard her murmur: 'A shark.'

*   *   *

147

By the time Joe left, at just after eight o'clock, the rain had eased to a light drizzle. He took a meandering route into town, exploring some of the narrow lanes and alleys that ran crossways to the High Street. In one, a couple of blocks up from the seafront, he found Derek Cadwell's funeral parlour.

It was housed in a modest two-storey building with blinds in the windows and only a few discreet posters advertising its services. There was a gated yard at the side, with a hearse and another Daimler limousine parked beside a single-storey adjoining building that might once have been a blacksmith's forge. There was no sign of anyone; probably still too early.

In the High Street, Joe passed a council truck clearing leaves from the gutters. There was a pleasant buzz of activity as the town came alive: shutters opening, stalls being set out on the pavement; enticing smells wafting from the bakery, which was already doing a brisk trade. Made it feel like a nice place to live and work.

It was ten to nine when he reached Leon's property. He pressed the button on the intercom. After a few seconds he heard a click, and the gate unlocked.

The front door opened as he ambled across the drive. He was greeted by the young man he'd seen outside the B&B yesterday morning, kicking at Diana's pampas grass while he smoked. Today he was in an LRS uniform, but looked no less surly or hostile.

'You're Carter, are you?'

Joe nodded. 'Can I see Leon?'

'He's not here. You got a message for him?'

148

'Tell him I accept,' Joe said. 'Providing the money's right.'

The man raised his eyebrows. 'It'll be what it is,' he said, and slammed the door.

*   *   *

Joe felt deflated. He'd envisaged agreeing the terms and possibly even starting work right away. Now at a loose end, he decided to find Alise and discuss how to approach her sister's former boyfriend.

His first stop was the café, but the only customers were a group of builders. Joe sent Alise a text as he returned to the High Street: **Are you free to meet today?**

The library was open, but there was a different woman behind the counter. Joe was chiding himself for feeling disappointed when a gently mocking voice said, 'Not you again.'

Ellie was heading towards him, her arms fully stretched to support the tower of books propped beneath her chin.

'Can I help with those?' he asked.

'I'm stronger than I look. And I have a reckless disregard for my personal safety.'

Joe followed her over to a display of large-print titles. She eased the books deftly onto a table and began adding them to the shelf.

'Have you seen Alise this morning?' he said.

'No. Why?'

'I ran into her yesterday. She told me about her sister.'

Ellie studied him carefully. 'You know she's far too young for you?'

'Jesus. Do you really think that's—'

'No.' She held up her hands. 'I was only teasing. But it sounds like she's ensnared you.'

'I feel sorry for her, sure. She's got no one else on her side.'

Ellie said nothing. Obviously she didn't dispute his assessment.

'Don't suppose you know where she lives?' he asked.

'No idea.' She turned away from him, arranging the books with small, efficient movements. A hint of her fragrance drifted into his range, and made him want to step closer. After a moment, she said, 'Did you check out the Shell Cavern?'

'I went up there. I didn't actually go into the cave.'

Playfully, she clicked her tongue. 'So you *do* need somebody to hold your hand. What have you got planned this afternoon?'

'Not a lot,' Joe said before he had time to consider. 'Are you asking me out?'

'Don't get ahead of yourself. I'm simply offering to be your tour guide.' Ellie turned, held his gaze for a second, her eyes dark and unreadable. 'Meet me here at two o'clock.'

*   *   *

Outside, Joe checked for messages, then tried ringing Alise but got the 'call failed' message. He had to zigzag up and down the street, chasing the phone signal as it danced in and out of range. Finally he had it, only to discover that Alise's phone was switched off.

Back to the café. He was gazing through the window like some forlorn character out of Dickens, trying to decide if he could afford a coffee, when a noise caught his attention. A trim silver-haired man in a dark grey suit was setting up an A-frame pavement sign for the Halcyon Gallery.

He made sure the sign was positioned correctly, then gave Joe a quick, furtive glance. Joe started towards him.

'Morning. Are you Patrick Davy, by any chance?'

The man nodded, his eyes narrowing with suspicion. He was about sixty, a few inches shorter than Joe, tanned and good-looking, with pale blue eyes.

'My name's Joe. Alise Briedis suggested I talk to you.'

The mention of her name didn't have the effect Joe intended. If anything, Davy grew more defensive.

'Did she now? What about?' He spoke with a soft Australian accent, but he sounded just as hostile as everyone else Joe had encountered in Trelennan.

'She told me that you own the gallery. Mind if I have a look round?'

Davy shrugged. 'It's open for business. You can do what you like.'

He turned and went inside, leaving Joe shaking his head in despair. *This town . . .*

*   *   *

The gallery was housed in a large, airy structure that had probably once been a barn, or maybe a granary. There was a mezzanine floor and three big skylights at the front that poured natural light into the building. The exhibits of many different artists

151

were displayed: a range of paintings, photography, ceramics and glassware, in styles that ranged from cute and corny to unsettlingly experimental.

Davy made for the counter by the door, slipped off his jacket and slung it over a stool. He was wearing a white cotton shirt that couldn't disguise a lean and muscular physique. A dedicated swimmer, perhaps, Joe thought.

The Australian picked up a stack of mail, pulling faces as he divided the envelopes into three piles. 'Bills, bullshit and miscellaneous,' he muttered to himself. Then he sighed. 'So what is it Alise has been saying?'

'Your name came up in connection with Derek Cadwell.'

'Aha. Not one of Alise's favourite people. Not one of mine, either.' Davy flashed Joe a quizzical look, as if to say: *And where do you stand?*

'From what I've seen, he's a creep. And I've only been here two days.'

That earned him another careful appraisal. 'You knew Alise from before?'

'No.'

'But she told you about her sister?'

'Kamila. Yes. I'm trying to help her.'

Davy's face went from suspicious to scornful, as if nobody could be that gullible.

'You know what Alise does for a living?'

Joe frowned. 'She's an actuary. But what's that got to do with—'

'And her boyfriend's name?'

'She did mention it, but I don't recall. Anyway, she dumped him because he wasn't being supportive. Said he was a prick.'

Davy laughed. 'Yeah. That's what she told me.'

152

'So why the twenty questions?'

Tossing the last couple of letters aside, Davy reached beneath the counter and came up brandishing a cricket bat. He wielded it, sword-like, in both hands, and took delight in the surprise on Joe's face.

'These days I believe in a cautious approach,' he said. 'The bastards tried brute force and it didn't work. I figure maybe next time they'll try something more subtle. Send in some bloke, pretending to be friendly . . .'

Joe nodded. 'So you are having trouble with Derek Cadwell?'

'Oh yeah. Him and his buddies. Leon Race being one of them.'

'You said they tried brute force. What did they do?'

Davy put the bat down and beckoned Joe closer. He bent forward and carefully parted his hair just above the crown, revealing a thick, bumpy line of scar tissue.

'Split my skull open.' He pulled his collar away from his neck to reveal several more scars in a pattern like raking fingernails. 'Came up behind me, smashed a bottle over my head, then swiped me with it as I fell.'

Joe whistled. 'That was Leon's men?'

'Yep. Couldn't prove it, of course.' Davy checked his watch. 'Tell you what, I'll hold off opening for another ten minutes and you can hear the full story.' His eyes twinkled. 'If you're really serious about helping Alise, you'd better bloody know what you're up against.'

CHAPTER TWENTY-NINE

Davy brought the sign back in and locked up. At the rear of the gallery there was a private area with a stockroom, toilet facilities and a small kitchenette.

'I used to have a tea room on the mezzanine,' Davy told Joe as he filled an ancient kettle. 'Fantastic views up there. Real hit with the tourists. It was run by the sister-in-law of the lady who owns the café along there. They had this friendly rivalry, you know? Who can make the best carrot cake . . .'

'And what happened?'

'Cadwell and Race frightened her off.' He found a couple of mugs, blew dust off them, then reconsidered and gave them a rinse under the tap. 'After that I couldn't find anybody else to replace her.' He hunted in the cupboards. 'There's coffee, tea and sugar, but no milk, I'm afraid.'

'Black coffee's fine,' Joe said. 'So why did they attack you?'

'Simple enough. Cadwell is keen to expand, and he wants this place.' Davy indicated the gallery. 'I guess the death trade is looking up, even if nothing else is.' His laughter had a bitter ring to it.

Joe was confused. 'A funeral parlour doesn't need a prime retail site.'

'Nope, you're spot on. But this is about status. Power. It's their town, so they'll get whatever they bloody well want.'

'And for that he half-killed you?'

Davy nodded. 'He made the first approach just over a year ago. A bloody silly offer. I guess he knew I was struggling. I said I wasn't interested but

154

he didn't listen. In the end I had to get my lawyer to tell his lawyer, in the usual polite legalese, to get stuffed. Fool that I am, I assumed that would do it.' He stared into the middle distance. 'But Derek didn't give up. He went running to Leon.'

*　　　*　　　*

They took their coffees up to the mezzanine, where the only remnants of the café area were an aluminium table and a couple of matching chairs. There was a stack of canvases in the corner, large expressionist paintings of turbulent oceans and grotesquely compelling portraits. Davy caught Joe admiring them and said, 'That's how I vent my frustrations. In oil and acrylic.'

'They're excellent. I like them a lot.'

'The tourists don't. They prefer tidy watercolours. Yachts and lighthouses and sandy beaches at daybreak. I make more from commission on other people's work than I do from my own.' Davy sighed. 'And I tell myself it still beats pen-pushing, nine to five.'

'If you didn't believe that, wouldn't you have given in to Cadwell?'

'Yeah. Fair point.' Unconsciously or not, Davy started gently rubbing his scalp. 'It was less than a week after I gave my final answer. In Newquay with a mate. We came out of this bar and got jumped from behind. Three of them, we think.'

'So it could have been anybody?'

'Not quite. As I fell I managed to take one of them down with me. Trapped his arm under my body.' He paused, the memory vivid in his eyes. 'Last thing I heard before I fainted was the crack

155

of a bone breaking. I was laid up for a month, but friends from here told me that one of Leon's bullyboys had his arm in a sling. Bloke called Reece Winnen.'

'Reece?' Joe said. He described the LRS men who had turned up during the incident with Alise and Cadwell.

'Yeah, that's Reece. The one with curly hair is probably Todd Ancell. I reckon he was one of them.'

'And the police couldn't do anything?'

'Nope. Reece claimed he fell off a ladder at Leon's place. There's some maintenance man who backed up the story.'

'That wouldn't be Glenn, would it?'

'Yeah. How'd you know him?'

Joe shook his head, a feeling of dread twisting in his stomach. *What was Diana playing at?*

'Doesn't matter,' he said. 'I suppose the police investigation fizzled out?'

Davy gave a caustic laugh. 'According to the boys in blue it had, to quote: "All the hallmarks of a homophobic assault."'

'Homophobic?'

The Australian laughed again. 'Don't be shocked that you missed the signals. I don't give out signals if I can help it. In that sense, the cops were dead right.'

'What do you mean?'

'It wasn't a homophobic attack *per se*, but Leon and his crowd aren't exactly fans of cultural diversity. I've been here eight years, and I reckon they only tolerated me because I'm white and I speak English—even if there are Poms who'd disagree. But now my time's up, because Cadwell's

156

set his heart on a morgue with a view . . .'

*   *   *

Joe gazed at the bank of windows that filled the gallery's north wall. The bay was obscured by a misty drizzle, an iron-grey sea rolling out of the murk. Gulls drifted like scraps of litter flung into the wind.

Davy's story sounded plausible, as had Alise's tale of woe, but Joe couldn't dismiss the possibility that both of them had an axe to grind. What he needed was corroboration from a more objective source.

He turned back to the Australian: 'Do you really think they'll try again?'

'Sure of it. But they'll vary their tactics, like they did before.'

Joe stared at him. 'Before?'

'Yeah. When Leon wanted Trelennan's taxi firm he used petty vandalism and fake bookings. Eighteen months of it, something different every night. Sent the proprietor insane.'

Davy leaned back in his chair, eyes half-closed as he reeled off the details. 'Whereas, with the amusement arcade, the police got an anonymous tip-off. Found child pornography on the owner's computer. Roger Pengelly, a nice bloke. He swore blind it had been planted, and luckily there were enough people with access to his office to cast doubt. They dropped the prosecution, but you know how it is.'

Joe nodded grimly. 'Mud sticks.'

'People wouldn't let their kids anywhere near the arcade. Leon made him an offer and Roger had no choice but to take it. Bloody effective way to build an empire, if you don't have to worry about reprisals.'

'And Leon Race doesn't?'

'Not round here. No one would dare.'

'And the police?'

Davy shrugged. 'The local station shut down a few years back. Wasn't needed, since the official crime rate is zero. I'd say it's also a fair bet that Leon has nurtured friendly relationships with one or two senior cops.'

Joe didn't respond. Allegations of police corruption aroused an instinctive desire to defend his former profession, even though he knew from bitter experience that there were a few rotten apples in the barrel.

He said, 'Did you know there's a journalist in town, writing an article about Leon?'

'Yeah? He won't be allowed within a mile of this place, then.' Davy grew thoughtful. 'Maybe if Alise had a chance to talk to him . . . ?'

'I'm not sure he'd be all that sympathetic, but perhaps it's worth a try. If I could get hold of her, that is.'

Davy sat upright. 'What the hell do you mean? Has Alise gone missing?'

*   *   *

The Australian's reaction set off a twinge of anxiety in Joe. 'Not exactly. I saw her yesterday afternoon, then she texted me a little later. Do you know where she lives?'

'I've got her address somewhere.' Davy steepled his fingers, held them upright against his mouth as if praying fervently. His eyes seemed to bore into Joe. 'You didn't like me suggesting the police might be bent. Are you a cop?'

'A long time ago.'

'I thought so. That's good. It means you have the expertise to help Alise. What's your honest assessment about Kamila? Do you think she's dead?'

'I think something serious has happened to her,' Joe conceded. 'As for what—and who did it—that's going to be very hard to establish.'

'But you're willing to listen. That's more than most people round here will do. I know Leon's involved, because I've seen what he's capable of.'

Joe raised a hand. 'The sort of intimidation you've described is terrible. But it's not the same as abduction and murder.'

'I disagree. To me, it's exactly the same. It's about greed. It's about getting your own way.' Davy's voice rose as the passion of the argument gripped him; he made an effort to bring it under control. 'Leon Race is a bully. A big, overgrown kid who never learned to compromise. He knows he's lacking in education. He's almost proud of it. But you know he's never had as much as a speeding ticket? As a kid he'd wreak havoc and then weasel his way out of taking responsibility. What I'm saying here, Joe, is that he's a bloody dangerous man, and he's all the more dangerous because he relies on being underestimated.'

Joe nodded. He decided not to reveal that he'd already met Leon and been offered a job by him. Better not to muddy the waters.

Davy glanced at his watch and gave a start. 'I should open up, in the vague hope of finding somebody willing to part with their money.'

He hurried downstairs, hunted behind the counter and located an old notebook. He licked his forefinger and dabbed the pages open.

'You got me worried about her now,' he muttered. 'Ah, here it is. Flat 5, 28 Lonsdale Avenue.' He gave Joe directions, then added, 'Be discreet. She's staying as an unofficial tenant with a girl . . . Karen somebody. Works in Gwynn's on the High Street. Karen or Sharon, anyway.'

'Okay. I'll let you know when I've spoken to her.'

They shook hands. Davy gave him a penetrating stare. 'You look like you could be pretty useful in a fight, Joe, but I'd have said the same thing about myself. It didn't count for much when three blokes clouted me from behind.'

'I hear what you're saying,' Joe told him. 'I'll watch my back.'

'Good. And if you need a hand, you know where I am.'

CHAPTER THIRTY

Leon was back home by half past nine, in a sour mood that he couldn't quite explain.

Last night, once the business with Alise was concluded, the clean-up had been assigned to Fenton. Leon and Cadwell drove to Bude, booked into a hotel, ate a late meal in the restaurant and then visited a couple of bars, making sure that plenty of people saw them.

Probably not necessary, but Leon was a firm believer in taking precautions. As it was, he had a nagging sensation that this was a misstep, and would come back to haunt him.

Fenton met him in the hall. 'You look as shitty as I feel,' Leon said. 'Are we all clean?'

'As the proverbial whistle.'

Leon inspected the living room, noting that the furniture was back in place. The polythene sheeting had been incinerated; every hard surface wiped down and polished for good measure.

Pam appeared. She was grey-haired, small and round and twinkly-eyed, like a granny in an American sitcom. 'Drinks, boys? Something to eat?'

Leon patted his belly. 'Cooked breakfast in the hotel. Not up to your standard, but . . .'

She smiled indulgently. 'Just cranberry juice, then, my love?'

'Perfect.' He scratched himself. 'I need to have a shower soon. Didn't have time this morning.'

'Joe Carter was here,' Fenton told him as they made for the office. 'He wants to accept the position, providing the wages are right.'

'Cheeky bastard. Where else is he going to earn anything?' Leon brooded for a moment. 'All right. Tell him to start tomorrow. Ten quid an hour: take it or fuck off.'

Fenton was already tapping himself a note on his BlackBerry. 'I've been thinking about that message on Alise's pho—'

'Ah, ah.' Leon raised his hand. 'We don't say that name now. Not any more.'

Fenton dipped his head in apology. 'Of course. But the text, the one she sent to Joe, we have to consider where it will lead . . .'

'Away from here. I'm fine with that.'

'But do we want this man, whom we're about to

employ, searching for the missing sister of a girl who is herself now missing?'

'Don't worry. We'll keep a close eye on him.' Leon studied the paperwork on his desk, then shook his head. Sighed. 'Last night,' he said. 'Do you reckon Derek was . . .?'

'What?'

There were tiny beads of sweat on Fenton's forehead. Leon stared at them for so long that he completely lost his train of thought.

'Dunno. Forget it.' He scratched himself again, gazing restlessly around the room. 'Hope there weren't any fucking bedbugs in that hotel.' The laptop prompted a memory. 'Those pictures we sent out. Any replies yet?'

'Only one. Mark Kowalski.'

'Ah, shit.' Kowalski was a semi-retired low-level cocaine dealer who'd say anything to anyone if it curried favour or earned him a few quid.

'I can tell him to take a running jump, if you like?'

'Yeah.' Leon burped loudly, then grimaced at the taste in his mouth: acid indigestion. 'No. Second thoughts, get his number and I'll call him.'

*   *   *

Lonsdale Avenue boasted a mix of properties: traditional Cornish bungalows, some Edwardian town houses—most of them converted into flats—and a few modern apartment blocks.

Number 28 was one of the Edwardian buildings, at the end of a terrace of five properties. It was four storeys high, with dormer windows in the roof: an ugly modern addition. Four steps led up to

162

the front door, which was half-glazed and had an industrial-sized letter box.

The house was in dire need of maintenance. The stonework was cracked and bleeding mortar. Most of the paint had peeled from the door. A gouge in the frame suggested that someone had tried to jemmy it open in the not too distant past.

There was no intercom; just a square plate on the wall with nine doorbells mounted on it, each with a name tag fixed under clear plastic. Some were blank; others practically illegible. On the one for 5 there was a single scrawled word: *Noye*.

Before pressing the bell, Joe tried the door. The ageing timber creaked and groaned, but the lock held fast. He rang the doorbell, then checked his phone. There was a signal, so he called Alise again. Still nothing.

After ringing the bell a second time, a net curtain swayed in a downstairs window. The lower sash opened and a man's bony arm emerged while his other hand fought with the curtain, clawing it over his head like a corpse escaping its shroud.

The man was in his seventies or older, pale and painfully thin, a rash of white stubble on his chin. Hollow eyes and a collapsed mouth. He smacked his lips a couple of times, like a goldfish, and Joe saw that he had no teeth.

'Who you after?' he said. The lack of teeth mushed the words into: 'Ooyouaffer?'

Be discreet, Davy had warned. 'Karen Noye,' Joe said.

The man squinted at him. Joe thought: *Damn: it's Sharon*.

'She's out. Who are you?'

'A friend. Are you the landlord?'

163

'Why?'

'No reason.' Ignoring the man's malicious scowl, Joe trotted down the steps and walked away. There was an alley that separated the terrace from a modern apartment block next door, but he couldn't use it without being seen from the landlord's window.

Instead he continued to the end of the street, made two left turns and found himself in a narrow access road that ran parallel to Lonsdale Avenue, serving a row of lock-up garages. The drizzle had let up slightly but still gave him good reason to hunch down into his collar, obscuring his face from anyone who might be watching.

Each building in the terrace had a modest backyard enclosed by a high stone wall. Joe hoisted himself up onto the wall, toes scrabbling for purchase on the mossy, rain-slicked stone, then slithered down into the yard. It was empty apart from an old rotary washing line and a rusted bicycle. Lying almost at his feet, as if thwarted in the act of escape, were the decomposing remains of what might have been a rat.

A wrought-iron fire escape clung to the back of the building, threading between two small balconies on each floor. Joe guessed that flat five would be on the second floor, assuming each floor had two apartments. He thought he might as well take a look through the windows and see if there was any obvious sign of trouble.

Even though he trod slowly, the metal steps reverberated with a dull clanging noise that must have sent vibrations right through the building. Reaching the second floor, he climbed over the rail onto the left-hand balcony and put his face to the window. The room was bare, with a patch of ceiling missing, lath and plaster dangling like severed limbs.

He moved back to the fire escape, then onto the opposite balcony, his heart beating wildly. If he was spotted now he'd have a hell of a job explaining himself to the police.

There were curtains up at the window, and what looked like women's clothes on the floor. He cupped his hands to shield his eyes from reflected light and examined the interior. More clothes in a cheap canvas wardrobe. Cosmetics on a chest of drawers. The room was untidy, but not suspiciously so. No evidence of a struggle.

Joe sighed. This wasn't going to tell him anything, and it might just land him in—

A heavy clunk from below: somebody jumping on to the bottom step. Then a voice: 'Down you come. Nice and slow.'

CHAPTER THIRTY-ONE

Of course, it wasn't the police waiting for him. Not in Trelennan.

It was an LRS patrol.

Worse still, it was the same one he'd encountered yesterday: stocky, belligerent Reece and curly-haired Todd. Two of the men who'd allegedly attacked Patrick Davy.

As Joe descended, each step slow and reluctant, he saw them exchange a knowing glance: *This is going to be fun.*

The moment Joe reached the ground Reece

swung in with a blow to the ribs. Joe was expecting it and managed to lean back, but the space was too restricted to evade it completely.

'You keep still now,' Reece told him. 'Or there'll be more where that came from.'

'That's him!' the landlord shouted, hobbling from a door at the side of the building. He was dressed in filthy pyjama trousers and a modern Puffa jacket. He'd put his teeth in, which gave his face a fuller, stronger appearance. 'Tryin' to break in, he was. Bold as fucking brass.'

Reece squared up to Joe. 'What have you got to say for yourself?'

Todd stepped closer. 'Say nothing, if you like. We'll beat the shit out of you instead.'

'I wasn't breaking in anywhere,' Joe said calmly. 'I was walking past and thought I saw smoke coming from one of the windows. I climbed up to check there wasn't a fire.'

'Bullshit,' Reece said.

'We caught you red-handed,' Todd snarled, saliva bubbling on his lips.

Reece grabbed Joe's right arm, twisting him sideways and securing his other arm. 'Your turn,' he said, and Todd grinned and punched Joe hard in the stomach. Joe managed to wrench one arm free, but too late. He doubled over, coughing and choking.

'Tell us what you're doing here,' Reece said.

'Let's get him inside, shall we?' Todd said.

'Why? Who cares if anyone sees us?'

Hearing Reece sound so unconcerned made Joe appreciate the risk he was taking. They seemed to have no idea that Alise lived here. He had to make sure it stayed that way. Exaggerating the effects

166

of the blow, he said, 'Leon's going to be pissed off with you two, treating a workmate like this.'

'What the fuck do you mean?'

Gingerly, Joe straightened up. 'Leon offered me a job.'

Both men looked dumbfounded. The landlord, watching from a safe distance, was enraged by the possibility of a truce. 'Go on. Give him a good kicking.'

'Speak to Leon,' Joe said, taking a step forward. Reece barred his way.

'Wait.'

'What you gonna do?' the landlord demanded.

Reece unclipped the phone from his belt. 'You can piss off now, grandad.'

The old man seemed about to object, until he remembered who he was talking to; then he hobbled away, muttering to himself.

Reece turned his back on Joe while he made the call. Joe heard a couple of exclamations, an enquiry cut short. Reece shoved the phone back in his pocket and jabbed a finger at Joe.

'We're going to finish this later, you and me.'

Joe shrugged. 'Any time.'

*   *   *

Leon was on the phone to Kowalski when Reece called, so Fenton took it on the other line. Leon tried to follow both conversations at once.

Kowalski was adamant that he recognised the man in the photo, and ninety per cent sure he was police.

'And when d'you last see him?'

Kowalski whistled. 'Oh, gotta be a good ten years

167

ago now.'

'We already knew he was a cop then. What else can you tell me?'

'I'm racking my brains, Leon. I really wanna help you with this.'

To his caller, Fenton said, 'Yes. Joe Carter. What was he doing?'

Leon frowned a question at Fenton, who shrugged. Leon asked Kowalski: 'So what about the name? Is he Joe Carter?'

Kowalski made a humming noise, and Leon growled, 'Don't fucking lie to me.'

'No, no. I can't say for sure, Leon. But it sounds right enough.'

'Anything else?'

'Not that springs to mind. That's gotta be a help, though. Gotta be worth something, eh, just by way of a thank-you?'

'Maybe at Christmas.' Leon slammed the phone down and growled, 'Santa says you're getting fuck all.'

Fenton said, 'No, that's correct. Best let him go.' He finished the call, shaking his head. 'That was Reece. Called to a suspected burglary and he finds Joe Carter on the balcony of a block of flats owned by Sean Collins.'

'That old scrote? What did Joe have to say?'

'Gave them a cock and bull story, according to Reece. But he hadn't broken in. He'd gone up the fire escape and was looking in through the windows.'

'Doesn't strike me as a peeping Tom.' Leon was troubled. 'Who lives there?'

'That's what I was wondering. It's gruesomely cheap accommodation . . .' Fenton's voice tailed off; and the idea struck them both at the same time.

'Our little foreign friend?'

Fenton nodded. 'Could be. Either Collins kept quiet, or he doesn't know.'

'Shacked up with somebody.' Leon sighed. Alise had proved surprisingly resilient last night. There were various things she hadn't told them; where she'd been staying was one of them.

'Not that it matters now,' Fenton said. 'But it shows how persistent Joe is.'

'You made the call yet?'

Fenton nodded. 'I left a message for him. Nine o'clock tomorrow.'

'Shame. We could have pulled him in this afternoon, found out what this is all about.'

'Best not change our plans now.'

A tap on the door. Glenn slipped into the room. Leon kept his focus on Fenton, who asked what Kowalski had given them.

'Fuck all.'

'But if he recognised Joe, the likelihood is that someone else will, sooner or later.'

Leon snorted. 'Is this your fucking "accentivate the positive" or whatever it is?'

'Accentuate,' Fenton said, and Glenn winced. Fenton was the only one allowed to correct Leon's use of English, because the superiority of his education was never in doubt. Besides, they all knew that—aside from his intellect—Fenton had precious little going for him.

'Whatever,' Leon said. 'You got me some better news, I hope, Glenn?'

'Not really. The journalist's here.'

'Ah, shit . . .' Leon looked at his watch. 'Already?'

169

'He's all done. Just wants to say goodbye.'

'Well, there you go,' Leon said drily. '*Accentuate* the positive. Before you send him in, I have a job for you. Should have thought of this last night.'

He opened a desk drawer and took out the pink Nokia. 'I need you to take this to Plymouth and send a text with it, later this evening. But whatever you do, don't turn it on till you get there.'

'Triangulation,' Fenton chipped in. 'Enables them to trace the whereabouts of a phone, even when it's not in use.' He glanced at Leon. 'Won't it disrupt the timing?'

'Chance worth taking, I reckon,' Leon said. He outlined the message to Glenn, whose lack of enthusiasm was visible in the droop of his shoulders.

'I was counting on finishing at six today,' he said.

'Stop moaning. This is important.'

Glenn just nodded, then stomped out to fetch the journalist. Fenton wriggled excitedly, the sofa squeaking under his weight. He'd asked permission to be present for the farewell, and since he'd provided some advice on the language and phrasing, Leon had granted his request.

*   *   *

Giles loped into the room, grinning his smarmy grin, sweeping his hair back from his forehead with a flick of his head. He strode up to the desk and struck out his hand. Leon pretended not to notice it.

'Mr Race, sir! May I say how grateful I am for your cooperation this week?'

Leon tipped his head forward once: *Yes, you may.*

170

Giles, thrown by the silence and by Leon's unwillingness to shake hands, nodded vigorously and ploughed on. 'Splendid. Because it has, ah, it really has been . . . refreshing, to meet such a . . . such a shining example of what can be achieved, after a bad start in life, through sheer . . . determination—'

'I get the message. Apology accepted, on one condition.'

Giles frowned. 'Apology?'

'For patronising me. You have a very patronising manner, Giles. And yes, I do know what the word means. How about that, eh?'

He beamed at Giles, who looked utterly lost. Fenton had a chubby hand clamped over his mouth, trying to muffle his laughter.

'I put up with it because you're my guest. That's the kind of guy I am.' A calculated pause, then Leon shook his head. 'No, that's bollocks. I put up with it because the story you're gonna write is extremely important to me.'

He leaned forward, elbows on the desk, his fists touching just in front of his chin, like a boxer waiting for the bell. Serious now, his voice low and menacing.

'See, I know what journalists can do. They twist things. Even after they've acted all nice and friendly, they go back and write a load of sneering, poisonous crap. If your story comes out like that, Giles, if I get even a whiff of you patronising me in print, then you'll have made one very serious enemy out of me. An enemy like nothing you've ever imagined. Are you clear on that?'

Giles was literally shaking: whether it was with fear, or rage, or a mixture of both, Leon had no

171

idea and he cared even less. What mattered was that the message had hit home.

Finally the journalist recovered his voice. 'I'll . . . I should be able to email you the article before it's submitted.'

'That sounds like a plan.' Leon signalled to Fenton, who hauled himself to his feet. 'Clive's gonna see you out. Travel safe, Giles.'

CHAPTER THIRTY-TWO

Slowly but surely, Jenny was reassembling her world. With each visit, she had decided she would try to learn a little more.

Today he had brought food: croissants and a bottle of Evian water. He had changed the bucket which she used as a toilet, and there was a packet of wet wipes. He wanted her to keep clean, for the sake of his own pleasure.

Before he entered the cell, he knocked. It might have seemed like a quaint courtesy, but it was not. It was an instruction to switch off the torch and lie down facing the wall.

At first, these rules had sent a thrill of hope through her. He didn't want her to see his face: therefore he intended to spare her life.

Then she remembered that she had met this man in a pub. She had chatted and laughed and drank with him, and then, probably drugged, she had left the pub in his company.

She knew his face. However much she tried, she could not *un-know* it, and he would never believe it even if she claimed to have done so.

172

She also knew his name, though she wasn't sure if he would remember telling her. She wasn't completely certain that she hadn't invented it. A false memory, snatched from her nightmares.

Either way, logic dictated that he would not permit her to live. Better to keep this knowledge to herself, though the restless, combative side of her character was only too willing to demand a response. He had reacted badly to a similarly blunt enquiry.

'Are you going to rape me again?'

'Don't call it that.' His voice loud and booming in the confined space, the voice of an ogre in a fairy tale. 'It's sex. We have sex. Okay?'

Jenny had been too cowed to say a word. He felt for her in the dark and slapped her face.

'Answer me.'

'Yes. We have sex.'

'That's right. And we're gonna have it now.'

*   *   *

Today she was better prepared. She waited until she judged it was safe to speak. It was incredible how acutely she could gauge his mood from the sounds he made: his feet shuffling or scraping on the concrete floor, the rustle of his clothes, the huff and snort of his breath, the fidgety movements of his hands.

'What time is it?'

'Why? It won't do you any good.'

'Please. It doesn't cost you anything.'

He deliberated for almost a full minute, then tossed his reply at her, like fluff from his pockets. 'It's about ten, ten-fifteen.'

173

'In the morning?'

'Yeah.'

'Thank you.' Emboldened by her success, perhaps deluding herself that her submissive charm could soften his attitude, she pushed on. 'Am I alone here?'

'What?'

'I thought I heard something . . . last night, I suppose it was. It sounded like a scream. A woman's scream.'

'Nah,' he said. 'You're imagining it.'

She sighed. 'Do you think so?'

The question, so measured and sympathetic, seemed to disarm him; maybe he'd expected a challenge. Laughing softly, he said, 'Being here, it's bound to send you mad, if you weren't already.'

'What do you mean by that?'

'Look, you're on your own, all right? You've always been on your own.'

*   *   *

Once he had gone, she wept for a long time. It was a despicable response, weak and self-pitying, but she couldn't stop herself. His comment about her sanity had wounded her deeply.

It's bound to send you mad . . . if you weren't already.

Finally she passed through it, forced herself to concentrate on her achievements. She had a time now, didn't she, or at least a vague sense of it. This was the morning. This meal was breakfast.

But on what day? That would be her next aim: to find out the day of the week. And then, the matter that bothered her intensely: how long had she been

174

here?

Several days, definitely. Beyond that, she couldn't say. Long enough to be missed, surely . . . ?

Jenny was twenty-two, blonde and slender, a bright, attractive young woman. That wasn't her own assessment: it was what other people had said about her. Until May this year she had been studying Classics and Ancient History at Exeter University, but she'd dropped out, without telling her family, as a result of illness.

Mental illness. Even now, when she considered herself almost fully recovered, she resented the stigma that attached to the notion of a breakdown. She had cracked under the pressure of work, combining her studies with two poorly paid menial jobs. That the pressure had been largely self-inflicted made it worse. She'd always driven herself too hard, had always felt that one day the wheels could come off . . .

In the first year at uni she'd had several dates. Nothing serious. Then Luke came along and she knew at once that this was different: her first genuinely 'grown-up' relationship. That had been a big factor in her decision to remain in Exeter after dropping out. Luke had hung in there, determined to ride out the bad times at her side, convincing her that soon she'd have her life back on course.

He was in the final year of an engineering degree, a solid unspectacular student, confident and likeable, with soft eyes and a hard body. Destined for a good, practical, rewarding career. Destined to be her husband, it had seemed for a while.

They'd both alluded to it, shyly, dropping hints, making jokes. *Not right now. God, no. Probably*

175

not for years. Too much to do before they could even begin to think of marriage and babies and mortgages. First there was travelling—for Jenny, revisiting some of the places that had so entranced her during her gap year—and some voluntary work, maybe. And partying, and . . . and just savouring their freedom, their youth.

And then came the bombshell. Her flatmate saw him sticking his tongue down the throat of a girl in a bar called Coolings, on a weekend when he was supposed to be visiting his mother in Kettering. When Jenny confronted him, he confessed to everything, almost gladly. Yes, he had lied to her. Yes, he'd been with a girl. Yes, they were having sex.

And it was fabulous sex.

He'd left the flat with a spring in his step, a burden lifted, and it had struck her then, with terrible force: *she was the burden.* He was free, but she would always be the burden.

After that, a relapse of sorts, and a flight to solitude. Jenny walked out of her jobs and moved, for reasons she could no longer fathom, to a cramped and dingy bedsit in Whipton. Her finances weren't great, but they weren't dire either. If she was careful, she had enough to last six months or so, while she got herself together and either made plans for the future or found the courage to do herself in.

Prior to this, prior to her abduction, she'd had virtually no contact with anyone for weeks. She had no flatmates here, and her neighbours were mostly older, anonymous and blunt in their lack of interest in her. She'd broken off contact with her friends, ignored their calls and texts. Didn't update

176

her Facebook page. Pacified her parents with an occasional email or text, pleading an overload of reading and socialising.

Sometimes she went out to drink, but always alone, always to distant pubs and cafés where nobody knew her.

And now she wondered: was it possible, when he met her, that he'd known what a mess she was in?

Had that been a factor in his decision to abduct her?

Oh no. No. She sat and shook her head, clutching the unlit torch on her lap, barely able to contemplate a truth this terrible. That she might have been targeted. Singled out because she was weak and lonely and vulnerable.

What reason was there to stay alive if she knew she could be kept here, abused again and again, for weeks or months . . . and no one would miss her?

He'd said: *It's bound to send you mad . . . if you weren't already.*

He'd also said: *You've always been on your own.*

And he was right.

CHAPTER THIRTY-THREE

Joe was at the library by five to two, having spent a couple of hours wandering around the town. He debated whether to go inside but decided it might seem too eager.

At three minutes past the hour Ellie came out, wearing a beautifully tailored but rather garish purple coat. She registered his presence and nodded to herself. 'You didn't find Alise, then?'

177

'How'd you work that out?'

'My guess was, if you found her you wouldn't turn up here.'

'I'm not like that,' he said. 'But I am getting worried.'

'She's fine. Probably taken a leaf out of her sister's book.'

'In what way?'

'They're young women. Free spirits. At that age you don't think twice about flitting off somewhere.'

Joe shrugged. Turned towards the High Street, but Ellie plucked at his sleeve. 'Car park's this way.'

'Aren't we going to walk?'

'It's raining.'

'Only a bit of drizzle.'

'You walk if you like. I'll see you there.' She smiled cheekily. 'You already look like a drowned rat.'

'Do I?'

'Well, half-drowned. You can come with me, but don't make the seat all soggy.'

*   *   *

Her car was a Renault Megane hatchback, four years old, parked in a staff car park that was shared with the town council offices: a monstrous cube of 1960s concrete.

Ellie was a confident driver, fast and a touch impatient, despite appearing to give the road only a fraction of her attention: the bulk of it was focused on Joe as he recounted his conversation with Alise.

'So basically you believe what she's been saying?' Ellie asked.

'Yes, though not necessarily that Leon Race was

178

involved.'

'Did you tell her that?'

'I pointed out the lack of evidence.'

'You see, my worry is that she's fixated on Leon—to the extent that she won't consider any other alternatives. Maybe you'll be able to talk some sense into her.'

'Is that what she needs?'

'Didn't you get the impression she's a little . . . flaky? Doesn't do herself any favours.' A beat of silence, then: 'Have you arranged to meet her again?'

'Not as such. I assumed I could find her fairly easily.' Joe told her about the unanswered calls, but not about his visit to the flat in Lonsdale Avenue.

'Perhaps you've called her bluff. She's been getting a kick out of going around appealing for help. The moment she actually enlists some support she runs a mile.'

'If so, that makes me a very poor judge of character.'

'Oh dear. I've wounded your ego.'

'I'll live,' Joe said drily. 'What I can't fathom is why you seem so hostile towards Alise.' *And practically everyone else*, he could have added.

'Not hostile. Sceptical.' Ellie braked hard at a junction, flicking the indicator on, and turned to look at him. 'I think Alise began with a genuine concern, but grew to enjoy being centre of attention. And I don't doubt her sister has vanished, but like I say there could be any number of reasons for that.'

'Free spirits?'

'Exactly.'

He nodded. 'Is this you speaking from

179

experience? Were you a free spirit once?'

Looking uncharacteristically solemn, Ellie avoided the question. 'My guess is that you, like most men, are a bit too gullible where helpless young damsels are concerned. I'd hate to see you being taken for a ride.'

'I'm being taken for one right now.'

She gave him a playful punch on the arm. 'That is a truly terrible pun, if you're being literal. And if you're implying that I'm trying to deceive you, I'm going to hit you even harder in a minute.'

*　　*　　*

There were several cars parked outside the cavern, with a gap that was just wide enough for the Renault. Shunning a larger space further on, Ellie drew alongside, glanced over her shoulder and expertly parallel-parked in one fluid movement.

She edged forward to straighten up, applied the handbrake, shut her eyes and tensed her shoulders. 'Don't say it.'

'What?'

'Don't compliment my skilful driving. And definitely don't say anything with an edge of surprise in your voice. You wouldn't congratulate a man on his parking.'

'I'd probably take the piss,' Joe said. 'That's what men do.'

They got out and faced each other across the car. Ellie gave him a narrow-eyed stare and bunched her fists: still in combative mode. Joe didn't bother to conceal his exasperation.

'I don't think you're trying to deceive me. But you're not being very sympathetic to Alise's plight,

180

and I don't agree that this is attention-seeking on her part.'

'So why hasn't she returned your calls?'

'I'll ask her, the next time I see her.'

The visitor centre was staffed by the same ageing hippie as the day before. He was serving an elderly woman who'd bought an industrial quantity of fudge. Other than her, and a middle-aged couple sceptically examining a dreamcatcher, the place was deserted.

'Doesn't do a lot of business,' Joe murmured.

'Seasonal,' Ellie said. 'It can get positively congested in summer.'

Joe dug in his pocket, but Ellie nudged him. 'My treat. You can pay next time.'

'Next time where?'

A shrug. 'If you're paying, you can choose.'

*   *   *

With Giles finally out of his hair, Leon rewarded himself with a run. For a big, bulky man, he prided himself on his fitness. He'd always been light on his feet, nimble and quick. As a youth he'd escaped arrest on numerous occasions by literally wriggling or dodging his way to freedom. If not for those skills he'd have a criminal record for sure, so in a sense he owed his business empire to that agility.

There was a gym of sorts in the house, with a treadmill, a cross-trainer and some weights, but every time he went in there he could guarantee an interruption within minutes, if not seconds.

So instead Leon ran the streets. He preferred being outdoors, in the fresh air: an ever-changing view. Thought of it as patrolling his precious little corner of the world.

He wore an iPod but didn't take his phone. Half the town barely had a signal, and in a grade-one emergency he could be located easily enough. This way it gave him a blessed hour or so of complete freedom.

Today, when he got back, Venning intercepted him as he made for the stairs.

'Better be good news, otherwise I'm having a shower first.'

'I dunno. Some bloke called for you. About that picture of Joe whats-his-name.'

'Oh, yeah. And what *is* his name?'

Venning looked blank, didn't get it. 'You mean Joe?'

'Never mind. Who was it that called?'

'He didn't say.' Now thoroughly confused, as well as worried. 'He wouldn't leave a number, neither. Said he'd ring back.'

Leon sighed, letting the air run out so slowly that he was calm by the time his lungs emptied; that way he wouldn't feel the need to beat the crap out of Venning.

'Sorry, Leon. I mean, I did ask him, like—'

'Never mind. When's he gonna call?'

'Later today. I told him you'd be here.'

Nodding, Leon stomped upstairs. After Kowalski, his expectations had lowered. Probably another bloody time-waster.

CHAPTER THIRTY-FOUR

It was a steep descent. The steps were narrow and uneven, the stone worn smooth and slippery. There was a handrail bolted into the rock face, with warnings to ignore it at your peril. Beyond the steps a narrow passageway led them deeper still, until they were perhaps thirty feet underground.

The air was drier than Joe had expected, cool and a little musty. The wall-mounted lamps threw out pools of eerie yellow light. There was no sound other than the echoing thud of their footsteps on the stone path.

'Is it all like this?' he asked, aware of a cold sweat prickling on the back of his neck.

Ellie said nothing. A second later the passage ended with a wide arched doorway. The chamber beyond it seemed to emit a silvery glow. Joe felt her hand gently brushing his arm as she ushered him through.

'*This* is what it's like,' she said.

*   *   *

The would-be informer rang again at twenty past two. Fenton had suggested taping the call: a doddle for Venning to set up.

It was Fenton who answered. Leon was in the living room, playing *Halo: Reach* on the Xbox. At a shout from Venning he threw the controller down and hurried into the office. Fenton kept the phone at his ear while Leon picked up the other handset and slumped on the sofa.

183

'This is Leon Race. Who are you?'

'I'm the man who can do you a very big favour.' The accent was vaguely London. An uneducated voice, and not young.

'I asked who you were.'

'Call me Billy.'

'What's your real name?'

The man chuckled: it sounded husky, clogged up. A smoker.

'All in good time, Mr Race. I seen that piccie of yours, doing the rounds.'

'So what can you tell me?'

'I'm not gonna come right out and say it, am I? Gotta be worth a few quid to you. In fact, I know it is.' He laughed again: not a chuckle, but a cackle. A man in his late fifties or sixties, Leon thought. A hard-lived life.

'I'm willing to pay for the information,' Leon said. 'How much exactly depends on what you have. A lot of bullshitters out there, and right now I think you're one of them.'

'Oh no, Mr Race. What I have is *solid fuckin' gold.*'

The phrase came out thin and wheezy. Leon pictured somebody scrawny, unhealthy, with a sly look in his eyes. But the enthusiasm wasn't faked: the man truly believed he had something valuable.

'Give me a flavour, then we'll talk terms.'

'First, you tell me this. The geezer in the photo—you've got him, have you? In your custody, so to speak?'

Leon started to reply, saw Fenton frantically shaking his head. He covered the phone and mouthed: 'What?'

Pressing his own handset into the folds of his

belly, Fenton hissed: 'If you tell him where Joe is, he could cut us out of the deal.'

Good point. Leon felt a rush of intense hatred for the man on the other end of the line.

'You're pissing me about,' he growled. He put the phone down and gestured at Fenton to disconnect as well.

'Was that wise?'

Leon shrugged, but his left leg was juddering with excitement. They were on to something.

'He'll call back.'

'What if he doesn't?'

'He will.' Leon rubbed his hands together. 'Accentuate the positive, remember?'

*   *   *

The cavern was an extraordinary sight: almost disturbing in its sense of otherness. It reminded Joe of how he'd felt, years ago, when he'd discovered a wasps' nest in his attic, perfectly and painstakingly constructed from scraps of newspaper. The awe he'd experienced at witnessing an essentially alien intelligence at work was replicated here.

The main cavern was rectangular, about twenty feet by ten, with three other arched doorways leading to what appeared to be smaller chambers. The roof of the cavern was dome-shaped, narrowing towards a central funnel which fed a soft ethereal light into the room.

The domed roof and the floor were fashioned from bare rock, but the walls, every square inch of them, were adorned with shells. Millions of shells in a variety of sizes, shapes and colours, placed with the utmost care and precision, to astonishing effect.

185

They were arranged in large rectangular panels. As Joe's eyes became accustomed to the sight, he started to discern shapes and symbols within the panels. Various animals were depicted, in styles reminiscent of Egyptian, Greek and Phoenician art; there were phallic symbols and trees of life and ancient gods and goddesses. But the location and the form continued to speak of an otherworldly culture.

'Who created this?'

'Nobody knows.'

'You're kidding?'

Ellie laughed softly, the sound echoing around them. Realising they were alone down here made Joe feel even more privileged.

'The whole thing is a mystery. Nobody has a clue who made it, or when, or why.'

'I can't believe I've never heard of it before.'

'I'm glad, in a way. I don't want to see it overrun, or Disneyfied. It's too precious.' She followed him as he moved from panel to panel. 'It would have looked even more spectacular when it was created. The colours have faded a lot over the centuries.'

'So what's the history? How many centuries?'

'It's anyone's guess. This wasn't discovered until 1835. There are caves and tunnels all round here. It was smugglers who found this. They broke through one of the antechambers and then excavated up through the dome. The hole at the top had been plugged by earth and rock. Now it's covered with perspex.'

She gestured at the walls. 'There's said to be over four million shells here. Even with a team of people, you're talking about a huge task: excavating the cavern, shaping it, then meticulously gathering

186

and transporting the shells here. And they had to be stuck to the wall while they were alive, apparently. But prior to the discovery there wasn't a single clue to its existence. No gossip, no local legends, nothing.'

Joe shook his head. 'That doesn't make sense. Can't they test the shells?'

'They tried carbon dating, but the Victorian lamps have coated everything in soot, so the results were meaningless.' She laughed again, with a child's delight. 'Scientists analysed the glue and drew a blank. It contains elements that can't be identified. They just don't know how it was done.'

With a sigh of rapture, Ellie gazed at the column of light in the centre of the room. 'We could be standing in a temple that pre-dates Stonehenge or Avebury. Built by a civilisation we know absolutely nothing about.'

Joe grinned. This was an utterly different Ellie, brimming with infectious enthusiasm and light years from the cool, acerbic persona he'd encountered before.

Slowly they explored the cavern. One of the antechambers had an alcove with what looked like an altar set into it. Ellie explained some of the theories about the sort of worship that might have been conducted here. One involved a solar calendar, with certain panels illuminated on the spring equinox and summer solstice.

'But it's all guesswork. They used radar on the walls and found hollow spaces behind the panels. But no one can countenance breaking through to find out what's in there.' Wistful for a moment, she smiled. 'I'm really glad you feel it too. The sense of wonder.'

187

'I don't see how you could fail to.'

'Oh, I know people who'd see this and think: a cave full of shells—so what?' She snorted at some private recollection. 'For me, this is a reminder that we don't have all the answers.'

'I've never been in any doubt about that.'

'Not you specifically. Human beings. We assume we're smarter than the people who went before us, because they lived in caves and wore animal skins, and we have central heating and iPads and hedge funds. The fact is, we don't have a clue what other civilisations might have flourished, thousands of years before us, and thrived to an extent we can only dream of. The people who built this might have been incredibly advanced, running happy, sustainable communities where people were healthy and looked after each other, worked hard but also had plenty of leisure time. To me, the Shell Cavern is like a hint, a clue to what our shiny modern world has lost.'

Ellie signalled the end of her speech with an awkward shrug.

Joe smiled. 'Phew.'

'Is that all you can say?'

'It's a very persuasive argument. But I would maintain that human beings are basically the same now as they've been for millennia. Some brilliant, inventive, compassionate; others mean and selfish and cruel. The essential struggle is between those opposing forces. Sometimes those forces exist within the same person.'

Energised by the debate, Ellie briefly rested her hand on his arm. 'Ah, but I'm an optimist, you see. I choose to believe that the ideal society can be achieved.'

Joe thought of Giles Quinton-Price, all set to proclaim that Leon Race had succeeded where many others had failed; never mind the methods by which that success had been achieved. He shivered.

'There are people who think Trelennan is pretty close to perfect.'

'They're wrong,' Ellie said. 'In fact, they couldn't be further from the truth.'

'Really?' He felt very cold. Had the lights just flickered, or was it his vision playing up?

The magnificence of the shells had caused him to forget where he was. Now he imagined the stone walls closing in on him, the weight of all that earth and rock pressing down, a voice in his head screaming: *You're in a cave. You're trapped.*

Ellie was talking. Joe had to make a physical effort to tune in: '. . . easier to make things look fine on the surface. I shouldn't say that, but it's true.'

She had drifted away a little, and when she turned back her lips were still moving but he couldn't hear a word over the sudden roaring in his ears. The light was wrong, too, brighter for a moment, then rapidly dimming. The floor tilted and he stumbled and then it went completely dark.

CHAPTER THIRTY-FIVE

Less than five minutes till the phone rang again. Leon picked it up but said nothing.

'Mr Race? I don't want to be wasting my time here. The fact is, I know a lot more than just *who* he is. But if you don't have him, it's hardly worth my while—'

189

'I know where he can be found.' Leon's voice was like flint. 'I also know he's on the run.'

A hesitation at the other end. *Stolen your thunder*, Leon thought. Then came the wheezy laugh.

'But who from? That's the nub. Who from, eh?' The man let the question hang for a couple of seconds. 'What are you going to offer me?'

'Ten grand,' Leon said. 'Paid once we know the information's good.'

'Make it a hundred thousand, and you're still getting a bargain. Cash, in used notes.'

Leon looked at Fenton, who was tight-lipped, shaking his head. Fat lot of use, Leon thought.

He said, 'Why don't we meet up, discuss this face to face?'

'Hmm. I gotta think about that. Trouble is, Mr Race, I don't trust you.' Cackling, he rang off.

Leon threw the handset down in disgust. 'Wanker.'

'We know him,' Fenton said.

'What?'

'His voice is familiar. That's why he's being so cagey. We know him from somewhere.'

Leon made a growling noise: neither agreeing nor disagreeing. 'If he's stringing me along, he's fucking dead.' He thought for a moment, shook his head. 'Nah. He's a dead man, anyway, talking to me like that.'

*   *   *

Danny Morton was hunting him, or was it Leon Race? Now they had him cornered, underground, in the dark. The roaring noise must be the river. He

190

pictured the cave, inundated with water, and felt panic crushing his chest. Someone cried out and he realised he wasn't alone down here—

Joe's eyes opened. He was sitting on the stone floor of the cavern. Ellie knelt at his side, one hand on his brow, the other feeling for a pulse.

'I'm okay. I'm okay.' He tried to get up but she held him back.

'Just rest for a minute.' She looked mortified. 'I'm so sorry. You told me you had a problem with confined spaces, and I didn't take it seriously.'

'I'm not sure if it was that.' Joe blinked a few times, chasing the nightmare into shadows. 'I don't know *what* it was.'

'We'd better go.'

Ignoring his protests that he could stand unaided, she helped him up, making him feel feeble and embarrassed. His head spun a little, but otherwise there seemed to be no after-effects.

Maybe it had been claustrophobia, or a panic attack. But why hadn't it affected him sooner? As they slowly climbed the steps, Ellie put forward an explanation.

'It was me, waffling on. You got so bored you keeled over. Wouldn't be the first time I had that effect on a man.'

Joe chuckled. 'I was very impressed. I saw a whole different side of you.' She looked blank, and he added: 'You weren't taking the piss out of everything.'

'Actually, you're right. That *is* a bit worrying . . .'

They left the visitor centre and strolled along the path. The rain had stopped, but low cloud still clung to the hillside. Joe was thinking back over the conversation they'd had: perfect societies. The

191

contrast between the surface appearance and the reality beneath.

'I met Leon Race yesterday,' he told her. 'He's offered me some casual work.'

'Wow. I wasn't expecting that. So what did you make of him?'

'I'm reserving judgement on that for now. But I've accepted the offer.'

'And how did your landlady react to the news?'

Now it was Joe's turn to be surprised. 'She seemed okay with it. Why?'

'Nothing.' Ellie concentrated on her bag, hunting for her keys.

'Are Leon and Diana enemies?'

'Oh no. It's not that.' She felt his gaze, saw he wasn't going to let the subject drop. 'I don't think Leon was all that keen on Diana's husband. Ancient history now.'

'Maybe, but I'd like to know. Roy was a good friend of mine. A mentor, really.'

A small smile from Ellie. 'You're a policeman?'

'I was. I left a few years ago. Why the amusement?'

'It explains a few things. Like why you're itching to help search for Alise's sister.'

Joe couldn't deny it. Nodding, he said, 'So what about Leon and Roy . . .?'

'When Roy and Diana moved here Leon hadn't been in business for long, but his reputation was already well established. You didn't cross him. I suppose Roy, as a retired copper, didn't take kindly to that.'

'Knowing Roy, that doesn't surprise me. Did he make trouble for Leon?'

'Possibly. I honestly don't know.'

Joe frowned. 'You're saying there was this bad feeling, and yet Diana told me that her new boyfriend works for Leon.'

'Hardly new,' Ellie said, the familiar sarcasm back in place. 'They've been together for years.'

'Have they? I got the impression it was fairly recent.'

Ellie shook her head, correcting his assumption while also dismissing the subject.

'Let's talk about the mess you're getting into. Off to work for Leon Race, and at the same time you're clearly on Alise's side. You know that's asking for trouble?' She looked deep into his eyes. 'You don't mind that at all, do you? In fact, I suspect you welcome it.'

Joe smiled. 'Are you always this perceptive?'

'Sadly, no.' Her sudden bitterness caught him unawares. 'But I'm working on it.'

                    *   *   *

He declined her offer of a lift home, said he had some shopping to do. When they exchanged mobile numbers, Ellie muttered, 'Not that you'll be in any hurry to see me again after this.'

'Don't be too sure. I choose the venue, though?'

'Above ground, presumably?'

'Definitely. No more caves for a while.'

Then an awkward moment, neither of them sure whether to kiss, shake hands, or refrain from contact altogether. Ellie decided for them by turning away. Joe started to walk, raising a hand in farewell as she drove past, and reflected on the wisdom she had shown.

Asking for trouble.

CHAPTER THIRTY-SIX

He called in at Gwynn's on his way home. The greengrocer's was in a key corner spot on the High Street: ample space for the trestle tables groaning with fresh fruit and vegetables.

Reckless devil that he was, Joe picked up a couple of peaches and carried them inside. The till was staffed by a young woman, plump and curvy, with white-blonde hair and a rash of acne on her cheeks.

'Seventy-eight pee,' she said, sniffing at the paucity of his purchase.

Joe gave her a pound coin. 'You're not Karen, by any chance?'

She was immediately on the defensive. 'Why?'

'I'm looking for Alise. I understand she's a friend of yours?'

'Who says?' Karen scanned the shop warily. There was only one other customer, an elderly woman, talking to another member of staff.

'I'm not here to make trouble,' Joe said. 'I just want to make sure she's all right. Is it true she's staying with you?'

Karen nodded unhappily. 'It's only casual, like. No one else knows.'

'I won't tell anyone. Do you know where she is now?'

'She didn't come in last night. I texted, but she hasn't got back to me.'

'Is that unusual for her?'

Karen struggled with the question for a moment. 'I don't know her well. I only offered her a place to

194

crash 'cause I needed the money.'

'If you do hear from her, can you tell her to call Joe? She has my number.'

'Yeah, okay.' Her expression turned sly. 'You know she's back on the market?'

'Sorry?'

'Ditched her feller, didn't she? I can see her falling for somebody like you, though. Good-looking older man . . .'

*   *   *

Joe ate the peaches as he walked, dawdling because he still felt awkward about inhabiting Diana's space. Caught himself hoping she'd be out, and then felt guilty about that.

She wasn't out. As he pushed open the door he heard music playing, the clatter of pans. A second later the smell hit him: his stomach did eager backflips. She was baking.

He shut the door with a thud, to announce his presence. Called out a hello and Diana called back: 'In here.'

The kitchen was warm and steamy, like a tropical garden. Diana was chopping up carrots, her hair tied back and her face flushed.

'God, that smells amazing.'

'Chicken pie,' she said. 'And there's a ginger cake as well. I hope you're hungry.'

'Starving.'

'We'll eat soon, then. My plans are already out the window.' She wiped her hands on a tea towel. 'I'd intended Glenn to join us. A nice way of introducing you to your new colleague.'

She smiled, anticipating his next question. 'They

rang earlier. Can you start at nine tomorrow? Ten pounds an hour, they said. I assume you knew that?'

'No, but don't worry. What happened with Glenn?'

'He's been sent on some sort of errand. Last-minute, as usual.' Diana sounded exasperated, but Joe couldn't help wondering if she wasn't also, secretly, a tiny bit relieved.

'Does that happen a lot?' he asked.

'More than it should. I've told him to try saying no occasionally, but he won't. Works too hard, too many hours.' She sighed. 'And you'll be next, I dare say.'

Joe shrugged. 'Who knows how long I'll last?'

*   *   *

Diana let him help prepare the vegetables, but only till she realised he'd been out in the rain for hours. Sent away to shower and change, Joe returned to find the dinner cooking, the dishwasher loaded, the wooden-handled saucepans washed up and not a single task remaining, except to open the wine.

'That would be very useful,' she said. 'Chenin Blanc all right with you?'

'Lovely.' He asked about her day, which had consisted of shopping, housework and coffee with a friend. In return, he described his visit to the gallery.

'Patrick Davy seems like a nice guy.' When Diana made no comment, he added, 'I also went to the Shell Cavern. Isn't it extraordinary?'

'I suppose. Roy and I tried it soon after we moved here, but it gave me the creeps. Of course, that was hilarious to Roy. He kept fooling around, making ghost noises. I couldn't get out of there fast enough.'

Joe commiserated, then said, 'I'm curious to hear what it was like when you came to Trelennan.'

She gave him a sidelong glance. 'There isn't a lot to say.'

'Well, what did Roy think of Leon Race, and vice versa? A retired copper moving to the town, I'd have thought they were destined to take an interest in each other?'

'Not really. Things weren't so—things were different then.' Diana smiled, as though to reassure him, but they both knew she had slipped up.

She'd been about to say: *Things weren't so bad then.*

*   *   *

In the interests of diplomacy, Joe let the matter drop. Over dinner they discussed the rigours of running a B&B. Diana confirmed his suspicion that the best and the worst aspects of the job were essentially the same thing: the people you met.

Suddenly the first bottle of wine was empty, and it was barely six o'clock. Dark outside, and raining heavily. Another glass or two and he'd be quite happy to go to bed.

Lightweight, he thought.

Diana suggested taking the second bottle into the living room. As he got up his phone buzzed. There was a text from Alise, sent nearly an hour ago. He must have failed to hear it.

Joe, I've decided to leave Trelennan. I've wasted too much time on this. My sister has

to go her own way in life. Sorry not to say goodbye. Xx.

He read the message a couple of times; became aware of Diana's interest and offered her the phone.

'It's from Alise.' After she'd read it, he pressed the call button, but got the same old message: *The mobile you are calling has been switched off.*

In the living room, he sank into an armchair while Diana took the adjoining sofa, sitting sideways with her feet tucked beneath her. Joe described his attempts to find Alise, and was forced to admit his temptation to get involved in the search for her sister.

'The minute you told me you'd spoken to Alise, I knew you'd want to help her.'

'Except she's given up and gone back home.'

'You can't blame her, can you?'

'No. It just seems an odd time to throw in the towel.'

Unless she'd been crying wolf, just as Ellie had suggested.

'If I'm honest, I'm not sorry to hear it,' Diana said. 'You have more than enough on your plate right now.'

Joe shrugged. He was still holding the phone, hoping there would be a call, a text. An explanation. He let it eat away at him for a while, and then said what was on his mind.

'The text came from Alise's phone. It didn't necessarily come from Alise. Every time I call, the phone's switched off. And the girl she was staying with didn't mention anything about her leaving.'

'Yes.' Diana sounded puzzled. 'And?'

'Well, bearing in mind the accusations that Alise

198

was making, I wonder if Leon might have taken some action of his own?'

'Are you saying he not only abducted the sister, but now he's taken Alise as well?' She shook her head. 'If you believe he's capable of that, how can you even consider going to work for him . . .?' She faltered, saw the apologetic grin on his face. 'Oh, Joe. Why can't you leave things alone?'

The question had the feel of a general lament. It prompted him to ask: 'Could Roy?'

But Diana went on as if she hadn't heard him. 'Lord knows, the last undercover work you did brought tragedy upon your family.'

He held up his hand. 'I took the job because the money will come in handy. Because I'm not comfortable accepting handouts, and because I can't just sit around doing nothing all day.' He gave a sad smile. 'I'm becoming a stubborn old fool, like my dad.'

'Happens to us all, I'm afraid. Turning into our parents.'

Another easy, gentle silence. Joe took a sip of wine before he spoke again. 'Diana, I really don't mean to pry, but I can't help thinking that something's wrong here.'

She looked at him, her eyes shining. 'Here?' she repeated.

He nodded. 'With you. Glenn. Leon. Alise. Trelennan. The whole place feels like it's off-kilter, somehow.'

She went on staring at him for a long time, then abruptly shook her head.

'I don't know what you mean.'

CHAPTER THIRTY-SEVEN

'Victor Smith.'

Leon gestured at Fenton to stop the tape. 'What?'

'Victor Smith,' Glenn repeated.

He was standing by Leon's desk, one hand on his mouth. While he listened to the recording he kept pulling his bottom lip out and letting it plop back into place. Leon had a stapler to hand; he'd seriously thought about throwing it at Glenn, or maybe stapling his lips together. Now, at last, there was something positive to distract him.

'Who the hell is Victor Smith?'

Glenn shut his eyes, pushed his fingers through his hair.

'One of the guys hanging round with Larry . . . Milligan, five or six years ago. The cut-and-shut merchants, up in Cheshire someplace.'

There was silence while they considered it: Leon, Fenton, Derek Cadwell and Warren Fry. Half-eight in the morning, and Glenn was a bit livelier than the rest of them. Fenton had teased him about it: 'Staked your claim last night, did you?'

'No, 'cause I had to go to Plymouth, didn't I? Traffic was shit. By the time I got back I decided on an early night.'

'Anyone else clued up on this Smith bloke?' Leon asked.

Shrugs. Blank looks. Then Warren said, 'It does ring a bell.'

'Rod Dutton might know,' Glenn said. 'He was connected to Milligan's lot.'

200

Fenton sat forward on the sofa, spraying flakes of his third croissant on to the carpet. 'So do we confront Smith with this knowledge?'

'No way,' Leon said. To Glenn: 'Where do you reckon he lives?'

'Dunno. I can ask around. Start with Rod. Do it subtle, like.'

'Yeah. Find out where he's likely to be right now. Then we plan the counter-attack.'

The phone buzzed: an internal call. Fenton took it and reported: 'He's here. Twenty minutes early.'

'That's keen,' Cadwell remarked. But he didn't like the idea of Joe working for Leon, and had made his views clear. Leon had ignored him. It was none of Cadwell's business.

'Off you go,' Leon told Glenn. 'Show him round, then rustle me up an address for Victor fucking Smith.'

*   *   *

Joe felt like a new boy on the first day of term. Not anxious, particularly; it was more a kind of weary anticipation of the processes that lay ahead. Knowing he'd have to find his way. Knowing, also, that his presence wouldn't be welcomed by some.

The front door was opened by a lean Welshman with dark hair and ears like walnuts, who introduced himself as Phil Venning. He told Joe to wait in the hall, then vanished into a side room. Joe glimpsed a desk laden with CCTV monitors.

The wine last night had left him with a thick head. He'd eaten breakfast with Diana, who seemed to have suffered no ill effects. The conversation didn't stray from neutral ground.

He walked up to Leon's during a dry spell between heavy showers. Alise's phone was still switched off, so he sent her a text, then put the whole issue aside. Time to focus on work.

*   *   *

The man who strode out to greet him was tall and ruggedly handsome, with strong features and big brown puppy-dog eyes. Joe could see how Diana had fallen for him.

'Joe Carter,' he said, offering his hand.

'Glenn Hicks.' Glenn had a crushing grip, and Joe had to make an effort not to wince. 'I hear you and Di go back a long time?'

'Yeah. I was friends with Di and Roy for years.'

A muscle in Glenn's jaw twitched at the mention of Roy's name. 'Right. Quick tour before you start. This is the base for most of our operations, so you'll be in and out a lot.'

He marched across the hall, and it struck Joe that this was also the man he'd glimpsed in an upstairs window on Wednesday, watching him out on the decking.

'Upstairs is Leon's private quarters. Totally out of bounds at all times.'

'Okay.' Joe wondered if every new employee received such a stern warning.

'Down here, it's pretty much all public.' Glenn pointed out the living room where Joe had first met Leon, as well as the larger room used as an office. Joe could hear the faint murmur of voices from inside the room.

'With the office, you knock first and wait to be called.'

202

Next was the kitchen. Joe was introduced to the housekeeper, Pam, a plump, homely woman in her sixties. She had two enormous frying pans on the go, filled with about thirty rashers of bacon. She paused in cutting open a stack of bread rolls and beamed at Joe.

'I do my best to keep you all fed and watered, don't I?' She gave Glenn a simpering look, and almost melted when he winked at her.

Then into the depths of the house, and a storage room full of boxes and cartons, their contents unspecified. Finally Glenn opened what appeared to be a cupboard door, revealing a set of stairs. 'Basement,' he said.

He led the way down to a large, comfortable den that reeked of maleness. A low ceiling, studded with spotlights. Walls painted dark brown, adorned with black and white prints of nude women that were just slightly too graphic to be called artistic. A thick beige carpet and black leather sofas placed like pews before a gigantic TV screen. Games consoles and DVDs and a rack full of men's magazines.

'You can hang out here between jobs.' Glenn showed him an alcove with a kitchenette. 'Tea and coffee in there. Toilet's the other side, but the plumbing's dodgy.' He snickered. 'If you're gonna drop a bomb, best use the upstairs loo.'

Joe said nothing. With no natural light, and the over-illumination of the spots, he imagined it wouldn't take too long down here to end up with a hell of a tension headache.

He had a sudden flashback to the Shell Cavern: the sense of being trapped; the pounding water; a scream in the darkness . . .

203

He shook off the memory, saw Glenn frowning at him, then realised the pounding noise wasn't just a memory. He tilted his head, listening hard. There was a deep thrumming sound, like blood heard through a stethoscope.

'The falls.' Glenn indicated the wall on which the TV was mounted. 'The ravine's about three feet away, but there's a state-of-the-art waterproof membrane. Nothing can penetrate it.'

As they headed back upstairs, he launched into an explanation of the process involved. It bored Joe rigid but he was grateful just to get out of there.

In the kitchen Pam was assembling a mountain of bacon butties on a silver platter. Both men helped themselves, adding brown sauce from a catering-size bottle on the unit.

Glenn wolfed his down in a couple of quick bites and opened the back door. It was raining hard again, rustling in the trees and beating on the roof. Under cover of the veranda, Glenn lit up as Joe followed him around the back of the house.

'No smoking indoors,' he muttered. 'Pain in the arse, but there it is.'

They reached the corner by the viewing platform. Two men were huddled close to the set of doors that Joe had used the other day. One was in an LRS uniform, a paunchy middle-aged man in glasses, introduced as Warren. The other one, in cargo pants and a lumberjack coat, was Bruce. About forty, broad and muscular, with short black hair and a closely trimmed beard. Joe made an effort to shake hands; Warren just settled for a nod.

They stood and made small talk, while Glenn sucked on his cigarette and glowered at no one in particular. Joe stepped out from the veranda and onto the viewing platform to take a look at the falls. The water was frothing and churning a little more wildly today, swilling leaves and other debris along with it.

'You wanna be careful,' Bruce called out. 'That rail's not very secure.'

'Yeah. Bloody cowboy builders,' Warren added. Both men were sniggering.

Glenn gave them a sour look. 'I built this,' he explained.

'Really?' Joe said. 'You're a useful man to have around.'

Without a hint of modesty, Glenn nodded. 'Yeah. I am.' And he turned and stalked back along the veranda.

*   *   *

Joe reached the kitchen door in time to hear a burst of giggles from Pam. Glenn had snatched another buttie from under her nose.

'Jesus, these are too good. You're gonna make me fat.'

'Ooh, I hope not.' She patted his belly. 'You look just right as you are.' She saw Joe and smiled. 'Are you having another one?'

'He hasn't got time,' Glenn said.

The next stop was the living room, and the big functional cupboard. Glenn took out a worksheet and attached it to a clipboard. 'Did Leon explain the set-up?'

'Not in any detail.'

'Right. Listen up.' He perched on the arm of a sofa. 'There are various businesses. Some of 'em, like the security firm, you won't get involved in

205

at all. Too many regulations. Same with the taxis. Insurance costs a fortune, and the bastards will jump on any reason to avoid paying out.' Glenn sighed, tapping the clipboard in his lap.

'With the vending company, the pubs and whatnot, we can be a bit more flexible. They're spread out all over the South-West, and most days we get problems. Someone goes sick, or has to change his shift. Your job's to fill in for any absences.'

'Okay.'

'The actual work's a doddle. An idiot could do it.' Glenn raised one eyebrow, cryptically, as though he hadn't yet decided if Joe fell within that definition. 'The money's not great, but on the plus side nobody cares how many hours you do. Especially as I hear you're completely off the books?'

He turned the statement into a question, so Joe had to nod.

'Of course we'll need some ID. Proof of a clean driving licence, as a minimum.'

Joe had a licence in the name of 'Joe Carter' in his pocket. He'd hoped they wouldn't ask to see it, but hadn't really believed he could be that fortunate. He showed it to Glenn, who plucked it from his hand and stood up. 'Just got to make a copy for our records.'

He slipped out of the room, and Joe felt a tiny chill creep along his spine. This was a stupid idea. Diana was right. He was crazy to be getting involved with an organisation like this. If they subjected the ID to any careful scrutiny . . .

Glenn was back, giving no sign that anything was amiss. He returned the licence and said, 'I'd better take your mobile number, as well.'

He jotted it down, then consulted the clipboard. 'Truro's gone to shit. Derek Stillwell and his slipped disc.' He indicated an address on the worksheet. 'Threemilestone industrial estate, just west of Truro. Ask for Brian. Once you're loaded, you've got five deliveries and a collection. The vans have satnav, and getting lost doesn't wash it with Leon. He'll work out the time and dock your money.'

'What about meal breaks?'

'Grab a burger or something. But don't take too long.' Back to the clipboard. 'Your last call is Padstow. Right next door is St Merryn. You need to collect a guy called Carl and drop him off at the Crow's Nest, which is a pub about a mile out of Trelennan.'

Joe nodded. He vaguely remembered seeing the sign on Tuesday night. That already seemed like a long time ago: Bristol, Ryan Whittaker, Lindsey Bevan . . .

'Earth to driver!' Glenn clicked his fingers in front of Joe's face. 'Any questions?'

'No.'

'Good. You're in the Vauxhall Combo. Make sure you're back before six, because that's when Carl's shift starts. He can't afford to be late, which means neither can you.'

He gave Joe a long stare, clearly debating whether to add something.

'What's on your mind?' Joe asked.

'How long you planning to stay at Di's?'

Joe kept his tone neutral. 'I'm not sure yet. A week or two.'

'A paying guest? I hear she's put you up on the top floor.'

'That's right.'

Glenn went on staring at him, nodding slowly until it was clear that Joe had got the message: *Stay away from my woman.*

As Joe got up to leave, Glenn murmured: 'You and Roy, eh? Best buddies?'

'What about it?'

A tiny, twitchy shrug. 'I never did like Roy.'

CHAPTER THIRTY-EIGHT

When Victor Smith called back at midday, Leon was ready and waiting.

'He's a total loser,' Glenn said. He'd spent the morning pushing his contacts for information. 'Been on the slide for years. His wife died. Kids buggered off somewhere. Milligan and that crowd won't touch him any more. He's said to be scraping a living, fencing stolen copper, and that's only because his brother-in-law's a scrap-metal dealer.' He gave Leon a rueful glance. 'Oh, and he's scamming the social for invalidity benefit.'

'Scum,' Leon spat. He didn't believe in social security: thought you should either stand on your own feet, or starve—and if you starved, tough shit.

Glenn had a look on his face like he was expecting a rant. Leon, taking a deep breath, decided to let it pass.

'If he's been ostracised,' Fenton chipped in, 'how did he get to see the photo of Joe?'

'He drinks in one of the pubs that Milligan's lot use. Sounds like he hangs round them, hoping to worm his way back in.'

'Is that going to happen?'

'No chance. Milligan's white-collar now. Making a fortune from insurance fraud—whiplash and all that. Cops don't give a toss. Money for old rope.'

Leon scowled. He'd had a chance to get involved in a couple of similar schemes and had declined. Was Glenn having a dig at him?

Irritably, he said, 'So where is he living?'

'Possibly Tunstall, wherever that is.'

'Stoke-on-Trent, if I recall correctly,' Fenton said. When Glenn continued to look blank, he added: 'The West Midlands. Between Birmingham and Manchester.'

'Geography's not your thing, eh, Glenn?' Leon said. 'Still, once you've been there you'll know it for the future.'

Glenn crumpled. 'You're not serious?'

'Course I am. I want an address, and I want it by tonight.'

*   *   *

Then the call itself. Leon didn't want Smith to be spooked by putting him on speaker, so Fenton and Glenn had to share a handset, squashed together like lovers in a cinema.

'Mr Race. I take it you've had some time to reflect?'

'Fifty thousand. If the information's good enough. You get half up front and the other half when we're sure it all checks out.'

'I said a hundred—'

'Fifty,' Leon repeated. 'Paid in two stages. I don't negotiate.'

'In that case, we won't be doing a deal.'

'That picture went out to a lot of people. I've

209

already had some promising calls.'

'Well, of course you would say that . . .'

They all heard the desperation creeping into Smith's voice. Leon sniffed.

'Yeah. I do say that. So stop wasting my fucking time. Fifty or nothing.'

A long, pensive silence. Then sweet surrender.

'Very well. Fifty grand in used notes.' Smith's tone became whiny and apologetic. 'You understand how I've gotta be careful? It's not an easy situation.'

'Look, I'm a businessman. I'm after a good deal, but I'm not going to cheat you. If what you've got is of value to me, then I'll pay for it. Simple as that.'

'So what about the details? The where and when?'

'For your sake, it needs to be tomorrow. I'm serious about those other calls. You know where I am, do you?'

'Cornwall, isn't it?'

'Yeah. North coast. A town called Trelennan. You got a pen to take my address?'

'I ain't coming to your gaff. No offence, but I could walk through the door and get clonked on the head or something . . .'

Leon sighed. He moved the phone away from his ear, knowing that Smith would pick up on the alteration in the background noise. He had anticipated this objection. Welcomed it, in a way.

Smith said hurriedly, 'It's not that I mind travelling. Maybe somewhere neutral, like?'

Leon pretended to think. 'There's a place called the Crow's Nest, a couple of miles out of town. A gastro pub.'

'Gastro . . .?'

'A pub that serves posh food. Saturday night, it'll be packed. Safe as houses. No one's gonna clonk you on the head.'

A few doubts lingered as Smith said, 'I suppose that sounds all right.'

'I'll be there at nine o'clock, with an associate of mine. Clive Fenton.'

'That the big fat fella?'

'Big-boned, is what his mum always told him.' Leon caught a glare from Fenton. 'And don't be rude about my right-hand man. It'll be his job to rustle up the cash.'

'Sorry. Sorry. No offence, like.' A smacking noise as Smith licked his lips. 'Twenty-five grand up front?'

'That's what I said. But this has got to be solid gold.'

'I promise you, Mr Race, you won't be disappointed.' Smith cackled away for a few seconds. 'But for your sake, you'd better not be shitting me—no offence, again. You'd better bloody have him.'

That sounded to Leon like a clumsy trap, easy to avoid. 'Tomorrow night,' he said.

He ended the call. Looked at Fenton. Looked at Glenn. Grinning like wolves.

'Oh, we've got him,' Leon said. 'We've definitely got him.'

*   *   *

Two hours later, Glenn's contact came through with an address. Tunstall, like they thought.

'We're talking, what, four or five hours in the car?' Glenn grumbled.

211

'So? You're gonna stay overnight. I want Reece and Todd to drive up separately. First you find Smith. Watch where he goes, who he sees. Tomorrow, when he sets off for the meeting, you follow him back here, see if he's bringing any backup. The other two need to turn his place over, make sure there's nothing about us. No notes, nothing on a computer or anything. Then we all rendezvous later at the pub.'

'Surely the Crow's Nest is too public?'

'It's perfect. He's less likely to come mob-handed if we meet somewhere safe.'

'True,' Fenton conceded. 'But then we have the issue of multiple witnesses . . .'

Leon smiled. 'Don't stress. I've got an idea or two brewing.'

They both noticed that Glenn was rooted to the spot, his hands making fists. Fenton discreetly rose, claiming a full bladder, but Leon waved him back down.

'Let's hear what Glenn's got to say.'

Once directly confronted, Glenn seemed reluctant to speak. He cleared his throat, which straight away sounded like an apology.

'This situation with Joe. Diana's positive he's not a cop any more, and we've taken her word for it . . .'

'You think she's lying to you?' Leon saw Glenn flinch.

'No. No, I don't. But she is only going on what Joe told her. Until this week, she hadn't seen or heard from him in years.'

Leon nodded: he got it now. 'So he could be lying to her.'

'Yeah. Or maybe he did leave the police, but went back in. More likely, he's moved into a different department. Secret stuff. *Undercover.*'

Leon had to stop and consider for a moment. The possibility that the authorities would try to infiltrate his organisation was never far from his mind. It had been a long, hard slog towards respectability, and there would always be those who remained suspicious, or resentful, or just plain disbelieving. *A leopard doesn't change its spots*, they would argue.

And in some ways, Leon thought, that was true.

'Fair point,' he said. 'But I don't see it, really. Why choose him, when he's known to Diana, and she knows he was once a cop? Why not send a complete stranger?'

Glenn was stumped. 'Uh, yeah, unless it's a sort of double bluff . . .'

'That's over-complicated,' Fenton said.

'I agree,' Leon said. 'Keep it simple every time. Nobody sent him here to spy on us. He turned up at Diana's without even a fucking toothbrush to his name. I think he's in trouble.' He chuckled. 'And we're gonna make that trouble a hell of a lot worse.'

CHAPTER THIRTY-NINE

It was a long and gruelling day. Not hard work physically, compared to some of the jobs Joe had done in recent years, but intensely wearying.

He was a competent driver, but the narrow twisting roads posed a severe test of his skills, concentration and patience. Half the time he was stuck behind something slow and impassable, while a succession of impatient local drivers sat on his

213

tail, waiting for the moment when they would veer out and roar past him on the wrong side of the road, oblivious to blind corners and the possibility of imminent death.

Other than the time pressure, the job was quite straightforward. Everything was carefully explained by Joe's contact at the distribution centre. Brian was in his late fifties, a small, dapper man with a neat moustache and reading glasses worn on a chain around his neck. Joe had the impression that he was well accustomed to dealing with temporary employees.

The five deliveries were to businesses that used Leon's vending machines. Joe was shown how to open and restock the machines. He was also told how to remove and replace the special lockable cash bags from those machines.

'We've had drivers trying to cream off some money,' Brian said in a languid voice. 'You don't strike me as the type, frankly, but I'm required to issue the warning. It's a very bad idea to steal from Leon Race. If you've met him, you probably get my drift?'

'Absolutely.'

Joe emerged from the office to find the van fully loaded with merchandise. According to the magnetic signs which had been attached to the vehicle, he was now a representative of the Trelennan Vending Co.

'Signs are removable because the vans get used for different businesses,' Brian told him. 'Just one of Mr Race's many superb ideas.' His tone was so dry that Joe had no idea if the admiration was genuine.

214

By the time he got back to the distribution centre, handed over the cash bags and removed the signs, it was gone five o'clock. He'd used the toilet at his last call, a car showroom, and he'd managed to gulp down a cup of water from a cooler at the same establishment. For food, he could have bought a snack from one of the machines he was re-stocking, but somehow being surrounded by boxes of chocolate bars removed all desire for them.

Roadworks on the A30 put him further behind schedule. When he pulled up in St Merryn, outside a nondescript sand-coloured semi, the front door burst open and a tall man in a shirt and tie came out at a run.

'Cutting it fine.' The man threw himself into the passenger seat, blew out a big sigh, then grinned at Joe. 'I'm Carl.'

'Joe Carter. Sorry I'm late.'

'Nah, don't sweat it. A few minutes won't matter.'

'I was told that punctuality was very important.'

'It depends,' Carl said. He was young, no more than mid-twenties, with a pleasant, guileless face and prematurely thinning brown hair. He gave Joe a quick appraisal. 'You're new, yeah?'

'Started today.' Joe recounted his itinerary, and Carl laughed.

'Sounds like a miracle you're here at all. That bodes well for you.'

'Does it?'

'Yeah. Some jobs, nobody gives a toss how much effort you put in. You work your bollocks off and still don't get a penny more than somebody who

215

does the basic minimum. Whereas here, if you show you're willing to do that bit extra, it doesn't go unnoticed.'

'So Leon's a good employer?'

'I'd say so. I mean, I don't have a lot to do with him. The Crow's Nest has a general manager. Leon leaves well alone.'

He paused, as if debating whether to elaborate. Joe kept very quiet. After a few seconds Carl added: 'Unless there's a problem.'

'Like what?'

'Mm.' Another moment's deliberation. 'I'll give you an example, you being new and everything. One of his other pubs is right out in the sticks. No reliable public transport, so Leon arranges taxis to ferry the staff home at the end of the night. He's got his own taxi firm.'

'Yes, I'd heard that.'

'So one of the drivers is doing this as a regular trip, and he gets the hots for this barmaid. She was only eighteen or nineteen, bloody gorgeous. The driver keeps coming on to her, but she's not interested. He's too old, and he's fat, and she already has a boyfriend.'

Carl slapped his hands down on his knees and sighed, a judder in his breath.

'One night, this guy just flips. Pulls into a lay-by and won't take no for answer, you know what I'm saying? I don't think he went as far as raping her, but it wasn't exactly pleasant, whatever he did.' Carl shivered. 'Anyway, the girl doesn't come into work the next day, and she doesn't call, so the manager drops by her house to find out what's wrong. Cut a long story short: two days later we hear the taxi driver had an accident. In his own car, late at night,

216

he somehow drove into a bridge. Broke both his legs, fucked up his spine and he's in hospital for a month. Not only that, but it turns out he was over the limit, so he's doubly fucked. That's the last we hear of him. Meanwhile, the girl is persuaded to come back to work, and Leon buys her a decent little second-hand car of her own, by way of apology.'

He looked at Joe, keen to see his reaction.

'You think the accident was arranged—'

'I don't speculate on things like that,' Carl said. 'And if you've got any sense you won't either.'

'Fair enough.' Joe checked the time. Almost six p.m., but the pub was only a couple of miles away. 'You get a lift to work every day?'

'It's only temporary.' Carl added ruefully: 'I got banned from driving.'

'Oh?'

'Nothing serious. Bloody totting up. Two of 'em were speeding convictions on the same day, when I went up to London for a concert. Took my girlfriend to see Lily Allen and I end up with six frigging points on my licence.'

'That's harsh.'

'Yeah. If it was someone decent it might have been worth it.' He laughed. 'I was sure I'd lose my job when I had to tell 'em I couldn't get to work. It was Leon who said they'd take care of it. Said I was too valuable to lose for something silly like that.'

'Shame more employers aren't so reasonable.'

'It is,' Carl agreed, as the pub loomed into view. He directed Joe towards the car park. 'Thanks, mate. Hope this job goes well for you.' He opened the door, then nodded towards the pub. 'Make sure you eat here sometime. The food is fantastic.'

217

'I'll bear that in mind,' Joe said.

* * *

And he meant it. After returning the van to Leon's, Joe had a brief conversation with the fat man, Fenton, who told him there was work available tomorrow if he wanted it. Joe said he'd be there for eight a.m. On the basis that it couldn't hurt to ask, he also got an agreement that tomorrow he'd receive payment for his first two days.

Walking back into town, he called Ellie on his mobile. 'How do you fancy dinner at the Crow's Nest tomorrow night?'

Ellie laughed. 'Do you get a staff discount?'

'I'll have to ask. Shall I pick you up around eight?'

'You have a car as well now?'

'Kind of.' Either he'd borrow Diana's, if it was available, or maybe see if he could use the works van. As a last resort, a taxi.

'Lovely. I'd better start saving myself, in anticipation of their banoffe pie,' she said. 'I won't let another calorie pass my lips.'

* * *

At the B&B, Joe found Diana preparing to go out. A bridge night with friends. He was welcome to come along if he wanted.

'Not my scene, really,' he said. 'But thanks for the offer.'

'All right. There's a casserole all ready to heat up. How was the first day at work?'

'Tiring, but it was nice to feel useful. I said I'd go

218

in tomorrow as well.'

'You'd better have an early night, then.'

He nodded. 'Does Glenn play bridge?'

'He does, actually, though he prefers poker. But not this evening. He's off on another errand, somewhere in the Midlands this time.' Diana raised her eyebrows. 'Ridiculous, on a Friday night. But if he won't put his foot down . . .'

After she'd gone, Joe mooched around in the kitchen. Drank some water while he waited for the coffee to brew. Having the house to himself made him realise the underlying tension that persisted between him and Diana, even while on the surface they appeared to be getting on fine.

And if he felt like that, he realised, it was almost certainly as bad, if not worse, for Diana. It meant that he shouldn't count on staying any longer than was necessary.

He drank his coffee while leafing through the local paper. He paid special attention to the round-up of news from the courts, found crime stories about Bodmin and Newquay, Padstow and Bude, but nothing in Trelennan. Not a single unpaid parking fine or drunk-and-disorderly.

Although he was starving, Joe decided to shower before he ate. Or a bath: better to soothe his aching muscles.

In the hall, the phone book caught his eye. He found a listing for the Crow's Nest. Dialled and waited: a busy place, judging by how long it took them to pick up.

Finally a young woman answered, sounding harassed. She interrupted when he got as far as 'tomorr—'

'Saturday night's all booked up.'

'Shame.' He was tempted to invoke Leon's name, but he hated people who did things like that, so he said, 'I was with Carl earlier. He recommended it to me.'

'I should hope he did,' the woman said. 'I'd recommend it, too. But we're still fully booked on Saturday.'

'You don't have any tables that you make available on the night?'

'Not tomorrow. Sorry.'

He put the phone down, his grand plan thwarted. He would need to find an alternative, but really he'd want a recommendation, from Diana or preferably from Ellie herself. Should he call her now, or would that look a bit . . .?

What, he wondered? Keen? Desperate?

'Where is this heading?' Joe murmured to himself.

He didn't know. He was too weary to think straight. Bath, dinner, TV, bed. Then call Ellie in the morning.

CHAPTER FORTY

Time slipping away. She'd always liked the phrase, thought it sounded romantic, prompting an image of a delightful couple romping on a beach, scooping handfuls of dry white sand into their palms and watching it spill through their fingers. Like time was something precious, yet abundant: there was always more when you needed it.

Now, for Jenny, time was like the drip of a Chinese water torture. A slow unending beat that compelled her to keep count, even while the impossibility of doing so dragged her ever closer to meltdown.

He visited daily, she concluded. Most often in the mornings. Perhaps not always, but often enough that it could give her something to cling to: a routine, a structure. If she could stay awake for long enough, marking out the minutes and hours, sleeping only once between each visit, she could keep track of the passing days.

Then she had a brainwave: scratch a calendar on the wall or the floor. A far better way to keep track, and still preserve what remained of her sanity.

She clutched this plan to her chest as though it were a Valentine's Day card from Luke. This one small thing would sustain her, the way Luke's cards, his calls, his texts had sustained her. A crumb of comfort. A grain of sand.

*   *   *

The next visit, she lay obediently in the darkness, eyes shut so that she wouldn't get so much as an accidental glimpse of his face. She sensed that his mood was angry, impatient, but still she asked the question. She had to take the risk. For calibration.

'What time is it?'

'Not that crap again.'

'Please. It's the morning, isn't it?'

'Yeah.'

'And the last time you came, that was yesterday morning?'

He didn't answer. Just grabbed the bucket, sloshing urine on the floor. She smelt it: sharp and foul. He shut the door, and she pictured him

221

stomping away, though she could not hear it. The cell was soundproofed, she guessed. The screams she'd heard must have been her imagination—or else they'd been horrifically loud, to have pierced the mute world of her prison.

And then he was back, the bucket refilled with clean water. The bleach made her nostrils twitch: almost as repellent as the waste.

'Food's by the door. There's a bottle of water, and another toilet roll. And batteries for the torch.'

'Thank you. Thank you so much.' A pause. 'What day is it?'

'You don't need to know that.'

She fell silent, defeated. To know the day: that was a step too far. But he didn't move. She could feel him standing there, in utter darkness. Staring in her direction, even though he wouldn't be able to see anything.

'Got the torch?'

'Yes.'

'Switch it on. Make sure it's pointed at you. Not me.'

She did as she was told, the torch now alien and clumsy in her hand, despite all the hours she had nursed it like a beloved pet. The light this time was shocking: it made her afraid in a way that it never usually did. But she obeyed his commands, directing the beam up and down the length of her body.

'You're not cleaning yourself properly,' he said, the disgust oozing out of him.

She didn't know what to say. She listened to his breath snorting in and out of his nostrils. Then he muttered to himself and went away. Came back and placed something on the floor.

222

'Soap,' he said. 'Next time, I want you clean. Who do you think I am, that I'd want to screw someone who smells like shit?'

'You're putting too much bleach in the bucket.' It wasn't courage: the words came from nowhere, before she could stop them. 'It'll burn me, especially . . . there.'

'Well, use the drinking water, then. Just clean yourself up.'

She could hear him opening the door, was suddenly overcome by recklessness.

'Leon?'

He froze: not even breathing. She felt the lack of vibrations in the air. Frozen physically, and emotionally as well. He *had* forgotten telling her.

Now he would lash out. She'd been foolish, should have kept that knowledge to herself—

'What?' he growled.

'How . . . how long will this go on?'

'As long as I want it to.'

The door shut with the usual terrible finality, and silence returned as other questions gathered in her mind, jostling like passengers denied access to a rush-hour train. Tired, angry, bitter. Self-pitying. Jaded. Suicidal.

Jenny fought them off. She'd survived this long: she wasn't going to throw herself on the tracks now.

He told you it's the next morning. Get your calendar started: from today at least.

First she switched on the torch and examined what he had brought her. A large bottle of Evian water. A couple of bananas and a big bar of Galaxy chocolate. The soap he'd referred to was a bottle of antibacterial hand soap, operated with a plunger. Better than nothing.

223

If she was going to scratch out the passing days, she needed a tool. But what? The bucket was plastic: even the handle was plastic.

There must be something, she thought. The cell seemed empty, but she hadn't conducted a really thorough fingertip search. Hadn't wanted to waste the batteries, but now she had a spare set. If she could find a nail, a pin, even a tiny stone . . .

Enthused, she set to work. She was brisk but methodical. She checked every inch of the cell floor and didn't find a thing. Then she moved on to the walls.

And that was when she saw the blood.

CHAPTER FORTY-ONE

Saturday morning, Joe's alarm went off at seven. He silenced it, then immediately fell deeply asleep for another ten minutes. Woke with a jump and thought: *work*.

Staying in bed had its appeal, but another part of him relished the fact that he had a reason to get up early. He spent a minute or two pondering the importance of routine; the reasons why human beings seem to crave it. Felt himself drifting off again . . .

He propelled himself out of bed and opened the window wide, letting the cold sea air shock him awake. There was a promising blue sheen to the hazy dawn sky. No sign of rain.

Washed and dressed, Joe crept downstairs. He opted for a quick breakfast: fruit juice instead of coffee, cereal rather than toast. He'd just finished when the back door opened and Diana came in, wearing her gym gear. She looked great: eyes bright, a ruddy glow in her cheeks. 'I woke at six. Couldn't get back off, so I decided to be virtuous.'

'You're putting me to shame.'

'It was also a form of punishment, for one glass of wine too many at bridge.' She lifted the kettle. 'I fancy a pot of tea. Do you have time?'

'Not really.' But he lingered for a minute or two. It felt rude to rush off, especially when they'd had a similarly brief contact the night before.

'Glenn seems like a nice guy,' he said. 'Pretty nifty with the DIY, if the decking at Leon's house is anything to go by.'

Diana nodded. 'He renovated this place, too. He used to have his own building firm.'

'So what prompted the change of occupation?'

'I'm not sure. Leon made him an offer he couldn't refuse, I suppose.'

'And is that how you two met? When he was working here?'

Diana was suddenly awkward. 'Probably. I can't honestly remember.' She busied herself with the tea, then said, 'Do you want anything in particular for dinner tonight?'

'Ah, actually, I'm eating out.'

She looked at him, intrigued. 'Lovely. Who with?'

'Ellie Kipling. The woman from the library?'

'Oh. I see. Good.' She turned away from him, fixing her gaze on the tendrils of steam rising from the kettle. Joe thought he heard her make a noise in her throat.

'What is it?'

'Nothing.' Diana waved him away. 'Go on, you'll

225

be late for work.'

*   *   *

He left the house, puzzled and disturbed by her reaction. He wasn't sure how long they could both maintain the pretence that all was well.

At Leon's place he was greeted by the red-haired guard, Kestle, who showed him into the living room. There was no offer of refreshments, no enticing smell of bacon frying. Maybe Pam didn't work weekends.

'You're in the Citroën Berlingo. It's okay, but the clutch can be a bugger.' Kestle handed Joe the details. 'Devon today. Only a couple of calls, so you'll be back for lunchtime. Then we'll get you sorted for this afternoon.'

'Where am I going this afternoon?'

'Dunno yet. No one's told me.'

Joe was heading for the front door when he heard movement behind him. He looked round to see Leon Race padding downstairs, barefoot and wrapped in a dressing gown. He was bleary-eyed and unshaven, his chubby features made vaguely sinister by the presence of stubble: like a corrupted baby.

'Settling in?' he asked.

'Yes, thanks.'

'Thought you would. And I'm not often wrong about people.'

Leon turned towards the kitchen: Joe's audience with the boss was over.

*   *   *

226

The Citroën was a pig to handle, but once Joe got used to its idiosyncrasies he settled back and enjoyed the drive. This early on a Saturday the roads were quiet, and he made good time to the distribution centre in Tiverton. It was the same routine as yesterday: loading up stock, magnetic signs attached to the van, and he was away with his list of deliveries.

Mid-morning, finding a place with a signal, he called Ellie and told her that the pub was fully booked.

'That's unusual, at this time of year,' she said. 'Shame.'

'Is there anywhere else you'd recommend?'

'Nowhere as nice as the Crow's Nest.' She thought about it, then added wryly, 'Might as well come to mine.'

'Are you sure?'

'It's perfectly safe. I won't molest you.' She laughed. 'Or poison you, if that's what you're thinking.'

'But it was supposed to be my treat.'

'That's all right. You can bring the wine.'

*   *   *

Leon spent all morning on the phone. There was a lot to organise: a lot of sweet-talking, a few palms to grease. Fenton worked alongside him, chipping in with advice when he had something useful to offer, keeping his mouth shut when he didn't. It was the secret of their successful working relationship.

And Fenton was buzzing with excitement, too, Leon thought. He was just better at hiding it.

'What d'you reckon?' Leon asked during a lull in

227

the calls. He sat back, lacing his hands behind his head.

'It's a masterstroke,' Fenton said, quite sincerely.

'There's no way he'll see it coming?'

'Absolutely not. In fact, neither of them will.'

'Mmm, I don't know about Joe. You got to remember he was a cop. He's a pro.'

Fenton shrugged. 'It's worth a try, in any case.'

'Yeah. But my bet is that he'll sniff it out.'

Then Glenn phoned and—as was so often the case with Glenn—managed to put a severe dent in Leon's mood.

'You're not gonna believe this bloke. Jesus, what a deadbeat.'

'What?'

'He's been on the move for an hour or so, right. We're in Stoke-on-Trent—'

'We?'

'I had to get Reece to help. I'm in the car, and Smith's on foot. He keeps stopping at bus stops, train stations. I'd have lost him otherwise.'

'So what's he doing?'

'He's been to a couple of houses, one of them quite decent. Wasn't there long, and he came out looking shifty, you know? Then he heads straight to a fucking pawn shop.'

'What's he doing in a pawn shop?'

'Like I said, you're not gonna believe it. I think he's trying to raise the cash for the journey.'

'You are shitting me.'

'I wish I was, Leon. Honestly, he's totally skint.'

'So it could all go belly-up because he can't afford to get here?'

'Looks like it. But I can hardly chuck him a few quid, can I?'

Leon was shaking his head. Far too soon to be building a rage, but he couldn't stop it. Fenton caught his eye and made a pushing gesture, palms facing down: *Calm.*

'Stay on him. If he takes a train or a bus, get Reece to follow. You and Todd do the house.'

'But I'm not a burglar,' Glenn protested. 'I'm a builder.'

'Yeah. So you know about locks and stuff. Perfect.'

Leon ended the call before Glenn could make him any angrier. Turned to Fenton and opened his hands in an appeal for understanding.

'It'll be fine,' Fenton said. 'Let's not get overly concerned.'

'Why did the stupid twat agree to come here if he couldn't afford it?'

'Because he'd be scared of appearing so weak. If you knew he was penniless, you'd never have agreed to fifty thousand in cash.'

Leon sat bolt upright, coldly furious now.

'He pushed me up to fifty grand, when he'd probably have settled for five hundred quid and a fucking bus pass.'

Fenton nodded, very tight-lipped, like he was just possibly biting back a laugh.

'That lousy fucker made a fool of me. He's gonna pay for that.'

It was a couple of seconds before Fenton replied. First he took a deep breath and made strange twisting motions with his jaw. The humour in his eyes vanished when he saw the way Leon was staring at him.

'He was always going to pay, Leon.'

CHAPTER FORTY-TWO

Joe's deliveries took him north across Exmoor, to Lynmouth, then east to Bridgwater in Somerset. He was tantalisingly close to Bristol: a couple of hours there and back, maybe.

Tempting. Only he didn't have a couple of hours. The roads were becoming increasingly choked with day trippers, tractors and the occasional out-of-season caravan, slowing him to a crawl.

He set off for Trelennan, vowing that he'd make the detour the next time a delivery took him out this way, even if it meant getting his wages docked. If he could recover the money he had stashed in Bristol, he wouldn't necessarily have to work for Leon: he'd be back in control of his own destiny.

*　　　　*　　　　*

He didn't reach Trelennan until two-thirty. Kestle opened the door and tutted.

'Thought you'd be here at lunchtime.'

'I was delivering in Bridgwater,' Joe said. 'Short of taking a helicopter, I don't know how I could've done it any sooner.'

Kestle snorted. 'Drive faster. Work harder. That's what the boss tells us.'

Joe didn't rise to the bait. 'Where next?'

'Make a sandwich or something. You can have twenty minutes, then there's some local trips.'

'Okay,' Joe said. 'Pam not here today?'

'No point when there's hardly anyone around.'

'So where are they all?'

230

Kestle shrugged. 'They don't have to tell me. Why would I tell you?'

Left alone in the kitchen, Joe made a ham sandwich and ate it standing at the counter. Drank a glass of water, used the toilet in the hall, and he was ready to go. The sooner he got back to work, the sooner he'd be finished.

The living-room door was open, but the room was empty. He checked the cupboard and saw several clipboards with worksheets on them, but he had no idea which one was for him.

Back in the hall he paused, listening. Aside from the usual ticks and groans of an old house, there was nothing to indicate another human presence. He called out: 'Hello?' and his voice echoed back at him.

Remembering the bank of monitors, he tried that room next. It was empty, although one of the swivel chairs had a jacket slung over the back of it. Kestle's, probably. He must have popped out somewhere.

Joe examined the monitors. Each one was receiving a live feed from several cameras. Some were mounted on the outside of the house, overlooking the drive and the gardens. One showed the decking, and Joe spied a couple of guys smoking on the viewing platform. Maybe everyone took it easier round here on a Saturday.

The other cameras were in a variety of locations, some of which seemed familiar: shops and offices in the High Street, and a few private homes. One looked down on a yard with a hearse in it.

Another showed the coast road and a sliver of the promenade by the harbour wall. Joe made a note to check the café the next time he went past.

231

He wondered if this was how Leon had known who Joe had been speaking to on Wednesday.

No wonder Alise and Patrick Davy had been so paranoid.

*   *   *

Joe returned to the hall. There was one room he hadn't tried: the office.

He knocked and waited, but he knew the room was empty. Over the years in the police he'd developed a sixth sense: an awareness of the vibrations that betrayed a human presence.

He knocked again, then tried the door. It wasn't locked. He opened it and leaned in. Empty. There was a laptop on the desk, the screen facing away from him. He could hear the quiet whir of the fan. A stack of paperwork next to it, and a plate bearing the remains of what might have been a croissant. Folded over the back of the sofa was a blazer that by its size could only belong to Fenton.

Joe was curious to explore, see what was displayed on the laptop, have a look through the paperwork, but the room had a bizarre *Marie Celeste* feel about it. Where was everybody?

The answer—two words—popped into his head and made the hairs on the back of his neck stand up.

Watching you.

There were cameras everywhere. Who said there wasn't one in here, concealed in a light fitting or a smoke alarm? Or a clock.

He concentrated on the desk. There was a small digital clock next to the laptop. Had that been there on Wednesday?

Shrugging to himself, as though baffled to find the room empty, Joe shut the door and returned to the kitchen. Ran himself another glass of water and heard footsteps. Kestle materialised, blushing slightly.

'All set to go?' he asked.

'Ready when you are.'

*   *   *

Upstairs, in one of the guest bedrooms, Leon, Fenton and Venning were watching the images transmitted from the covert cameras: a wall clock in the kitchen, smoke alarms in the living room and the hall, and a clock on the desk in the office.

When Joe checked out the office there was a chorus of gasps, followed by groans from Fenton and Venning as Joe changed his mind, shut the door and walked away.

Leon didn't groan. He said, 'Told you. He's rumbled us.'

'Not necessarily,' Fenton said.

'Yeah, he has. Shame.' Leon gazed at the empty office on-screen. 'I tell you what—tonight had better be a damn sight more successful than this.'

*   *   *

They'd had another update from Glenn. With Victor Smith safely installed on a train to Cornwall, via Birmingham, Glenn and Todd had broken into Smith's flat.

'I was right. He hasn't got two sticks to rub together.'

Leon hadn't heard the phrase before, wasn't

233

totally sure that it *was* a proper phrase, but he got the gist. 'Definitely the right flat?'

'Oh yeah, no doubt about that. There were clothes and stuff. But no furniture. A ratty old mattress and a couple of blankets, a little transistor radio that looks thirty years old, and that's it. No cooker or fridge. No chairs to sit on. Not even a fucking bath.'

'You what?'

'There's broken tiles and cobwebs and shit where the bath used to be. The floorboards beneath it are all rotten. All the pipework's gone, of course. Just a sink and a toilet left. A load of newspapers next to the toilet, and most of 'em weren't readable any more, if you get my drift. I wouldn't shake hands with the guy if I were you.'

He paused, maybe expecting a laugh, but Leon wasn't amused. In his view, this was just more evidence of Victor's nerve. *Temerity* was the word Fenton used afterwards. *Taking the fucking piss* was how Leon saw it.

Glenn coughed, a bit embarrassed, and went on. 'No sign of a mobile phone. He might have one with him, but there was no charger, either. I reckon he's been using a call box.'

'Well, that would be something, at least,' Leon said. Accentuate the positive.

The fewer traces that Victor left in his wake, the better.

CHAPTER FORTY-THREE

The afternoon's deliveries weren't for the vending business. Joe was given half a dozen thick brown envelopes and told to deliver them to various private addresses in Trelennan and some neighbouring towns: Port Isaac, Camelford, Boscastle.

From the feel of them, the envelopes contained thick bundles of paper that could, in Joe's estimation, be money. Strips of transparent tape had been used to seal them, but one or two had loose edges that could perhaps be prised open without causing any visible damage.

He thought about it as he drove to Port Isaac, but concluded that this bore the traits of another test. It would be simple enough for someone to booby-trap an envelope with flour or ink. Not worth the risk.

At each address he had to wait for the householder to collect the package by hand. In every case Joe had the feeling that the delivery was expected. Four men and two women took the envelopes from him with little more than a grunt of acknowledgement.

He was back at Leon's by a quarter to six, and was relieved to see Fenton waddling across the hall. Joe was given his wages in an envelope identical to the ones he'd just delivered, albeit much thinner. That answered the questions in Joe's mind. He *had* been delivering cash, and it probably had constituted another test.

By his reckoning he'd worked approximately eighteen hours over the two days. At ten quid an hour, cash in hand, he was expecting a hundred and eighty pounds. But Fenton—or Leon—evidently thought otherwise. They had paid him two hundred.

It was a pleasant surprise; totally unexpected in the light of the mostly negative things he'd been told about Leon Race. Then again, it chimed with what Carl Ennis had said. Work hard, and they'll look after you.

*　　　*　　　*

Diana was busy with housework when Joe got in. He felt a twinge of guilt as he set down the bag containing the wine he'd bought for this evening.

Upstairs, he found her running a brightly coloured Dyson along the landing. She saw him and started, one hand clamped to her chest. He yelled an apology, and she nodded.

'It's all right. I'm done now.'

They went back downstairs, Joe carrying the Dyson. In the kitchen, while Diana made coffee, Joe surreptitiously placed the wine in the fridge, then counted out a hundred pounds and tried to give it to her.

'What's this?'

'I got paid for the first two days. This is part of what I owe you.'

She stared at him. 'Joe, I did this as a favour. We're friends, remember?'

'I can't stay here and not contribute to the running costs.' He pressed the notes into her hand. 'This is me, putting my foot down, okay? No arguments.'

Reluctantly, Diana accepted the money. She was smiling, but Joe thought there might have been a

236

tear or two glistening in her eyes. He was reminded of the conversation they needed to have, the blunt, honest questions he had to ask. Now would be a perfect opportunity, but he was tired, and running late.

Those were the excuses he gave himself. More than that, perhaps, he was scared of the answers he might receive.

But it was Diana who broached a difficult subject. 'Joe, I know this can easily be misconstrued, but I'm worried for you. Please go carefully with Ellie.'

'What do you mean?'

'She's . . . God, I don't know how to put this. "Damaged goods" sounds a bit harsh, and I don't mean to be bitchy, truly I don't . . .'

'Di, we just got talking, struck up a friendship,' Joe said. 'That's all it is.'

'You may think that. What about her?' She gave a quick shake of her head, as though irritated by her own line of thought. 'Oh dear. I sound like your mother, don't I?'

Joe shrugged. 'A bit.'

'Well, I'll shut up now. I'm sorry.'

'Hey, it's fine,' Joe said. 'I promise I'll be very cautious. Both feet touching the floor at all times.'

*   *   *

The comment was more or less forgotten until Ellie opened her front door, wearing a simple but figure-hugging sleeveless black dress, high-necked and scooped in the back. It cleverly revealed a lot of flesh, but none of it in places that could be considered overtly sexual.

237

She greeted Joe with a smile; he leaned forward and kissed her cheek. *Only to be polite*, the voice in his head assured Diana.

She turned to let him in. The sight of her bare back, the delicate bumps of her upper spine, made him shiver. Her skin was the colour of honey, clear and smooth and taut, with good muscle tone in her arms and shoulders. It occurred to him that all kinds of things were possible while still keeping both feet on the floor.

He held up two bottles of Sauvignon Blanc. 'I hope these are okay. I'm not much of a wine buff.'

'Me neither,' she said, taking them from him. 'Cold and wet is my usual criteria.'

Ellie waited while he removed his jacket and hung it by the door. He could almost see her mind working: registering that he'd made sure the wine was chilled; that he was scrubbed clean and smartly dressed and smelled good. That he looked exactly like a man going on a date.

'What did Diana have to say about this?' she asked.

'Not much,' Joe said. 'We're not joined at the hip.'

Ellie laughed, softly mocking. 'No. But I bet she told you to be on your guard.'

*   *   *

She led him through to the kitchen, where he was greeted by the aroma of slow-cooked beef. The splendour of the room—a huge kitchen-diner with hand-crafted maple cabinets and granite worktops—took him by surprise. From outside, the house was only a modest semi, probably three

238

bedrooms, with a grey slate roof and rendered walls painted the colour of clotted cream.

'This swallowed up half the garden,' Ellie admitted. 'Luckily, I was never much of a gardener.'

'It's wonderful.' Joe was struck by the similarity to Diana's kitchen. The dimensions and the layout, and even the units themselves, were virtually identical. 'Was it like this when you moved in?'

'No. We added this part a couple of years after we bought it.' Ellie waited to see if he would query the plural. 'My husband did it.'

'Oh. You're married, then?'

Poker-faced, she said, 'Frankly, I'm concerned it's taken you this long to ask. Or do I resemble the cliché of the lifelong spinster librarian?'

'Absolutely not. I just didn't like to pry.'

'Really? Is that so you don't have to answer questions in return?'

'Partly,' Joe admitted.

'Well, pry away,' she said drily, 'because I intend to.'

She had put one bottle of wine in the fridge; the other she handed back to him, together with a Christmas-tree corkscrew. 'Would you do the honours?'

He stood beside her at the counter as she opened an overhead cupboard and took out a pair of large full-bodied glasses.

'You're separated?' he said.

'We split up six years ago. Now we're divorced. Full and final.' She moved aside a step and watched him pour the wine. 'And much better off without him.'

'But you've not remarried? Not met anybody else?'

239

'I've seen a couple of guys. The first was a disaster, the classic rebound case. The second one . . .' She pulled a face. 'He kept acting like he couldn't believe his luck.'

'Understandable.'

'Ha ha. Thank you. The keener he got, the less I wanted to know. Makes me think I should stick to the single life. What about you?'

Joe grinned at the speed with which she'd switched the focus.

'I'm separated. Four years or so.' He tried to keep the emotion out of his voice, but he was sure she spotted something.

'Children?'

'Two girls. Amy and Hannah.' He smiled, as he always did when he talked about them. He wished Ellie wasn't watching him so closely.

'You don't see them very often.' An observation, not a question.

'It's complicated. How's that for a cliché?'

She picked up on his sadness, reflecting it in her own expression. 'You know, normally I'm a nosy cow. But on this occasion I'm not going to push it.'

'I appreciate that.'

Ellie held up her wine. 'To families, absent and otherwise.'

'To families,' Joe said, and they touched glasses, a quiet brittle clink that could have been the sound of a heart breaking.

*   *   *

Dinner was going to be a while yet, she said, and suggested they move into the lounge. It was smaller than the kitchen, with pale blue floral wallpaper

240

and a thick cream carpet. There were shelves piled with books either side of the chimney breast, and a gas fire in a modern chrome surround.

For seating, Joe had a choice between a sofa and two armchairs. He took one end of the sofa, and Ellie took the other, pulling out a nest of tables for their glasses.

'Was it an amicable split from your husband?'

'Not at first, but we get on reasonably well these days. I can't say the same for his current partner, I'm afraid.'

He caught the sourness in her voice and grimaced in sympathy. At the same time he'd noticed a couple of photographs on the mantelpiece. They showed a handsome, broad-shouldered young man, perhaps eighteen or nineteen, with a mop of dark hair and a killer smile. Joe immediately saw the likeness to Ellie, but there was another resemblance, too—

'You look puzzled,' Ellie said.

'Sorry, but is that . . .?' Joe pointed at the photographs.

'My son, Alec. He's twenty-one. Studying English at Durham.'

Joe went on staring, transfixed by the photos, by the similarity . . .

In a voice that seemed to come from miles away, he said, 'Your ex-husband did the extension? So he's a builder?'

'*Was* a builder. He gave it up, rather inexplicably.' She added wryly: 'I put it down to a mid-life crisis.'

Joe groaned. Now it was there in front of him, he couldn't understand why he hadn't worked it out sooner.

241

'It's Glenn, isn't it? You were married to Glenn Hicks.'

CHAPTER FORTY-FOUR

Victor arrived early and loitered in the shadows outside the pub. Scared to go inside. Desperate to go inside. It was another world in there, another universe. Busy and bright, probably expensive, somewhere he would never belong.

So he stood a while longer, shivering from the cold, trembling with anxiety. He needed something to calm his nerves. Anything would do: he wasn't fussy. Booze, fags, weed, benzos ... anything.

But he had none of those. He had nothing. He'd smoked the last of his cigarettes outside the station at Bodmin Parkway, and now, after taking a fucking taxi to Trelennan, all his money was gone. Every last penny, literally. That included the cash he'd got from pawning some shitty earrings and a camera, stolen this very morning from his ex-wife's aunt, who had Alzheimer's and had believed him when he'd said he was from social services.

If, God forbid, something went wrong tonight and he didn't lay his hands on the cash, he had no idea how he would get home. He'd thought to buy a return ticket for the train, but Bodmin was miles away: further than he'd walked in his whole life. He'd never make it.

So it had to come good tonight. There was no alternative. No Plan B.

Time to start thinking positive, he told himself. Act confident. Act like he was a player. Otherwise

Leon Race would make mincemeat of him.

At least the Crow's Nest was just as Leon had described it. Vic had been fearing a trap. Told himself that if he got here and found a tiny deserted boozer in the middle of nowhere, he'd turn right round and get the hell out. He wouldn't have, of course, because the money meant too much to him, but at least now that was one less thing to worry about.

Although it *was* in the middle of nowhere. Leon had said a mile or so out of Trelennan, but Vic couldn't see any lights in the distance. Maybe trees or a hill in the way. No street lights along here, either. Under a cloudy sky, still dripping a few dregs of rain, it was darkness like he'd not seen in years. Fucking countryside . . .

Positive, remember. The windows had fancy blinds on them, and the glass was steamed up, but he could tell from all the messy silhouettes that the pub was packed to the rafters. And the car park was stuffed full of decent motors. Vic wished he'd brought along a few acquaintances, people who could have had these lovely Beemers and Mercs spirited away while he was doing his business with Leon, and no one any the wiser.

Safe as houses, too. Out here in the country you probably didn't see the filth from one day to the next.

Inducing a little rush of confidence, he dragged one foot into the air and urged it forwards, followed by the other, and before he knew it he was walking in a fast, slightly uneven gait towards the entrance. No turning back. No more nerves. All you wanna think about now is *the money the money the money*.

243

He pushed the door open, into a sort of lobby, then through another door into the main room, and the warmth and the smells of rich fresh food and alcohol were so intoxicating that they made his head spin. He took a deep breath and swallowed greedily: more calories in the air than in anything he'd had all day. In fact, he realised he hadn't eaten a single thing for nearly twenty-four hours.

What had Leon called it? A *gastro*-pub? Victor hadn't really understood what that meant, but he saw it now. A nice upmarket place, with the quality and style of a restaurant and the relaxed atmosphere of a pub. It was all very sleek: beautiful wood floors and matching tables, a kind of posh rustic look. Plain walls painted a deep maroon colour and lots of modern squiggly artwork, hanging beneath lamps like silver eyelashes. No horse brasses or beer mats; definitely no fruit machines or dartboards. Soft tinkly piano music, barely audible above the chatter of conversation, and staff in crisp black and white uniforms like waiters Vic recalled from a holiday in Venice, many years ago.

One of them ghosted up now, stood beside him and then took a deliberate step back. Looking at Vic in an uncertain way, his face set in a pre-sneer.

'Uh, the name's Vic. I'm meeting someone. Leon . . .'

'Ah, Mr Race's guest.' A hundred-watt smile, all of a sudden. 'If you'd like to follow me.'

He threaded a path through tables full of happy, wealthy-looking people. All of them white, most middle-aged or above, apart from a sprinkling of young men with their girlfriends. No kids in sight, but not a bad thing in Vic's view. Letting rugrats into pubs had always struck him as a terrible mistake.

His table was in a prime location at the back of the room, which Vic now saw had a magnificent view out to sea. Okay, so it was pitch black and drizzling, but Vic could use his imagination.

'Great place,' he muttered.

'Thank you, sir. Mr Race said to inform you that he's running late. Can I get you a drink while you wait?'

Vic hesitated, that agonising, unmistakable hesitation of the impecunious, and the waiter glided in with: 'Mr Race also suggested you could dine here as his guest . . .'

That was more like it. Vic nodded away the pause as if he'd merely been debating what to have. 'Glass of still water, please.' He smacked his lips. 'Got a hell of a thirst on me.'

The waiter nodded, every bit as puzzled as Vic wanted him to be.

'Very well, sir—'

'Plus a pint of Guinness. And a double brandy. Hennessy if you have it.'

The waiter turned away. Vic grinned. He caught a man at the next table giving him a surreptitious glance, and he nodded a greeting. The man quickly averted his gaze.

He chuckled. So no one wanted to look him in the eye? Who gave a fuck when there was free food and drink on the way, and a big cash payout for afters?

He didn't fit in, he knew that. He was unshaven, dressed like a tramp. Probably stank to high heaven, if the behaviour of those girls on the train was anything to go by: vicious little tarts dancing past his seat, holding their noses and singing, 'Poo, poo, poo!' to each other. If he'd had a knife on him, he'd have . . .

'And fucking enjoy it too,' he growled. 'Bitches.'

'Your drinks, sir,' the waiter said. Made Victor jump, the denial already forming: *I wasn't serious. I never touched them.*

He shook himself like a dog on a beach, forced his clenched teeth open and remembered: *Positive.*

His drinks. The water had ice cubes and lemon, as clean and clear as a polar morning. The Guinness had a perfect white foamy head, like the Irish Sea on a stormy night, and the brandy sat in its fat glass like a wicked uncle with a dark gleam in his eye.

Sup up, my lad, and see where I can take you . . .

Victor licked his lips. His reduced circumstances meant he'd been more or less dry for months. And now this.

Gonna be one hell of a night . . .

CHAPTER FORTY-FIVE

Joe stared into his wine glass, rotating the stem between his fingers while he tried to decide if he was more amused than irritated, or vice versa.

'Why on earth didn't you tell me? Why didn't Diana?'

'I can't answer for her. In my case, it just wasn't that important. Glenn and I have very little to do with each other.'

'But you were curious to see whether Diana would tell me first?'

'Are we going to fall out?' Ellie asked, a mischievous look in her eye.

'Of course not. I just don't understand why you both let me put my foot in it.'

'For the entertainment value?' She laughed. 'Seriously, I didn't say anything because I don't think it's relevant. Diana might feel differently. The way she deals with her guilt is to view me as a rival. A bitter, resentful woman desperate to lure her husband back. Your presence here could be seen as giving me a more appropriate form of revenge.'

Joe shook his head. 'You've lost me now.' But that wasn't quite true. He said: 'In what way is Diana guilty?'

'Glenn and I were still married when their affair began. A perk of his job, you see?' She gave a chilly smile. 'I could never understand why he seemed to prefer renovations and extensions rather than new-builds. After we split up he admitted it was because there was more chance of shagging a bored housewife, a stay-at-home mum. Much more fun than some muddy site full of blokes in low-slung jeans.'

'Is that when it started, during the building work?' Joe asked. 'But Roy was still alive . . .'

'I don't know for sure,' Ellie said quickly, and he wondered if she was just trying to spare his feelings. 'Put it this way: I don't think Glenn would have been deterred by the fact that Diana was married. I'm sorry.'

Joe sighed, ran a hand through his hair. 'I'm stunned. It isn't what I'd expect from Diana . . .' He thought of the retirement party, and Diana's

247

lament: *It's not my future.* Joe had been guilty of dismissing her fears, and Roy perhaps even more so. 'It must have been devastating for you,' he said.

'Yes and no.' She avoided his gaze for a while, staring at her glass. 'Things were never that great between us, to be honest. I'd always suspected that he played around. At that point I didn't know he'd slept with one of my best friends two days before our wedding.'

'That's appalling.'

'It is, but he can't help himself. A born charmer.' In unison they turned to look at the photographs on the mantelpiece. Joe saw now that Alec was the image of his father: the same strong features, the same cheeky glint in his eyes.

Reading his mind, Ellie said, 'Don't. It's my worst fear. I just hope I've managed to instil a bit more respect. A greater sense of loyalty. Not that Glenn hasn't been a pretty good dad, to be fair.'

'This is very rude of me, but if your son's twenty-one, how old were you when you had him?'

She laughed. 'It's not rude. I'm choosing to take it as a compliment. Alec was conceived when I was sixteen. I was a mum at seventeen.'

'And Glenn?'

'He was twenty-two. Five years older.'

'Bloody hell. I bet that was popular with your parents?'

'They didn't know.'

'What?'

'I ran away from home when I was three months gone.'

*   *   *

248

Ellie popped out to check on dinner, returned with the wine and refilled their glasses. She explained that she'd grown up in Oxford, with regular family holidays in Trelennan. At fifteen she had a holiday romance with Glenn, rekindled a year later, after which she discovered she was pregnant.

'I knew my parents would go ballistic. They'd envisaged sending me to uni, where I'd get a great degree, have a career, meet some lovely middle-class professional and deliver grandchildren at the appropriate time, and not a moment sooner.'

'So you ran away? And Glenn took you in?'

'Not exactly. I turned up here one night and announced that I was "with child". Scared him half to death. His mum, bless her, gave me a place to stay and more or less forced Glenn to do the right thing.'

Joe nodded. It would be insensitive to suggest the relationship was doomed from the start, but that seemed to be the inference.

'In time he came round to it. Obviously I know now that he had his little diversions whenever he wanted them. And his mum could see that I was a positive influence. I encouraged him to complete his apprenticeship, and after a few years to set up on his own.'

'And what about you? Your plans for university?'

'They went on hold.' Ellie gave him a sad, wry smile. 'I finally did the degree a few years ago, through the Open University. Not quite the debauched artistic melting pot I'd dreamt of, but hey. I had Alec, and I wouldn't have exchanged him for anything. Life doesn't always go the way you plan . . .' She faltered, seeing something in Joe's face that he didn't know was there. 'I suspect you're

249

probably the last person who needs to be told that.'

'You could be right.' Eager to change the subject, he said, 'I see now why you feel so strongly about Alise and her sister.'

Ellie nodded. 'I suppose my natural sympathies do lie more with Kamila. When Alise told me, all I could think was: *Maybe she doesn't want to speak to you. Maybe she doesn't want to be found.* That's incredibly painful for the family of a runaway to accept, but sometimes it's true.'

'You really believe Kamila could be intentionally ignoring her sister?'

'Absolutely. Once you've made that break, it takes huge determination not to go crawling back home. A single phone call or text can be enough to demolish your resolve.'

'I hadn't thought of it like that,' Joe said. 'Still, it's academic now.' He described the message he'd had from Alise. Before Ellie could seize on it as proof of her 'cry wolf' theory, he added: 'And yet, the day before, she sent me the details of this guy that Kamila originally ran off with. Why do that and then abandon the search?'

Ellie was perplexed. 'I agree. That makes no sense. What are you going to do?'

'I don't see there's a lot that I *can* do.'

'If you've got this man's details, there's no reason why you couldn't carry on making enquiries.'

'Do you think I should?'

'I've no idea.' She tipped her glass slightly in his direction. 'But I can sense that you want to, so I'm trying to make it easier for you to decide.'

Joe couldn't help laughing. 'You're always two or three steps ahead of me. I don't know. Maybe I will.'

Ellie sat up, had a gulp of wine. 'Time to eat now. And open another bottle. Perhaps, through an alcoholic haze, the answers will become clear.'

*   *   *

Dinner was a delicious beef stifado with salad and French bread. They ate in the dining room, which had the feel of a room kept for special occasions. Lots of family portraits in here, including one of Ellie as a new mother, looking little more than a child herself.

'I've been puzzling over the timeline,' Joe said as they came to the end of the meal. 'You and Glenn splitting up, Glenn going to work for Leon, and his affair with Diana. Did they all happen around the same time?'

'And is there a link? That's what you're wondering.' Ellie shut her eyes, sifting through her memory. 'I think the job at the B&B came first, and obviously that's when he met Diana.'

'She and Roy had just moved here?'

'Within the first year or so. The job went on for a few months, on and off. Then he was contracted to work at Leon's home, so for a while he was going back and forth between them. And then he just announced one day that he was winding up the business and going to work for Leon.'

Joe nodded. That fitted perfectly with his hunch. 'And it came as a shock?'

'Absolutely. He'd worked so hard to make his business a success. Why throw it all away to become . . . I don't know . . . arse-licker-in-chief to Leon Race?'

'And he never gave you an explanation?'

251

'At that stage we were barely talking. The marriage was well and truly on the rocks, even if I hadn't found out about him and Diana.'

'And nowadays,' Joe said. 'Looking back on it, do you understand it any more than you did at the time?'

'Not really. I can only put it down to a kind of hero worship.'

'Of Leon?'

Ellie nodded. 'That was always the impression I got, even though Leon is five or six years younger than Glenn. And it applies to a lot of other people he employs, and the hangers-on. Creeps like Derek Cadwell and Councillor Rawle.'

'But why?' Joe asked. 'What inspires such adoration?'

'Now we've reached the million-dollar question, and I need pudding before embarking on a reply. What do you say?'

Joe patted his stomach, which had seemed full to bursting. Now he realised there was a tiny space he'd been reserving for a dessert.

'Sounds good to me.'

CHAPTER FORTY-SIX

It didn't take long till all three glasses were empty. A magical process, Victor thought. Osmosis or some shit like that.

Just reading the menu was a thrill, like a top-quality porn mag that hit all the right buttons. He was stuck on whether to order two main courses, though he also wanted a starter.

Without being asked, the waiter had brought him a selection of bread, which might have been home-baked, it tasted so fresh. The bread came with a couple of little bowls with liquid in them. At first he'd confused them with those bowls you use to clean your fingers, but then he realised they contained something edible. Oils of some kind. Tasty.

He devoured the lot, mopping up every last drop of oil and licking his fingers with noisy appreciation. He had one grimy forefinger stuck in his gob when the waiter reappeared. The smarmy smile wavered for a second.

'Ready to order, sir?'

'Yeah. I'll start with pâté, then the salmon thing with pasta, but can I have the chicken with the wine sauce as well? Kind of a side dish?'

'Of course, sir. Anything else?'

'Chips.' Vic winked. He was feeling warm, expansive. 'Gotta have chips with a good pub meal, eh?'

'And something else to drink?'

'Yeah. Same again.'

'Guinness, brandy and water?'

'Don't bother with the water.'

*   *   *

He watched the waiter glide away, and sighed contentedly. Around him the buzz of conversation went on, but it seemed curiously muted now, as though his brain was tuning it out. He sat back in his chair and stretched. He felt gloriously warm and comfortable and light-headed. No wonder: tipping booze into an empty stomach, chased by the bread

253

and oil . . .

When he opened his eyes, the drinks were being placed in front of him.

'Fucking great service—' *Whoops*. Bit posh here for that sort of language.

'Sorry,' he said. The waiter had already moved away. Another one, a girl, was bringing him the pâté. He beamed, but she seemed to be concentrating on a spot just over his shoulder. Maybe it wasn't advisable, a great big smile, when he had so many missing teeth. Better just to grin.

'Thanks. Lovely.' The words sounded slurred. He should eat this before he touched any more booze.

Except the brandy glass was empty. How the f—- did that happen?

Oh well. He picked up a knife, smeared pâté on a triangular sliver of toast. Get some proper grub inside him and he'd be fine. Clear his head, concentrate on what he came for.

The payday of his life. This was going to be his retirement fund, and with it he fully intended to drink, smoke, snort, swallow and inject himself to death. Maybe he'd last a year, a year and a half. Go out early, but happy.

*   *   *

The pâté was incredible. Vic wished he'd eaten it more slowly, savoured it, but hey ho. It seemed like only two minutes after the plate was cleared away before the main course arrived, with the chicken on its own plate and a bowl full of chunky posh chips. There was another pint of Guinness. Another brandy, too.

Had he ordered those?

254

'Jesus, you guys are quick off the mark,' he told the waiter, who murmured his thanks. Vic wondered if everyone got this treatment, or was it just because of Leon Race?

He looked round the room, still full of people eating, drinking, talking. Still avoiding his eye. Certainly they all looked happy to be here, and why not? Great food, great service. There was just one tiny niggling worry, but he couldn't for the life of him think what it was.

Never mind. The salmon next: light and fluffy, melting in his mouth. Even the vegetables were tasty, albeit very crunchy. He wasn't used to food that required a lot of chewing; it made his jaw hurt. The chips went down easily enough, but the extra order of chicken defeated him. He had to give up halfway through.

Vic pushed the plate away, sat back and burped. Jesus, he felt stuffed. Like that feller from the Monty Python film. Not funny, though. He didn't want to throw up in here, in front of all these people . . .

That niggle again. What was it?

He glanced at the door, then at his wrist. *Old habits* . . . He'd pawned his watch months ago. The waiter was hovering, ready to clear away; Vic beckoned him over.

'All finished, sir?'

'Yeah, but leave the chicken. I might have another go at it. What's the time?'

'Two minutes past ten, sir.'

'Don't suppose you know when . . .?'

There was a noise from across the room; the inner door opening. A gust of cold air blew through, because the outer door hadn't closed in time. The waiter smiled.

'Here he is now, sir.'

*   *   *

Now Victor knew what was niggling him, but there wasn't time to think about it properly because Leon Race was striding towards him like he owned the place, big and bold, shoulders thrown back. Another man waddling behind him: Fenton, just as Leon had said. Fenton the money man. The paymaster.

That door hadn't opened before now. Vic had been here nearly an hour and a half, and in that time no one else had come or gone . . .

Unless he'd missed it. He was pretty pissed, after all. But the place had been full when he'd arrived, and it was still full now. That seemed a bit weird.

Then Leon was standing over him. Taller and broader than Vic remembered from the only time they'd met before. Blond hair and a pink round face, like a chubby toddler. But the eyes didn't belong to any toddler.

'I know you, don't I?' Leon was squinting, as if searching his memory, but it struck a slightly false note.

'Vic Smith. We met a few years ago, when I was working with Larry Milligan.'

'You worked for Larry. That's right.' Leon looked at Fenton, who nodded, as though this was a pleasant chance meeting of old friends. It made Vic nervous, but he reminded himself that Leon had kept to his word: just him and Fenton, in a busy restaurant. And he certainly hadn't stinted on the hospitality.

'Sorry about the, er, deception, Mr Race,' he

256

said. 'I just wasn't sure how to, like, approach you without . . .'

Leon nodded away the apology. 'I understand.'

'And thanks for the meal. Best I've eaten in months.'

'Yeah, nice little place here.'

'Doing a roaring trade, as well.' Vic gazed upon his fellow diners. Was it his imagination, or had it gone a lot quieter since Leon arrived?

'This is my colleague, Clive Fenton,' Leon said. 'The big fat feller.'

Vic squirmed, but Fenton didn't seem to take offence. They shook hands. Fenton's grip was limp and moist. Leon's wasn't. Fenton took the seat to Vic's left, Leon sat opposite. The waiter returned, and both men ordered water. Vic declined another drink. He felt breathless, a bit sick. Maybe he'd had enough for now.

He could always have one for the road later, a final brandy to celebrate.

They did a bit of small talk: stuff about Cornwall, Trelennan, the train service. The waiter delivered a carafe of water, ice cubes clinking busily against the glass. The noise set Vic's teeth on edge. He winced, then realised it was being amplified by other high-pitched sounds: the clatter of crockery, the scrape of chairs on the wooden floor, like a whole class scratching their fingers down a blackboard.

At first he thought his ears must have been blocked up and had suddenly cleared, but it wasn't that. All round the room, the other diners were getting to their feet. Every single one of them. At some tables the plates were cleared; at several there were desserts that looked virtually untouched. Glasses full of wine, just abandoned: a

257

heartbreaking sight to a man who'd gone without for so long.

And apart from the clatter, it was being done in total silence. No one said a word. None of the diners acknowledged the fact that everybody else was leaving at the same time.

The doors opened and stayed open as forty or fifty people filed out. The temperature plummeted, but Leon and Fenton didn't seem to notice. They sat and sipped their water. From behind the bar, the staff emerged with their coats on, everyone brisk and a little tense, as if responding to an alarm that Victor alone could not hear.

It was an evacuation.

Outside, cars revving up, all those fancy Mercs and Beemers. Rich fumes drifting inside. The gastro-pub was empty but for the three of them. The last man out was the waiter, but he didn't shut the inner door. He held it open for the people coming in.

Three men. You didn't have to be a genius to know they were Leon's crew. One of them was strangely familiar. Vic had a feeling that he'd seen him on the platform at Birmingham.

The three men had jobs to do. Locking the doors. Closing the last few blinds. Leon and Fenton ignored them, the way Larry Milligan had once ignored Vic.

'Now,' Leon said, 'what shoes are you wearing?'

'Shoes?' Vic was in shock. The alcohol was keeping the panic to a manageable level, but it was also dulling his responses. He knew he wasn't thinking straight; knew he ought to be a lot more scared than he was.

'What kind of shoes?' Leon repeated.

Gripping the table for balance, Fenton eased his head down to have a look. 'They're boots.'

Vic nodded. 'Timberlands.' He was proud of those boots: the only decent item in his wardrobe. He'd stolen them from an upmarket gym a couple of years ago; some wealthy pillock in too much of a hurry to use the lockers.

'Are they in good shape?' Leon asked. 'Any holes in 'em?'

'No. They're top-quality, Mr Race.'

Vic had decided he'd better start ingratiating himself. Maybe Leon was a pervert, a foot fetishist or whatever it was. The evening had taken such a strange turn, it felt like anything was possible now.

'Good,' Leon said. 'So they won't leak?'

CHAPTER FORTY-SEVEN

Dessert was a homemade chocolate hazelnut mousse with a raspberry coulis. Joe managed two helpings, to Ellie's great amusement. Afterwards Ellie suggested coffee, but Joe said he was happy to wait a while. He wanted to hear about Leon Race.

'All right. But you must have formed an opinion yourself?'

'I've only been here a couple of days, but it's certainly an impressive set-up. Way beyond what you'd expect from someone with his background.' He mentioned the theory that Leon's fondness for tracksuits and trainers were to remind people of his humble origins.'

'I'd add another reason. Dressing as he does encourages people to underestimate him, which he can use to his advantage.'

'True,' Joe said. He recalled Patrick Davy making the same point.

'Part of Glenn's fascination with him was to do with Leon's childhood. The whole family were notorious. You know how the media sometimes get hysterical about "neighbours from hell"? Well, the Races were like a textbook example. Leon was the youngest child. One of three, I think, but far and away the worst. He was always tall for his age, and terrorised his classmates virtually from the beginning. Tall and strong and fearlessly aggressive.'

'The big fish in a small pond,' Joe murmured. *A shark.*

'Exactly. By the age of nine or ten he was out of control. Kids of fifteen or sixteen running scared of him. But he was really smart, too. Not in a conventional sense—schools couldn't hope to control him, much less interest him in the curriculum.'

'Streetwise?'

'Yes, but more than that. Glenn says he's brilliant with numbers. A very sharp brain. But his real skill in those days was in avoiding getting caught. Even when he did he somehow managed to talk his way out of trouble.'

'Hence a clean record,' Joe said, 'thereby enabling him to work in the security industry.'

Ellie nodded. 'Some time in his mid to late teens he got his act together. Went off somewhere and came back a couple of years later, having transformed himself into this calm, focused entrepreneur.'

'Any idea what happened to cause the

260

transformation?'

'Afraid not. If Glenn knows, he's never said. And it wasn't quite that obvious, to be honest. Leon's first foray into business was with door security, providing bouncers for pubs and clubs along the coast. The big step-up came when he took over a taxi firm here in town.'

'Ah. Patrick Davy mentioned that, as well as the methods Leon used to persuade the owner to sell up.'

'Harassment?' Ellie said. 'I can't say I'm surprised.'

'Does all your knowledge come from Glenn, or are Leon's practices known to the whole town?'

Ellie shrugged, gave a curious smile. 'An interesting question, with no easy answer. It's not as though we get together to compare notes. Most people avoid talking about him at all, just in case.'

'So there would be reprisals if people did challenge his behaviour?'

'Oh yes, but it would be done in such a way that you could never know for sure.'

'Nothing to take to court?'

'Exactly. Not that anyone in their right mind would ever give evidence against Leon. It was the same when he moved into domestic security. As you've probably noticed, Trelennan has a lot of expensive property. Quite a few holiday homes and rental cottages. The owners pay handsomely for Leon's guards to patrol the streets, especially out of season when the homes are empty. But when he first starting touting for business there wasn't much interest.'

'I suppose crime in these small towns has never been a huge problem?'

'Not really. But guess what? Suddenly there was a spate of burglaries and vandalism . . .'

'Which stopped as soon as they signed up for his patrols?' Joe sighed. 'The oldest trick in the book.'

'You've got it. But one of the consequences was that crime in general just plummeted. On the rare occasion that somebody did run amok, they had to answer to Leon. A few broken bones later and everyone got the message. If you've got uniformed thugs patrolling the streets, no one's going to break into a house, whether it has one of Leon's alarms or not.'

'And to the outside world it looks as though he's wrought a miracle.'

'Absolutely. Another thing you can't fail to notice here is the absence of ethnic minorities. I'm ashamed to say it, but I suspect there's a lot of unspoken support for Leon's racism, even if no one wants to consider too closely what he might be doing to discourage black and Asian people from settling in Trelennan.'

Joe was reminded of the taxi driver's taunt: *You're gonna fucking love it here, you are.*

'Why do people stand for it?'

Ellie rubbed her thumb and forefinger together. 'The financial benefits. No crime, no vandalism: that equates to more tourists, more money being spent. A lot of businesses have flourished under Leon's regime.'

'So everyone's happy?' he said sardonically.

'You sound like me. A born cynic.' Ellie picked up her wine and then thought better of it, pausing with the glass almost touching her lower lip. She shook her head.

'No, not happy,' she said. 'A whole town walking

262

on eggshells isn't conducive to happiness.'

*   *   *

First, they broke his toes. Before they asked a single question, they broke his toes.

Vic couldn't believe it. Even when they tied him to the chair, he felt sure there'd be a chance to talk his way out of trouble. But Leon wouldn't have it.

'You'll have an opportunity to explain later. First there's punishment for taking the piss on a grand scale.'

They used a set of giant steel bolt cutters. The man who did it was called Reece, Vic gathered. The one he'd seen in Birmingham. Dimly, through the alcoholic haze, he worked it out. They must have recognised his voice, traced him to Tunstall and followed him down here.

Before Reece went to work, they stuffed a rubber gag between Vic's teeth and put tape over his mouth so he couldn't spit it out. To muffle the screams—but not because someone might hear and come to the rescue.

Because they didn't want to listen to a lot of noise.

True to their word, his boots were kept on to reduce the mess. He couldn't say for sure how many toes were broken: a couple on each foot, at least. A quick, efficient process, the steel jaws tightening beyond painful, down into a crushing, splintering agony the like of which he'd never known, and then . . . *snap snap.*

Sweat broke out over his whole body: a river of it, soaking his clothes as effectively as if he was standing out in a monsoon. When they were done

263

there were puddles on the floor and he'd sweated out the alcohol, the last of his defences.

By the time they removed the gag he was brutally sober. He was proud that he hadn't fainted, but he couldn't stop himself from throwing up. They'd anticipated that: caught it in the towels which they used to mop up the sweat.

After vomiting himself ragged, Vic was too exhausted to scream or cry. The broken bones were throbbing like bass drums, his feet swelling against the rigid leather. He couldn't have taken the boots off now if he'd wanted to.

'No more bullshit,' Leon told him. 'You answer every question truthfully. If you do that, and I'm happy with the answers, you might not have to suffer too much more pain. Clear?'

Vic nodded. Tested his voice and croaked, 'Yes. Yes, Mr Race.'

'First up, how does a hopeless old scrote like you get hold of information that's supposed to be worth a fortune?'

Vic shut his eyes while he gathered his thoughts. He had no intention of crossing Leon, but despite everything—the abandoned restaurant, the merciless damage they had done to him—he couldn't completely let go of the idea that there was something to be salvaged from this. A payment, no matter how modest. Enough for the taxi fare to Bodmin and a bottle of cheap Scotch.

'Prison,' he said. 'Couple of years back. It was bollocks, I got fitted up by these bastard filth—'

'Victor,' Leon crooned. 'Confusing us with people who give a fuck . . .'

'Sorry. Anyway, I got eighteen months. Shunted round to various nicks, like you do. For a time I

264

was in Belmarsh with a load of well-serious faces. Premier League, they were.'

'Oh yeah? Like who?'

'Well, maybe not the very top. Not the Man U's or suchlike, but a Newcastle, a West Brom.'

'What about Arsenal?' Fenton said, sounding pleased with himself.

'A lot of Arsenals in jail,' Leon added, chuckling. Even Vic managed a smile. He couldn't begrudge them a bit of light relief, now could he?

'So a bloke in there, he's nursing one hell of a grudge against your man.'

'Joe?'

'Uh-huh. Had a photo of him in the cell. Not a great picture. Copied lots of times and gone all grainy, like. But it was him. Your feller.'

'Got a name?'

'I been racking my brains, honest I have. "Joe" sounds right to me, but I don't recall the surname. I ain't gonna lie to you and make it up.'

'No, you're not,' Leon said.

'Why the grudge?' Fenton asked.

'This Joe, he's filth,' Vic told them. He expected more of a reaction than he got.

'He's still serving in the police? You know that for sure?'

'Well . . . no. But at the time, he was. That's not all . . .'

Vic paused, wanting them to appreciate what he had. His eyes wouldn't stop watering, blurring his vision. Leon and Fenton swimming in and out of focus, standing over him. Not happy. Not impressed.

'He was working undercover, see. My bloke in Belmarsh had planned a major job. Bullion. This

265

Joe infiltrated the gang and put a fucking stop to it. Blew 'em apart from the inside.'

CHAPTER FORTY-EIGHT

Joe felt reluctant to press on with his questions. This was the kind of evening he hadn't had in years, an evening heavy with potential, dangerous and thrilling.

They'd returned to the lounge. Ellie seemed more relaxed now the meal was over: her voice softer, her movements languid. He was continually drawn to her eyes; each time they captured his attention he found it almost impossible to look away.

'Go on,' she said, breaking his reverie. 'What's on your mind?'

My wife, he could have answered. And guilt, like a dentist's drill, vibrating through his skull.

He said, 'Does Leon have any police officers on his payroll?'

Ellie gazed at him, as if trying to read what his question was designed to conceal.

'I don't know. From what Glenn has let slip over the years, it may be that there are "arrangements" in place. Then again, Leon is smart enough to allow that rumour to flourish, as further discouragement to his enemies.'

'So either way it makes him pretty impenetrable.'

'I take it you don't believe he earns an honest living these days?'

'I'm sure he does in part. What makes me dubious is the nature of his businesses. They all

266

lend themselves to criminal activity.'

'Do they?' Ellie twisted on the sofa so she was facing him, wide-eyed and keen to hear more. Her chin rested gently in one hand, cradled by long elegant fingers.

Joe stifled a shiver. 'The taxi firm and vending business give him a distribution network. They both involve mainly cash transactions. Same with the amusement arcade: more cash, and no inventory. Perfect for money laundering. Then the security firm: a lot of muscle on tap for protection, intimidation and extortion.'

'And now you work for him, too.' She stopped abruptly. 'Why would Leon risk employing you if he was still involved in crime? He must have heard about your past.'

'He knows I used to be a cop. Why he offered me the job, I haven't yet fathomed.' Joe was silent for a moment. 'Ellie, there's something else.'

He relayed Patrick Davy's account of the attack in Newquay. It turned out that Ellie was vaguely aware of it, but not the possibility that Leon's men had been responsible.

'In this case it appears the police did investigate, but Reece and the others had a watertight alibi. One of the people who backed them up was Glenn.'

'So you're wondering if Glenn is a villain, too?' She stared hard at the floor. 'The truth is, my heart wants to say no, but my head says it could be true. I don't think he'd participate in an assault. That's not him at all. But afterwards, if he was asked . . . no, if *Leon* asked him to give someone an alibi, then I think he would do it.'

'And Derek Cadwell? Would he be up to his neck in it?'

267

'That's harder to say. Outwardly he's a lot more respectable than Leon. I'd suggest theirs is more of a strategic alliance, so it's quite possible the attack was arranged as a favour for Cadwell.'

'Alise hinted that Leon has a particular hold over Cadwell, because of certain . . . proclivities.'

Ellie looked simultaneously thrilled and appalled. 'No! I'd like to believe that, because he's such an arrogant turd.'

'You've never heard any rumours like that?'

'Nothing at all. And like I said, I'm a nosy cow. Did you ask how she found out?'

'She wouldn't say. Just pleaded with me to take it on trust.'

'Hmm. No offence, but I think you misjudged things there.'

'That's pretty much what Diana said.'

'Well, there you go. We agree on something.'

Joe frowned. 'Oh, you agree on a lot more than that.'

Ellie shifted position on the sofa. 'Really? I'm not sure I like the way you said that. Are you cross with us?'

'Confused more than cross. I hear all these negative rumours about Leon—and Glenn for that matter—and yet both of you seem inclined to stick up for them, even though you concede that many of the rumours may be true.'

'"Innocent until proven guilty." That principle just about applies these days, doesn't it? But maybe you're right. You can't have failed to notice how isolated this place is. That breeds a certain insularity, I suppose. It's us against the world.'

'I just don't want to see either of you ending up on the wrong side.' Joe raised a hand, forestalling

268

any objections. 'Sorry. That sounded patronising. Not what I meant.'

Ellie looked amused rather than affronted. 'Then you'd better hurry up and find the truth for us. What rank were you, by the way?' She sprang the question so quickly that he saw no good reason to evade it.

'Detective sergeant, when I finished.'

'A detective? How exciting. Did you ever do anything dangerous? Any undercover work?'

'You said you wouldn't pry.'

'You can always refuse to tell me. Official secrets or whatever.'

'Okay. I can't tell you.'

'Spoilsport.' She pulled a face. 'I'm at a disadvantage. I don't have the benefit of your professional interrogation techniques.'

Joe snorted. 'You have techniques that more than match what I'm capable of.'

'Oh yes? Like what?'

'That sulky lip, for one thing. And those eyes.'

'What about my eyes?'

'Forget it. I've had too much wine.'

'So have I. It's nice, isn't it?'

'Was. We drank it all.'

'I mean the effects of it. Present tense.'

'I am a little, actually.'

Ellie burst out laughing. He felt himself blushing. 'It wasn't that funny.'

'Ah, but I have a fatal weakness for wordplay.'

Joe smiled, said nothing. They were so close now that he could feel the heat radiating from her body, her thigh almost touching his.

'Why did you leave the police? Is that an official secret?'

269

'Yes.'

'Hmm. So here's a real leap in the dark. Does leaving your career also explain why you're estranged from your family?'

'More than you can possibly know, I'm afraid.'

And then, sensing what her follow-up would be, he decided to be reckless rather than indiscreet.

He blocked the question with a kiss.

*   *   *

'So who is this feller in Belmarsh?' Leon said.

'Look, Mr Race, I came here in good faith. You told me yourself: you're a businessman, but decent with it. Fair-minded.'

'Tell me.'

'I will. But this has to be worth a . . . a gesture, at least. Let's say a grand? That's small change to you.'

Leon shook his head. 'As bargaining positions go, yours isn't the strongest I've seen.'

'I'm asking you to see sense. I mean, all these people know I was here—'

'Believe me, Victor, nobody saw a thing. Take my word on that.'

'But Mr Race . . .' Victor groaned, some of the fight going out of him. Leon was surprised he'd had so much to start with. In other circumstances he might have found some admiration for the man, but he couldn't forget the fury that Victor had inspired, trying to extort a hundred grand out of him.

Leon had nurtured that anger, kept it bubbling under until it was needed. Now he turned to Reece, who was lurking a few feet away, cradling the bolt cutters in his arms.

'Break his fingers.'

'No, Mr Race, please—'

'Give me the name.'

'All right. All right.' Pale as a ghost, Victor began to weep, snot leaking from his nose. 'Doug Morton. The bloke in Belmarsh was Doug Morton.'

Leon shrugged, but Fenton said, 'Rings a bell.'

'He's West London,' Victor told them. 'A serious face in his day. So were his dad and his uncles before him. Most of the family's dead or banged up.'

'And Doug's still inside now, is he?'

'Yeah. But he's burning up with hate for Joe. He's got this picture, like I said. The screws don't know about it. He shows it to everyone. "If ever you set eyes on this bloke, you let my boy know." That's what he says.'

'And who's that?' Leon asked.

'Danny Morton. Doug had two sons. Danny's the youngest. The way Doug tells it, he's dedicated his life to finding this Joe.'

'So how come you didn't go straight to the Mortons?'

Victor grinned, weakly, the sort of smile you'd give on your deathbed. 'That's what you thought I was planning, eh?'

'If you could have got away with it, you would have.'

'No. I wouldn't dare. Not unless I had this Joe locked up somewhere. If I sold him to Danny Morton and couldn't deliver, I'd be a dead man.' Vic managed a bark of laughter at the irony. 'Danny Morton's a head case. I thought—huh—I thought it would be safer to deal with you.'

Leon had to smile at that. He noticed Fenton

271

mulling over something.

'You said Doug Morton *had* two sons?'

'Yeah,' Victor said. 'The eldest . . . ah, Gary, I think it was. He died when the bullion job went tits-up.'

He looked up, held Leon's gaze. Leon felt a shiver run through him as he guessed what Victor was going to say.

'This bloke Joe killed him. He murdered Doug Morton's son—Danny's big brother. That's why they want him so badly. They'll give anything to lay their hands on him.'

CHAPTER FORTY-NINE

In one sense, it was the easiest thing in the world to kiss her. It required virtually no movement and even less deliberation: he just did it.

In another sense, it was much more difficult. What thoughts Joe had as their lips came together were simple but painful, amounting to no more than two images and a single concept.

Helen.

Diana.

Betrayal.

Then the kiss absorbed him completely, blotting out everything but the intense, thrilling *hereandnow* sensation of close physical contact. Nothing else mattered. Nothing else intruded. A perfect moment, and like all perfect moments it was over far too soon.

They separated, staring at each other.

Ellie said, 'Oh my God.' Her hand floated

upwards, fingertips gently caressing her lower lip, as if to confirm where it was, and what it had done. 'It's just been so long. I'd forgotten . . .'

Joe nodded. 'Same here.'

She thought about it, then said, 'Can we do it again?'

'Yes,' he said.

The second time was both better and worse. More practised, obviously, but also more self-conscious. Another break, gasping for breath. This time Ellie ran her tongue over her lips, top and bottom, very slowly. She didn't appreciate the effect it had on Joe until he tore his gaze away.

He moved towards her, but she reached out with both hands, gripping his shoulders.

'Joe, this is wonderful . . .'

'But?'

'I'm tired. And a bit drunk. Possibly a lot drunk. And I'm excited, but also confused, and scared, I suppose . . .'

'Time for me to go?' he said, and she nodded, reluctantly.

'I think that's best.'

*   *   *

'Danny Morton.'

Victor nodded. He'd been slumped in the chair, head lolling, eyes closed: Leon thought he'd passed out. But he said, 'Danny Morton, right you are. That's who you want.'

'Don't suppose you've got his number?'

Victor couldn't have heard the sarcasm. His eyes opened wide and focused on Leon. Set into the face of a dead man, they looked more alive and alert

273

than they had any right to be, full of mad hope.

'Yeah, yeah, I can get it for you. In fact, I might have his address back home—'

'You haven't.'

'Honestly, Mr Race. No word of a lie, I can help you.'

'It's not in your flat. Take my word for it.'

Leon held his gaze for a full ten seconds before Victor let out a despairing groan. Finally it had sunk in that he'd given them everything they wanted and he wasn't going to get a thing in return.

Well, tough shit, Leon thought. *Teach you to push your luck with me . . .*

He surveyed the room: Reece, still holding the bolt cutters, eager to get back to work. Todd sat just behind him, thrilled to have witnessed his hero at work. Glenn was perched on a bar stool with his back to them, sipping from a bottle of beer.

'Glenn, over here!' Leon drew Fenton aside. 'I reckon we've got everything we need.'

'Except contact details for this Morton character. But if what Victor says is true he shouldn't be too hard to locate.'

Leon frowned. 'You don't think Vic's been lying to us?'

'A figure of speech.' Fenton smacked his lips with pleasure. 'In my view this is completely authentic. And it's solid gold, just as he claimed.'

Glenn heard him and looked at Leon, who gave a grudging nod. 'Good work, putting us on to him.'

Fenton coughed quietly. 'Would it not be wiser to return him home, or abandon him by the roadside somewhere?'

'Normally it would, Clive. But not this time.' Leon studied Victor, his mangy head still bowed,

274

his skeletal frame distorted by the cords that bound him to the chair. 'I mean, look at him. Fucker thought he was gonna con a *hundred grand* out of me.'

The three of them turned to examine their prisoner. Fenton made a busy humming noise, which meant he was reluctantly coming round to Leon's way of thinking. Nothing from Glenn, of course.

'Well?' Leon snapped.

Glenn jumped as if he'd been shot. 'If you say it's the right thing to do . . .'

'It is.' He told Fenton to call Derek. Then a nod to Reece to get started.

*　　　*　　　*

Reece and Todd took up position behind the chair. Both wore latex gloves. Victor was quietly moaning to himself, his feet jumping and twitching as though in their own death throes. Leon grabbed a chair and placed it directly opposite, within touching distance of his prisoner.

Fenton finished his call and said, 'On his way.'

'Perfect.' Leon caught a glimpse of movement: Glenn edging towards the door. 'Where the hell are you going?'

'Thought I'd grab some fresh air.'

'Fuck that. Come and sit down.' Leon glowered at him until he complied. 'You're part of this. You can see it through to the end.'

Glenn didn't respond. Victor had lifted his head and was staring at them. Maybe it was the words 'the end'. Or maybe he had just tuned in to the atmosphere in the room.

'Hold him tight,' Leon said. 'That's gonna be the key thing.'

'Mr Race . . .' Vic's plea for mercy was drowned out by a rasping whip crack as Reece noisily unrolled a strip of duct tape. As the tape was slapped over Victor's mouth, Leon sensed everyone relaxing a little. If Victor couldn't beg for mercy, then mercy could be set aside, forgotten.

Leon still felt the man was getting off lightly. Far more satisfying to beat him to death, but that would be messy. Leon wanted the Crow's Nest open for Sunday lunches tomorrow.

Taping his eyelids proved to be tricky, involving a certain amount of violence to make Victor comply. By now he understood what they intended to do, and he wasn't going to make it easy for them.

A sudden stench made them all recoil. 'He's bloody shit himself,' Todd exclaimed.

'Ah, fuck. Hurry up, or we'll have to fumigate the place.'

Leon watched as Reece and Todd grasped Victor's head and shoulders, wedging their legs against the sides of the chair. When they were sure he couldn't move an inch, Reece simply reached over and pinched Victor's nostrils together.

His eyes bulged in their sockets; another panic sweat broke out on his forehead and he made a terrible keening noise in his throat.

Leon settled back in his chair. At least by doing it this way he could comfortably observe every second of the man's death. That had to be a bonus worth savouring.

It wasn't often you got the chance to see the lights go out.

CHAPTER FIFTY

They stood up, moving apart by a couple of feet. There were awkward smiles and exaggerated sighs and some unnecessary bustling around as they took their empty glasses through to the kitchen.

'We were going to have coffee,' Ellie said.

'I'm full to bursting. Another time, perhaps?'

'Yes. Absolutely. Look, you don't mind . . .'

'No. Of course not.'

Out in the hall she became uncharacteristically subdued. 'You remember what you said the other day, about Diana having a boyfriend? Well, at first I thought you must know I was Glenn's ex-wife, and you were rubbing my nose in it.'

Joe was shocked. 'Why would I do that?'

'I don't know. I suppose it's what I've come to expect. This is a cruel place.'

*   *   *

He put his jacket on, mulling over the implications of what he had learned tonight.

'You said Glenn can't help himself. Do you think he's still having affairs?'

'More than likely, unless you believe a leopard can change its spots. But you mustn't tell Diana I said that. It'll only feed her distrust.'

Ellie opened the front door. Peeked out. 'There'll be curtains twitching as you leave.'

'Are you worried about word getting back to Glenn?'

'Diana will tell him, won't she?' she said, and

Joe felt foolish for not having thought of that. Of course she would.

And once Glenn knows, Leon will know.

'What about Leon's relationships?' he asked. 'Is he married? Gay? What?'

Ellie folded her arms across her chest and shivered. 'I don't know. I think he's had girlfriends in the past. Occasionally you see him with a glamorous woman on his arm, but Glenn claims that he hires escorts for social events. Anyway, most of the time he's got that entourage of his at the house. I don't see how any wife or girlfriend would put up with that.'

'Not to mention how he treats people,' Joe said, adding quickly: 'Allegedly.'

She smiled. Didn't rise to the bait. He stepped over the threshold, then turned back to say goodbye. Their farewell kiss carried some heat, but there wasn't the same turbocharged connection they'd had in the lounge.

'See you again soon?' he said, and she nodded enthusiastically.

'I hope so.'

Joe walked slowly along her street, aware that he was pleasantly drunk, and in an equally pleasant kind of turmoil. He carried a kiss to remember, but nothing he regretted.

It was a perfect night for a slow walk: clear and perfectly still. A sky rich with stars and moonlight shining a silver path across the glassy sea. A few birds sang, eccentrically, in the trees of a large, unkempt garden. Apart from that, and the distant gentle rasp of the tide, there was silence.

In a dreamy mood, a line from *Under Milk Wood* came to him: *And all the people of the lulled and*

278

dumbfound town are sleeping now.

But they were not. There was a light on at the funeral parlour.

*   *   *

The main building was in darkness, but the gates were standing open. The light came from the flat-roofed building at the rear of the yard. The limo was parked where Joe had seen it the other day, with the hearse tight alongside to make room for a third vehicle: a black Transit van, backed up to a set of double doors.

Joe studied the scene. He couldn't rule out the possibility that this was another trap, but it seemed unlikely. Still he waited a minute or two, until he was satisfied there was no one observing him from the shadows. He was about to move when he recalled the images he'd seen in Leon's comms room. Feed from a security camera in this very yard.

But by now his curiosity was piqued. Reflecting that CCTV was no deterrent to a drunken idiot, he hurried across the yard, head down, staying mostly in the shadow of the main building. Up close, he saw that the double doors were firmly shut. A dim, uncertain light shone from three small windows, but the glass was opaque. Nothing to be seen.

Then he realised the same flickering illumination was visible above the building. Joe retreated, stood on tiptoe and spotted the protruding edge of a skylight. He wouldn't have given it another thought, except that the hearse was close enough to make a perfect stepping stone.

This is madness, the sober voice in his head

was shouting as he climbed onto the vehicle. He took care not to dent the bodywork, or to leave fingerprints anywhere. He managed to clamber up with barely a sound; just a low metallic *whump* as he lifted his weight off the car.

The roof of the building was clad in felt with a layer of stone chippings. Impossible to traverse without making a loud crunching noise. Only by keeping to the very lip of the roof could he move safely to within a foot of the skylight. Just beyond it there were a couple of extraction units, their fans whirring away.

Gingerly, Joe knelt down and leaned forward, just far enough to see into the room. As he'd guessed from the double doors, this was where the bodies were brought for preparation. It was full of equipment, a lot of gleaming stainless steel: embalming tables and hydraulic trolleys for transporting coffins, sluice sinks and a set of cold-storage chambers, like oversized filing cabinets.

The peculiar lighting was explained by the fact that only one of the room's fluorescents was lit; it was augmented by half a dozen candles, placed at intervals around the only table currently in use. The warm, pulsating glow looked utterly inappropriate in such a cold, sterile environment. It sent a shiver of revulsion through him, even before he caught sight of Derek Cadwell.

*   *   *

The undertaker was attending to the corpse of an emaciated old man. Possibly a tramp, judging by the pile of tatty clothing which lay on the tiled floor.

280

The man had filthy grey hair, missing teeth and bruises all over his face and body.

Cadwell wore disposable polypropylene overalls, gloves and a mask. The dancing shadows played over his pink, shiny scalp and for a second Joe was put in mind of a medieval grave-robbing scene, or the good Dr Frankenstein at work on his monster.

It was eleven-thirty at night. What the hell was going on?

His best guess was that a homeless man had been found dead and brought in, but Joe would have expected more activity than this. Where were the police, the other funeral-home staff to take care of the paperwork?

Joe moved sideways a few inches to get a clearer view of the body. The old man's feet were swollen and mangled, caked in dried blood. Perhaps a car had run over them, he thought, although the rest of the body was relatively intact. A very unusual road fatality, if it was that.

He considered calling 999. Let the police make sure this was all above board. But he knew that an anonymous call, this late on a Saturday night, would invariably be given a low priority, assumed to be a drunken hoax.

And what, exactly, would he be alleging? As proprietor of the funeral home, Cadwell was entitled to work at any time that suited him. That it was an unsettling sight probably owed more to what Alise had told him about Cadwell. But there was no proof of that. And no Alise.

Below him, Cadwell fetched a bottle of fluid: disinfectant, maybe. His head bobbed as though he was talking to someone. Joe tried to adjust his position but lost his balance, his knee thudding against the roof, Cadwell reacting, turning towards the skylight . . .

* * *

The Transit was the nearest vehicle. Joe didn't even think about it. He sprang up and jumped the gap. Hit the corner of the Transit's roof, his toes barely making contact before he crouched, hands splayed on the roof while he threw his legs over the side and dropped like a gymnast descending from the bars.

He didn't land much like a gymnast, clumsily turning one of his ankles. Stifling a groan, he dashed across the yard and heard the double doors open. An angry voice shouted: 'Who's there?'

So they hadn't seen him clearly, if at all. Thank God.

Joe kept on running till he was within fifty yards of the B&B, adrenalin beating off the effects of a large meal and too much wine. Finally he slowed to a walk, muttering a string of curses, furious that a man of his age could have done something so reckless, so stupid. It was only as he reached the front door that he started laughing.

CHAPTER FIFTY-ONE

This time, when he came in, everything felt different. What little routine he had established was broken.

And *he* was different. As soon as he stepped into the cell Jenny could feel the energy coursing from his body. The smells he brought with him were a

282

mix of food and alcohol and nicotine, sweat and fear and violence.

He was keyed up, thrilled, but also on edge, as though he'd been close to danger and survived but couldn't yet accept that survival. She pictured a man staggering across a motorway after a pile-up, turning back to survey the wreckage and noticing the bodies of those who hadn't been so lucky.

*   *   *

His first words were: 'Before you ask, it's three in the morning. Middle of the fucking night.'

Day four, Jenny thought. She had been here longer than that, perhaps much longer, but this was the fourth day since she'd begun to grasp the passage of time.

The first set of batteries had failed during her fingertip search. That was when she realised she could scratch a thin line on the stone floor, using the edge of a dead battery to mark out a calendar.

The batteries might have other uses, too, if she could only force her brain to be more inventive, more constructive. She feared he would demand them back, but probably not during this visit. He had come here with a very specific purpose in mind.

'Switch the torch on,' he ordered. 'Shine it on yourself.'

He wanted to see if she was washing thoroughly enough. As the beam of light wobbled across her body she felt the waft of air that meant he had stepped closer, and she knew then why she was picking up so many scents from his skin.

He was naked. He had come to her naked.

'That's better,' he grunted. 'Light off.'

She complied, expecting him to move in, but he remained where he was. She listened to him breathing, and once again a dangerous sense of abandon overcame her.

'Why do you hide your face?'

Silence.

'I mean, I've seen you before. I know who you are.'

Silence.

'I think you're ashamed. That's why you won't let me look at you. Because you're a better man than this.'

A laugh, scornful but amused.

'You are. There are people who love you. Family. Friends. They wouldn't want to imagine you're capable of this.'

'You don't know a fucking thing about me.'

'Let me go.'

'That's what you're really after.'

'Can you blame me?'

Silence, but Jenny could tell she had struck home. She visualised his morality as a tiny maggot, furling and unfurling in the neglected soil of his innermost soul. She knew there was shame lurking there, but she also knew that shame, in a man like this, could easily be transformed into rage.

His answer, when it came, was no answer at all.

'Open your legs.'

*   *   *

Afterwards, in what he might have regarded as a

display of tenderness, he said, 'You enjoyed that, didn't you?'

Jenny didn't trust herself to speak, but managed: 'Mm.'

'See? I don't like having to do it this way, but I can't help it. Nobody's fault. It's just one of those things. One of those situations you get into, and you can't get out of.'

'You're going to kill me.'

He gave a sharp intake of breath. 'Why do you say that? I'm being nice to you, aren't I?'

'Let me go.'

'I can't. Not now.'

'When?'

'I don't know. Let's . . . see how it goes, shall we?' As though they were discussing taking their relationship to the next stage.

She felt him moving in the dark. Climbing to his feet, brushing the dust from his knees. The breeze chilled the tears on her face.

'You've done this before.'

'What?'

'There's a bloodstain on the wall.'

Silence. His breathing was heavier, almost panting, as if steeling himself for action. He could kill her now, if he chose to. But if he did, would she care?

'The girl before me, did you let her go?'

He didn't move. She was still alive. He made a noise that she identified as a chuckle. 'Are you a lawyer?'

'That depends. Let me go, let me finish my degree, maybe I'll become a lawyer.'

Bullshit, of course. Had she told him what she was studying? Would he really care?

285

All he said was: 'Maybe you will.'

'What was her name, the girl before me?'

'Kamile. Kamila. Something like that. Foreign.'

Distaste in his voice, and in hers, too. 'You killed her, and now you don't even remember her name?'

'I didn't kill her. She died.'

'How long did you keep her?'

'Not long. She kept wailing and blubbing. Drove me crazy.'

'Did you promise Kamila that you would let her go?'

'Yeah, not that it shut her up. But I would have.'

'Then why . . .?'

'Because,' he said, and for a moment Jenny thought that was it. A one-word answer; the response of a petulant child.

Because.

Then he said: 'Because she tried to make me her friend, same as you're doing. When that didn't work, she mocked me. Said I didn't have the balls to go through with it. So I taught her a lesson.'

'You killed her to prove that you could do it?'

'I told you, I didn't kill her. She died. There's a difference.' He grunted. 'You'll learn.'

CHAPTER FIFTY-TWO

Sunday began in a panic, Cadwell banging on the door at eight o'clock. Leon was never really one for a lie-in, but this was taking the piss . . .

He padded downstairs in time to see the night-shift man, Opie, hurrying across the hall. Opie looked like shit: worse than Leon felt.

286

'You've been sleeping at your desk again.'

'I weren't, Leon, honest,' Opie gabbled. 'I was in the bog.'

'Is Glenn up yet?'

'Dunno. Haven't seen him.'

Cadwell marched in, flapping his arms to indicate the urgency of the problem.

'Office,' Leon said, because Opie wasn't part of the inner circle. The door was barely shut when Cadwell turned on him, red-faced and spluttering.

'Someone was spying on me.'

'What? When?'

Cadwell looked at him as though he was stupid: a look that Leon wouldn't forget.

'Last night. An intruder on the roof of the damn preparation room, while I had your bloody victim on the table.'

'Keep your voice down. Jesus.' Refusing to be worked into the same frenzy, Leon walked over to his desk and sat down. 'You sure there was somebody on the roof?'

'Ben was with me. We both heard it. He saw a man running away.'

'Any description?'

'No. Too dark.'

Joe, Leon thought. But he didn't say as much. He teased out the silence, staring coolly at the undertaker until he stopped pacing and collapsed onto the sofa.

'So you had a body on the slab. So what? I take it the cops didn't turn up? And you've got a plan to get rid of it?'

Cadwell nodded. 'A burial Tuesday. Elderly man, no family to speak of.'

'Room for a small one.' Leon chuckled. 'See?

287

Two days and it'll be done with.'

'This went well beyond the call of duty, Leon. I hope you appreciate that.'

Leon said nothing. A sudden yawn split his face open. Not much chance that Cadwell would piss off and let him go back to bed. He summoned Opie, who looked like he'd been splashing his face with cold water.

'Put the kettle on, and do me some juice and a bagel. And wake Clive and Glenn. Lazy bastards should be up by now.'

*   *   *

Fenton's arrival coincided with the coffee and bagels, which Leon suspected was no accident. He'd shaved, but hadn't put his contact lenses in: he wore Harry Potter specs with Coke-bottle lenses, blinking at Leon like something from an aquarium. He stank of the cigars they'd shared last night, partly in celebration, partly to chase the smell of Victor Smith from their throats.

'Where's the fire?' he drawled, only half in jest.

Cadwell responded: 'There was an intruder last night, while I was cleaning up your mess. Literally, I might add.'

'It's what you do for a living, Derek,' Leon reminded him. 'It's your *vocation*.' He managed to make it sound like a dirty word. Cadwell caught his meaning and went pale.

'Have you checked the CCTV?' Fenton asked, and Leon had to conceal his annoyance: he hadn't thought of that.

'Nothing remotely useful,' Cadwell said. 'At one stage you see a shadow flitting between the cars,

288

and that's it.'

'Perhaps you need to upgrade,' Leon said.

'The new high-res cameras offer stunning quality,' Fenton added, helping himself to a bagel.

'Can we forget the sales patter for now?' Cadwell snapped. 'This could jeopardise everything. Thirty years I've worked in this town.'

Leon ignored the comment. 'Where's Glenn?'

'Snoring to wake the dead, as of five minutes ago,' Fenton said.

Leon got back on the intercom and was bawling Opie out when Glenn sloped in, wearing jeans and a T-shirt but barefoot. He rubbed his jaw and sighed.

'Early for a Sunday.'

'Lazy bastard,' Leon muttered. 'Sit down. We've got things to discuss.'

They gave him a quick recap, and between them concluded that there was no serious harm done. No other candidates in the frame but Joe Carter.

Glenn swelled a little at that. 'Told you he might be undercover, didn't I?'

Leon shrugged. 'He *was* undercover. I don't buy the idea that he's still a cop.'

'Neither do I,' Fenton said. 'But that's not to say he doesn't represent a danger.'

'Did you search his stuff?' Leon asked.

Glenn twitched uncomfortably. 'What? No. Not after you offered him a job . . .'

'It needs doing, Glenn, but carefully.' Leon stared at each of them in turn, a look of fierce determination on his face. 'Every step from now on has to be bloody careful.'

*   *   *

289

The previous night, after his brandy and cigars, Leon had been too wired to sleep. Instead he'd gone online and trawled for information about the Morton family.

He found plenty to corroborate what Vic had told them. The Mortons were a serious outfit, successful over many years. Wealthy and powerful, with a reputation for extreme violence. Not to be taken lightly.

The media had been up in arms over the bullion robbery shoot-out that had left one of the cops dead and a couple more badly wounded. Markedly less concern for the four gang members who'd died, one of whom had indeed been Gary Morton.

Some of the longer investigative pieces confirmed that an undercover cop had infiltrated the gang. There were suggestions that the operation had been compromised by the existence of one or more corrupt officers on Morton's payroll. A couple of the top brass were mildly reprimanded for various procedural failures, and the world had moved on.

But Doug Morton hadn't.

Now, chomping on a bagel, Glenn made what he obviously believed was another brilliant suggestion. 'We know this guy's a risk. Why don't we just keep him prisoner till we're ready to do the deal?'

Fenton weighed in: 'We must bear in mind the outside possibility that Victor lied to us. Even if he genuinely encountered Morton in prison, Joe's involvement could be a fabrication, or even an error. He admitted that the photograph he saw wasn't very clear.'

The thought made Leon feel sick. Sighing

morosely, he said, 'Good point, Clive. But we've gotta keep a close watch on him. Can't let him slip from our grasp now.'

'We mustn't spook him, either. This is a man on the run for his life, remember?'

Leon nodded. He said to Glenn: 'Go round Diana's, check how the land lies. Reckon you can do that?'

'Subtlety is the order of the day,' Fenton added. 'One sniff . . .' He fluttered his stubby fingers in mid-air, like no bird they'd ever seen. 'And he'll be away.'

*   *   *

Once Glenn had left, they discussed how to approach Danny Morton. Leon had identified an associate in London who would be tasked with securing a phone number. Making contact with the man wasn't the hard part. It was what they actually said to him.

'If a penniless no-hoper like Vic Smith was going to roll us, you can bet Morton would jump at the chance.'

Fenton agreed. 'Play our hand too early and he'll bite it off.'

'The way I see it, we're gonna have to tell Morton who we are up front. But not a word about Joe until we've met this feller face to face and seen what we make of him.'

'What will you say, then?' Cadwell asked. Leon had reluctantly agreed he could have a share of the proceeds, in return for his assistance in disposing of Smith's body.

Fenton said, 'I'm sure we can work out some sort

291

of generic business proposal.'

They were still talking it over when the phone rang. Leon put the call on speaker. It was Glenn, sounding panicked.

'He's not here.'

'What?'

'I'm at Diana's. Well, I'm outside. Said I had a call to make. Joe's not here.'

'Where is he?'

'She doesn't know. He wanted to use her car. Didn't say where he was going.'

Leon took a deep breath. 'So he's coming back, though?'

'I hope so. But after what you said about last night. If it was him at Cadwell's . . .'

Leon glanced at the other two, both looking to him for an answer. He gritted his teeth. 'She must have some idea. Make her tell you.'

A pause from Glenn, as though he was tempted to bite Leon's head off. 'You said to be subtle.'

'Have you checked his room?'

'How can I do that without her knowing . . .?'

'For fuck's sake. Just go and have breakfast with her. I'll be there in ten minutes.'

CHAPTER FIFTY-THREE

Joe told himself he was doing it for Alise, but the reality was a lot more complicated than that—or so he finally had to admit.

The road conditions were perfect for a long journey: dry and sunny, hardly any traffic, inviting the sort of autopilot driving that allowed him plenty of opportunity to think.

Of course he knew it might prove to be a waste of time. A 250-mile round trip, perhaps five hours or more, for nothing. He'd decided not to call ahead, fearing an unhelpful or hostile reaction. But what else did he have to do on a bright and brittle autumn Sunday?

Not stay in the B&B with Diana, that was for sure.

*　　*　　*

He'd opened his eyes at six o'clock, instantly wide awake. The first thing he remembered was the kiss. A wonderful image, immediately superseded by that of a dead body on a stainless steel table.

What had possessed him? He couldn't even count on having made a lucky escape—not until he knew whether Cadwell's security cameras had picked him up. If they had, at the very least Leon would fire him. No more than he deserved.

Back to that question. The answer wasn't so difficult. He'd done it because Alise had believed every word she'd told him about Cadwell, about Leon, about the darkness that they brought to Trelennan. And at the time, listening to her, his instinct had been to believe it, too.

But there were also inconsistencies, not least the contrast between the Leon who had allegedly abducted Kamila, and the protective employer described by Carl, meting out punishment to a driver who'd been accused of a sexual assault. Or was that just Leon acting to safeguard his own reputation, his own secrets?

While Joe brooded, one of Ellie's observations

kept bumping against his conscience. It stayed with him while he showered, dressed and crept downstairs.

He had the details of Kamila's former lover. What was to stop him making his own enquiries?

*   *   *

Diana was already up. Her hair had been brushed, but she wore no make-up. She looked pale and drawn. There was a pot of tea in front of her, and a half-read John Grisham paperback propped open, face down on the table as though in disgrace.

'Not having a lie-in?' Joe's voice had the forced bonhomie of a chat-show host.

She shook her head. He tried again, toning down the enthusiasm.

'Hope I didn't disturb you last night?'

'No.'

'Good. I got back around midnight. Safely unmolested.' He tried a grin, but there was no response.

Joe poured some juice, slotted bread into the toaster, waiting for the questions that didn't come; instead, an icy silence, crystallising the air around them.

It could be that she wanted him to make the first move. After all, she must have anticipated that Ellie would reveal the link with Glenn. Maybe she'd spent the whole night fretting.

'Would you rather I hadn't gone?' he asked.

She made a non-committal sound, while trying to appear unconcerned.

Joe sighed. 'If I'd known what I know now, I probably wouldn't have agreed to it. But I didn't know. Because neither of you told me.'

Diana carefully put her cup down. 'I don't want to discuss it. I can't.'

'What do you mean?'

She stood up, heralding a burst of anger unlike anything he'd witnessed from her.

'I won't be interrogated, Joe. This is my house. I gave you shelter, and I was glad to do it. But there are limits. I can't deal with this . . . this *continual pressure.*'

She gave him a look of pure despair. He didn't really understand what she meant, but saw that yet more questions would be counter-productive.

'All right. I'm sorry. Forget I said anything.'

The toaster popped, an almost comical intrusion. Diana's temper fizzled away as quickly as it had flared. But she remained standing, as if poised to flee.

'I was hoping to borrow the car,' Joe said, 'but that seems like adding insult to injury.'

'Take it. You're welcome.'

'Are you sure? You weren't planning . . .?'

'No. Take it.' She walked over to the units and found the keys. Dropped them into his palm and gave him an awkward, conciliatory smile.

'I think it would be better if you went soon. Perhaps another two or three days?'

He nodded. 'Okay. Fine.'

Diana's eyes were shining with tears. She held Joe's gaze for a couple of seconds, then left the room without another word.

CHAPTER FIFTY-FOUR

When she heard a tap on the back door, Diana assumed it must be Joe. Either he'd forgotten something, or he'd come back for another attempt at the conversation he was so desperate to have—and which she was so desperate to avoid.

To find that it wasn't Joe, but Glenn, should have lifted her spirits. Except that he was part of the problem, too.

'Hey, sweetheart.' He stepped inside, kissed her on the mouth, holding his lips on hers for that extra half-second that always set the furnace burning within her.

She studied his face. 'You look shattered. Tell me you've been to bed.'

'Work kept me up.' He kissed her again, hugging her tight. She wasn't certain, but she thought he might have sniffed, tentatively. 'Did you have a late night?'

'Not especially,' she said, puzzled and a little disturbed. 'Just didn't sleep well. I was up by half past five.'

'Wish I'd known. I'd have come over and taken you back to bed.'

She had a light-bulb moment: *He was sniffing for aftershave. Joe's aftershave . . .*

'I doubt it, if you'd seen the state of me.'

'You're beautiful, Di. Anyway, with you it's *inner* beauty.' Flashing his eyes as he emphasised the word. He was being especially charming, which usually meant he wanted something—or had bad news to deliver.

296

In this case, as it turned out, it was both.

* * *

Diana made a fresh pot of tea, although Glenn said it wasn't necessary. She wished she could slip away, put on some lipstick and mascara, if nothing else.

He followed her to the counter, standing close behind her, his groin almost but not quite touching her bottom. He placed his hands on her shoulders, nuzzled the side of her neck, chuckling as he made her shiver.

'Don't.'

'We could go back to bed now.'

She squirmed, wriggled him off. 'Maybe later. Do you want toast?'

'No. I want you.' His voice changed as he spotted the plate with crumbs. 'Is Joe up?'

'He's gone out. I lent him my car.'

'I thought it must be in the garage. Where's he off to, then?'

'I don't know,' she said, thinking: *Thank God I didn't ask*.

'You must do. You wouldn't just let him take your car.'

'Why not? I trust him.'

'What if he doesn't come back?'

She moved sideways, so she could turn and confront him. What she saw in his face made her take another step back.

'Joe's an old friend. He's not going to steal my car, for goodness sake.'

'Did he say how long he'd be?'

'No. We're not joined at the hip, Glenn.'

She knew it was a mistake as soon as she said it.

297

Any reference to physical contact between them was bound to set his mind racing. He gave her a dubious glance and reached for his phone.

'Gotta take this,' he said.

She nodded, but she hadn't heard it ring or vibrate. *He's making a call*, she thought, and the implications filled her with dread.

* * *

He was back a couple of minutes later, finishing a cigarette and looking even more strained. Sitting at the table, he accepted his tea, then reached out and stroked her arm. Diana made to move away but his fingers curled around her wrist and held her tightly.

'Sit down. Let's talk about this.'

'What?'

'Joe. How much do you really know about him? You say he used to work with Roy, but then he left the force. Well, is there any proof of that?'

'I don't understand what you mean. Or why you need to know, for that matter.'

'You understand,' he said, his voice so quiet that she might have imagined the note of menace. 'It's not just me, is it?'

'Leon, then. Why does Leon need to know?'

Glenn shook his head, as if thoroughly disgusted. 'Use your brain, Di. Imagine the shit I'll be in if it turns out he's still a cop?'

She gaped at him, aware that she had to get a grip on her panic. 'If Leon had any worries on that score, why on earth did he offer him work?'

'Christ knows. But if it goes wrong it won't have been Leon's idea, will it?'

'Frankly, Glenn, I wish neither of you worked

298

for him. Maybe it's time to get the construction business up and running again . . .'

Glenn's withering look told her what he thought of that. He drank his tea, slurping greedily. The noises Roy had made when he ate and drank had always irritated Diana beyond reason, whereas with Glenn it only seemed to emphasise his masculinity: such a big strong man ought to devour his food like a wild beast.

He wiped his mouth with the back of his hand, his eyes heavy-lidded as he studied her. 'So what did you two get up to last night?'

'We didn't do anything. I stayed in, and Joe went out.' She wouldn't have said that much, except that a glimmer of light had appeared: a way to divert Glenn's interest away from Joe's identity, his history. 'He had dinner with somcone.'

'What? You mean he's getting his leg over?'

'I'm hardly going to ask him that, am I?' Too late to backtrack. This was going to make things worse even as it made other things better. But it was a question of priorities . . .

'Who is it?'

'You should be pleased. This proves you've been worrying for no good reason.'

'So tell me who it is.'

'Ellie.'

'*My* Ellie?'

If the phrase had been deliberately intended to wound, Diana would have taken a lot more offence. As it was, Glenn seemed to recognise his clumsiness.

'You know what I mean. Is that where he's gone today?'

So tempting . . . but she couldn't risk an outright

299

lie. 'It might be. I didn't ask, and he didn't say.'

'I don't bloody believe it.' Glenn exhaled loudly. Diana had the impression he was both infuriated and simultaneously very relieved. She chose to share the latter emotion.

Then the doorbell rang, and that relief evaporated like mist over a summer meadow.

CHAPTER FIFTY-FIVE

Poundbury was a brand new community on the western fringes of the ancient market town of Dorchester. Built on land owned by the Duchy of Cornwall, it had been designed according to the classical architectural principles espoused by Prince Charles. Joe recalled various points of controversy over the years: fears that the alleys and walkways would encourage crime; architects who insisted that design had to look forwards, not backwards. Joe decided he had sympathy with both sides.

It was strikingly different, and the period architecture was grandly impressive, but the pristine stone and brick, together with the absence of modern street signs or road markings, lent it an oddly artificial air. As he got out of his car, Joe felt he'd strayed onto a movie set, or perhaps an elaborate folly. It reminded him of Portmeirion, the Italianate village on the Welsh coast which had provided the location for the 1960s TV series *The Prisoner*.

And whilst he admired the ideas which underpinned the development, he was reminded of his conversation with Ellie in the Shell Cavern.

300

No matter how honourable the intentions, perfect communities weren't something you could create on a drawing board. Or impose by force.

* * *

Poundbury remained a work in progress, with a large sector to the south excavated for the next wave of construction. Even in the completed areas, the streets were unnaturally quiet. Many had no separate pavements, and the road surface was covered with a layer of pea gravel, adding to the 'costume drama' feel of the place.

The address he had for Pearse was a three-storey Georgian-style town house. Joe knocked on the front door, which was opened swiftly by a tall, elegant woman in her early thirties. Mrs Pearse, he presumed.

She had long, straight blonde hair, brilliant blue eyes and just enough of an elitist sneer to be sexy rather than obnoxious. She was immaculately turned out in close-fitting slacks and a pale blue cashmere sweater. Subtle make-up accentuated a face that looked fresh and untroubled, despite the clamour of what sounded like several young children somewhere in the depths of the house.

'May I speak to Jamie?' he said. 'I'm Joe Carter, a friend of Kamila's. From London?' He employed the rising inflection for its disarming effect.

Unfazed, the woman smiled. 'Yes, yes, of course. Do come in, but would you mind . . .?' She indicated several robust doormats that covered a couple of square yards of the spacious hallway.

Joe stepped inside, wiped his feet, then decided to stay where he was. Not worth removing his shoes

301

if he was about to get kicked out.

Moving away from him, the woman glanced back. 'Joe? A friend of Kamila's?'

Joe nodded, marooned on the doormat as she disappeared into the kitchen. The hall carpet was pure white and spotlessly clean, and he had a vision of the children forced to wear protective overshoes at all times. Or maybe they never went out . . .

He heard the woman speaking, a good-natured appeal for quiet, and then a man's voice, one word emerging clearly from the murmured conversation. 'Who?'

*　　　　*　　　　*

Seconds later, he stepped into view. Jamie Pearse was an inch or two shorter than his wife, not unattractive despite narrow shoulders and a weak chin. He was around fifty, with sandy grey hair and bushy eyebrows. He wore dark blue jeans and a brown Tattersall shirt. With his wife hovering at his shoulder, he beamed at Joe as though they were old friends.

'Joe, hi! I completely forgot. We need to talk about the Lambert account.' Undetectable in his voice, his expression frantically signalled that Joe should pretend to understand.

Feeling like a louse, Joe had little option but to nod enthusiastically. 'If you can spare the time. I thought, seeing as I was in the area . . .'

'Yes, why not? Good man. We have nothing on this morning—'

'Lunch with the Vinalls,' his wife interjected.

'Oh, bags of time yet. This won't take long.'

He grabbed a light brown cord jacket from a

hook. 'I say we get a coffee. Not fair to inflict our business woes on the family, eh?'

'Quite,' said Joe.

Pearse exuded relief as he called a farewell to the children and shut the front door behind him. He led Joe along the deserted street, the only sound their footsteps on the gravel.

'Awful, isn't it? Crunch crunch crunch. Drives you mad. Anyone strolls past, it sounds like a bloody regimental parade. And the mess! Ruins your carpets, scratches the wooden floors to buggery. All because it looks nice from the air, apparently . . .'

'You didn't know about it before you bought the house?'

A sly laugh as Pearse acknowledged Joe's dig at him. 'Oh, yes. Small quibble, really. We were one of the first here. Bought two, one for the investment portfolio, and saw prices double in three years. Not a bad return.'

Joe made no comment. What had started as a mild distaste for the man was rapidly transforming into a full-on loathing.

Once they were at a safe distance from the house, Pearse gave him a confiding look. 'Apologies for the spot of subterfuge. Better all round to keep shtum. Now, d'you want to explain who you are and what this is all about?'

'I'm doing a favour for a friend,' Joe said. 'Kamila's sister.'

'Ah. Alise.' Pearse wrinkled his nose, as if at a bad smell. 'How did you find me?'

'The hotel where Kamila worked.'

Pearse frowned, but not at Joe's use of the past tense. 'Bit naughty of them. Data protection and

303

what have you. Not a mad axe murderer, are you?'

He guffawed, then abruptly stopped. 'Or police,' he added thoughtfully. 'That would almost be worth the grief. If you're here to tell me you've found her.'

Joe stopped dead. Pearse took a couple more steps before he noticed that Joe was no longer keeping pace. He turned, his feet scraping the gravel like a cyclist slewing to a halt.

'You know Kamila's missing?' Joe asked.

'Missing? I should think she's bloody missing.' Pearse was grinning until he saw Joe's face and understood that they'd been talking at cross-purposes. But he must have mistaken Joe's confusion for a sense of fellow feeling.

'Oh dear,' he said ruefully. 'Don't tell me you're the latest victim?'

CHAPTER FIFTY-SIX

Glenn went to the door and returned with Leon Race. That explained the phone call, Diana thought.

Leon wore a broad smile, but his eyes were as cold as the sea in winter. Diana stood up as he opened his arms and embraced her, kissing her cheeks like some exuberant Italian nephew.

'Di! You're looking great. It's been too long, hasn't it? Glenn never brings you over.'

'No.' Her own smile was an invitation to dispense with the soft soap.

'Drink, Leon?' Glenn said.

'Glass of water, thanks.' Leon sat opposite Diana, in the chair that Glenn had vacated.

'This is a surprise,' Diana said, a microscopic pause where the word *nice* had been omitted.

'Well, to be honest, Di, I've come to talk about this Joe . . . Carter? Glenn probably told you, we're a bit worried.'

Glenn gave Leon his water, then jabbed his thumb over his shoulder. 'Need a pee.'

Diana didn't watch him leave, in case it betrayed her fear. Glenn's excuse had all the feel of a contrived exit. They were working as a double act, she realised: so grimly ironic that in better circumstances she might have laughed.

Good cop, bad cop.

*   *   *

'You don't have anything to worry about,' she told Leon. 'I've said this to Glenn.'

'I know. I know you have. I appreciate that.'

There was a weighty silence. She heard a creak from overhead: Glenn, climbing the stairs. But there was a toilet on the ground floor. Why would he need—?

Joe's room. Of course.

She said, 'Why did you offer him a job?'

'Spur-of-the-moment thing. He sounded useful. He was short of cash. And I was keen to take a look at him, you know?'

'He's not spying on you,' Diana said, and knew at once it was a mistake. She had no choice but to press on. 'He's not a threat.'

'Yeah, but I have to be the judge of that, Di. Not you.' Leon shrugged. 'Trouble is, right now he's starting to remind me of Roy.'

Diana flinched. Leon took a measured sip of

305

water. 'Joe's not here today, then?'

'No. He asked to borrow my car.'

'Do you know where he's gone?'

'Last night he had dinner with Ellie Kipling. Somewhere with her, perhaps.'

Leon's lips formed a sordid little grin. 'What did Glenn have to say about that?'

'Not much. Their marriage ended years ago.'

'Oh, but you know how it is, Di. A flame still burns.'

'Maybe.' He was just trying to rile her, she knew that. But it was working.

'Don't tell me you haven't got a flame burning for dear old Roy?' Still grinning, Leon lifted one hand to his chest, clamped a fist against his heart. 'Dear. Old. Departed. Roy.' With each word he thumped his chest, imitating a slow-beating heart.

Tears rolled down her cheeks. Leon watched them, waiting for a sob, a wail, but Diana didn't make a sound.

Glenn returned. He registered her tears and his gaze moved swiftly on.

'Find anything?' Leon asked, as though Diana wasn't present.

'Just clothes. Toiletries.' He hung back, sheepish, not meeting her eye.

Leon frowned at Diana. 'Vince at the Britannia said he didn't have any luggage. When I saw him Wednesday he'd bought shaving gear and deodorant. Who comes to stay and forgets stuff like that, eh?'

He spread his hands in a question, but wasn't perturbed by her lack of a reply. This was more a demonstration of his knowledge and power.

'He's been talking to that foreign bitch about

306

her sister. We caught him nosing round outside my house. Do you expect me to believe he's pure as the driven snow?'

Diana could feel herself trembling. If Leon got a whiff of Joe's secret, he wouldn't fail to capitalise on it. There was a mantra running in her head: *Nothing about Joe's past. Nothing about undercover. Nothing about Joe's past . . .*

'You believe what you want to believe, Leon. Whatever I say will make no difference.'

'Try me. Do you swear he's not a cop?'

His tone was so reasonable that she hesitated, fearing a trap. Leon might be dressed like someone on *Jeremy Kyle*, but he was as wily and sharp as any barrister.

'Yes,' she said. 'I swear.'

'Why did he leave the police?'

'I-I don't know why. We'd already lost touch by then.'

His lips tightened. He didn't believe her. Glenn was hanging back in the kitchen, examining a National Trust calendar as though it was the most fascinating thing he'd ever seen.

Leon pushed his chair back and stood up. 'I'm gonna leave it there, Di. But if I were you, I'd make sure Joe doesn't follow in Roy's footsteps. I don't take kindly to betrayal . . .'

The words floated in the air like poison gas. With a curt nod at Glenn, he walked out.

* * *

The front door shut and Glenn jerked to life, hurrying towards her. Concern in his eyes, eyes that for years had held her spellbound. It was all Diana

307

could do not to slap his face.

She held her arms against her chest, palms out to ward him off. He stopped a couple of feet away from her.

'That was a bit strong. Betrayal. I'll have a word with him about that.'

'You will, will you?'

'Yeah. I'll go and see him later.'

'What was wrong with now, Glenn? What stopped you from speaking up on my behalf *right now*?'

'It's not that—'

'Get out.'

'Di. Come on.'

'No. I want you to leave.'

She spun away from him, waited for what felt like an age until the door shut for a second time and she was alone.

CHAPTER FIFTY-SEVEN

Pearse led Joe to a rather featureless café and ordered coffees. After exchanging greetings with a couple of other customers, he chose a table at a discreet distance from them and sat down, throwing aside a discarded supplement from one of the Sunday papers.

'Kamila's vanished,' Joe told him. 'Alise last spoke to her at the end of August. Since then there's been no contact whatsoever.'

'Well, I can't help you there. She ran out on me well before that.' Pearse explained that he ran a successful executive recruitment agency, a job that entailed plenty of domestic and international travel. His family home was in Poundbury, and although he had an apartment in London he didn't always use it.

'I have a grown-up daughter from a previous marriage who sometimes breezes in for a week or two, not always when it's entirely convenient. I can't indulge my dalliances in her presence, so I take myself off to a hotel. That's how I met Kamila.'

He laughed to himself, but there was a sour look on his face. 'Damn clever, these Eastern European girls. Know exactly what they want and how to get it. Devious bitches.'

Joe knew he couldn't afford to antagonise the man, much less punch him in the face, so he sipped a bitter espresso and let him continue.

'After a marvellous night, I invited her for a few days in Gloucestershire. I have a cottage in Bourton-on-the-Water. Use it as a bolt-hole when I have reports to write or need some space to chill out, away from the brats . . .' Pearse smirked. 'Didn't get much work done then, though. A bloody demon between the sheets. Did all those things the wife will never countenance. Too good to be true, I thought, and of course it was.'

'What do you mean?'

'I woke one morning and she'd decamped with nearly two thousand pounds from my safe, plus jewellery and a Rolex worth another three grand.'

Joe was instinctively suspicious. 'Why did you have so much cash?'

'Self-preservation.' Pearse snorted. 'How's that for ironic? I've experienced the hazards of a stray receipt here, a bank statement there. To dally in safety takes cold hard cash.'

'Did Kamila know it was merely a "dalliance"?'

Pearse regarded Joe as though he'd let the side down. 'Oh, come on. You must get plenty of interest from the ladies, am I right? You ought to know the score.'

'So you didn't tell her you were married?'

'Look, we're not talking about some innocent little maiden here.'

'I was given the impression that Kamila was quite naive, actually. I was wondering if she found out you'd been lying to her—maybe that was what prompted the theft?'

Pearse grunted. 'Is that the spin she put on it for her sister?'

'I don't think Alise knows anything about this.'

'There you are, then. She set out to rob me. I dare say that's why you haven't heard from her since. Boil it down to basics, these girls are whores, that's all.'

When Joe said nothing, Pearse's gaze drifted towards the newspaper supplement. He gave a wistful sigh, as though it represented the kind of day he should be having.

'I assume you didn't go to the police?' Joe said.

'Of course I didn't. In the scheme of things it's not a great deal of money. I took it on the chin and resolved to be more careful who I play with in future.'

'And you've had no contact with Kamila since the day she left?'

Pearse shook his head, but his eyes slid away. 'Not really.'

'So you have?'

He shrugged irritably. 'She also took an old phone. I use several at a time, and upgrade

310

regularly, so it was a couple of months before I realised. I tried calling but didn't get an answer. Then, out of the blue, she phoned me.'

Anticipating Joe's question, he frowned. 'It could well have been late August. It was very brief, along the lines of: "I've spent your money and it serves you right." I told her what I thought of her, in no uncertain terms, and she responded with another taunt.'

Pearse looked down at the coffee he'd neglected until now. He took a sip. Over his shoulder Joe saw a familiar figure advancing on the café.

'Which was?' he asked quickly.

'Basically, that I was a stepping stone, and she'd hooked up with somebody far more profitable.'

'Did she say anything else about him? A name? Where he lived?'

The café door opened forcefully enough to capture Pearse's attention. He half-turned while replying to Joe: 'Not that I recall.' Then he gave a spasm as he realised it was his wife bearing down on them. 'Hello, darling. What brings you—?'

'Don't you try and sweet-talk me. I've just spoken to Denny Sorrill. There's no one called Kamila working on the Lambert account. No Joe Carter, either.'

She faced Joe, while gesturing at her husband. 'He's been screwing around again, hasn't he? What are you? The husband? Lawyer? Private detective?'

'Darling, it's not like that. Please let me explain—'

Pearse started to rise, but his wife spun and landed a solid blow to his cheek, knocking him off-balance. He stumbled against the chair and fell as it toppled backwards under his weight. As

311

he lay sprawled on the floor, there was a moment when she seemed tempted to kick him in the balls. Instead she gave him a scornful glance, as though he wasn't worth the effort, then turned and marched out, oblivious to the shock and amusement of the other customers.

Pearse looked stunned. He didn't move as Joe stood up, shaking his head.

'I have to say, that's far less than you deserve.'

*   *   *

Leon thought the meeting with Diana had gone well. Running through it later with Fenton, they agreed he'd got the tone just right.

'Given what's happened, it's quite natural for us to be suspicious of Joe,' Fenton said. 'Therefore we have to remain suspicious, even though we know precisely who he is.'

It had been Leon's idea to employ reverse psychology. Deliver a warning that Joe had to stop snooping, and it was bound to have the opposite effect. He'd aimed to give Diana just enough of a scare that Joe would feel duty-bound to stay and protect her.

'I imagine Glenn felt rather compromised?' Fenton said.

'Nah, he was okay.' Leon told him about Joe hooking up with Ellie Kipling. Fenton giggled, rubbing his chubby palms together.

'Wonderful! Another reason for him to stay.'

'Though Christ knows what they all see in her. Mouthy bitch. I keep telling Rawle he ought to shut that fucking library down.'

Fenton looked troubled. 'Of course, when we sell

312

Joe to Morton and he disappears, we'll now have Ellie to contend with, as well as Diana.'

'I know. Cross that bridge when we come to it, eh?'

But it might not be too far off. Their contact in London was confident he'd have a phone number for Danny Morton by tomorrow morning.

All coming together nicely, Leon thought. Just as long as Joe hadn't done a runner today.

CHAPTER FIFTY-EIGHT

The journey back to Trelennan took longer. A lot more traffic on the road, and a slower average speed, but thankfully not too many hold-ups. Nothing to distract Joe from his thoughts.

Pearse's account seemed plausible, including the tacit admission that he'd lied to Kamila. Joe could well envisage a creep like Pearse posing as a wealthy bachelor, offering the prospect of a genuine relationship. Perhaps Kamila had discovered the truth and taken revenge by stealing from him.

Then again, maybe she was the bad apple in the family, or simply an untamed spirit who felt entitled to a tangible reward in exchange for sex with Jamie Pearse. Either way, Joe didn't doubt that she'd used the proceeds to pay for a couple of months' travelling before ending up in Newquay. Since then, perhaps shame or guilt—plus the fear of prosecution—had deterred her from returning to London.

From Joe's perspective, he'd made some enquiries, which had proved inconclusive, and there

313

was no one to whom he could report his findings. That ought to be the end of it.

Stopping to refuel at a service station near Okehampton, he bought himself a sandwich and a Coke. He wanted five minutes to sit back, shut his eyes and let his mind wander.

After stealing from Pearse, Kamila hadn't completely gone to ground—she'd remained in touch with her sister for weeks. She had a penchant for wealthy, powerful men, and she had taunted Pearse about finding a better candidate. Her final conversation with Alise had mentioned Trelennan, and Leon Race. And now Alise appeared to be missing . . .

Too much there to dismiss. But Diana wanted him gone within a few days. If he intended to keep digging, he would have to find new accommodation.

Another option was to head for London. Someone at the hotel where Kamila had worked might have an address for Alise. But after his narrow escape in Bristol, going anywhere near the Mortons' home territory seemed almost suicidally dangerous.

Joe made it back to Trelennan without reaching any firm decision. Now he had to steel himself for another confrontation with Diana. She had talked of *continual pressure*. Well, the best way to relieve that pressure was to get the truth out in the open.

He opened the front door, calling her name. There was a response from the lounge. Not a voice, but the clunk of glass on wood.

*　　　*　　　*

He found her slumped in an armchair, one arm

314

bent into her lap, the other stretched towards a low table, her hand loosely enfolding a heavy glass beaker as though she couldn't quite bring herself to let it go. The beaker held an inch of whisky. A half-empty bottle of Glenfiddich sat on the table.

She struggled to lift her head and focus on him. Her cheeks were bright red and stained with tears, her eyes puffy and unbearably sad. She could have been twenty years older than the woman who had opened the door to him on Tuesday night.

'Oh God, Diana . . .' He was furious with himself for having departed on bad terms, but Diana was shaking her head.

'Glenn,' she said, then clamped her mouth shut. A shudder ran through her. The glass slipped from her hand, toppling to the floor in a splash of single malt.

'Come on.' Joe helped her up, Diana suddenly frantic: a clumsy uncoordinated panic as he frogmarched her to the downstairs toilet. They made it with about a second to spare.

He held her while she vomited, lightly rubbing her back, making soothing noises. He hadn't done anything like this for years. Not since he'd ceased to be a father to his daughters.

When she was done, she washed her face with cold water and he handed her a towel. She wiped her mouth. Tried to smile but couldn't quite bring it off. She was still unsteady on her feet, so he took her arm and led her back to the lounge, batting away her apologies.

He put the kettle on, fetched a glass of cold water and a packet of Nurofen. Found a cloth to mop up the whisky.

'I'm so sorry, Joe.' Already her voice was clearer.

'Don't tell me you've spent all day drinking?'

'No. Slept some of it. And wept. Slept and wept.' She giggled, gesturing at the Glenfiddich. 'That's Roy's. Found it in the cupboard. I don't even like whisky.'

'Good job. You might have drunk the whole bottle otherwise.'

He rinsed the cloth out in the kitchen sink, made strong coffee with plenty of sugar and encouraged her to eat a couple of biscuits. She was crying again, her chest heaving gently as she stared at the coffee mug cradled in her hands.

'If it felt like I've been interrogating you, it's only because I'm worried.' Joe said nothing more until she made eye contact with him. 'Ever since I arrived I've had the feeling that you're in trouble. Even when you keep insisting you're fine. But you're not, are you?'

*   *   *

Diana shook her head, as forlorn as a little girl caught cheating in an exam. Her hands trembled as she lifted the coffee and drank. She swallowed, then exhaled gratefully.

'I've been lying to you, Joe, for your own sake. That's why I didn't want you to get involved with Alise, or Leon. I know what you're like.'

'Stubborn,' he said. 'Same as Roy.'

She sniffed. Rubbed her nose with the side of her hand. 'They were here this morning—Leon and Glenn. Asking where you'd gone.'

Joe was intrigued by that, but set it aside for now. 'Let's start at the beginning, when you moved down here. Something happened between Roy and Leon

316

Race, didn't it?'

'Why do you say that?'

'Because he was a good cop, with the best instincts for people that I ever saw.'

Diana smiled sadly. 'When Glenn came round to quote for the extension, Roy thought he was a flash bastard. Said he could charm the knickers off Mother Teresa.'

Joe winced. But there was no going back now. He had to tell her.

Then Diana said, 'The first year we were here, a woman came to stay with us. She was searching for her missing daughter.' She stopped, fearfully, as though she expected Joe to rage at her. But he merely nodded: *Go on.*

'It was similar to the tale Alise told you. A young woman had vanished without trace. From St Ives, I think, but some vague reference had led her mother to Trelennan.'

'And Roy offered to help?'

'He jumped at the chance. For all his dreams of a new life, this wasn't really what he wanted. There was always a ton of jobs to do, but nothing that got his adrenalin pumping. Whereas this, a bit of bona fide detective work . . .'

'How did it get onto Leon's radar?' Joe asked.

'You said it yourself the other day. Not much happens round here without him knowing. Roy was already convinced that Leon was up to his neck in crime, so that made a place to start.' Diana sighed. 'Even when the mother gave up and went home, Roy refused to let it go. He was making a nuisance of himself, following the security vans, trying to call in favours from the local police. Of course, they took a dim view: this retired big-shot London cop, trying to show his country cousins how to do their job.'

'Hmm. Roy wasn't always the most tactful of men.'

'Quite. All he did was rub them up the wrong way.'

'And incurred Leon's wrath at the same time.' Joe hesitated a moment, then pressed on. 'Look, Diana, I'm sorry but I have to say this, but it's not just about Leon. It's Glenn, as well.'

'What do you mean?'

He had to force himself to say it. 'I think he was deceiving you from the beginning.'

CHAPTER FIFTY-NINE

Glenn called Leon at three o'clock to report that Diana's car was parked on the drive.

'I haven't actually seen him. I could go in, but after this morning . . .'

Leon agreed it wasn't wise. 'So was he with Ellie?'

'No. I've just been to see her.' Even allowing for the slight distortion caused by the speakerphone, Glenn sounded miserable as hell. Leon grinned at Fenton, whose shrug seemed to say: *Everyone knows women are nothing but strife.*

'Sent you away with a flea in your ear, did she?'

Glenn ignored the question. 'I've told her if she sees him any more she's in trouble.'

Leon ended the call, and smiled pleasantly at Fenton. 'Relief that he's back.'

'I'd feel more secure if we knew where he went.'

318

'Yeah, but I don't want Glenn barging in there now. We gave her a good scare this morning. Now we play it cool.' He thought for a moment. 'You remember that text we saw on the other one's phone, about some feller in Dorset? I bet he followed up on it.'

'So still probing, then.'

'It doesn't matter, not now we have Danny Morton on the horizon.'

He glanced at his laptop, saw a new email from Giles Quinton-Price. He scanned the message, then opened the attachment that came with it.

'Problem?' Fenton leaned forward, puffing as his belly squashed against his knees.

Leon didn't respond immediately: too busy reading.

'It's from the journalist. The article's all ready to go.'

'Favourable, I hope?'

Fenton sounded uneasy: Leon could have taken offence at that. But he was in a good mood. Joe was back within their grasp. Diana had been put in her place. And now this . . .

He beamed. 'What else could it be, Clive? Didn't you have any faith in the man?'

*   *   *

Diana said, 'First, let me just say I have no defence. What I did was unforgivable.'

'Your affair started when Roy was still alive?'

She nodded, then gave a hopeless laugh. 'It all went wrong when we came down here. Running a B&B is like being a housewife, multiplied by ten. Roy had this image of himself as "mine host", swanning around with a drink and a cigar while I did the cooking, and the cleaning, and the laundry. That only drove us further apart.'

'So when Glenn showed an interest . . .'

'I succumbed. I know it's appalling, but I was so lonely. So unhappy.'

'Di, I do understand. I remember how you felt on the night of the retirement party. You don't have to justify yourself.'

'But I do. It's been eating away at me for years.'

'When it began, was Glenn working at Leon's place?'

'I think so. There were months where he was going back and forth, and doing other jobs as well.' Her voice was stuttering with shame, and then she saw the look on Joe's face and said, 'What do you mean—Glenn was deceiving me?'

'If Roy was being a nuisance, then Leon needed to neutralise him somehow. But with an ex-cop he couldn't do anything too drastic. The wisest option was to find out precisely what kind of threat he posed. And the best way to do that was to place a spy in the camp.'

Joe tensed, anticipating every sort of reaction except the one that he got.

Diana nodded, quite calmly. 'You mean Glenn was told to seduce me? It's almost funny. If you'd suggested this to me at any time prior to this morning I'd have thrown you out on your ear. But I've spent most of the day working myself towards the same conclusion.'

'It wasn't necessarily quite so mercenary. To have lasted this long, there had to have been some genuine feelings.'

'Maybe. I don't know any more.'

320

'What happened today? Did they threaten you?'

'Not exactly,' Diana said. But then she shuddered. 'Leon's clever. He just said that you were starting to remind him of Roy, which I took to be a warning of sorts.'

Joe was shocked. 'Did Leon have something to do with Roy's death?'

'He contributed to it. When Glenn landed the contract at Leon's, Roy thought he could exploit that. He made a somewhat ham-fisted attempt to entrap Leon, but it went wrong. Afterwards, Roy refused to talk about it. He was never the same again. The fight went out of him. His health deteriorated.'

'What about the affair? I don't see how Roy wouldn't have been aware of it.'

'No.' Diana sounded deeply ashamed. 'I kept it secret for a while. He was so preoccupied with Leon. But eventually he worked it out.'

'And how did he react?'

'Look, Joe. Some things have to . . .' Her voice choked up. 'He was . . . he took a sensible view. We'd had no sex life to speak of for years.'

'But even if he forgave you, surely he wasn't happy to let it continue?'

'He wasn't given the choice.'

'What?'

'That's another thing I've only just worked out. I think Leon forced him to accept it.'

*　　　*　　　*

They took a break, moving to the kitchen because the smell of spilt whisky was making Diana nauseous. Joe refilled the coffee machine and made

321

cheese on toast, and all the time he was trying to process what he'd heard. *Leon forced him to accept it.*

'Okay, so they told you to warn me off,' he said. 'But what are they hiding?'

'I really have no idea. And frankly I don't care.' She took his hand and squeezed it. 'I have a lot of horrible mistakes on my conscience. I don't want to add you to that list.'

He grinned. 'Neither do I.'

'I'm serious.' She told him what Leon had said to her this morning, picking away at Joe's past. 'If they had any inkling of your history they wouldn't hesitate to capitalise on it.'

'But you didn't give them anything?'

'No. When they asked where you'd gone, I suggested you might be with Ellie. I thought that was a fairly safe way of shifting their interest.'

'Good idea,' Joe said, though he would have to make sure that Ellie wasn't at risk of any reprisals.

'Are you seeing her again?' Diana said, none too subtle code for: *Are you sleeping with her?*

'Maybe. We're only friends, Diana.'

'It's none of my business. Of course, I take back what I said about you leaving. Although, to be honest, it might be safer if you went.'

'Let's take it a day at a time, shall we?'

'All right.' A tense moment, before she said, 'Will you carry on working for Leon?'

Joe sighed. There was no denying that he was in a perilous position. The fact that Roy had tried to bring Leon down meant that Leon would be especially vigilant against further attempts, perhaps to the point of paranoia.

'I know you want me to say no. I know it's

322

probably the wisest thing to do. But I can't give in to bullies, Diana. And I can't shake off the idea that Alise's disappearance is linked to the fact that she was seen talking to me.'

Once again, Diana surprised him with her response. 'You make me even more ashamed of the coward I've become. You're never going to take the easy way out, are you?'

'Believe me, I wish I could,' Joe said. 'I guess it's just not in my nature.'

CHAPTER SIXTY

Jenny woke to confusion, to fear and self-loathing. Was this the fifth day, or was it still day four? How long had she slept: a nap, or a full night?

It was impossible to say. His last visit had been in the middle of the night, or so he had said. Afterwards it occurred to her that she had been awake when he came, which meant her sleeping patterns must be badly off-kilter.

Since that visit she had slept at least once, but possibly twice, and now she had absolutely no idea what time it was. Her precious calendar was already worthless.

And she was overdue a visit. She knew that from the state of the bucket, from the smell that clung to her nostrils. Something was wrong: some kind of crisis or interruption to his own routine, which invariably had repercussions for her.

If she was in the mood to take any comfort from the situation, she could tell herself that at least now she knew the score. What had he told her?

I didn't kill her. She died.

She didn't understand the distinction. It hardly mattered that there was one, if the end result was the same.

* * *

Now it seemed she had a simple choice: accept death, in which case she was better off trying to kill herself, rather than let him select the manner and timing of her departure from the world.

Or escape.

Get out.

Put like that, in such short snappy little words, made it sound almost easy. Feasible, certainly. Just make a plan and get to work on it. She wasn't chained up. She was still reasonably healthy, despite her confinement. Still reasonably strong.

She had a working brain, didn't she? So use it.

She had illumination, and a set of dead AA batteries that could just about scratch a mark on the stone floor. Nothing really sharp, though. Nothing she could use as a weapon or as a tool.

So find something . . .

* * *

Another fingertip search proved futile. The door was made of timber, thick and heavy and covered in gloss paint. The floor was bare untreated concrete, completely impenetrable. The ceiling was plywood and the walls had been crudely plastered. There were no cracks, no holes, no obvious weak spots at all.

She tried gouging the plaster with one of the

324

dead batteries, but all it produced was a bit of dust. Then she had a brainwave of sorts.

She used the filthy water from the bucket, pouring it slowly over a patch of the wall in the corner furthest from the door. By soaking it, then scratching back and forth with the battery, she found she could slowly erode the surface layer of plaster to expose what lay beneath.

What she found was plasterboard; and beneath that, rough yellow timber. This was a stud wall, not brick or blockwork.

Jenny had seen stud walls before. She understood their design, and she was thrilled.

Because stud walls had gaps between the timbers.

She redoubled her efforts, despite the pain from her bruised hands and broken fingernails. She worked her way to the edge of the vertical timber, soaked and scratched and dug until the plasterboard yielded, and finally had a space large enough to get her hand into. Now she could work much faster, ripping the plasterboard off the frame.

But she paused, knowing this was a crucial decision. From here on there would be no concealing the damage. She had to make it worthwhile.

She had to escape.

The fist-sized hole gave back nothing but darkness. She shone the torch on it for a long time, wondering, worrying. There was something missing. Something wrong.

She reached into the gap. What she felt made her recoil. It was soft and warm and slightly spongy. Some sort of quilted fibres. She pulled out a handful, sniffed it, examined it in the weakening beam of her torch. These batteries were dying now.

It was insulation, she guessed. Not to keep her warm, but for soundproofing.

Okay, she thought. Not insurmountable. Remove the soundproofing and enlarge the hole big enough to squeeze through. It should be a breeze from now on.

And she laughed. She really did. Because now she understood what was wrong.

'Should be a breeze,' she said aloud, and laughed again, her voice creaky and unused, shocking in the silence. The voice of a madwoman.

She put her face up to the hole and kept completely still, not even daring to breathe. Didn't feel as much as a tickle on her skin.

There was no breeze. No fresh air coming through the hole she had created.

She reached in, dug through the insulation and her knuckles hit solid rock. She pulled back, twisted to find another angle, tried again. Cold, smooth rock.

She punched it in frustration. Solid rock. No way out.

She was in a cell, and the cell was in a cave.

CHAPTER SIXTY-ONE

Monday dawned dry and blustery. Joe came down at seven to find Diana in the kitchen, singing along to the radio.

'No hangover?'

'No, I feel fine. Going to bed at eight o'clock probably helped.'

326

They ate breakfast together, without dwelling too much on yesterday's conversation. Seeing Diana so relaxed and chatty made Joe appreciate just how oppressively the weight of her past must have been bearing down on her.

'This wasn't a day I'd have wished on myself,' she had told him last night. 'But now it's happened, I'm glad. I feel liberated, in a way. And you've helped with that.'

Joe had denied being of much use, but decided privately that one reason to stick around was to ensure that her new-found liberation wasn't threatened by Leon or Glenn.

As he walked to work, he thought about confronting them right now: perhaps issue a few threats of his own. Tempting, but ultimately counter-productive, he decided.

Yesterday's insight continued to gnaw away at him. Leon's paranoia made the man a lot more dangerous. If he perceived Joe as a threat, how far would he go to neutralise it?

*　　　*　　　*

Kestle opened the door, wearing a Monday-morning face: not quite all there. He pointed Joe at the kitchen and shuffled away.

Glenn was busy schmoozing while Pam made bacon butties. She spotted him first, and asked about his weekend. Glenn turned and interrupted Joe's bland reply.

'You're out west today. Come on.'

'Hold up, my love,' Pam said. 'Let the poor man have a bite to eat.'

'Not hungry, thanks,' Joe said.

327

Glenn turned on him as soon as they were out of the kitchen. 'You keep away from Ellie, you hear?'

'She's divorced, because you cheated on her. It's for her to decide who she sees.'

Glenn shook his head, his lips clamped tightly shut, as though he didn't trust himself to speak. At the door to the living room Joe stopped and raised his hand: his turn.

'You upset Diana yesterday. If that happens again, I'll make you regret it. Do *you* hear *me*?'

'You don't talk to me like that, you fucking—' Glenn drew back his fist. A shout from the stairs caused him to freeze.

It was Leon, clad in his usual tracksuit bottoms and a baggy sweatshirt. Glenn's arm fell to his side. His frustrated growl sounded to Joe like an attempt to save face.

Leon gestured at the office. 'In here.' At the same time, Fenton emerged from the comms room, slipping something into his pocket. He looked startled by the tableau that greeted him. 'See to Joe,' Leon said, while Glenn followed him meekly into the office.

Joe grinned at the bemused Fenton. 'Monday mornings, eh?'

Fenton said nothing, just fetched a worksheet and the keys to a Ford Transit. Joe was crossing the hall when Reece and Todd came in. They saw him and broke apart, letting him walk between them. As he drew alongside both men leaned together, bumping Joe's shoulders. He might have been back at school, running the gauntlet of the kids whose self-esteem depended on constant petty violence.

'Unfinished business,' Reece muttered once Joe was past.

328

Joe turned, nodding. 'I haven't forgotten.'

*   *   *

His first stop was Truro, but before leaving town he called in at the greengrocer's. Karen was serving the shop's lone customer. Joe picked up a bunch of bananas and took it to the till.

'Don't suppose you've heard from Alise?' he said, handing her a five-pound note.

Karen frowned. 'Not a thing. The cow's done a bunk on me. I've got rent due next week and she was supposed to be paying half.'

She delved into the till to gather his change, then hesitated, as if hoping he might donate it to the shortfall in her rent.

He held his hand out for the coins and said, 'What about her things?'

'She hasn't got much. Just a few clothes and stuff. Though her case isn't bad. Gucci.' Karen brightened a little. 'I could sell it on eBay, I suppose.'

Since the van was facing downhill, Joe continued on to the plaza but found the library was closed. He'd have to call Ellie later.

At the seafront he went left, glancing at the gallery as he passed. That too was shut. Turning back to the road, he found a cyclist cutting across his path, heading for a section of dropped pavement. It was Patrick Davy, bundled up in a Berghaus ski jacket.

Joe braked, pulled in at the kerb and opened the passenger window. He leaned over the seat as Davy smoothly dismounted and rolled towards him, standing on one pedal. The Australian peered into the van, recognised Joe and came to a stop.

'What are you doing?' Davy said. He sounded confused, unhappy.

'I wanted to see if you've heard any more from Alise.'

Davy exhaled slowly. 'You've got a bloody nerve.'

'What?'

'This.' He rapped loudly on the roof of the van. 'This is one of Leon's. Christ, Joe, what do you take me for?'

Joe shook his head, cursing his own foolishness. 'It's not like that, I promise—'

'Oh yeah? You remember when I said they'll be smarter next time? I gave you the benefit of the doubt. Now here you are driving round in one of his bloody vans.'

Joe started to explain but Davy straightened up, only his outstretched palm visible in the window.

'Save it. Ever since they split my skull open I've had a low tolerance for bullshit.'

*   *   *

Mid-morning, Leon went for a run. The house was crowded and the mood tense: if he didn't take a break he'd end up with a migraine.

He'd had to give Glenn a dressing-down about his attitude to Joe. What had he been told yesterday? They'd all agreed it was vital to back off, keep tabs on the man but without spooking him until the deal with Danny Morton was completed. Fuckwit.

It was a cold, bright day, normally ideal for running, but there was a savage force to the wind. A fresh fall of leaves lay piled in the gutters and

330

skittered across the pavement into his path. Leon aimed for them when he could, enhancing the rhythm of his pace with the satisfying dry crunch of a crushed leaf.

He was almost at the seafront when a shout made him break his stride. He turned and saw Venning coming up fast. The small, lithe Welshman had once run marathons on a regular basis, and he kept himself in good shape.

Leon groaned. 'What's happened?'

'Nothing.' Venning had the decency to sound slightly out of breath. 'I wanted to talk to you . . . away from the house, like.' He looked around, checking the street was deserted. 'It's about Clive.'

'Yeah?'

'He asked me to do him this favour, said it was all fine with you. But I'm starting to wonder.'

'Go on, then. Spit it out.'

'Last Wednesday evening, you had a woman round?' When Leon's eyes narrowed Venning raised both hands. 'I don't know anything else, and I don't wanna know. I haven't even looked at it.'

'Looked at what?'

'The tape,' Venning said. 'Clive asked me to rig up a covert camera in the living room. He wanted to record what happened, so I made a tape, put it on a USB stick. But I don't have a clue what it contains, I swear.'

'Anyone else see it?'

'No. Well, nobody that works for you, that is.'

Leon put his hands on his hips. He leaned threateningly towards Venning. 'What the fuck do you mean by that?'

'The way Clive was talking, I got the impression Mr Cadwell was getting a copy.'

CHAPTER SIXTY-TWO

From Truro, Joe was sent to restock vending machines on a route that, just before midday, brought him to Newquay. As he descended into the town along Henver Road, he wished he knew more about Kamila's time here. Even the name of a café or pub she'd frequented would have been a place to start.

But he had tried Alise's phone again, to no avail, and the only other person who might know more was Patrick Davy. Joe suspected he would face an uphill battle to regain the Australian's trust.

At the next stop, in Perranporth, he spotted a fish and chip shop and awarded himself a brief lunch break. After he'd eaten, he called Ellie. She answered promptly, but with a certain wariness that didn't bode well.

'I wanted to warn you that Glenn knows about Saturday night.'

'He came round yesterday, tried laying down the law. I told him to piss off.'

Relieved that she was unscathed, Joe suggested they have a drink tomorrow night, and she readily agreed. Afterwards, as he put the phone away, there was a spiteful voice in his head, asking what on earth he thought he was doing, making plans and looking to the future, as though he could hope to live a normal life. Who was he kidding?

*   *   *

Leon sent Venning away, then crossed the road to

332

the beach and took a walk along the shore. A better place to get his thoughts in order.

The timing couldn't have been worse: just when he needed to focus on the deal with Danny Morton. They'd got a contact number this morning, and agreed that Fenton should be the one to get in touch. Now he tried to remember *whose* idea that had been. Every discussion, every decision would have to be re-examined in the same way.

But he mustn't overreact, either. Fenton and Cadwell weren't necessarily plotting against him. There were other, far more simple reasons why the pair would want film of Alise being tortured.

Perverts but maybe not traitors. That conclusion cheered him, until he realised that he hadn't actually planned to hurt Alise on Wednesday night. Why had they got the cameras set up in advance?

Because they know me so bloody well. He might have to shake things up a bit. Spring a few surprises.

By the time he reached home he was worrying again. Regardless of their motives, the crucial fact was that they now had solid evidence of Leon committing a serious crime. It was like they'd placed a bomb beneath him and set it ticking.

He found Fenton quivering with excitement. 'It's done. Two o'clock tomorrow, at a hotel near Ascot.'

Leon scowled. 'Morton's choice of location, then?'

Fenton gave him an uncertain look. 'Well, yes. It required a great deal of persuasion just to agree a meeting without divulging the reason for it.'

Realising that he ought to be pleased, Leon managed to lose the scowl. 'What d'you make of him?'

Now it was Fenton who turned sour. 'Normally I'd recommend giving him a very wide berth, but needs must.'

'This is too good a chance to miss.'

'Precisely.' Fenton went on studying Leon. 'Is everything all right?'

'Yes, thanks, Clive. Just a lot on my mind.'

Leon tried to relax. Fenton had no reason to betray him. If he did, where would he go? He'd had a high-flying career with a big accountancy firm, but had departed in a hurry as a result of 'personal issues'. He wouldn't talk about it, but Leon knew there had been numerous complaints from his female colleagues.

With Cadwell, it was different. Derek's business would continue to thrive, no matter what happened to Leon. And Cadwell might see this as payback: a richly appropriate form of payback.

As if he'd read Leon's mind, Fenton said, 'I've suggested that Derek come over this afternoon. Get our heads together about tomorrow.'

'Do we need him in on that?'

Fenton took it calmly enough. 'I don't see why not.'

Leon stared at Fenton, his eyes cold. He clamped his jaws together.

'The more the better, surely?' Fenton added.

Leon shrugged. 'If you say so, Clive.'

*   *   *

An accident on the A39 delayed Joe's return to Trelennan. It was relatively recent: an ambulance and two police cars arrived while he was waiting, some thirty cars back.

It wasn't until the traffic began edging forward that he spotted the paramedics working on someone at the side of the road. A cluster of civilians stood nearby, one of them being comforted, sobbing and gesturing while a uniformed officer tried to get information from her.

A couple more cars got past, and Joe saw a bicycle lying on the verge, the rear wheel mangled out of shape. The casualty was a young boy, a teenager. One of the paramedics had placed an oxygen mask over his face. Someone else was holding his hand.

Joe shivered. As a child he had been knocked down by a car. He still dreamed about it occasionally, saw himself lying there while the newly qualified doctor who'd happened to be passing saved his life.

The car ahead pulled away, but for a moment Joe was back in the Shell Cavern, cold and disorientated, trapped; someone crying out in the darkness . . .

Then he was past the scene, and thinking of the missing women: Kamila, Alise, the girl Diana had mentioned; others, possibly, over the years.

Joe knew that seaside communities were a magnet for runaways, partly for the seasonal employment opportunities, as well as for the anonymity inherent in towns whose populations swelled with tourists. From his own experience, Joe felt there was another reason, too: the melancholy pull of the sea itself.

The official figures were extraordinary: over two hundred thousand people went missing every year in the UK. Even with ninety-nine per cent of cases resolved swiftly, that still left a couple of thousand people who vanished into thin air, year after year. Joe, like many police officers, had always believed a significant number were murder victims whose bodies were never found—and their killers never caught.

That was the key point here. And from what Joe had seen, some kind of conspiracy was certainly feasible, perhaps using Derek Cadwell to dispose of the bodies. But Joe also knew that conspiracies were inherently unstable. People got scared. They made mistakes, spoke out of turn. They were prey to blackmail and extortion. For Leon to be getting away with it for so long he'd have to be very careful, or very lucky, or both.

With that thought came an image, an idea; it floated through Joe's mind but stayed tantalisingly out of reach. He was still chasing it into the shadows when he reached the big stone house and parked under the car port. Kestle signed him off for the day, then told him to be here an hour earlier tomorrow.

'You've got deliveries in Glastonbury.'

'Okay,' Joe said, careful to conceal his excitement. Glastonbury was only twenty or thirty miles south of Bristol. Touching distance.

*   *   *

Cadwell turned up at five. He didn't seem to notice anything amiss, despite the anxious glances Fenton kept casting in Leon's direction.

An afternoon nap hadn't done much to improve Leon's state of mind. Sitting in the office with Fenton, Cadwell and Glenn, toying with the CCTV feed on his laptop, he could feel the distant pulse

336

of another migraine, like a storm gathering over the horizon. He wasn't sure now if he could trust any of them.

Even Glenn had a question mark over him. He'd done plenty of building work for them both over the years. Fenton in particular had wanted Glenn to remodel his entire house, despite spending most of his time here.

'It's essential to get this right,' Fenton kept saying. 'We mustn't overplay our hand the way Victor did. Equally, we mustn't fail to exploit the full potential of this opportunity.'

'Got to be worth a million or two,' Glenn said. 'The Mortons are loaded, I take it?'

'Not officially,' Fenton said. 'They have a network of shell companies. Perfectly adequate,' he said with a sneer, 'but not as sophisticated as our own set-up.'

'That won't stop them from treating us like yokels,' Leon said.

'All the more reason to present ourselves as professionals. Ambitious, not greedy.'

'Rather than just cash,' Cadwell interjected, 'what about going for a stake in their operation?'

From the exaggerated way that Fenton was nodding, Leon guessed they had discussed it in advance. He gave a thin smile as Fenton said: 'It's an option to explore, from a tactical viewpoint if nothing else.'

'How do you mean?' Leon asked.

'If they baulk at paying out so much cash, we suggest an equity deal. Suddenly our original request doesn't seem so unreasonable.'

'I like that,' Cadwell agreed, wagging a finger. 'That could work very nicely.'

Leon had to choke down a sarcastic comment. Glenn, who looked every bit as bored with it all as Leon, scratched his head and said, 'So who's going tomorrow?'

'Me, you and Clive,' Leon said. 'We need some muscle with us as well.'

'Not Reece,' Fenton said. 'He flies off the handle at the slightest provocation.'

'Could show them we mean business . . .'

Fenton shook his head. Leon sensed that Cadwell agreed but had suddenly gone shy.

'It's your decision, obviously,' Fenton said. 'But Morton, by all accounts, is a volatile individual. The last thing we want is an all-out war because Reece didn't like the way someone was looking at him.'

'And they probably will try to intimidate us,' Glenn added.

'Maybe Bruce, then.' Leon winced at a spasm of pain. Shut his eyes.

'Sore head?' Glenn enquired.

'Migraine.'

'Another one already?' Fenton said.

Cadwell tutted. 'You ought to go to the doctor.'

'One day.' Leon spat the words out. All this fucking advice, he'd never really seen it for what it was: manipulation. Pushing and pulling and nudging him into the position that suited them best.

He willed the pain away. Opened his eyes to find Joe Carter, caught on CCTV as he parked the van.

'Keeping him busy?' he asked Glenn, who nodded, still sulking over this morning's confrontation.

Leon switched cameras, followed Joe into the house and studied him carefully as he talked to Kestle. At least Joe's body language was relaxed:

338

that was one good thing.

He didn't have a clue, Leon thought.

CHAPTER SIXTY-THREE

On Tuesday Joe woke to light but steady rain. Once again, he came down to find Diana already busy in the kitchen. Only a week and they were settling into a routine.

Last night he had told her that he would probably revert to his original plan and leave at the end of the week. Diana had dismissed his fear of reprisals. 'They wouldn't be that stupid.'

'Has Glenn been in touch since Sunday?'

'He keeps calling and texting.' She smiled. 'I've ignored every one of them so far.'

With no sign of the rain letting up, she insisted on driving him to Leon's. He was wearing the jacket he'd bought in Bristol, and for good measure he had the cap with him as well: a disguise for his return to Lindsey Bevan's.

Kestle had his paperwork ready. There was no sign of Pam—or anyone else, for that matter. 'They're out today. Big meeting somewhere.' Then he clammed up, perhaps aware that he'd said more than was advisable to a colleague who was still far from trusted.

Before Joe left, Kestle popped into the comms room, came out with a newspaper and offered it to Joe, who shook his head.

'Not to my taste, thanks.'

'Leon's orders.' Kestle slapped it into his hand. 'Everyone gets a copy.'

One of Leon's cast-iron rules was that any vehicle he travelled in wasn't to exceed the speed limit, particularly outside of their local area. It was because of something he'd been told about Al Capone, how after years of criminal activity he'd finally gone down for tax evasion. Same with keeping the fleet roadworthy, properly taxed and insured.

'If they can't get you on the big things,' he'd been warned, 'they'll be just as happy to get you on the little things. All they need is a way in.'

Today, with Bruce behind the wheel of a brand-new Range Rover, there was a constant danger that Leon's rule would be broken. He got tired of reminding him to slow down, and the others got tired of hearing it.

'I don't reckon you should worry, not now.' Glenn was on the back seat, next to Fenton. He tapped the newspaper spread out over his knees. 'If the cops pull us over, you just have to show 'em this. You'd get away with anything.'

Leon snorted, trying not to show how pleased he was. Since receiving an advance copy of the article on Sunday, he'd already memorised the key phrases.

The town that puts 'Broken Britain' to shame: he liked that.

He's an unlikely-looking saviour, the article began, then spoiled it with a snooty put-down of his dress sense before going on to say: *but this rough-and-ready bruiser from the wilds of Cornwall could teach us all a lesson about the creation of a safe,*

340

family-friendly society.

There was a giddy atmosphere as they pored over the article, reading sections aloud to each other and mildly taking the piss out of the photos. Leon thought they were superb: a nice big portrait of him out on the veranda, and then the photo-op from last week, cropped to show just Leon, some mayor in a dodgy toupee, and the chief constable.

Glenn quoted the caption beneath the portrait. *'Leon Race: A shining example of the Big Society at work.'*

Leon scoffed. 'Don't have a clue what that means.'

'I could explain, but it's horribly dull and a lot of nonsense,' Fenton said.

'Services coming up,' Bruce announced.

'Hope you got a pen on you,' Glenn said.

'What?'

'For the autographs.'

'Ha, ha.' Leon made a play at leaning into the back and swatting Glenn, but they could all tell he was delighted by the idea.

*   *   *

Joe decided it was a good omen that Leon was away from Trelennan. With any luck he'd sneak over to Bristol for a couple of hours and no one would be any the wiser.

After loading up at the depot in Glastonbury, he studied the delivery route and decided to make the detour from his fourth call of the day, in Trowbridge. He was thrilled by the prospect of regaining his possessions; being able to make plans for the future.

Tonight, when he saw Ellie, he would have to tell her that he was leaving soon. Not without regrets, because there was no denying the attraction he felt towards her. But he was never going to be settling down to a life of domestic bliss in Trelennan, not least because—as Ellie had pointed out—at heart he was still married.

And he wasn't a delivery driver. He wasn't a painter and decorator, a hotel porter, a farm worker, or any of the other roles that had sustained him over the past few years.

He was a police officer. A detective. An undercover cop. He was a man who had flourished in a world of lies and deception. That was why he had gone to work for Leon Race. That was why he continued to pursue the mystery of Alise's disappearance. A sucker for lost causes, perhaps.

Because he was a lost cause himself . . .

His phone buzzed. He was on the A303, doing a steady forty in a line of traffic stuck behind an Eddie Stobart truck. He glanced at the display. An unfamiliar number, from a landline. The area code was 01503. Not Trelennan.

There was a junction coming up, bordered by a wide grass verge. Joe swung the van off the main road and bumped up onto the grass, fumbling with the phone before he lost the call.

'Hello?'

'Joe? Is that you?'

The voice was female, but low-pitched, guttural, as though the caller had a bad throat infection. He wouldn't have identified her, had it not been for the accent.

'Alise?'

CHAPTER SIXTY-FOUR

Silence.

'Alise?' he said again. 'Are you there?'

What he'd taken for the buzz of static was her breathing, close to the mouthpiece.

'Joe. Will you help me?'

'Where are you? I've been trying to reach you for days.' He was trying not to sound exasperated, but a hint of irritation must have shown. She gave a sob.

'They take my phone. I had your number in my head, but I could not call. I was in hospital until last night.'

'Hospital? What happened?'

Another sob. 'It was Leon. Leon tried to kill me.'

*   *   *

The meeting wasn't until two, but Leon had insisted on an early start. The migraine had receded overnight and he didn't want to give it any reason to come storming back. That meant a nice steady journey. No stress.

That was the key thing today. The newspaper article had lifted his spirits, and after a greasy, overpriced breakfast he settled back and let the motion of the car lull him into a pleasant state of semi-consciousness.

As they skirted around Reading the rain petered out and the clouds thinned to a pale grey membrane stretched across the sky. Leon roused himself, sat up straight and had a few gulps of water from the bottle that Glenn carried.

Time to focus. Like an actor, Leon had to think himself into the part he was playing. The main thing to remember, he told himself, was that he held the winning hand.

The hotel was set in acres of manicured grounds, complete with its own golf course. It was accessed via a private road, lined with mature trees ablaze with autumn colours. Leon wasn't normally one for nature, but even he was impressed by the dazzling reds and golds.

The lawns were like the baize on a snooker table. In the distance he spotted little white carts trundling back and forth, golfers in their ridiculous costumes ambling across the greens.

The hotel itself was like a palace from a fairy tale, a sprawling white building with towers and turrets galore. Bruce parked as close to the entrance as he could get. Leon opened his door and stepped down onto the gravel. The air was rich with wood smoke, but what it truly reeked of was money.

For reasons he couldn't explain, Leon took against the place at once.

At Fenton's suggestion, to save them from rushing back, they'd booked rooms at another hotel nearby. Once the deal was concluded they could retire for a celebratory dinner. The champagne would be waiting on ice when they checked in.

Leon wasn't fussed either way about that, but he was glad they'd chosen another hotel. He hadn't even set foot inside this place and already he was eager to get away.

They clustered at the rear of the Range Rover, keyed up, anxious to project the right image. As a concession, Leon had worn jeans and a shirt with a collar. Fenton and Glenn were in suits, while Bruce had gone for cargo pants and a tight muscle vest that advertised his brute strength.

It was one-thirty. Leon rubbed his hands together. His palms were slightly damp. This felt like a job interview, or a court appearance. Something to be endured.

'Ready?' he said.

There were nods, a few encouraging murmurs. For a second he thought of getting them all to bump fists or high five, like a sports team before the whistle blew.

But that was all bollocks. It would either go well or it wouldn't.

'Let's do it,' he said.

             *   *   *

Joe had been heading towards Wincanton when Alise called. It turned out she was in Looe, over a hundred miles south-west of him—and in the opposite direction to Bristol. Going to see Alise now would mean abandoning the chance to retrieve his possessions.

He wasn't conflicted for long. Dreaming up an excuse took even less time. He rang the number he'd been given for Leon's home. Kestle answered, and Joe gave him a convincing account of a mysterious engine failure.

He claimed to be near Yeovil, in case they sent someone looking for him, and said a local garage was sending a breakdown truck. Kestle started on about one of their guys in Shaftesbury who might be able to help, so Joe pretended the signal was failing. He cut the call and switched his phone off.

The route to Looe was simple enough: a

345

succession of A roads with stretches of dual-carriageway. The downside was that the rain hadn't let up, and in places the road surface was treacherous. Joe had to find a delicate balance between driving safely for the conditions while also urging the most speed he could get from the tired, noisy van.

It took him nearly two and a half hours, with only a swift toilet break at the Harcombe Cross services. He drove with his full attention on the road, deliberately refusing to let his mind wander; not brooding or speculating on anything.

Descending into the Looe valley, between undulating hills of woodland and fields, he was struck by the contrast with the wild and rugged north coast of Cornwall. The landscapes in the south seemed gentler, more tamed, but in their own way just as beautiful.

Looe consisted of two settlements either side of a river mouth. Despite the dreary weather, Joe's first sight of the wide tidal estuary took his breath away. Nestled snugly in its valley, the town had the feel of a natural sanctuary from the world; by contrast, Trelennan crouched on its wooded slopes like something lying in wait for the unwary.

He followed the directions he'd been given and parked close to the railway station in East Looe. Then a short walk to the seafront, through a maze of narrow streets filled with gift shops and restaurants.

It was half past one when Joe entered a large, characterless café close to the beach. He hadn't eaten anything since breakfast, but what appetite he had vanished the moment he set eyes on Alise.

He had to stop and stare before he was sure it

346

was her. She was in a booth, sitting tight against the wall, her handbag and a menu placed strategically on the edge of the table, as if to shield her from the other patrons. She was wearing a grey roll-neck jumper and a white knitted beret, as well as a comically large pair of sunglasses. Retro style, he guessed.

As Joe approached, she glanced round, smiled weakly and removed the sunglasses. There was nothing comical about what they had concealed.

Her face was a mass of bruises and abrasions. A large swelling around her left eye caused her temple to bulge outwards, the skin black and purple, stretched so tightly that it looked like it was about to burst. There were scabs on her lip and a laceration on her chin that had needed half a dozen stitches: he could see the raw pinpricks where they had recently been removed.

Alise rose to her feet, as frail and unsteady as a woman twice her age. Her hands were scratched and bruised. She embraced Joe, clutched him tightly and thanked him. Joe brushed off her gratitude as unneeded, almost inappropriate.

He wouldn't say it out loud, but what he thought was quite straightforward, and totally resolute.

Thank me when I've dealt with the men who did this to you.

CHAPTER SIXTY-FIVE

Leon hung back in the hotel lobby, content to let somebody else go to the desk. He felt excluded enough without having the staff looking down their

347

noses at him.

Fenton returned with directions and led them into the depths of the hotel. It was all marble floors and chandeliers and statues; an atrium with a bloody great fountain. Leon tried not to notice because he knew he was supposed to be impressed, and he didn't want anything in here to impress him.

He found he was clawing at his leg as he walked, literally trying to get a grip on himself. A voice chattering nonsense in his head, like a madman in the corner of the room.

What was wrong with him, for Christ's sake?

Morton had hired one of the hotel's conference suites. In similar rooms they glimpsed rows of sad suits, hypnotised by spreadsheets on a whiteboard. Fenton and Glenn were joking about 'death by PowerPoint' but Leon growled at them to shut up. It was white noise, and all it did was draw the next migraine a bit closer.

The anteroom outside the Branson Suite was guarded by two men in suits. Not the usual gorillas: they were smaller than Glenn, let alone Bruce, but they had a quiet, purposeful manner that conveyed a lot of menace. Leon could see a slight bulge in their jackets, about where a shoulder holster would be.

He felt his mouth go dry. He turned to gauge what the others made of all this, but no one would meet his eye. Then Fenton was handing him a phone, though Leon hadn't even heard him take a call. *What the hell . . .*

He grabbed the phone, backing away from the guards. 'Yeah?'

It was Kestle. 'Thought you should know, boss. I just got a call from Joe. The van's broke down on him and he can't make his rounds today.'

'What?' Leon must have shouted: everyone was staring at him. 'Where is he?'

'Yeovil. Says he's been on to a garage and he's waiting for them to come out. I've tried ringing back to find out more, but his phone's off.'

Leon groaned. He didn't have a single clear thought that made any sense. At the door, Fenton was talking quietly with one of the men. Glenn, listening in, turned to Leon and shrugged a question. As though Leon was a bloody mind-reader.

He was still focused on Joe. The vans did a lot of mileage. From time to time things went wrong with them, so the breakdown could be genuine. On the other hand, it could mean he'd got wind of their plan and was doing a runner . . .

Victor Smith's words came back to him: *If I sold him to Danny Morton and couldn't deliver, I'd be a dead man.*

'Keep on it,' he told Kestle. 'Let me know as soon as you speak to him.'

Glenn was ready with the next problem. 'They want us to hand over our phones.'

As Leon marched over, one of the guards shifted his stance, his jacket falling open. 'These are our standard security measures,' the other one was saying. 'Not negotiable, under any circumstances.'

'What are they?' Leon asked.

The guard turned to a small table and picked up two hand-held body scanners. 'You submit to a check with these. No phones, watches, jewellery or electronic devices allowed through. And a maximum of three people go in.' He pointed at Bruce. 'I suggest he remains with us.' His voice

349

was well educated, with that strange honking tone people had in the South-East.

Talking through their noses as well as looking down them, Leon thought. He pulled Fenton aside. 'Joe called to say his van broke down. Now he's turned his phone off.'

Fenton's eyes widened. He did his gulping-goldfish act.

'Yeah, I dunno what it means either,' Leon snarled. 'Let's just get this done.'

He stepped towards the guards, opening his arms in surrender.

*   *   *

Six days ago Joe had sat in a café with Alise and listened to the account of her sister's disappearance. Now he heard the story of her own.

She'd been abducted by three or four men, just a couple of hours after parting from Joe. Probably while Leon was offering him a job. Later she got a look at them; from her descriptions he identified Reece and Todd, and possibly the man he'd met out on the deck the other day. Bruce somebody.

That night she'd been taken to Leon's home and interrogated, brutally, by Leon himself. He had inflicted many of her injuries, the worst of which was a fracture to her eye socket. The doctors had told her she was lucky to have kept her sight.

Joe felt overcome: by shame, because he'd been so tempted to dismiss her allegations; then by shock at the severity of her injuries. Next came guilt, because essentially Alise had been punished for talking to him.

Finally, deep down, building slowly and

350

methodically, there was rage, and a desire for vengeance.

Once Leon had had his fun, Alise was force-fed a bottle of vodka, driven to the Rame Peninsula, south of Plymouth, and thrown over a cliff. Her body had rolled down the steep grass bank and onto the rocky beach below. By pure fluke she'd landed just above the high-tide mark, otherwise she would have drowned.

'A man with his dog found me the next morning. My body was so cold, he thought I was dead. In hospital they say I had one more hour, maybe less.'

Rushed to intensive care, Alise didn't properly regain consciousness until Saturday. It was only when a duty psychiatrist came to conduct a mental-health assessment that she realised the assumption everyone had made.

'They think I have tried to kill myself. Exactly as Leon plans it to be.'

Joe couldn't argue with that. The fall onto the rocks conveniently explained her injuries, and her backstory—a futile search for her missing sister, the threatened loss of her job and her relationship—completed an ideal scenario for suicide. Joe felt certain that would have been the coroner's verdict at the inquest.

'Did you tell anyone what really happened?'

'A policewoman came while I am still confused. The things I say make no sense. Later, when I start to feel better, I see there is no point telling the truth. I cannot prove it happened this way. So next time I say I don't remember.' She leaned towards him. 'You see why Leon is so dangerous? You believe me now that he killed my sister?'

Alise's hands were gripped together to stop them

351

shaking. Joe placed his own hand over them. He nodded.

'Yes, I do.'

* * *

Being patted down and checked with the electronic wand was humiliating. Leon endured it by closing his eyes and pretending he was at an airport, where everybody had to put up with this shit.

They gave his shoes a thorough going-over before handing them back, but they held on to his watch and his belt. Fenton and Glenn must have sensed how close he was to storming out because they shuffled into formation behind him, blocking his exit.

The Branson Suite was big enough for about fifty people. In one corner there was a stack of tables and chairs, piled up the way they used to be at school. A couple of tables had been placed end to end in the centre of the room, like a barrier, with chairs on each side. Three vacant seats with their backs to the door: for Leon's team.

On the other side, three more chairs. The middle one was empty, the other two were occupied by men who looked far from comfortable in their tight suits. Not neat and civilised, like the guards on the door. One had long matted hair and the other had a buzz cut around a bald spot the size of a saucer. Both were unshaven, with bad skin and bad teeth. They looked mean and greasy and savage. Thugs.

At the sight of them, Leon relaxed a little. These were men from his own world: council estates, broken families, vicious competition for scarce resources and feral, ruthless violence from the

352

moment you could grab and run.

Leon spotted movement across the room, almost lost in the shadows of the colossal floor-to-ceiling drapes. A man and a woman, standing close together. The woman had long black hair, in dazzling contrast to her crisp white blouse.

Glenn noticed her, too, and blew out a loud breath in appreciation. She was slim and curvy, in a tight grey pencil skirt, split to show a sliver of thigh. Like a secretary in a decent-quality porno, Leon thought.

By comparison, the man was pretty forgettable. Unlike the others, he was in jeans and a black T-shirt. He was average height, wiry, with short spiky brown hair. Although he must have heard them come in, he kept his back to them, as though he couldn't give a shit who had just joined the party.

With a terse nod at the other two, Leon pulled the middle chair a foot or so back from the table and sat down. Glenn and Fenton followed suit, sitting each side of him.

Finally the man at the window turned and wandered towards them, sighing with vague irritation, as though this was another minor chore on a long list. He was rubbing absently at his cheek, and when he dropped his hand Leon saw the puckered scar of an old puncture wound.

'Mr Morton?' Fenton rose to his feet and extended his hand.

The man nodded. He sat down without responding to the handshake. Leon snorted, remembering how he'd done the same thing to the journalist.

'Thank you for agreeing to this meeting,' Fenton went on. 'I'm confident that you'll agree it will be

353

tremendously beneficial—'

'You're in charge, yeah?' Danny Morton flapped a hand at Leon. His eyes were small and dark, like buttons.

'Yeah. I'm Leon Race.'

'So how about you do the talking, while Mr Blobby here shuts his fucking cakehole?'

Silence. Morton's men smirked. Leon couldn't see Fenton or Glenn's reaction, and he didn't want to look. The woman was still by the far wall, ignoring them completely.

'You ever heard the word "entrapment"?' Morton asked.

'What?'

'Entrapment. You know what it means?'

Leon took a deep breath. Told himself this didn't matter. It was like Glenn had said: Morton was trying to wind him up.

'Course I know what it is. Why?'

'Are you the filth?'

'What? No, I'm not the fucking filth.' The caution he'd given himself just a second before was instantly forgotten. He wanted to tear Morton's heart out.

'You're working for them, though? An undercover agent or something?'

Fenton tried to speak: 'Mr Morton, I can't for the life of me conceive what—'

Morton silenced him with a shake of his head. 'You were sent here by the cops, weren't you?'

Leon was speechless. This was just about the worst insult he could imagine. He felt his pulse racing; the answering thump of his migraine as the bugle call of stress rang out: *Yes, I'll come and play . . .*

354

He got hold of himself, took another deep, steadying breath and gave Danny Morton his best man-to-man, straight-talking look. 'What the *fuck* do you mean by that?'

Morton raised one arm in the air, as if hailing a cab. The woman marched over and slapped a rolled-up newspaper into his hand like a relay racer passing the baton. Morton opened it out, slapped it down on the table and jabbed a finger at the photograph of Leon, glad-handing the mayor and the chief constable.

'This,' he said. 'This is what I *fucking* mean.'

CHAPTER SIXTY-SIX

Joe ordered coffee and a ham sandwich. Alise accepted a glass of juice. She wasn't eating much, she said, partly because the pain medication left her slightly nauseous, and partly because several teeth were loose. It was touch and go whether they'd heal.

'What made you come here?' Joe asked. 'Why not back to London?'

'Because I have nothing there. In hospital I was able to check email. My company have made me redundant.'

Joe tutted. 'I'm sorry to hear that.'

'Plus I am still seeing doctors in Plymouth. Someone had told me Looe was nice, so I thought . . . why not? I like it here. The lady at hotel is very kind.'

'And what about the other reason?'

To her credit, Alise didn't pretend to be confused by his question. What he got was a short, harsh sigh.

'Now more than ever before, I have to know what happened to Kamila.'

'Is that why you called me?'

'I suppose. You believed in me. I went away so happy, so excited, sure that you would help me. Now Leon has done this, it is certain he hurt Kamila.' Her voice became cold. 'Killed her, probably. This is what we have to think now, yes?'

'What happened to Kamila isn't necessarily the same thing that happened to you.' Alise started to protest, but Joe raised his hand to placate her. 'I want to know more about Derek Cadwell. No one else seems to have heard this rumour you mentioned.'

She withdrew into herself. He could see pain in her eyes. And guilt.

'Please,' he said. 'If you really know something, tell me how you found out.'

'You remember the man we see in the café? Ben?'

'He told you the secret?' Joe recalled how the man had glared at Alise.

'Yes. He was at the funeral home one night. Cadwell thought he had gone. There was the body of . . . a young girl.' Alise shuddered. 'Cadwell . . . was undressing.'

'And Leon filmed it?'

'Later Ben hears about a camera hidden in the room. Leon knew this is valuable information, but not if rumours get out, because then Cadwell's business is finished. It is kept very secret.'

'So how come Ben told you?'

Her eyes closed and opened in a slow, deliberate blink: *You work it out.*

356

And then he did. 'Oh, Alise. I'm sorry.'

She gave a defiant flick of her head. 'Why sorry? It is my decision, my shame. For Kamila, I become a whore.' A quiet sob escaped from her throat.

'That's not what you are.'

Alise shrugged. 'I don't care. To stop Leon, I would do anything.'

This was the first time she'd stated an objective beyond learning what had become of her sister. It was perfectly understandable under the circumstances.

'I can appreciate how you feel, but it's not quite as simple as that.'

'You tell me this? You think I do not know?' She shook her head in disgust. 'The police will not listen, so we must do something else.'

'What?'

'Kill him.'

Joe automatically glanced round, but the café's other customers appeared to be taking no interest in them. When he looked back Alise was studying him carefully, a sympathetic smile on her face. Behind the smile, rock-solid determination.

'If you say no, fine. I understand. I do it myself. I wait till I am stronger, and then kill him.'

*　　　　*　　　　*

'What d'you come here for?' Morton asked. He was slouched in his seat, legs splayed, as if to demonstrate how angry he could be when he was relaxed.

'It's a business proposition,' Fenton offered.

'Not the monkey. The organ grinder.' Morton spat the words, staring hard at Leon.

357

'We want to do a deal with you.'

'What kind of deal?'

Once again, Leon was struck dumb. Start off cagey and it would look weak, suspicious. But if he came right out with it, he'd have no other cards to play.

'I'm not going into detail till I know if we can trust you.'

Morton laughed. 'Why'd you think I'd be interested in a deal with you?' He put one foot on the table, stamping his heel on the newspaper. 'This says you're squeaky clean. Got your tongue up the arse of any number of cops and politicians and fucking journalists.'

Leon shook his head. 'Ignore what that says. It has nothing to do with this meeting. I didn't even realise it was coming out.'

'You didn't realise—or maybe you thought I wouldn't see it,' Morton echoed. 'Either way, you fucked up big time.'

The comment drew sniggers from the men either side of him. Even the woman, who'd retreated to the back of the room, turned and smiled. Leon looked away in disgust and caught Glenn eyeing her up.

'The article's bullshit,' he told Morton. 'But it gets the police off my back.'

'A deliberate strategy on our part,' Fenton confirmed. 'Whatever your concerns, please believe that we are quite genuine. We have a very valuable proposal for you.'

Morton didn't seem any more convinced. 'Babe,' he said, clicking his fingers.

The woman approached, her head tilted to one side. Her expression indicated that she was listening

358

to something. Leon leaned slightly and saw she was wearing an earpiece.

'We safe?' Morton asked her. 'Nobody listening in?'

'Absolutely.'

'Good.' He dragged his foot off the table, slapped his knees and sat up straight. 'The thing is, Leon, I'm a villain. I make a living from the proceeds of crime, and I'm proud of it. I'm also proud that in more than twenty years I've only spent three of 'em inside, and I don't intend to ever repeat that experience. But what I won't do is go sucking up to the filth. If my picture's in the paper it means something's gone seriously fucking wrong.'

More laughter, but Morton wasn't done yet. He signalled at the woman, who stood at his shoulder, gazing serenely into the middle distance. She cleared her throat and began to speak.

'Leon Race, age thirty-six. Born and resides in North Cornwall. Parents deceased. Undistinguished family, no accomplishments of note.'

Her voice was like a TV newsreader's, calm and smooth. The words rolled out so swiftly that Leon barely understood them, but he felt a sick heat prickling the pores on his face.

'Raised on a council estate, Race was a hooligan and small-time criminal until the age of seventeen. He then spent approximately three years living in Cheltenham as a result of meeting Terence Povey-Jones, alias Raymond T. Lockhart, disgraced peer, convicted fraudster and predatory homosexual.'

'What about that, eh?' Danny was addressing Clive and Glenn, realising they were in the dark. 'Your boss shacked up with Pervy Povey, as I think

359

he used to be called.'

Leon was rigid with shock. He'd never told anybody about the man who had set him on the path of a careful, lucrative and seemingly law-abiding career.

'He was a poof, but he never went near me,' Leon said. Danny Morton just raised his eyebrows and motioned for the woman to continue.

'The exact nature of their relationship is unknown,' she said, and somehow that snide phrase hurt Leon more than an outright accusation. 'Following Povey-Jones's death in 1994, from an AIDs-related illness, Leon returned to his home town with the funds to launch his first business. Originally involved in the drugs trade, in recent years his illegal activity has been restricted to money laundering on behalf of several long-term associates. His current earnings are primarily achieved through legitimate means.' A brief smile, and she was done.

What followed was the most excruciating silence Leon had ever known. Danny Morton watched him through narrowed eyes, a born predator.

'You think I'd let you come swanning in here without knowing anything about you?' He shook his head. 'Sure, you haven't done bad, given your start in life. But you're still a fucking hick, running a two-bit outfit in the back of beyond. What can you offer us?'

Fenton opened his mouth, shut it again at a look from Morton.

'Either you've got ideas above your station, and you reckon I'll agree to a deal where you do better out of it than me. Or it's some kind of trick. Maybe your buddies in blue thought sending a dumbfuck yokel would make me less suspicious. But I ain't falling for it.'

Leon didn't respond. He wasn't processing the words any more. Morton was just a noisy snarl of hate. Instead he concentrated on the voice in his head, working on him like anaesthetic, softly chanting: *You're never gonna get him. You're never gonna get him. You're never gonna get him.*

Fenton made a last attempt at rescue. 'Mr Morton, please. None of what you've said is relevant to the offer we have for you.'

'So what is it?' Danny said. 'If you're genuine, put your cards on the table right now. If you're not, fuck off out of my sight and don't ever come back.'

But Fenton wasn't authorised to say. He sent Leon a silent plea: *Please tell him. Put us all out of our misery.*

Leon understood the desperation, but he couldn't do it. He'd been humiliated to a point beyond his worst nightmares. He would rather die than give this man anything at all.

'I don't trust you,' he said. He knew he sounded like an amateur. Compared to Morton, he *was* an amateur.

'So what the fuck are you doing here?'

'I-I thought we could talk—'

'Ah, that's nice. Get to know each other first?' Danny put on a simpering voice, pursing his lips into a kiss. 'You don't go all the way on a first date, is that what you're saying?'

Leon wanted to throw himself across the table and throttle Morton with his bare hands, but the men who guarded him were alert to that possibility. They'd cut him down in a second.

Suddenly Leon knew that never in his life had

he felt as stupid and worthless as he did right now. There was no way back from this, no way out but defeat, and the only thing that allowed him to keep any pride or dignity at all was the knowledge that he could at least deny Morton the ultimate prize, even though Morton himself wouldn't know it.

Joe's all mine, and you're never gonna get him.

CHAPTER SIXTY-SEVEN

Joe ran through what had happened since last Wednesday. He was cautious when it came to explaining how and why he'd gone to work for Leon Race. The last thing he wanted was a repeat of the reaction he'd provoked from Patrick Davy, but if anything Alise was too excited about it.

'So you see Leon, at the house? You can get close to him?'

'Alise, I'm not going to assassinate him.'

With a certain reluctance, she nodded, listening patiently as he described his visit to Jamie Pearse.

'He says Kamila called him, around the time she last spoke to you, boasting that she'd found someone else.'

'Leon,' Alise murmured.

'Possibly.' Joe paused. 'Pearse also claims that Kamila ran out on him after stealing a lot of money and valuables.'

Alise sighed so heavily that Joe felt awful for adding to her burdens. 'I keep asking her, how do you pay for this travelling? How much did this man give to you? Always she hid from the questions.'

She dabbed at her eyes, very gingerly, with the

362

edge of her hand. 'If Kamila did this, she would have a reason. It changes nothing for me.'

'Nor me,' Joe said. 'And I'll do what I can to help you.' To avoid a show of gratitude that he knew he didn't deserve, he added, 'But I'm worried about you staying here.'

She shrugged off the concern. 'No one knows I am in Looe.'

'Maybe not. But they're probably monitoring the local news, waiting to hear that your body was discovered on the Rame peninsula. If they think you've survived, they might already be on the search.'

She absorbed the warning, her expression solemn, then said simply: 'I will take the chance.' The glint in her eyes told Joe he'd achieve little by arguing.

He could see she was getting tired, so he accompanied her back to her hotel, which turned out to be virtually opposite the railway station. Alise moved slowly and with difficulty, limping from a badly sprained ankle, her posture affected by a couple of cracked ribs. Joe did the best he could to help, letting her cling to his arm as she walked.

When it came time to say farewell, Joe kissed her on the cheek and promised to do everything he could to get answers for her.

Back at the van, he thought about how best to manage his absence. It was now almost three-thirty, and very tempting to make straight for Trelennan. If he chose to return to the depot in Glastonbury he was looking at another four or five hours on the road.

Then again, he decided, a late return to Leon's

363

might not be a bad thing.

Climbing into the van, he spotted the newspaper that Kestle had thrust at him this morning. He leafed through it, and quickly saw why Leon wanted everyone to have a copy.

Joe read the article in a state of incredulous fury. It took exactly the line that Giles had promised to take: portraying Leon as the unlikely poster boy for Little Englanders everywhere. It wasn't so much fiction as a dangerous fantasy, and it made Joe determined to disprove every word.

*　　*　　*

Leon said nothing, gave no warning. Just got up and strode out of the room. Taken by surprise, Fenton and Glenn scrambled after him.

Morton burst out laughing, shouting: 'Send my regards to the chief constable!'

In the adjoining room, Leon's hands trembled as he collected his watch and phone, stuffing them in his pockets, the guards grinning like it was a huge joke. Leon ignored them, racing back to the lobby. He burst through the exit like a drowning man breaking the surface. When the others caught up he was at the Range Rover, slapping his hand on the rear screen, not caring if he smashed it.

'Why didn't we bring guns?' He turned on Bruce. 'You were the fucking hard man. What fucking help were you?'

'They wouldn't let me in—'

'We should have had fucking guns!' Leon yelled, then saw a party of golfers frowning in their direction.

'Let's get in the car,' Glenn said. 'Talk in there.'

Grudgingly Leon complied. From the front seat he could feel Fenton, sitting behind him, almost vibrating with the desire to speak. If the fat bastard uttered a word Leon was going to climb over the seat and punch his lights out.

When the Range Rover pulled away, Leon stamped his feet on the dash and let out a roar of frustration.

'What the fuck happened there?' Now he was muttering to himself, and for once they had the sense not to interrupt. 'We had what Morton is longing to get. If he'd just shown a bit of respect—a tiny bit—he could have had it. I'd have given it to him, and we'd all be coming out happy as Larry. So what happened?'

'There's nothing, Leon,' Glenn said. 'You didn't put a foot wrong.'

Fenton made a smacking sound with his lips. 'Perhaps there's a way to salvage—'

'Shut up, Clive. I don't wanna hear it.'

'But—'

'No. Listen to me. That is bordering on fucking mutiny at a time like this.' Leon turned, glaring at Fenton for long enough that maybe some telepathy did its work: *I know about you and fucking Derek plotting against me . . .*

With a harrumphing noise, Fenton broke eye contact and stared out of the window. Leon straightened up and went on to his next grievance.

'That was a pack of lies they were telling about me, but if they've been digging around it could mean they've had people in Trelennan. Watching us.'

'Christ, I hope not,' Glenn said. 'They could spot Joe at any time.'

365

'Ah, shit.' Leon went cold.

'What?'

'Maybe they have. Maybe that's what all the breakdown stuff was about.'

*   *   *

Joe was back in Glastonbury by five-thirty. The supervisor at the depot wasn't impressed.

'Kestle kept trying to phone you. It doesn't take all chuffing day to send out a breakdown truck.'

Joe played dumb. The supervisor made him unload the stock and warned him that he wouldn't be getting a penny for today. Joe grumbled for the sake of appearances, but it was no less than he'd expected.

Considering he'd had to put in thirty quids' worth of diesel, it had been a costly day in financial terms. But it had also brought clarity to his task, and that made it a price worth paying.

En route to Trelennan he remembered that he was due to be seeing Ellie tonight. He pulled in and sent a text, said he was running late but would get to her around nine.

A little optimistic, perhaps, he thought when he rolled onto Leon's driveway at ten to eight. The rain had stopped but the clouds still hung low overhead, as if too exhausted to move on. Joe stood for a moment in the murky darkness. Water dripping from the trees made for a hushed, secretive concerto, a counterpoint to the pounding of the falls on the far side of the house.

Joe was surprised to see Kestle. 'Not finished yet?'

'I stayed to find out what the hell happened to

366

you.'

Joe shrugged, easing past him and walking confidently towards the kitchen.

'So why couldn't I get hold of you?' Kestle demanded.

'Problems with my phone.'

'What, your phone *and* the van went on the blink?'

'That's right. You never had a day like that?' Joe found a glass, ran the cold tap. Kestle was in the doorway, surly but also uncertain; out of his depth.

'Well, yeah. But this isn't on, not calling in.'

'Hey, I left here at eight this morning. Twelve hours ago. I got the engine fixed on my own initiative. If that was wrong, tough. I returned the stock and then I brought the van back. I know I won't get paid for today, and I'm not going to argue with that, but what I won't do—' he jabbed a finger at Kestle, making him wait while he gulped a mouthful of water, '—is take any more crap, from you or anyone else.'

Kestle gave a petulant shrug. 'For Christ's sake, it isn't me that makes the rules.'

'I know. And if Leon wants to sack me, fine. Go and get him.'

'I can't. They're still out.'

Thank you, Joe thought. He refilled the glass. 'Got a thumping headache,' he said. 'I think I'll crash for ten minutes before I get off home. Glenn told me I can use the basement.'

Kestle looked uneasy, but nodded. 'I'm going now, anyway. It's Venning's shift.'

True to his word, the front door opened and shut while Joe was descending the stairs to the basement. With any luck, that left only Venning,

367

probably in the comms room. If he was careful, Joe should have a good opportunity to explore.

First he decided to leave it for a few minutes. He took a look around the basement, but he didn't expect to find anything down there, and he was right.

He was about to go back up when he heard movement at the top of the stairs. His initial reaction was disappointment: the search would have to be postponed for a while.

Then Joe saw who was descending the stairs, and his disappointment melted away.

CHAPTER SIXTY-EIGHT

Reece Winnen, with Todd Ancell at his shoulder, both grinning like hungry jackals. They were delighted, and why not? They had Joe exactly where they wanted him: outnumbered two to one, trapped, helpless. As far as he could tell, there weren't even any cameras down here, so Venning wouldn't know what was happening. All in all, a perfect set-up for them.

What they didn't realise was that Joe was just as delighted. He'd been hoping to encounter them soon, while the sight of Alise's wounds was still so sharply imprinted on his mind.

He walked towards them, apparently unconcerned. Reece stopped, four stairs from the bottom. He looked confident, saw no reason to move. Right now they didn't just outnumber Joe: they also had a height advantage.

Joe came up to the foot of the stairs. From

here, Reece could easily kick him in the face. Joe watched him reach the same conclusion: an urgent twitch of his right leg signalling his desire to do just that.

But first he'd want to speak: threaten, taunt, gloat. Or maybe he'd wait until Joe asked him to stand aside. Then Reece could refuse, and that would be the cue for battle to commence.

So Joe acted first. An impatient sideways shuffle, as though he was expecting them to continue down the stairs. Todd, being less practised at intimidation, automatically tried to comply, jostling against his partner on the stair in front. For half a second Reece was off balance, having to push back against Todd to stay upright.

Joe lunged, grabbed Reece's left leg with both hands and pulled it forward. Reece cried out, arms flailing uselessly as his right foot slipped off the stair and his body was momentarily airborne. Joe stepped back, forcing the leg as high as he could get it, not letting go until Reece landed with a crash, his coccyx hitting the second stair and his head bouncing back into Todd.

Reece gave a screech of pain and rolled to the side, collapsing onto the basement floor. Then Todd launched himself off the stairs in a clumsy flying drop-kick. It was the sort of attack that looked hugely impressive, and probably worked brilliantly when Todd was playing on his Xbox.

In reality it wasn't so effective. Joe only had to take a single step to his left to avoid him. As Todd landed, Joe twisted at the hip, raised his right arm and jabbed his elbow into the young man's temple. Todd stumbled but stayed on his feet, swinging a clumsy punch. Joe cut inside it and drove his palm against Todd's nose, then kicked him in the kneecap.

Todd collapsed, blood gushing from his nose. Joe turned and saw Reece trying to get up, hampered by what Joe hoped was a nasty injury to the base of his spine.

'Not so easy when your victims aren't helpless, is it?'

Joe had more to say, but there was a sudden cry from above them. Venning. The horror on the Welshman's face brought Joe to his senses. He climbed the stairs, forcing Venning to back up.

'We had a tiny disagreement,' Joe said. 'Strictly between us.'

Venning nodded meekly. 'Fair enough. I got no argument with you.'

Joe left the house, aware that he'd probably created a whole world of trouble for himself, but at the same time unable to regret a moment of it.

*   *   *

Fenton argued that they should still go to their hotel, and Leon reluctantly agreed. Four or five hours from home, there was nothing they could do in a hurry.

Leon made straight for his room. Said he didn't want to be disturbed, unless it was to confirm that Joe was back. By now he thought there was a very real possibility that he was gone. He was surprised to discover how much it mattered to him.

The room was supposed to be one of the hotel's best, but to Leon it looked shabby. There were hunting scenes on every wall and the carpets were a deep maroon colour that made him think of blood.

Third-rate compared to the hotel they'd come from, although the staff were just as snotty.

And the migraine was still creeping forward. After taking his Maxalt, he lay on the bed, intending to rest his eyes for a few minutes. The next thing he knew it was gone eight in the evening and his phone was ringing: Kestle. Joe was back, safe and sound.

Leon celebrated for all of ten seconds, until it struck him. This was Joe's fault. All this humiliation, disappointment: the whole frigging disaster was down to Joe.

He roused himself, then found the others. They were in the bar, weary but relaxed. Plenty of booze on the table.

Glenn said sheepishly, 'Sorry, Leon. We'd have invited you, but you said—'

'Yeah, yeah. Listen, I know how we fucked up. It was Joe.'

A lot of blank faces. 'What was Joe?' Fenton asked.

'The reason Danny Morton is such a head case. It's because Joe got inside the gang. Killed his brother. Got his dad banged up. That's what we didn't allow for, that he'd be so paranoid about somebody trying it again.'

Fenton sighed. 'You're right. And that damn newspaper article sealed our fate.'

'But we weren't to know,' Leon said, smarting at the insult. He realised that in fact he *had* known: the email from Giles had told him the article was due out today. He just hadn't given it a thought in relation to Danny Morton. Why would he? The two issues were completely separate.

'Anyway, Joe's come back. He's still ours. Finish

371

up, so we can get moving.'

They regarded him with astonishment. 'What?' said Glenn.

'I wanna get back tonight.'

Bruce scratched his head, looking like he'd just woken up and remembered he was late for something. 'I, uh, I've had a few beers, boss.'

'Who said you could do that?'

'Sorry, Leon. I thought we were staying over, like.'

'I can drive,' Glenn said. 'I've only had one.' He pushed a nearly full pint across the table to Bruce, who pretended not to notice it.

'Actually,' Fenton said, 'are we sure this is wise? I mean, a night here might be what we need. The restaurant has an excellent reputation . . .'

'You and your bloody stomach,' Leon growled.

'It's also an opportunity to reflect, regroup. You've made a valid point about Morton's paranoia. It may be that a second meeting would be more constructive.'

'Uh-uh,' Leon said. 'I will die rather than give that wanker what he's after.'

Glenn winced. Bruce shrugged. Fenton looked sick. But nobody argued.

Leon managed his first smile in what seemed like hours.

'Meet out front in ten. Roads'll be quiet. We can be home by midnight.'

*   *   *

From Leon's, Joe made straight for Ellie's. He felt exhausted, sweaty and grimy from a long day's driving, but knew that if he went back to the B&B

to shower and change he would never summon the energy to go out again.

He was on the corner of her street when his mobile buzzed. It was Venning.

'Listen, Joe, I'll have to tell Leon what happened here. All I can say is . . . well, they're a couple of twats, to be honest with you, and I'm not the only one that thinks so. They've been boasting about how they were gonna do you in, so I don't blame you for fighting back. I'll make sure Leon hears your side of it, all right?'

Surprised but grateful, Joe thanked him and reached Ellie's house in good spirits. She opened the door and gave him a wry smile. 'You made it, then?'

'Straight from work, I'm afraid.'

'I can see. You're dead on your feet.' She ushered him inside, touching his arm briefly, but there was no greeting kiss.

She looked wonderful: her hair dark and glossy; those bewitching eyes. Her make-up was a little more overt than before, her lipstick a darker shade of pink.

'Drink?' she said. 'I have wine on the go.'

'I'd better stick with coffee.'

To explain his fatigue, Joe gave her an account of the day he was supposed to have had: deliveries in Devon and Somerset, plus the fictional breakdown, just in case she had cause to swap notes with Glenn. He was on the verge of mentioning Alise, wanting to say that the 'cry wolf' theory couldn't have been further from the truth, but at the last moment he clammed up. Sensible discretion—or didn't he trust her?

Ellie made coffee while he sat at the kitchen

373

table. At one point she laughed and he jerked his head, realising his eyes had shut; not quite asleep, he insisted, to her amusement.

Then into the lounge, where the TV was playing quietly: a Met Office weather warning for more heavy rain.

'That'll make a change,' Ellie quipped. She'd poured herself a refill; now she took a big gulp of wine. 'Shall we get the awkward part over with?'

'What awkward part?'

'The Saturday snogfest. What's our official communiqué? Blame it on the booze?'

Although Joe chuckled, inside he felt slightly hurt. He hoped her flippancy was a mask to conceal genuine feelings for him.

'Why did Glenn give you a hard time about it?'

'Because he's a stinking great hypocrite. Anyway, nothing happened, did it?'

'No,' he agreed. There was a relaxed, thoughtful silence.

'For what it's worth,' she said, 'on Saturday night I wanted you to tear my clothes off and drag me into the bedroom.' She spoke slowly and deliberately, taking care not to stumble over the words. He wondered how much wine she'd had.

'And now?' he asked.

'Now I'm rather less sure. I have a hunch that you won't be around for much longer.'

He realised she was waiting for an answer. Dipped his head to indicate it was possible.

'And while a one-night stand would be pretty glorious, I think we'd both end up feeling a bit shabby.' She studied him closely. 'You might be separated from your wife, but it seems to me you're still married in your heart. God, that sounds slushy,

374

but you know what I mean, don't you?'

'I do. And you're probably right.'

'So go,' she said. 'Leave now, before I change my mind and keep you chained up here for ever as my sex slave.'

They both smiled, but Joe felt a cold shiver along his spine. Thinking of Alise, and Kamila, and any number of women before them.

Ellie picked up on his discomfort. 'Scary image, eh? You look like you did when you flaked out on me in the Shell Cavern.'

'I'm fine,' he lied. 'Just tired.'

He followed her out to the hall, feeling both touched and disappointed. At the door she leaned close and kissed his cheek, her lips soft on his skin for a microsecond longer than he expected.

'You know something, Joe Carter?' she said. 'You're a gentleman. And if you're still here by Friday, you're welcome to take me to the Crow's Nest for a farewell dinner.'

'I'd love to,' he said. But even though he meant it, he was aware that it felt like one of those pledges that was destined not to be met.

CHAPTER SIXTY-NINE

Jenny hated her captor. She loathed him. Feared him. Resented him

Now, more than any of these things, she missed him.

Her plan to mark the passage of time had been hopeless, but even without it she knew it had been at least three days since he'd visited; perhaps longer. The stench of human waste was appalling.

All her food was long gone; the bottle of Evian water, doled out in the tiniest sips, no more than a sweet, delicious memory. Her lips were so dry and swollen that it hurt every time she brought them together.

She no longer felt hungry. She had gone beyond hunger. What she felt was a lightness that had spread throughout her entire body; a sensation that she no longer existed. She drifted like a balloon, her mind barely anchored in the real world . . . for she had made sense of his curious distinction.

I didn't kill her. She died. There's a difference.

And the warning that had followed:

You'll learn.

He wasn't coming back. He had left her to die.

*   *   *

Now even the knowledge of her abandonment couldn't rouse much feeling. In her lucid moments she understood that it was because of her physical weakness, the lack of food and water, robbing her of the will to react.

And yet it hadn't always been so. There had been a time, many hours before, when she had drawn upon miraculous reserves of energy and determination. Recovering from the disappointment of burrowing through the stud wall, only to hit solid rock, she had challenged herself to examine the problem and come up with a solution.

Her conclusion, brilliant in its simplicity, was that she should try another wall. The wall with the door. It stood to reason that there must be some sort of access beyond the door, otherwise how else would

376

her captor come in and out?

The idea had been enough to sustain an attack on the plasterboard, using the same method of alternating splashes of filthy water with a frantic digging using the battery and, inadvertently, her fingertips. She had lost several fingernails in the process, and her hands ended up bruised and soaked in blood, but she had broken a small hole through the inner panel before the exhaustion and delirium set in.

In the hours that followed she had lain slumped against the door, one hand gripping the hole as if waiting for the instruction to get back to work. An instruction that never came.

*   *   *

Then she was awake, not merely drifting but abruptly, vividly conscious of her surroundings and her predicament. If she didn't find liquid soon, she would die.

The thought set her heart thudding madly, as though she'd just been running for her life; the last dregs of adrenalin were pumping energy into her system and she had to make that count for something.

Jenny found the torch, the second set of batteries long dead. Then knelt, groping in the darkness until she had positioned herself level with the new hole. Before she could change her mind, she drew back the torch and beat it against the wall with all her strength until the plasterboard yielded, leaving a hole large enough for her fist.

The torch had been smashed in the process, but that was irrelevant. She put her hand into the void and wrenched out the soundproofing material, tossing the fibres over her shoulder with a mad abandon. This new-found strength might desert her at any moment.

A sudden sharpness made her gasp. When she withdrew her hand she could feel something protruding from her palm. Unable to see, she reached out tentatively with her other hand and identified it as a nail. She couldn't tell how far it had penetrated, but knew it had to come out.

The pain was like hot, wet lightning. She felt blood running from the wound, and with revulsion she instinctively pressed her hand against her mouth, smearing blood over her parched lips. Hot and salty, it offered little relief.

She explored the contours of the nail with her fingers. It was about three inches long, bent into the shape of the letter C.

A gift. She had a tool to work with.

Holding it like a dagger, she eased her hand into the gap and thrust the point of the nail against the outer panel, stabbing and gouging while the blood continued to run from her palm, her whole hand now throbbing like an abscessed tooth.

She cried out when the nail punctured the plasterboard. Crouching down, she peered through the inner hole and saw something remarkable. A pinprick of weak light.

She had broken through.

As well as the light, she realised, there was sound. It seemed to echo her own ravenous heartbeat: a living, breathing, pumping noise, low-pitched and thrumming. The wound on her palm had stopped bleeding before she worked out what it was—and the irony pierced her more

378

sharply than the nail.

It was water. Water in huge volumes, flowing quickly and very close by, but utterly beyond her reach.

CHAPTER SEVENTY

Leon felt the noise rather than heard it, vibrating through the bed for so long that he thought it might be a minor earth tremor. Only when it occurred a second time did he lift his head and recognise it as thunder, very distant.

He settled back and lay still until his decision was made. When he got up, it was with a clear head. He seemed to move more freely, as though a physical burden had been lifted.

He was back on his home turf. Yesterday was done with, irrelevant. He knew the way forward.

In the shower he caught himself singing, with conscious irony, 'London Calling' by The Clash, bellowing out the chorus while he thought about how he was going to stick it to Danny Morton.

Padding downstairs at eight, he took a wander around the ground floor, the thunder growling quietly every few minutes, like a neglected dog.

Fenton hadn't yet surfaced, but Glenn was up, sweet-talking Pam. Leon collected some juice and a couple of chocolate croissants, then he and Glenn retreated to the office.

'What's the latest?' he asked.

'A&E patched up Todd's nose. He's going to look stupid for a week or two.'

'No change there, then.'

379

'It's wounded pride more than anything. Same with Reece.'

'Fuckwits,' Leon muttered. Venning had made it plain they'd been spoiling for a fight. 'But what was Joe doing in the basement?'

'Having a lie-down, according to Kestle.'

'I don't buy that.' Leon consumed half a croissant before he spoke again. 'I want you to get his van checked over by a mechanic. It'll be obvious if anyone's worked on the engine recently.'

'You think the breakdown story was bullshit?'

Leon nodded. 'And call Reece. Tell him and Todd to come in, soon as they can. I want everyone else out of here this morning. Just them two, plus Bruce.'

Glenn loitered, clearly hoping for an explanation. When Leon didn't supply it, Glenn said, 'Sure you want Reece and Todd back here so soon?'

'Yeah.' Leon smiled. 'I'm arranging a treat for them.'

*   *   *

Joe had set his alarm for seven, but when it started bleeping he switched it off, turned over and went back to sleep, vaguely aware that there was a storm approaching. The thunder intruded into his dreams, became the rumble of stone walls collapsing all around him . . .

He woke in a cold sweat. Sat up and waited for the shock to subside. He wasn't sure if he should go into work, but he showered, shaved, and went down for breakfast. It was almost eight o'clock, and Diana looked relieved to see him.

'I didn't know if I ought to wake you.'

380

'I'm not due in till later,' he said. As with Ellie, he hadn't told her about Alise, or the fight with Leon's men. He felt he'd brought enough trouble upon them all. From now on he had to resolve this himself.

'Did you hear the thunder?' Diana said. 'Sounds like it's going to be another foul day.'

In more ways than one, Joe thought.

*   *   *

By the time Fenton sloped in, at half past eight, Leon's plans were well advanced.

'I just spoke to Claudia Watson,' he said cheerily.

Fenton, baffled, said, 'Oh? Why's that?'

'Just a bit of business. You remember Claudia?'

'Well, yes, of course.'

'Oh yeah, she was your birthday present. Your fiftieth, wasn't it?'

Leon sniggered, and Fenton looked away. He was drinking tea from a prissy little cup, complete with saucer. He even stuck his finger out as he drank. Leon had never really noticed before, and it added to his doubts about the man.

'Where was Glenn off to?' Fenton asked.

'Getting Joe's van checked, to see if the engine thing was genuine.'

'Hmm. Why would he fake a breakdown?'

'To give him cover for what he was really doing.'

'Which was . . . .?'

'I dunno for sure, but I'm going to find out.'

There was another peal of thunder, slightly louder than the last. Still no lightning, no rain, but the wind was getting up. Leon could hear the veranda creaking with every gust.

'I wonder if it was another mission on behalf of our foreign friend?'

'Alise.' Leon savoured the name, enjoying Fenton's surprise. 'Don't worry,' he added. 'The room's clean. I got Venning to do a thorough sweep.'

'You don't think Morton's people are spying on us?'

Good try, Leon thought. He said: 'Spies can be anywhere, Clive.'

Fenton didn't seem to understand what Leon was getting at. 'Do you really think she survived?'

'She must have done. Unless the body got washed out to sea, it would have been found by now.'

'Then let's hope she's feeding the fishes. Otherwise she remains a threat. Especially if Joe is working on her behalf . . .'

Leon flapped his hand. 'That's not a worry. Clive. I need you to make a phone call.'

Fenton brightened up, an excited rattle as he set the cup down. 'Ah, yes. Now you've had time to sleep on it, surely you can see the wisdom in making another approach?'

Leon said nothing. His silence gave Fenton encouragement.

'What I'd suggest is that we put it to him quite bluntly, in the kind of language he understands. *We have Joe. If you want him, the price is a million pounds*. Almost like a ransom demand.'

Leon pretended to consider it. 'I will tell Danny Morton where Joe is,' he said. 'But when I do, it'll be to tell him he blew his chances. Because by that point Joe will be dead.'

CHAPTER SEVENTY-ONE

The landline rang at ten to nine. Diana passed the phone to Joe. It was Clive Fenton.

'Good morning, Mr Carter. Were you planning to come in today?'

'I hadn't decided,' Joe said, assuming that Fenton would tell him not to bother.

'Regarding last night, I've received a full account from Reece, as well as from Phil Venning. Now I wish to hear your side of it. Shall we say ten o'clock?'

'Fine.' Joe put the phone down, impressed that Venning had kept to his word.

Diana was loading the washing machine and didn't turn round until he finished the call. 'Has something happened?'

'Why do you ask?'

Crossing her arms, she gave him a stern look. 'I was married to a policeman, remember? I know when something's not right, just like you do.'

It was a pointed reminder that on Sunday she had given Joe the truth. Now he owed her the same candour.

He told her about the call from Alise, driving to Looe and finding her with terrible injuries. 'They were clever. Too many people knew of her feud with Leon for her to simply disappear. Faking a suicide was the perfect solution.'

'But now she's survived, surely she'll go to the police?'

'She says not. There's no evidence, and Leon is bound to have arranged for another solid alibi.'

'So he'll get away with it again—' Diana stopped abruptly. 'Oh, Joe. Please tell me you're not thinking of taking him on alone . . .'

'Not as such. I know I'm outnumbered. What I'm hoping to do is get hold of some evidence that incriminates him. Then I'll gladly leave it to the authorities.'

Diana didn't look reassured. 'So what was the phone call about?'

'Uh, a minor altercation I had with a couple of the security guys.' Joe grinned. 'I'm sure I can talk my way out of it.'

*   *   *

Nine forty-five. The storm was pushing closer, the skies darkening. A squally wind rattled the tiles above the porch as Joe prepared to leave.

Diana hovered anxiously. 'Are you sure you don't want a lift?'

'It's not raining yet. If I hurry I'll be there before it starts.'

'I'm not sure you should be going at all.'

'I have to face them at some point.'

'Do you?'

He said nothing. They stared at each other for a moment, then embraced. Holding him tightly, Diana said, 'Please be careful, Joe.'

When they separated, Joe had a sense of how much had been left unsaid. He knew Diana would be thinking of Roy, and the mistakes he'd made in trying to confront Leon. Afraid that Joe was preparing to make the very same mistakes.

Joe couldn't put her mind at ease, because he feared she might well be right.

384

*   *   *

As he left the house, a Range Rover pulled up and backed onto the driveway, its brake lights a vivid red in the dull gloom of the day. The driver opened his window and beckoned to Joe. It was the man he'd met out on the veranda on his first day. Bruce.

'Clive said you were going in for ten, and I was down this way. Hop in.'

Joe glanced up at the sky. Any second now it was going to tip it down. Silly to refuse.

Climbing into the passenger seat, he caught Bruce grinning at his hesitation.

'Reece and Todd are idiots. You gave 'em a right pasting, according to Phil. Done a bit of fighting in your time, have you?'

'A bit.' Not a route he wanted to go down, so Joe said, 'You?'

'Bloody loved a scrap, I did. Got in a lot of trouble over it. Luckily I ran into Leon, and he gave me a second chance.'

'You like working for him?'

'Oh yeah. Leon's a top man.' Bruce gave Joe a conspiratorial glance. 'Clive's a weirdo, but easy enough to deal with. You'll probably get a slap on the wrist for this. Just keep your head down in future and you'll be okay.'

Joe nodded. 'Thanks for the advice.'

*   *   *

A loud crash of thunder commanded their attention as they got to the house. Sheet lightning flashed above the trees to the west.

385

'Raining in Padstow, I bet,' Bruce said. 'Be us next.'

They entered the house. Bruce told him that Fenton would see him in the office. As he peeled away to the comms room, Joe called, 'Is Venning still here?'

'Nah, finished at nine. He's on nights.'

That was a shame, Joe thought. He knocked on the office door, waited for a summons, and walked in. Fenton was behind the desk. With a self-important, headmasterly air, he laced his chubby fingers together and announced: 'Leon has requested that I deal with this on his behalf.'

'Where is he?'

The big man bristled at Joe's impertinence. 'He's away.'

'Anywhere nice?'

Fenton ignored the question. He cleared his throat. 'You'll be pleased to hear that Reece has decided he won't be pressing charges for assault. Neither will Todd.'

Joe shrugged. 'They came looking for trouble. I responded.'

'Yes, well, there are conflicting opinions. Suffice to say we won't tolerate any repetition of this behaviour. That's clearly understood, I hope?'

'Perfectly.'

There was an awkward silence. Fenton seemed unnerved by Joe's composure. At last he said, 'Good. We'll regard the matter as settled. Now, I haven't looked at the schedule yet, but I believe there's work available for you today.'

The phone rang. Fenton answered, then told the caller to hold on.

He addressed Joe: 'Glenn's due back shortly.

Help yourself to a coffee and either he or I will sort something for you.'

As Joe stood up, there was a faint high-pitched noise from above them. Joe frowned, and Fenton muttered, 'It's just the wind.'

Joe left the room, shutting the door behind him. He was reflecting that he'd got off lightly—almost too lightly—when he heard it again: a long, piercing screech.

Sometimes the wind could make a sound like this, he thought, when it was funnelled through a narrow space at high speed. But that wasn't the case here.

What he'd heard was a woman screaming.

CHAPTER SEVENTY-TWO

Joe raced up the stairs. At the top there was a wide landing, with passageways leading left and right. Half a dozen doors within sight, all of them shut.

He paused, the first doubts creeping in. Less than a minute since Fenton's warning and already he was courting trouble.

The next sound was a whimper, like that of a beaten animal. It came from the second room to the right. Joe crept forward, cautious now. He grasped the door handle, twisted, felt no resistance.

He stood to one side as he opened the door, to avoid presenting an easy target. The widening arc revealed a pale green carpet and an antique dressing table with a large mirror above it. Reflected in the mirror was a double bed with an ornate brass frame. A woman lay face up on the bed, tied to the four corners by leather cords. A cloth gag had been stuffed into her mouth and secured with tape, but she'd managed to dislodge it enough to make a noise.

Her eyes widened as she saw the door opening. She was completely naked, a young woman with a thin frame and large breasts that barely splayed towards her armpits. She had a small tattoo of a bird on her inner thigh and another, more elaborate butterfly design on her left breast.

Joe didn't sense any other presence, but he went in fast, ready to fend off an attack. The room was empty. The only other furniture was a chest of drawers with peeling lacquer. There was a sink in one corner, but no en-suite. No hiding places.

Shutting the door, Joe raised a finger to his lips, urging silence. 'It's all right. I'm going to untie you.'

The woman seemed to trust him, but there was still panic in her eyes. He pulled the tape away from her mouth. She spat the gag out, gasping for breath.

'Quick! Before Leon gets back.'

'Leon's here?'

She nodded. 'About ten minutes ago.'

Joe started on the cords that bound her feet. The knots were thick and unwieldy. 'How long have you been held prisoner?'

'Since last night. Please hurry,' she said.

Finally he untangled the knot and her left foot was free. He moved to the next corner and felt the woman tense. The door was opening.

Joe turned, helpless, as Leon Race entered the room. He didn't seem remotely surprised to see Joe. If anything, he looked delighted.

And he was holding a gun.

It was a Glock 9mm. Of course, it could be a fake. Lots of criminals used imitation firearms because they were cheaper and easier to obtain, and just as effective as a threat.

The question was, did Joe want to take the chance?

Leon gestured for him to move round to the far side of the bed. The woman was slumped in defeat, glaring crossly at Joe.

'Like playing the hero, don't you?' Leon said. 'I bet you couldn't believe your luck. *Joe Carter to the rescue!* The brave undercover cop saves another victim.'

'I'm not an undercover cop.'

'I don't care what you are. Other than a fucking nuisance.' Leon approached the bed, urging Joe back against the far wall. Taking a flick knife from his pocket, he popped the blade and cut away the remaining cords.

'What are you going to do with her?' Joe said.

'Shut up,' Leon said. When the last of the bonds had been cut, he folded the knife and reached out towards the woman. Instead of shrinking away, she took his hand and let him help her up. Joe got ready to throw himself at Leon if he took aim at her.

But Leon merely stood and watched as the woman reached under the bed, retrieved a silk robe and put it on. There was a loud crash of thunder, almost directly overhead. The woman shivered.

'All done?' she asked Leon.

'Yeah. You were brilliant, Claudia. I'll get somebody to drive you home.'

389

'Thanks, hon.' She gave Leon a peck on the cheek and hurried out of the room without sparing Joe another glance.

Leon was still smiling. 'Now the real fun begins,' he said.

*   *   *

Joe was utterly bewildered, and saw no point in hiding it. Leon was twitchier than usual, his face pale and drawn. A wild look in his bloodshot eyes. Not a well man, but this was his grand set piece and he clearly intended to enjoy it.

'You thought you had me red-handed, didn't you? These missing women. You think I'm raping and murdering them?'

Joe met his gaze and said, 'Yes. I think you are.'

Leon snorted. 'So did Roy Bamber. Silly bastard didn't have a shred of proof, but he wouldn't stop digging away.'

'I know. That's why you arranged for Glenn to have an affair with Diana.'

Grudging admiration from Leon. 'He didn't take much persuading. Glenn would shag a Hoover if there was nothing better on offer.'

'What happened when Roy found out?'

'He went ballistic, but it was too late. She was in love with Glenn by then.' Leon paused, rubbing sleep from his eyes. 'You know Roy tried to fit me up? Came here one day, said he wanted to discuss a building project. He'd smuggled in one of those tiny voice recorders. Took me all of ten seconds to guess what he was doing. I should have rammed the fucking thing up his arse.'

Joe didn't respond. He knew Leon was trying to

goad him.

'Anyway, I called Glenn in and asked him outright: do you wanna go on screwing Roy's missus? Well, Glenn said she wasn't bad for an oldie, so I gave him permission, and I made Roy give his permission, too.' Leon laughed at the memory. 'Didn't surprise me one bit when he dropped dead. Sent him to an early grave, trying to bring me down. That's a lesson you could have learned.' He jabbed a finger at Joe. 'Where did you go yesterday?'

'Glastonbury. Then the van broke down.'

'No, it didn't. I checked. Alise is still alive, isn't she?'

Rather than answer directly, Joe said, 'I know what you did to her.'

Leon was unfazed. 'What happened to her has nothing to do with this.' He gestured at the rumpled bed covers. 'Alise had a vendetta against me. Getting rid of her was self-defence, pure and simple.'

'That's not how I see it.'

'Huh. Once a cop, always a cop. What about Sunday? A trip to Dorset, was it?'

Joe saw no reason to lie. 'I was following up on Kamila's disappearance. Trying to find the evidence that would put you away.'

'It won't happen,' Leon gloated. 'Round here, I'm invincible. I'm fucking fireproof. I own this town, and you made a big mistake, crossing me.' As his voice rose in pitch and volume, he sounded like a madman; not far short of foaming at the mouth. Joe decided he had nothing to lose in making a run for it: even if the gun was real, Leon might not shoot straight.

Then Reece and Todd trooped in, putting an end to that idea. Todd had a dressing on his nose. Both men looked as though they would gladly tear Joe apart with their bare hands.

Bruce came in behind them, carrying a bottle of cheap vodka. Leon made sure Joe had seen it, then said, 'It worked okay with Alise. It's gonna work even better with you.'

CHAPTER SEVENTY-THREE

It was funny, Leon later reflected, how because of one thing, another thing happened.

He descended the stairs slowly, because he was exhausted and unsteady on his feet. They hadn't got back from Ascot until nearly one in the morning, and then Leon had lain awake for hours, waiting for his fury to subside.

Glenn had just come in, so the door to the office was open. Because Leon took the stairs so slowly, he didn't make any noise. And because they didn't hear him coming, Fenton and Glenn went on talking as if Leon wasn't there. Glenn must have asked for an update, and Fenton made a disgusted noise.

'It's insane, tossing Joe into the bloody river Allwyn. As he floats away on the tide, so does our chance of a spectacular payday.'

Glenn's comment was drowned out by a clap of thunder. When it echoed away to silence, Fenton was saying: 'How can anyone look such a gift horse in the mouth?'

'I don't know. But Leon didn't exactly get a fair

392

hearing. I wouldn't want to go crawling back to Morton after that . . .'

'There are ways and means, Glenn. The trouble is, he's become entrenched. Won't listen to a word I say. I've asked Derek to come over, and you should work on him, too. He's always had a soft spot for you.'

'Dunno about that any more,' Glenn muttered.

'The past day or two, it's like he's taken leave of his senses. He won't listen to reason.' Fenton's tone became even more confidential. 'In fact, I've started to wonder if it isn't time to move on. I've built up quite a contingency fund. I assume you've done the same?'

Glenn made a non-committal sound. 'Bit early to be jumping ship, isn't it?'

'Is it? I don't know. With a million pounds at stake, I'm sorely tempted to call Danny Morton myself.' Glenn must have looked disapproving, for Fenton sounded defensive when he spoke again. 'Wouldn't you say it's a risk worth taking?'

*　　　*　　　*

'What risk is that?' Leon shoved the door open, letting it crash against the wall.

Fenton lurched out of his chair, one hand slapping against his chest as if he might need to restart his heart. Glenn barely moved: just a little colour in his cheeks as he nodded a greeting, before deftly changing the subject.

'You got Joe here all right?'

'Bruce played it perfectly. So did Claudia.' Leon winked at Fenton. 'You know she still looks as fit as she did at eighteen?'

393

'Wonderful,' said Fenton drily. He took a deep breath. 'Leon, ah, Glenn and I were just discussing whether it isn't worth one final approach to Danny Morton . . .'

'Not gonna happen, Clive. And if you try going behind my back, it'll be the last thing you ever do. Understand me?'

Fenton gulped like a bullfrog, then silently rose, allowing Leon to take his place behind the desk.

'Have you got a key for Diana's?' he asked Glenn.

'Not any more. She took it back on Sunday.'

Leon fished in his pocket, producing a key and an envelope. 'There's a letter in here, written by Joe. His are the only fingerprints on it. I want you to leave it for Diana to find, and get Joe's stuff while you're there.'

'What if she's at home?'

'Lure her somewhere,' Fenton suggested.

'She's not taking my calls.'

Leon snapped: 'She must go shopping or something. Sit outside all morning if you have to. Just get it done.'

Glenn nodded miserably, perhaps realising that Leon was putting him out of harm's way. 'I don't get what the plan is.'

'We're faking a suicide, same as with Alise. But I want Diana to think that Joe's left of his own accord. Otherwise she'll start making trouble, and then we'd have to deal with her.' To make sure Glenn had got the message, he added: 'The same goes for your ex-wife.'

Glenn's mouth tightened but he didn't protest; instead he exchanged a worried glance with Fenton. It happened so fast, they probably thought Leon hadn't noticed.

Once Glenn had stalked out, Leon settled back and shut his eyes: the picture of relaxation. 'All going nicely to plan, isn't it?' he said.

'If you say so.' Fenton sounded grumpy. 'There are no guarantees with a faked suicide.'

'We can learn from last time. They're gonna drown him in the river first. High tide's at two, so they'll dump him just as it turns. And the currents from the Allwyn go way out into the Celtic Sea. Once he's gone, he won't be coming back.' He opened his eyes, saw Fenton looking dubious. 'With any luck, this storm will raise the river levels even higher.'

Right on cue, there was a soft thud outside: a large drop of water hitting the veranda. Then another. Then a heavy burst, drumming ferociously on the house. Leon beamed. Fenton gaped at him as though, just for a moment, he could believe that Leon had mystical powers.

*   *   *

The rain was so sudden, so intense that everyone stopped to listen.

Todd groaned. 'We're gonna get soaked.'

'It's good,' Reece said. 'There'll be no one around.'

Joe knew precisely what they were planning, for Leon had explained it to him. First he'd been searched, relieved of his keys and his money, as well as the passport and driving licence in the name of 'Joe Carter'. Leon had snorted as he examined the documents, as if he knew they were false.

Bruce put on a pair of latex gloves, left the room

395

and returned with a sheet of writing paper and a pen. Leon pointed the gun at Joe's chest.

'Write a note for Diana, saying you've had to leave in a hurry. Tell her you've done all that you can here, something like that.'

'She won't believe it.'

'All right.' Leon gave him a knowing look. 'Why don't you say your past has caught up with you?'

Joe felt a coldness along his spine. Surely Leon couldn't have found out about the Mortons?

'I can see that's hit home,' Leon said. 'Now get writing.'

No, Joe thought. *If they knew, they wouldn't be doing this. They'd hand me over.*

'What if I refuse?' he asked, with an involuntary glance at Reece.

Leon saw it and said lightly, 'Oh, we won't torture you. We'll torture Diana instead.'

It wasn't a bluff. Joe knew Diana would only be safe if she accepted his sudden departure as genuine. He had no choice but to write a convincing note.

Once it was done, Leon made him place it in an envelope, then took it off him. He said, 'This is self-defence, remember that. Same as with Alise. You brought it on yourself.'

Joe didn't bother to respond. Clearly irked, Leon left the room, taking the gun with him. Evidently confident that three of his men were more than capable of dealing with Joe—either that or the gun was a fake, in which case Joe would bitterly regret not having made a fight of it.

For the next stage, Todd fetched a chair and tied Joe to it, padding his wrists and ankles with towels so the cuffs wouldn't leave marks on his skin. The whole time Joe could feel violence radiating from Reece and Todd: it was taking every ounce of their self-control not to lash out.

Bruce was a lot more matter-of-fact. 'I should get an Oscar,' he declared. 'I suckered him big time.'

It was Bruce who did the honours with the vodka, while Reece stood behind the chair, holding Joe's head in place.

'Little sips are fine,' Bruce said, easing the neck of the bottle up to Joe's mouth.

'No hurry,' Reece added. 'We're waiting for high tide.'

Joe took an involuntary nip of vodka. Thought about spitting it out but knew there would be another after that, and another; so he swallowed. He had no choice. They weren't going to force it down his throat, because that would make him vomit. Small sips were just as effective . . .

Half a dozen and he felt agreeably light-headed. At least he'd be going out happy.

He fought against that idea. He had to stay sharp. Think of what he had to lose: his daughters. His wife.

Today he might be gone from the world, and no one who cared would ever know what had become of him.

CHAPTER SEVENTY-FOUR

Two hours after it began the rain was still pelting down. Wishing she'd gone out earlier, Diana took the car and parked on double yellow lines in the High Street. All she needed was milk and sandwich

397

meat from the Co-op. The shop was all but deserted, and she was back home within ten minutes.

Glenn's Toyota was on the driveway. Diana parked next to it, turned her engine off and sat for a moment, composing herself. Then it occurred to her that he was nowhere to be seen.

As she got out of the car, the front door opened. Glenn saw her and froze. Braced against the wind, she put her head down and ran inside, forcing him to retreat into the hall. He was hiding something behind his back.

She wiped the rain from her face, then gave him the full blast of her fury. 'What are you doing here? How the hell did you get in?'

Shamefaced, he displayed a key in his palm.

'That's not yours. And what have you got there?'

Slowly he brought the other arm into view. He was holding a carrier bag, bulging with clothes. *Joe's clothes*.

*   *   *

A brief battle ensued. Her heart said throw him out. Her head said get some answers first.

'Kitchen,' she said, snatching the bag from his grasp.

But the kitchen brought another shock. A sheet of paper rested innocently on the table. Purportedly from Joe, claiming his past had caught up with him and he'd had to flee.

Diana turned on Glenn. 'I don't believe Joe wrote this. Not if you brought it here. And you used his key . . .' She tailed off, saw the hopelessness in his eyes as he stood in the centre of her kitchen: such an imposing presence, a man she had loved

398

and yet knew nothing about.

Glenn gave her a pleading look: *Don't make me explain.* 'It's all gone to shit, Di.'

She had another insight: 'You waited till I was out?'

He nodded. Glanced at the unit and said with feeling: 'Christ, I need a drink.'

'Then put the kettle on. I'm not your skivvy.'

'I mean a *drink*.'

'Go on, then.' She reasoned that, by staying calm, she stood a greater chance of finding out the truth, and ultimately helping Joe.

She sat down, brooding while Glenn hunted for the brandy. Without being asked, he brought two glasses over. Poured a generous measure into each. Diana regarded hers with distaste.

'Where is Joe?'

'I don't know.' A long pause. 'Leon wants rid of him.'

'Rid of him how?'

Glenn sat down, drained his glass in a single gulp and poured another. 'Just . . . getting him out of town.'

Diana's eyes narrowed. She realised that even now, after all that had happened, she wanted to believe him.

'Joe told me about Alise. What Leon did to her. It's all true, isn't it? Alise's sister, and the girl Roy was looking for . . .' Her voice had become too shaky to continue. She swallowed a mouthful of brandy and grimaced. 'Were you involved?'

'No!' He turned away, wounded. 'We both know what Roy thought, but there's never been any proof.'

'There is now. There's Alise, beaten up and left

399

for dead. And I want to know if you took part in that.'

Glenn shook his head. 'I swear I had nothing to do with it. I'm guilty of lots of things, Di. Guilty of being weak, and stupid. Guilty of turning a blind eye when I shouldn't have. But I've never gone near the sort of stuff Leon does.' He shuddered. 'Him and Clive Fenton.'

'What about Derek Cadwell? Does he just "turn a blind eye", or is he an active part of the conspiracy?'

'He's close to them. Closer to Fenton than he is to Leon, probably. But they're all rotten. Rotten to the core.'

Ashamed, he stared at his brandy as though it could provide the answer he needed. Diana let him brood for a minute. Having initially faked a sense of composure, she now felt genuinely calm.

'You have a big decision to make,' she said.

*　　*　　*

Glenn went for the brandy but Diana got there first, moving it beyond his reach. He didn't protest; just glanced at her, then hung his head again. A savage gust of wind threw rain at the house.

'Leon's lost the plot. He won't listen to any of us. Yesterday he made a complete frigging disaster out of—' He stopped.

'What?'

'Doesn't matter. Just something he buggered up.' A heartfelt sigh. 'I'm tempted to walk out.'

'Then do it.'

'It's not just that.' Now he met her eye. 'The past couple of days it's really hit home, you and me

400

splitting up. I don't want to lose what we had.'

'And what did we have?'

Glenn heard the coolness of her tone, and seemed surprised by it. 'I don't . . .'

'It was a happy coincidence, was it, you seducing me just as Roy made a nuisance of himself?'

'Who put that idea in your head?' He snorted. 'Joe, I suppose?'

'Tell me the truth. Was it Leon's idea?'

Glenn gazed longingly at the bottle of brandy. Diana had it clutched in her hand as though ready to club him with it.

'He suggested that I should . . . get to know you. But I fell for you, Di. Honestly. Hook, line and sinker. Leon wasn't happy about that. After Roy died he told me to end it, but I refused.' To her dismay, he couldn't resist injecting pride into his voice.

'I betrayed my husband in the worst possible way, and now I find out the whole thing was engineered by *Leon bloody Race*.'

'I'm truly sorry. But my feelings for you were genuine. Would I still be here if they weren't?'

He reached across the table and laid his hand over hers. Diana found that she didn't have the strength to push him away.

'You can't let this happen, Glenn. You have to do the decent thing.'

He grunted. 'I'm surprised you still think I'm capable of that.'

'So am I. Maybe it's the brandy talking.'

'You've hardly touched yours.' His fingers tightened around hers. 'We did have some good times, didn't we? Best relationship I've ever had.'

'Then do what you can for Joe,' she said. 'For the

sake of a fresh start.'

Glenn stared at her for a long time. 'You mean that?'

She nodded. He checked his watch, and Diana automatically looked at hers. It was twenty to two.

'I need to make a phone call,' he said.

CHAPTER SEVENTY-FIVE

They fed him the vodka, slowly and patiently, for what seemed like hours. Joe had no choice but to submit to it. Any hope of survival he had lay not in violent resistance, but in the skills he'd perfected in his former life.

An undercover cop is essentially an actor, and Joe had prided himself on his ability to inhabit a character, living as a criminal among criminals, for days or weeks at a time. That had often meant drinking heavily, matching his associates pint for pint, but in a situation where any slip-up could be fatal he'd developed a strategy to avoid becoming hopelessly drunk.

During the first stage his surface persona would exhibit the full effects of the alcohol, while underneath the real Joe remained sober and sharp. To achieve this, he set himself memory challenges and conducted mental arithmetic, even as his eyes lost focus and his mouth became slack.

He'd had a bacon sandwich for breakfast, plus two cups of coffee with milk. Not a bad intake in terms of fat and protein to line his stomach, though a fry-up would have been better still.

With just an inch of vodka left in the bottle,

Bruce fetched a box of paracetamol and a mortar and pestle. He began to grind the tablets into powder, whistling like a busy chef.

Reece objected. 'It's too early. He could be dead before we get there.'

'So what?'

'That's not the plan.'

'Ask Clive?' Todd suggested, after the other two had spent a long minute glowering at each other.

Reece sloped away and returned looking smugly vindicated. 'We'll give him the last bit once we get there.'

Joe was glad to hear it. He had a method for fighting the booze, but not pills.

'I need a piss,' he declared, his voice slurred, but not too slurred. When playing drunk, he knew the tendency was always to overdo it.

'Fuck off.' Reece consulted his watch, and told the others: 'We're about ready to go.'

'Imeanit,' Joe said, lolling his head slightly. 'Gotta go now. Or wet myself.'

Bruce groaned. 'I don't want him pissing in the Range Rover.'

'What if he tries something?' Reece complained.

'What?'

'We should keep him cuffed.'

'So how's he gonna . . .?'

'I ain't holding it for him,' Todd said quickly. 'Or going in with him.'

Bruce took the lead. 'For Christ's sake. As long as he can't get out the window. There's three of us. Better to let him take a leak so we don't have to clean up the car.'

Reece nodded reluctantly. He kept a close eye on Joe as the other two removed the cuffs and hauled him to his feet. Joe felt his head spin and realised he was quite genuinely inebriated: never mind the performance. And yet there was also the sober core of him, perhaps half in control: like a car being operated by a learner driver and an instructor at the same time.

*   *   *

They led him into a bedroom with an internal en-suite shower room: no windows, no escape route. *One up to them.*

Being macho men, none of them wanted to get too close to the doorway after they shoved him inside. He stumbled back against the door, flicking his heel to make sure it shut while giving the impression it was down to clumsiness.

He didn't have long. The need to void his bladder was real enough, but there were other, more important considerations. The next stage of his strategy was to empty his stomach, very rapidly, and without drawing attention to himself. If they heard him retching they'd only force more vodka down his throat to replenish what he'd lost.

After urinating, Joe shoved two fingers down his throat while simultaneously pushing the lever to flush the toilet. In the gurgling rush of water he crouched down and vomited, with a minimum of noise. This was the method that had once enabled him to drink the Mortons and their associates under the table.

Then he turned, gripping the sink as black spots danced across his vision. He could feel another spasm coming on but fought it back. The gurgle of the cistern refilling wasn't loud enough to disguise

404

a second bout. Instead, running the cold tap, he cupped his hands and frantically drank as much water as he could throw into his mouth.

The door started to open. An angry voice called, 'Get a frigging move on.'

'Yeah.' Joe bumped against the door frame on the way out, still fumbling with his zip. His hands left damp patches on his jeans and the men around him instinctively recoiled.

They directed him back to the landing and down the stairs. Once or twice Joe tripped and had to be held upright by Todd and Bruce. He kept his mouth tightly shut so they wouldn't smell the bile on his breath.

There was no one in sight as they reached the hall, and the office door was shut. Joe wondered if all the other staff had been banished.

Before they left, his captors put on thick plastic coats, overtrousers and boots. Heavy-duty waterproof gear, designed to protect them from the elements. Joe wore only jeans and the thin plastic jacket he'd bought in Bristol, a week and a lifetime ago.

*   *   *

Joe was marched quickly to the Range Rover. The other three ducked their heads, while Joe turned his face up to the sky, the rain so hard and fierce that he could barely keep his eyes open.

'Thirsty?' Reece gave a scornful laugh. 'You're gonna have all the water you can drink soon enough.'

He was put in the back, forced to crouch in the footwell behind the passenger seat. Reece took the seat next to him. He held a leather sap. 'You just give me a reason, all right?'

From the driver's seat, Bruce tutted. 'We ain't supposed to mark him.'

'What's it gonna matter if his head gets split open? The rocks and tide'll make a mess of him.'

They set off, the windscreen wipers struggling to combat the torrent of water, Bruce grumbling about the driving conditions, Todd about how unpleasant their task was going to be, and Reece just sitting silently, staring at Joe with murder in his eyes.

The footwell was a tight space, so Joe wasn't thrown around too badly, but the motion of the car did little to ease his nausea. It was worse with his eyes shut, so he kept them open, staring at Reece's booted feet and thinking: *I'm sober. I'm sober. I'm sober.*

He tested his muscles as best he could, flexing one or two at a time: tiny cautious movements. He played out how the attack might develop, like a choreographer preparing several permutations of a dance routine. If he got a chance—*when* he got a chance—it had to be exploited without hesitation.

He stayed positive, except for the odd moment when an image of his wife and daughters broke his concentration and left him with the desperate, heartbreaking knowledge that one day they might be informed of his suicide and not doubt it for a second.

They would believe that Joe had given up on them, and somehow that thought was more unbearable than the idea of death itself.

CHAPTER SEVENTY-SIX

When Cadwell turned up Joe was still having the booze poured into him. Leon affected surprise at the news of the funeral director's arrival. 'I'm too busy to see him now.'

Fenton stayed by the door, fighting the temptation to plead. Leon glared at him till he left the room, and was then beset by doubts. Wasn't this reaction going to supply more fuel for the conspiracy against him?

To demonstrate to himself that he was a reasonable man, he went back over it all. It wasn't too late to rethink. They could keep Joe here. Phone Danny Morton and see what was on offer.

But every time he played it out, all he saw was Morton sneering at him. Calling him a *fucking hick*. Calling him a *dumbfuck yokel*.

And Leon couldn't do it. He couldn't give Morton the satisfaction. No matter how much money was involved, Morton would feel he'd got the better deal. He would come out the winner, and Leon—the dumbfuck yokel—would be the loser.

There was no way he'd let himself end up like Victor Smith, begging for whatever scraps Morton cared to throw him. No way on earth.

But Joe had to go. Leon had no qualms there at all. One way or another Joe was determined to bring him down, and he possessed the skills to do it. For the sake of Leon's own survival, Joe had to die.

* * *

It was twenty to two when they took Joe out. Leon slipped upstairs, stood at a bedroom window and watched the Range Rover drive away. The rain was churning the gravel driveway into a series of miniature lakes. Perfect conditions for the task ahead.

Back downstairs, Fenton met him in the hall, his face grave. 'You need to see this.'

To Leon's surprise, he was beckoned in the direction of the basement. His first reaction was to suspect a trap. Were Cadwell and his men hiding down there . . .?

He made Fenton take the stairs first, stayed alert for any sound or movement. But the den was empty.

He sniffed. Pulled a face. 'It stinks. What is it?'

'This.' Fenton placed his palm against the outer wall, next to the plasma TV. When Leon looked closely he could see that a patch of the wall was darker than the rest. He laid his own hand on it. Damp.

Fenton said, 'The river level must have risen above the damp-proof membrane.'

They inspected the rest of the room. In the toilet there was a puddle of water on the floor.

'Glenn guaranteed this would be waterproof,' Leon said. 'He can bloody well get it fixed.'

'Probably have to wait until the storm passes.'

'Whatever. Anyway, he should have picked up Joe's stuff by now.'

Returning to the office, he tried Glenn's mobile, but there was no answer. He was dimly aware of noise in the hall: that must be him.

Then Fenton came in, Derek Cadwell looming over his shoulder. He was wearing a dark suit with a

408

white shirt but no tie, and a black fedora glistening with rain.

'Not now, Derek.'

'You don't have a choice.' There was more steel in Cadwell's voice than usual. Always grim, the funeral director had a bleak determination on his face that gave Leon pause, but the conciliatory approach wasn't his style.

'I've been over it with Clive. I'm not changing my mind. Anyway, you're too late.'

Cadwell pulled out one of the conference chairs and sat down, while Fenton took his usual position on the sofa. Enough space between them that Leon couldn't look at them both at the same time. Was that a deliberate tactic? he wondered.

'This isn't about Morton. Or Joe Carter.' Cadwell sounded weary, as though he'd spent so long time building up to this conversation that he barely had the energy to go through with it.

'No?'

'No. It's about you and me, Leon. Our working relationship. It's been far too uneven for far too long.' Cadwell reached into his jacket and produced a USB stick. 'This,' he said, 'is going to restore the balance.'

CHAPTER SEVENTY-SEVEN

Joe wasn't able to see out of the Range Rover's window, so he couldn't track his route. All he had was a rough estimation of the direction and the time it took them to get there.

At first they ascended, driving south out of

409

Trelennan, then turned left, heading east. For ten or fifteen minutes they travelled on flat, winding terrain, the rain hammering on the roof and gusting against the windows. Then the road dipped and rose and dropped again more violently, twisting through a series of switchbacks as they descended towards the coast.

Joe guessed they were about four or five miles east of Trelennan. The coast along here was rocky and inhospitable, with only the occasional hamlet or farm nestled in the hills.

Finally the Range Rover came to a halt, Bruce ratcheting the handbrake, and then there was only the sound of the rain, trying to pummel the world into submission.

'Come on.' Reece was the first to get out. Rain blew into the car, hitting Joe in the face. Reece shut his door and stood by it to prevent Joe from escaping.

Todd opened the rear door on Joe's side, and Reece joined him as Joe manoeuvred himself backwards out of the car. Bruce was last to appear, abandoning the fight to keep his hood up.

Joe stood in docile silence, swaying in the wind. Cold rain poured down his neck but he tried not to shiver. Drunks tend not to notice the cold. With heavy-lidded eyes he took note of his surroundings.

The Range Rover had descended a steep wooded hill and parked on a muddy track beside a narrow river mouth. A grassy bank led down to a spit of dark grey slate, curving out to sea as if directing the river to its rightful home. In both directions Joe could barely make out the shore, lost in the spray of a raging sea. There wasn't another living soul in sight.

410

'This is some shitty weather,' Todd complained, shouting to be heard over the crashing waves. He and Reece took hold of Joe's arms and escorted him around the Range Rover towards the riverbank. Then Reece stopped abruptly and yelled at Bruce: 'The vodka.'

Joe said a prayer: *Thank God they hadn't forgotten it.*

* * *

Bruce returned to the vehicle and retrieved the bottle, while the other two fumed at the delay. Every second out here made them colder and wetter and angrier.

As Bruce approached, Joe was turned to face him. He now had Reece to his left, standing side-on to the riverbank, and Todd to his right, on the path directly in front of the Range Rover. Joe could feel their grip on him relax a little. He knew they would tense up again as Bruce made him drink the spiked vodka.

Anticipating that response, Joe let his body sag, his shoulders slumping and his arms bending at the elbows. He kept his hands suspended just above his waist. Shut his eyes and rehearsed the move; trying to allow for the fact that, despite his best efforts, he wasn't fully sober. His coordination wouldn't be at its best.

Bruce slowly removed the bottle's top; of the three, he seemed the least affected by the rain. He grinned at Joe, eyes shining with malice.

'Remember I said how fighting got me in trouble? It was with the filth. A bloke and a girl. Tried to arrest me for driving uninsured, so I beat

411

the living crap out of them.'

As he spoke, the rain coursed down his face and tumbled into his mouth. He spat it at Joe, who barely flinched as the water hit his chin.

'So drink up, 'cause ever since I've been hoping to go one better and kill a pig.'

Bruce lifted the bottle. Joe's mouth drooped open, offering no resistance. As he expected, he felt the grip on his upper arms tighten viciously, but his hands remained level with his stomach, only inches away from the bottle.

Joe let the alcohol flow for just long enough to establish his compliance. Then he moved, grabbing the neck of the bottle with his right hand. He wrenched it free and rammed the solid base of it into Bruce's face, then drew his right arm back and swung the bottle outwards, swatting Todd on the side of his head; simultaneously he used his left arm to shove Reece down the slope.

Reece cried out as he lost his footing and fell towards the rushing water. Bruce also stumbled backwards, his mouth a mess of blood and broken teeth. Todd wasn't badly hurt, but of the three he was the least experienced, and unlikely to have the stomach for a straight fight.

Joe didn't give him the opportunity. He jabbed the bottle into Todd's nose, at the site of his earlier injury. Even over the storm, Joe heard the bone give way. Todd screamed, doubling over. Joe grabbed the collar of his coat and hurled him down the bank in Reece's wake. No half measures now: it was kill or be killed.

Bruce came at him with a bellow of rage, the rain-diluted blood streaming over his bearded chin. Joe ducked sideways, surprising Bruce by going left,

412

towards Reece, who was trying to clamber up the slope on his hands and knees. Bruce's fist missed Joe's head by less than an inch. Now off balance, Bruce hesitated rather than follow Joe down the bank.

Reece was equally astonished to see Joe leaping towards him. Instead of flattening himself down on the grass, which might have saved him, he instinctively rose up, chest out and fists raised, ready to fight.

But Joe had the momentum of the steep slope in his favour. He leapt into the air and struck Reece in the chest with both feet. Reece was flattened by the impact, Joe landing in a heap next to him, and in a tangle of writhing limbs they slithered the last few feet onto the narrow slate beach.

Up close Joe could see the awesome power of the tidal flow, sucking at the slate as it rushed past, while the storm drove vicious waves across the surface, drenching them both with a foaming spray.

Joe recovered first, gaining a vital advantage by levering himself above Reece, who was pointed in the other direction, feet up on the bank and his head almost in the water. Joe grappled with him, trying to slide his body into the current, but Reece thrashed and fought to stop Joe getting a purchase, his wet-weather gear as slippery as the hide of some aquatic beast. Then, for a second, his resistance ceased, his gaze shifting to a spot just over Joe's shoulder.

There wasn't time to look, and the raging sea muffled any noise. All Joe could do was move—and hope. Keeping low, on his hands and knees, he drove his legs backwards as if doing a squat thrust. His feet connected with something, with *someone*,

413

and as he dropped and rolled he saw Todd falling, not directly into the water but close enough for a wave to catch him.

Briefly immersed, Todd panicked, wrenching his head and upper body away from the edge. But in doing so his legs went in deeper; his heavy boots were swamped with water and after that he didn't stand a chance: the current sucked him beneath the surface and he was gone.

*   *   *

It was over so quickly that Joe could hardly believe what he'd seen. Desperate not to suffer the same fate, Reece threw himself at Joe, clubbing and pawing at his head. Joe butted Reece in the face and wrestled him closer to the water. He was committed now. With Todd having been snatched away like driftwood, Reece had to follow.

Joe got his hands round Reece's neck, forcing him closer and closer, but to submerge him part of Joe's own head and shoulders were in the water. It took all his strength to hold Reece down. Breathing was almost impossible: an occasional gulp of air that came saturated with spray and lined his mouth with salt. Reece was snarling and spitting, raw terror in his eyes because he understood that Joe was ruthless enough to do it.

Freezing cold waves broke over them. Even at the very edge, only inches deep, the outgoing tide exerted a tremendous force, tugging at their hair, their jackets, while the rain slashed down on their bodies and the slate beach seemed to writhe and shift beneath them. Joe was dimly aware that they were both screaming with desperation and rage,

414

each knowing that it came down to nothing more or less than sheer determination: only one of them was going to survive, and it would be the one who wanted it most.

For Joe, it was never in doubt. Even with Reece clawing at his face and neck, even with starbursts distorting his vision and his blood pumping so hard that he felt his heart or head might burst; even then he knew it was going to be him. *He* wanted it the most.

At the end he shut his eyes and kept them shut. Not because he couldn't bear to look, but because his mind had taken him somewhere else, and when he came back he was dangerously cold and the water was pushing and pulling him over the slate, teasing him closer, and Reece lay flat on his back with his head beneath the surface and his arms splayed out in surrender.

Joe shoved the body into the water, let it be claimed by the greedy sea. Then he crawled a few feet up the slope before stopping to be violently, painfully sick.

He spat bile and rain from his mouth, wiped his face and looked up to where Bruce was waiting for him on the path. He'd known all along that Bruce was the main threat, the real fighter of the three.

This had been the easy part.

CHAPTER SEVENTY-EIGHT

Cadwell slipped the USB stick back into his pocket and waited to see how Leon would react. But Leon, who knew exactly what was on it, decided to say

415

nothing.

Cadwell quickly tired of the silence. 'So Alise survived?'

Leon nodded. 'Joe's spoken to her. That's one of the reasons he had to go.'

'That doesn't remove the threat.'

'Alise isn't a threat to me.'

'Oh?' Cadwell said. 'I wouldn't be so sure about that.'

Grinning, Leon laced his hands behind his head. 'Why? Because of that little stick of yours?'

'Correct.' If Cadwell was disappointed that Leon had stolen his thunder, he hid it well. Fenton wasn't so smooth, his goldfish mouth opening and closing in astonishment.

'You're on that tape as well,' Leon said. 'The way I remember it, you were practically wanking yourself off.'

Cadwell flushed. 'I made sure I stayed out of range. And it was recorded without sound.'

'Lucky you. So what are you planning to do with it?'

'Nothing. It's what used to be called "mutually assured destruction".' A condescending smile. 'You're with me up to this point, are you?'

Leon ignored him, staring at Fenton. 'You two cooked this up together?'

'No. It wasn't so calculated. The tape was originally intended for . . . well . . .'

'Private pleasure,' Cadwell finished for him. 'We had no idea you'd get so enthusiastic. As you laid into her, I spotted the perfect opportunity to flush you out.'

Leon frowned. 'What do you mean?'

Cadwell leaned forward, his beaky nose

416

wrinkling, as though he didn't much care for the sight in front of him. 'I needed an incriminating tape of you because you have one of me. But do you?'

'Of course I do.'

'Then I want to see it. Otherwise I'll have to conclude that you've been bluffing all these years.'

Leon was struggling for a response when Fenton, unwittingly or not, threw him a lifeline.

'Leon, please. Neither of us wanted it to come to this, but your refusal to countenance a deal with Danny Morton . . . It's madness.'

'He's right,' Cadwell said. 'You've allowed your ego to get in the way of common sense.'

Leon couldn't maintain his relaxed pose any longer. He unclasped his hands and slapped his palms on the table. 'Whatever we did, Morton would have found a way to screw us. Maybe you've got your heads stuck so far up your arses that you can't see it, but I can. And to blackmail me for something as stupid as that . . .'

'No. No. Not blackmail—' Fenton had both of his pudgy hands up in the air.

'Actually, Clive, I beg to differ,' Cadwell broke in. 'Maybe it didn't start out that way, but it's blackmail now, and why not?' He squared up to Leon again. 'It all comes down to the tape you claim to have. If you do, then prove it.'

'Or what?'

'Or you step down from your little empire and cede control to a new holding company, run by Clive and myself. You'll be retained in an advisory capacity, providing you cooperate fully.'

'Piss off,' Leon spat. 'I've been eating twats like you for breakfast since I was a kid.'

417

Fenton looked pained. 'Leon, please. From our perspective—'

'Forget it, Clive.' Still focused on Cadwell, Leon said, 'What do you think you're gonna do, take that tape to the cops? Go ahead. I'll talk my way out of it.' He gave a sly smile. 'But I don't think you'd risk it. Not when you just buried that extra body.'

Cadwell produced a matching smile. 'Your Mr Smith isn't buried anywhere. He's being stored safely, at an undisclosed location, for just such an eventuality as this.'

As Cadwell spoke, Leon concentrated on Fenton's reaction, saw him suppress a gasp, to which Cadwell responded with an angry glare.

Leon pounced. 'He's taking you for a fool, Clive.'

Fenton started to speak, but a sudden deep rumbling brought an end to the conversation. The whole room shook, as though a bomb had gone off close by. Leon's chair jerked an inch or two across the floor. A document tray toppled off the desk, and pictures fell from the wall.

As the noise subsided, the divisions between them were temporarily forgotten. Fenton had dived to the floor and now lay panting like a beached whale. Cadwell was gripping the arms of his chair as though on a roller-coaster ride. Both men turning to Leon for an explanation—and the most obvious one was also the most outlandish.

They were under attack.

*   *   *

The water was like some kind of miracle. Something she had prayed for, but had never expected. If you didn't believe in God, how could He possibly answer

418

your prayers?

Jenny had given up the fight. Her body was shutting down, taking with it her will to resist, to survive. *You should be dead by now*, the voice inside her kept saying.

She had been so stupid. Bewitched by the prospect of escape, she had blithely used the waste water to soften the plasterboard, never suspecting that she might need it to assuage her thirst. Back then the very idea would have appalled her: inconceivable that she could ever stoop to such depravity.

She knew differently now.

It was in a dream that she smelled it. She hadn't known that water possessed a smell, but her eyes opened and made out a dull gleam on the floor of the cell. She had been lying unconscious by the door and now, somehow, there was a tiny moist patch just an inch or two from her head. Any further away and she might never have known it was there.

The energy to move, the craving, was immediate and extraordinary. It occurred to her as she lowered her head and scraped her tongue on the concrete that she was an animal now: a mindless, primitive creature who existed, but barely lived.

And she didn't care. Lapping water from the ground, weeping with the knowledge that this might only prolong her agony, she didn't care how it looked or what it made her. Nothing mattered except this.

You should be dead by now.

But she wasn't. She was alive, and her body rejoiced. She licked the floor dry, rested, still desperately thirsty, then lowered her mouth to the ground and found more water. The puddle had been replenished.

Jenny gasped. And drank again.

Truly, a miracle.

CHAPTER SEVENTY-NINE

Bruce wasn't stupid; at least, not as stupid as his late colleagues. He didn't even attempt to descend the slope. He was in a winning position and had no need to relinquish it.

Joe was trapped. If he tried moving left or right Bruce could easily intercept him. A direct assault was almost impossible: he had no weapons, and just climbing the bank would require all his concentration. But if he stayed where he was, he would quickly succumb to exposure. He was already shivering uncontrollably, his body drenched by rain and seawater.

He began to climb, using his hands and feet for better purchase on the slippery grass. Every couple of paces he looked up at Bruce and tried to think of a way past. And every time he came up blank.

Bruce stood on the edge of the path, arms folded, water streaming down his face. An intimidating sight, like a massive tree that had to be felled by hand.

Closing the gap to a few feet, Joe stopped. 'You should let me go,' he said, yelling to be heard over the crash and roar of the storm. 'Don't make the same mistake as those two.'

'I haven't,' Bruce shouted back. 'They were losers, the pair of them.'

420

'So what are you getting out of this?'

'I'm not interested in avenging them.' Bruce spat a mouthful of blood in Joe's direction. 'When I kill you, it's gonna be for my own enjoyment.'

Movement along the path caught Joe's attention. He turned his head, frowning.

'Fuck off,' Bruce shouted. 'Oldest trick in the book.'

But then he sensed it, too. Risked a glance and saw a big Toyota truck thundering down the track towards them.

Glenn.

Bruce was disappointed, and Joe guessed why. Mobile phones wouldn't work out here. Any change of plan and Leon would have to send someone in person.

'Gonna help me up?' Joe said, half joking, extending a hand towards Bruce.

Bruce ignored him, waiting until the Toyota pulled up behind the Range Rover and Glenn got out. He was alone, wearing jeans and a short quilted coat that wasn't going to keep him dry for long. That suggested an urgent mission.

Bruce must have thought the same. He took a couple of steps back from the edge and turned towards Glenn. 'Don't say he's changed his mind?'

Glenn cocked his head, trying to decipher the words before they were lost in the wind. Then he nodded grimly, leaned close to Bruce and said something that Joe couldn't hear.

In response, Bruce swept out his arm to indicate the churning river mouth. 'Drowned 'em both,' he cried, turning towards Joe. There was a flash of silver and a spray of blood and Bruce staggered away, dropped to his knees and collapsed onto the

421

muddy track.

Glenn stared at the body, as if he couldn't quite believe what he had done. He was holding a large adjustable wrench. He didn't move until Joe had taken the last cautious steps onto the path. They regarded each other warily for a moment, and then Glenn offered a hesitant smile.

'Glad I made it in time.'

'Why did you come here?'

'To save you.' Another rueful look at Bruce. A dark puddle of blood spread out from beneath his battered skull. Glenn shuddered, turned away and hurled the wrench into the sea.

'Was this Leon's idea?' Joe asked.

'Diana's.' Glenn sighed. 'Leon would kill me for this. He'd kill us all.'

*   *   *

Leon ran to the comms room, barely registering an unfamiliar draught of cold air as he crossed the hall. Wishing he'd arranged for Venning or Kestle to return sooner, he examined the bank of monitors. There was no movement at the front of the house, no unfamiliar vehicles on the drive. The side cameras showed nothing wrong, although the one above the rear decking must have come loose in the storm: the image was slanted at an angle, tight up on the corner of the building.

Fenton eased past him and brought up a different selection of cameras. 'The north-east corner is out.'

'That's the kitchen,' Leon said. Had somebody tried to break in at the back?

He was first into the room, but didn't notice

422

anything amiss until Fenton pointed towards the adjoining utility room. Part of the ceiling had come down. Chunks of plaster covered the washing machine and tumble dryer. There were cracks in the outer wall large enough to put your hand through. Rain was already blowing inside.

'What the hell did this?' Irrational or not, Leon couldn't get the idea of an explosion out of his mind.

'I don't know,' Fenton murmured, 'but I have a horrible feeling . . .'

'What?' Leon asked.

Fenton said nothing, just hurried back out and made for the basement. Leon caught up with him on the stairs. There was a lot more damage down here: big cracks in the ceiling and the outer wall. The movement had been enough to shatter the TV screen. Leon groaned when he saw it.

'Subsidence,' Fenton said. 'The foundations must have been undermined.'

Leon was already crossing the room, casting uneasy glances at the ceiling. Looked like the whole thing could give way at any moment. In the toilet, the puddle from earlier had covered the floor and was creeping over the threshold.

'Fucking Glenn. He swore it could never flood.'

Leon turned, suddenly aware that Cadwell wasn't with them. He rushed upstairs and found the funeral director emerging from a room they used for storage.

'More cracks in there,' he said. 'This is very serious.'

As Fenton caught up with them, Leon said: 'Get Glenn over here now.'

Cadwell shook his head. 'A jobbing builder

423

isn't much use. You're going to need structural engineers. Experts in underpinning.'

'This is Glenn's problem,' Leon said, 'and he's damn well gonna put it right.'

The three men returned to the office. Cadwell made for the doors to the veranda. 'We'd better check the river level.'

He didn't need to spell it out. Leaving Fenton on the phone, Cadwell and Leon stepped into a blast of wind and rain, which intensified as they moved out of the relative protection of the veranda.

Cadwell was first to reach the viewing platform, testing the handrail before he leaned on it. Leon heard an exclamation as he drew alongside.

The surface of the river was only a couple of feet below the deck, swirling madly around the struts that supported the viewing platform. All kinds of debris was being swept along: branches and fence posts and a tangle of barbed wire, a yellow plastic bollard, a wheel that might have come from a motorcycle; then a dead seagull, dirty white and crumpled like an old pillow, twisting helplessly in the current.

Cadwell turned to Leon, rain coursing down his face. 'You need to evacuate. If the water gets much higher, the whole house could collapse.'

As if to emphasise the point, there was a ferocious rending noise from further down the hillside. The upper reaches of a tree shivered and disappeared from sight.

'Gonna be a lot of damage downstream,' Leon said. But he didn't sound—or feel—the least bit concerned.

Cadwell started to move away. Leon put a hand on his arm. 'There wasn't a tape.'

'What?' Disbelief, or maybe Cadwell hadn't heard him over the raging water.

'There wasn't a tape,' Leon said again. 'I put a camera in, but it didn't work. I had a good idea what you were up to, so I blagged it. And because you found the camera, you believed it.'

Cadwell was incredulous. 'It's all been a bluff?'

'Yep. I've got nothing on you. Never have had.'

'But now I've—' Cadwell fell silent as it dawned on him that Leon shouldn't be admitting to this. Shouldn't be handing him such an easy advantage . . .

The funeral director was a big man, about four inches taller than Leon and probably a couple of stone lighter, but he wasn't in good shape. Too keen on his rich foods, his fine wines and his single malts and his Cuban cigars; he never took any kind of exercise.

Leon, on the other hand, was plumper but also stronger and fitter. Younger. More determined.

And, when it came down to it, a lot more ruthless.

Leon's punch was fast and powerful, low into Cadwell's gut. The older man had no defence. Winded, he clutched his stomach, tried to breathe and made a desperate *uhuhuh* noise while Leon grabbed him with both hands and rammed him against the guard rail. It splintered but didn't give way.

Cadwell finally found the breath to scream, a thin, hoarse noise easily lost in the storm. His arms batted at Leon, but there wasn't much strength in them. Leon ducked, got Cadwell by the legs and flipped him over the rail.

One second Cadwell was there: a rival, a traitor,

a threat. The next second he was gone, lost to the muddy swirling water. A tragic victim of the flood.

And probably not the last.

*　　*　　*

The water restored Jenny to life, as though she'd been reduced to some kind of freeze-dried powder: now the addition of moisture gave her substance and strength once more. She could almost feel her body's cells swelling, her blood flowing faster, the normal functions restarting, gearing up for a prolonged survival.

Hope bloomed, like a flower in the desert.

And then she had drunk her fill, but the water kept coming. Now strong enough to sit up, she was leaning with one hand on the floor when she felt the water tickle her skin.

It took her some time to process the information, for the flower to wither and die. She didn't know how long, precisely, but it was equivalent to the time it took for a thin membrane of water to spread around her body and cover the floor of her cell.

Jenny shivered. The temperature, which had remained constant throughout her captivity, seemed to be rapidly falling away. She grasped the fact that her environment was changing, becoming more hostile. She had to respond in some way.

First she groped for the broken torch, switched it on and off several times, but nothing was going to restore it to life. The pinprick of light from the hole in the outer wall made no appreciable difference to the illumination in the cell. All she could rely on was her sense of touch.

She felt her way along the bottom of the cell

426

door, and determined that the water was seeping in underneath. The gap seemed very narrow, which struck her as important, even though she didn't completely understand why.

Jenny moved along to the hole she had made in the wall, where she had another shock. The lower part of the wall was wet to the touch. When she put her hand through the hole she found water, a couple of inches deep, in the partition.

The noise she'd heard earlier was subtly different. There was still a pounding, pulsing river, but now it also splashed and echoed and dripped; it was the busy, joyous sound of water breaking into new territory, invading tunnels and caves, drowning everything in its path.

As she sat and listened, the water in the partition reached the hole she had made and began to dribble over the lip of sodden plasterboard. At any moment, Jenny realised, these walls might melt away.

If they did, could she escape through the studwork before she drowned in the flood?

CHAPTER EIGHTY

'Did you really kill Reece and Todd?' Glenn asked. He and Joe were in the Toyota, bumping up the hill away from the shore. With Glenn's help, Joe had rolled Bruce's body into the sea. The Range Rover had followed, the tremendous force of the current pulling the vehicle under as though it were a child's toy.

Despite this, Joe still hadn't decided if Glenn

427

could be fully trusted. He said nothing.

'Right vicious bastards, they were,' Glenn added. 'I wouldn't have taken them on. I mean, I know you were a cop once, but that took some doing. You weren't a secret agent or something, were you?'

Joe snorted. 'Nope. Just an ordinary plod.' Before Glenn could speak again, Joe had his own blunt question: 'Did Leon kill them?'

'What?'

'The missing women. Alise's sister, most recently. I think there were others before her. What did Leon do with them?'

Glenn gave an uneasy laugh, as if he might be in the company of a lunatic. 'I don't know if any of that stuff's true. Like I said, I came out here for Di's sake. That's all.'

'But you must have a gut feeling about him. Tell me: if I searched his house from top to bottom, would I find anything?'

Glenn sighed. 'The honest truth is that I loved working for Leon, and now I've betrayed him, helping you like this. So even if I don't end up in jail for whacking Bruce on the head, I haven't got a bloody clue how I'm going to earn a living.'

*   *   *

They drove on in sullen silence, Joe's mind trawling through everything he'd seen and heard. He was tormented by the idea that he had enough raw material to find a solution to the puzzle, if he could just catch a glimpse of the design.

Once they crested the hill, the effects of the storm became more apparent. The narrow lanes were flooding fast, the rain washing large quantities

428

of mud into the road. Even the heavy Toyota struggled to get traction at times.

The heater was turned up to the maximum, but Joe didn't stop shivering until they were descending into Trelennan. Here the roads were littered with wind-blown debris and criss-crossed with streams of flood water. Mini-lakes spread out from drains choked with leaves, and the trees bowed under the weight of the rain pelting down on them.

There was a desolate air to the town, the streets deserted in the early dusk, every door and window tightly shut. A community under siege, huddled down and hoping to ride out the storm.

*   *   *

Diana was ecstatic to see them. Fighting off tears, she threw her arms around Joe, hugging him so tightly he could barely breathe. Then she embraced Glenn, who seemed taken aback by this show of affection.

'You're soaked, both of you. Dry off and change before you do anything else.'

Neither of them was about to argue. Joe trudged up to his room on the top floor, stripped off and stood under a scalding-hot shower until he felt human again. He dressed in clean clothes and was back down within ten minutes.

Diana had coffee waiting for him, and there was bread in the toaster. She'd just heard a news report on the local radio.

'It's absolute chaos. Trees down, roads blocked. Flood warnings right across the South-West. The police are advising people not to travel unless it's essential.'

429

Joe nodded, satisfied that his own objectives fell within that definition.

'Where's Glenn?' he asked.

'Taking a shower in my room.' She gave Joe an uncertain smile. 'I'm so relieved that you're all right. What happened?'

'They tried the same tactic they used with Alise. It probably would have worked, if not for you.'

'And Glenn,' she pointed out. 'I gave him an ultimatum. I wanted to see if he was capable of doing the right thing. It turns out that he was.'

Joe glanced at the doorway. 'I think it would still pay to be cautious there . . .'

'Oh, don't worry, I will. One tiny step at a time.'

*   *   *

Glenn wandered in, rubbing his wet hair with a towel. He was wearing a pair of paint-splattered jeans and a denim shirt: old decorating clothes. He accepted a coffee, then joined Joe at the table. Diana brought over the first batch of toast and urged them to tuck in.

Joe said, 'I want to know if the allegations that Alise made are true.'

Glenn had just picked up a piece of toast. He paused, then took a bite, indicating with a nod that he was composing a reply.

'I know Leon wanted her to disappear. She was damaging his reputation. Same thing with you,' he added, waving the half-eaten toast at Joe. 'Leon's a businessman, simple as that. Everything I did for him was totally legitimate.'

'And you never saw any evidence of illegal activity? No money laundering, for instance?'

430

Glenn raised his eyebrows in surprise. 'I don't have a clue about money. Doing my own accounts used to send me mental—just ask Ellie.' He snorted, then gave Diana an apologetic glance. 'That's one of the reasons I went to work for Leon. Anyway, Clive Fenton handles all the financial stuff.'

'You're saying Fenton is the brains of the outfit?'

'In a way. Though you can't get much past Leon, either.' Glenn picked up another piece of toast, took a bite and shrugged. 'Well, not till lately.'

'What do you mean?'

'His judgement's gone haywire. An opportunity came up at the weekend, a chance to make a lot of money. Leon turned it down flat, just 'cause he felt he'd been insulted. Fenton and Cadwell were seriously pissed off. In fact, it wouldn't surprise me if they're hatching a plan to take over.'

Joe considered this. For all Glenn's apparent candour, there was something that made Joe uneasy, something that didn't quite ring true.

He said, 'Would Fenton or Cadwell know what happened to the missing women?'

There was a heavy silence, broken only by the sound of Glenn chewing. Joe looked down at his own plate. He knew he should eat, but he didn't have much appetite.

Gently, Diana said, 'Please, Glenn. If you know anything that can help . . .'

'I don't. Not really. But maybe it's true. They're a bunch of perverts, all three of them. Me and the others, we joke about it behind their backs.'

'But it's not a joke, is it?' Joe said, struggling to contain his temper. 'We're talking about women who might have been abducted and murdered.

431

Now, are you saying that the others are involved? Is Cadwell disposing of the bodies? Is that why Leon's so sure he won't be caught?'

Joe saw immediately that he'd struck home. Glenn's guard dropped, but before he could respond there was a loud bang in the distance.

And the lights went out.

CHAPTER EIGHTY-ONE

Soaked by the rain, Leon dived back into the office and grabbed a fleece, using it to dry off. Fenton had the phone to his ear, waiting impatiently.

'Signal's going haywire. When I do get through he doesn't pick up.'

'Useless twat.' Leon glanced at his watch. 'Isn't Reece back yet?'

'I tried him, too. And Bruce's phone. Nothing.' Fenton looked from Leon to the veranda doors, then frowned. 'Where's Derek?'

'Derek? Oh, he's moved on,' Leon said, his tone light and cheery.

Fenton did the goldfish thing again, then managed a single word: 'What?'

'You knew him better than me. Never much of a swimmer, was he?'

Slowly, as if operated by wires, Fenton lowered the phone and collapsed onto the sofa, his face white. It was a full minute before he found his voice.

'You murdered him?'

Leon tutted. 'Clive. You know better than that. I've no idea what happened to him. Lost in the flood, I suppose.' He wagged a finger at the fat man. 'But if it can happen once, it can happen again. You wanna think carefully about that.'

*   *   *

The whole house seemed to exhale, the electrical appliances groaning as they powered down. Plunged into shadow, the room felt instantly colder, the murky twilight crowding in on them. Without the normal hum of background noise, the rain was louder than ever.

'Power cut,' Glenn said.

'It sounded like an explosion.' Joe hurried through the hall and ran upstairs. One of the guest bedrooms had views down the hill. He could just make out a lick of flame and a smudge of black smoke coming from a gap between two white stone villas.

When he went back down Diana and Glenn were in the hall, checking the electricity meter in the cupboard under the stairs.

'Substation's blown,' he told them.

'Oh my God,' Diana said. 'I'll find some candles. Torches.'

A knock on the front door made them all jump. Concerned that Leon might have sent reinforcements, Joe checked the side window and through the frosted glass he saw a single diminutive figure.

Ellie.

*   *   *

He opened the door and ushered her in. She was

433

soaking wet, and possibly crying. Her relief at seeing him turned to apprehension when she spotted Diana and Glenn. For a second Joe thought she was going to bolt. He reached out and took her arm.

'Are you all right?'

'Just about. The river's burst its banks and flooded the High Street. All the shops had to be evacuated. I tried to get home but one of the footbridges has collapsed. I didn't know . . .' She glanced at Diana and shrugged. 'This was the only place nearby that I could think of.'

'You were quite right,' Diana said firmly. 'Come on. Let's get you dry.'

Glenn said nothing: he'd taken out his phone and was staring intently at the tiny screen. Just as studiously, Ellie ignored him as Diana placed a comforting arm around her shoulder. For Joe, the sight of Ellie being helped along produced a powerful jolt of recognition.

He followed them back to the kitchen and waited, impatience gnawing at him, while Ellie dried off with a towel and finally sat down, a mug of coffee warming her hands.

'You remember saying the Shell Cavern was probably discovered by smugglers?'

They stared at him, trying to understand the context of the question.

Ellie nodded. 'As far as anyone knows.'

'And there are other tunnels up there?'

'Supposedly, yes.'

Glenn had slouched in and was now leaning against the kitchen units, keeping a wary distance from his ex-wife. The phone was still in his hand, and he looked distracted.

Joe eyed him suspiciously. 'How far is Leon's

house from the Shell Cavern?'

Glenn seemed confused for a moment; then he let out a groan, as if winded. 'Oh, shit.'

'What?' Diana snapped. 'What do you know?'

'There's a tunnel, isn't there?' Joe said. 'Beneath the house.'

Now unwillingly the focus of attention, Glenn approached the table. He pushed a hand through his hair.

'It was years back, when I remodelled the basement. Leon said he had another job. All top secret. He'd located a passageway that ran under the house and he wanted me to put in a strongroom.' He bit anxiously at the tip of his thumb. 'He said it was for storing important documents, money—stuff like that.'

'But it wasn't?'

'I've no idea. He keeps it padlocked. And it's not easy to get to. There's a panel that comes off, behind the toilet. I haven't had any reason to go near it for years.'

'Who knows about it? Just you and Leon?'

He spread his hands. 'Clive Fenton, maybe.'

'And Cadwell?'

'Leon wouldn't have told him. But if Clive knows . . . it's possible.'

'And this room,' Joe said. 'It's big enough to keep someone prisoner?'

Glenn sighed. He looked mournful, defeated. 'It's got shelves for storage, and I helped Leon carry a filing cabinet down there. But get rid of those, and what you'd have left is a prison cell.'

* * *

It was Diana who spoke first, recognising the determined look on Joe's face. 'Tell me you're not going to Leon's now?'

'I have to,' Joe said. 'If Alise's sister is there, she might still be alive.'

'You should call the police.'

He gestured at the window. 'Look at the conditions out there. The emergency services are going to be swamped with calls. No one will have time to listen to some vague accusation about a missing woman and an underground room.'

Glenn held up his phone. 'I've got messages from Clive, demanding that I get back. He says the house has serious flood damage.'

Joe stared at Diana. 'All the more reason to act fast.'

He stood up and started across the room. Glenn made to follow him, but Joe shook his head. 'It's best if you stay with these two.'

'What, the helpless little women?' Ellie said in a mocking voice.

Joe shook his head. 'It appears to be safe enough here, but if you need to get out in a hurry you'll stand a much better chance in Glenn's truck.'

'That's a good point,' Diana said. 'In the meantime I'll get a fire going in the front room. With the power off it'll be freezing in here soon.'

*   *   *

Before he left the house, Joe made sure he was properly equipped. Diana had found him a better waterproof jacket, as well as a small rucksack and a sturdy Maglite torch. She also suggested that he take a first-aid kit. Glenn fetched the toolbox from

436

his truck, and Joe borrowed a ten-inch crowbar, a Stanley knife and a set of heavy-duty Knipex bolt cutters.

The two women came to see him off, while Glenn stayed in the kitchen. He'd agreed not to respond to Fenton's messages, and Joe had discreetly asked Diana to make sure he kept to his word.

Diana returned the door key that Leon had taken from him, and offered him the use of her car. Joe thought it would be safer and probably quicker on foot.

'If you're sure,' she said. 'Please take care.'

'I will.'

She looked into his eyes for a moment. He sensed that she wanted to say something more, but perhaps Ellie's presence inhibited her. She settled for a brief kiss on his cheek, then turned and walked away.

Ellie smiled sadly. 'She's been a good friend to you.'

'She has,' Joe agreed. 'So have you.'

Their embrace was different: harder, fiercer, with an undercurrent of passion and a poignant sense of opportunities squandered. They kissed, lips pressed together for a long time, and when they broke apart he found that a tear had transferred from her cheek to his.

She swallowed heavily. 'I shouldn't say this, but if you find . . . what you expect to find . . .'

'Go on.'

'Even if he's arrested, you know Leon will find a way to get out of it. It's what he does best. Avoiding responsibility. Blaming others.'

'What are you saying?'

437

'I think you know,' Ellie said. 'If you get a chance, you should kill him.'

CHAPTER EIGHTY-TWO

Clive Fenton was many things, but slow on the uptake he wasn't. Even Leon was surprised by how rapidly he adjusted to the new reality.

'I suppose, from a business perspective, it's no great loss. I always had my doubts about the man, as you know.'

'Do I?' Leon said, acting baffled.

'Well, yes.' Fenton's face was bright red, but he brazened it out. 'I often warned you that he was privy to far too much confidential data. That always made him a threat.'

Leon nodded sceptically. 'Anyway, what I need to know is where *you* stand.'

'With you, Leon. One hundred per cent. You can be sure of that.'

'Except I can't. Not in view of what was said earlier. You're gonna have to earn my trust all over again, Clive. Starting from scratch.'

Fenton looked uneasy. 'Very well.'

'What do you know about this stunt Cadwell pulled with Smith's body?'

'Nothing. That was a surprise to me, I can assure you.'

'I reckon he was bluffing. I want you to find out, and while you're at it make sure he didn't have any other tricks up his sleeve.'

'Good idea.' Fenton cast an anxious glance at the rain-lashed veranda. 'As for the immediate priority,

438

I think we should vacate—'

'We're not going anywhere yet. Ring Glenn one more time.'

While Fenton made the call and waited for an answer, Leon used his mobile to try Reece, then Todd, then Bruce. He couldn't get through to any of them.

'Where the fuck are they?' he yelled, hurling the phone across the room.

Fenton flinched, even though it had missed him by a mile. 'Perhaps the weather's delayed them. It's probably disrupting the phones, too.'

Leon gave an incoherent growl of frustration. He stalked over and retrieved his phone. The cover was cracked, but it was still working. Functioning, but useless, he thought: *just like the people I employ.*

*   *   *

Joe set off at a run, the tools clanking in his rucksack, the rain pelting his face as he descended the hill, dodging the streams of dirty water that gushed from every driveway and drain. Greasy smoke was worming from the substation, but the fire appeared to have been extinguished by the rain.

Along the front, gigantic waves battered the shore, hurling great white plumes of spray onto the promenade, exploding across the road with a sound like machine-gun fire. The sea was a leaden grey beneath a low black sky, lit by the occasional flash of lightning. Several small boats had been torn from their moorings and driven, pulverised, onto the beach.

By the time Joe reached the gallery he was soaked to the skin and shivering again. The CLOSED

439

sign was up; the door locked. Joe put his face to the glass and peered inside. There were no lights on but he could see movement at the back of the room.

He hammered on the door. Patrick Davy approached, gripping a mop in both hands.

'What?' he mouthed.

'Let me in, please!' Joe shouted. 'I don't work for Leon any more. He tried to kill me.'

Davy looked unconvinced, but when Joe showed no sign of leaving he unlocked the door and let him in. 'This better not be a try-on.'

'I promise.' Joe indicated the mop. 'Has that taken over from the cricket bat?'

'Not exactly. The bloody roof sprang a leak. Practically everything on the mezzanine is ruined.'

'Do you have insurance?'

Davy snorted. 'Sore point. The premiums were crazy, so I cut down, didn't bother with cover for my own stuff.' He pointed to a stack of ruined canvases. 'I don't mind admitting, I'm about ready to throw in the towel. Let Derek Cadwell have the place.'

'I wouldn't do anything too hastily. Things might be changing round here.'

'Glad to hear it.' Davy gave him a careful appraisal. 'So how come you've made an enemy of Leon Race?'

'For one thing, I found out what happened to Alise.' Joe quickly relayed the story, describing how they had tried to dispose of him in the same way. 'I'm sorry about the other day, rolling up in one of Leon's vans.'

'No, mate, I'm the one who should apologise. I did wonder afterwards if you'd gone undercover. I couldn't decide whether that makes you very brave

440

or very stupid.'

'Both.'

Davy laughed, but there was little humour in his eyes. 'So what now?'

'I'm going after Leon. And I need your help.'

*   *   *

For Jenny, the irony of her predicament was almost unbearable. A woman who had been dying of thirst now faced death by drowning.

The water was steadily rising, both in her cell and in the tunnel beyond. She had managed to prise off enough of the saturated plasterboard to see that escape was impossible. The studwork was constructed with thick planks of wood: what her dad would call four-by-twos. The horizontal timbers were spaced only three or four inches apart, like bars on a cage. She could barely get her hand between them.

From what she could see, the cell was situated in a natural alcove in a low, narrow tunnel. There was very faint illumination to her right, just enough to see the dark water as it rushed and gurgled along the tunnel, flowing from the other direction. The noise of the river was hideously loud, pounding against the rock wall.

She was so weak that she could hardly stand upright. The water was up to her knees, rising imperceptibly when she stared at it but alarmingly fast if she shut her eyes and tried to pretend it wasn't happening.

And it was cold. She couldn't feel her feet. Her calves ached and throbbed. She wrapped her arms around herself and shivered and prayed, shivered and prayed.

The prayers made no sense, but God didn't mind that, did He? He'd make allowances for a situation like this.

She had done everything possible to escape. But it hadn't been enough.

*   *   *

Patrick Davy confirmed what Ellie had said about the state of the High Street, but said they could probably reach the top of the hill in his Land Rover. He put on a Barbour waxed jacket and leather bush hat, and caught Joe's knowing look.

'A practical concession to my heritage,' he said. 'Minus the corks, you'll notice.'

Before locking up, he slipped behind the counter and picked up his cricket bat. Joe grinned, but said nothing.

It took them nearly fifteen minutes to wind their way up through the backstreets, passing gardens waterlogged and trashed and trees and hedges withering under the onslaught of the storm. Many of the roads were partially flooded, but Davy's battered old Land Rover coped ably with the conditions.

At the top of the hill, crossing the main road bridge, they saw the river level was surging to within a couple of feet of the road. The surrounding fields had turned into giant lakes, feeding the torrent. For the first time they encountered traffic, almost all of it travelling in the opposite direction.

'Doing the sensible thing and getting out,' Davy muttered.

'I was never big on sensible,' Joe said. 'But drop

442

me off and turn round if you want.'

Davy chuckled. 'Nah. Fact is, I'm relishing a chance to get even.'

As they reached the junction for the road to Leon's they caught sight of the High Street, curving away below them. The river had burst from its channel at roughly the point where Joe remembered stopping to phone Maz. From there it gushed down the street, flooding offices and shops and flattening everything in its path. Cars were being carried in the flow; others had come to rest smashed against each other or piled up like trash in the doorways.

There were half a dozen fire engines and police vehicles parked at the top of the street, but other than rescuing anyone who remained trapped there wasn't much the emergency services could do, other than stand by and let nature take its course.

'This'll kill off the town completely,' Davy murmured.

Joe disagreed. 'With the right people in charge, Trelennan can recover from this.'

The darkness was closing in as they parked at the kerb, some fifty yards from Leon's home, but there was light streaming from the neighbouring properties.

'Power's still on up here,' Joe said as they got out. 'Watch out for CCTV.'

Davy hefted the cricket bat. 'I have my handy deactivation tool at the ready.'

The main gates were open. There was a limo parked in front of the house: Derek Cadwell's. A Mercedes sat under the carport, along with the Citroën van that Joe had used on Saturday, but there were far fewer vehicles than normal. That corresponded with what Glenn had told him: there should be only Leon, Fenton and maybe one or two others present.

They studied the front of the house. There were a couple of lights on, but no sign of movement. Joe mapped the layout in his head, working out a route to the basement stairs.

'I need to go in through the back door,' he said. 'Preferably without being heard.'

Davy nodded. 'You'll want a noisy diversion out front, then?'

CHAPTER EIGHTY-THREE

Diana was reluctant to acknowledge the extent of her doubts about Glenn. But when she sent him to the garage for firewood she found an excuse to go along, and while he got a fire going she bustled around the lounge, lighting half a dozen candles. Only when Ellie joined them did Diana regard it as safe to leave the room.

Returning with a tray of sandwiches, the sound of a toilet flushing made her heart lurch. But it was Ellie who had slipped out. Glenn was kneeling by the fire, idly probing at the flames with a poker, no sign of his phone anywhere.

'Fantastic!' he said. He chose to sit close to Diana on the sofa, consuming the sandwiches with a noisy, exaggerated pleasure, accompanied by frequent glances at his ex-wife. Ellie, idly thumbing through a glossy magazine, took no notice.

All these years, Glenn had fostered Diana's insecurity by encouraging her to believe that Ellie

444

still hankered after him, but maybe it wasn't true. Maybe it had never been true. And the knowledge that Ellie didn't want him helped to crystallise Diana's own feelings.

She didn't want him either.

Glenn finished his sandwich and burped, proudly, before directing his gaze once more at Ellie. 'You planning on a future with Joe?'

'Not particularly.'

'So he wasn't Mr Right, then?' Glenn laughed. To Diana, it sounded needlessly callous.

Without looking up from the magazine, Ellie said, 'A halfwit could see what you're trying to do here, Glenn. I'm not about to fall for it, and neither is Diana.'

Embarrassed, Glenn mumbled something—it might have been *'Mouthy bitch'*—then he took out his phone and stared at it longingly. Diana felt her heart rate increase. *Here it comes . . .*

But, to her relief, he put it away. Sighed. Checked his watch.

'Anxious?' Diana said, attempting to keep the mood congenial.

'Mmm.'

'I'm so worried for Joe. Do you think he'll be all right?'

'He's got to be,' Glenn said, with unexpected conviction. 'He's got to be.'

*   *   *

Leon didn't want Fenton to see that he was worried, but where the hell were Reece, Todd and Bruce? They were the only ones he trusted for the serious work—the illegal stuff. He needed them back here.

Reluctantly he let Fenton show him the basement again. The sofas were almost lost from sight, the water two feet deep and rising; filthy brown with bubbles of scum on the surface. The room stank of mud and waste. Leon took one look and marched back upstairs, Fenton panting and wailing behind him.

'Leon, please. I can't emphasise this enough. It's not safe here.'

'Fuck that. Give it another hour. Keep trying Glenn.'

Fenton sighed. 'Please understand that I genuinely have your best interests at heart—'

'If Glenn doesn't answer in the next ten minutes, you can go and find him. Bring him back here, then we'll talk about evacuating. Okay?'

Made restless by his anger, Leon headed for the comms room again. Despite knowing that the damage had been caused by the weather, he kept checking the monitors, gripped by the idea that he was under siege. As he stepped into the room, a shadow flitted beneath the viewpoint of the camera that covered part of the driveway.

'D'you see that?'

'What?' Fenton was too slow, as usual.

Leon switched cameras, catching a much larger shadow near the front door. A blur of motion was followed by a loud crash, and then the screen went black.

*   *   *

The sound of glass breaking was Joe's cue to move. The back door had a good lock and a small double-glazed window. For a fast entry, Joe used

446

the crowbar to prise the door away from the frame. Messy, and noisy, but he hoped the distraction out front would protect him.

Crossing the kitchen, he peered out at the hall. The front door was standing open: someone had gone to investigate the disturbance. There was no one in sight.

As he opened the door to the basement, the smell hit him at once: like sewage and rotting vegetation. Joe was halfway down the stairs when he realised the shadows were too high, too even, as though the floor had been raised. Then his foot splashed into water.

He stopped, found his torch and switched it on. The room was flooded to a depth of about two feet.

Drowning. You dreamed you were drowning in a tunnel.

Joe pushed the thought away. Everything rested on a simple question: Did he really believe that Kamila could be down here?

The answer was yes. On that basis, the choice was made for him.

He plunged into the water, felt the bitter cold penetrate his clothes and his shoes. Breathing in shallow gasps, trying not to dwell on what was causing the stench, he waded towards the toilet. He remembered Glenn saying that the plumbing didn't work properly. Had that been a bluff, to deter people from using the room?

He was examining the wall above the cistern when he heard a commotion upstairs. He hoped Davy wasn't in too much trouble: the Australian had made him agree that nothing should divert Joe from finding Kamila.

Spotting a gap in the panel, Joe attacked it with

447

the crowbar, levering it away from the wall. At first it stretched and bent, then popped out as a couple of tiny screws were dislodged.

The entrance to the tunnel was about two feet wide and three feet high, positioned at chest height but easily accessible if you used the toilet bowl and the cistern as steps. Gripping the torch between his teeth, Joe climbed up, squeezed through the gap and lowered himself back into the water.

He could feel the rough stone floor of the tunnel beneath his feet. The walls and ceiling were also bare rock, but there was a single weak bulb set above him. Beyond its range the tunnel vanished into a tight dark circle.

Joe shivered, and he was back in the Shell Cavern, the walls closing in, crushing the breath from his lungs . . .

Gripping the torch tightly, he shone it straight ahead. The tunnel must be flooding slowly from some small ingress, but the river above him was roaring like a freight train. He couldn't help but wonder at the thickness of the rock that was holding back the main body of water. At any moment that opening could be overwhelmed and the tunnel would flood in an instant.

He swore softly to himself. Not the way to be thinking . . .

Then the beam of light picked out a shape, about twenty feet away. A straight edge: man-made. It was the corner wall of Leon's strongroom.

Joe pushed through the water, feeling the current pressing against him. He broke out in a cold sweat, prickling through his hair and down his neck. If he slipped and went under, it wouldn't be the flood that destroyed him; it would be the panic.

Then something bumped against his stomach. A rat? Debris swept in from the river?

Heart thudding, he pointed the torch down and saw a grimy white sheen, something long and smooth floating on the surface. Because his police career had incorporated all manner of grim discoveries, Joe identified it immediately.

It was a bone. A human femur.

CHAPTER EIGHTY-FOUR

The attack's begun at last, Leon thought as he wrestled the front door open. In a strange way, it came as a relief.

He had no real idea *who* the enemy was. Could be Cadwell's men, or the authorities—or even Danny Morton. Whoever it was, Leon was braced for a fight to the death. Reece and the others had failed to return. There was nobody left that he could trust. His house was collapsing around him. Why not go out in a blaze of glory?

He'd had the foresight to grab the Glock. It was an imitation—a harmless replica—but it had fooled Joe well enough earlier. Might buy him some time, at least.

Leaving Fenton in the comms room, Leon rushed outside and found just one man, far from young, dressed like a hiker and wielding a cricket bat. He'd used it to smash the camera above the door and now, grinning like a maniac, he turned on Leon. It was Patrick Davy, the Aussie who'd fallen out with Cadwell after refusing to sell the gallery.

'Tried to kill me, you bastard!' he roared,

whipping the bat down in a two-handed grip. Leon dodged sideways but the bat caught his gun hand full on: he felt the bones in his wrist crack in a white-hot explosion of pain.

Leon shrieked. Saw Davy raising the bat for another strike and lunged towards him, using his height and weight to knock the older man off balance. As Davy stumbled, Leon rained blows on him with his left hand, clumsy but brutal, until Davy dropped the bat and his legs gave out and he fell to the ground.

*   *   *

Joe pushed on through the tunnel, fighting revulsion and claustrophobia. The torchlight swept over the water and revealed other debris, other bones. The strongroom was just a few feet away, jutting out from what seemed to be a natural alcove in the rock. As Glenn had said, the door was secured by a padlock, now just a couple of inches above the flood water.

And Glenn was right about something else. It *did* look like a cell.

Joe tried to rest for a second or two. The pressure of the water was making it harder to stay upright. Bracing himself against the side of the tunnel, he turned to check that his exit was still clear, but the torch beam was swallowed by a much deeper darkness to his right. There was another opening in the rock, a chamber reaching back several yards at least.

Joe was shivering so violently that he could barely hold the torch steady. He shone it into the chamber and saw her straight away.

450

Kamila.

*   *   *

The water had reached above her waist and was lapping just below her breasts, but Jenny didn't feel it. Didn't feel anything. She longed to sink beneath the surface, fill her lungs with water and have it ended. But she couldn't. Some primitive, obstinate instinct refused to let her give in.

So she was still upright, propped against the damaged wall, slipping in and out of consciousness, when she registered a flash of light in the darkness. Maybe some kind of hallucinatory flare, the product of a dying brain, synapses firing their last desperate signals.

An image came to her: Mum and Dad, finally alerted to her disappearance after . . . how many days or weeks? She pictured them years later, slipping towards death themselves, corroded by the agony of the questions no one could answer. The mindless torture of *not knowing*.

The water sloshed against her, as if the current had been disturbed. A noise like kids in a paddling pool. A fresh misery plucked at her heart: children she would never have.

She bumped her forehead against the wall, as if she could beat out the bad thoughts. A moan escaped her and she prayed: *God willing, this should be my last breath . . .*

*   *   *

The body was floating face up in the water, naked, the skin blackened and putrefied. The abdominal

451

cavity had burst open, and the limbs were only loosely connected to the torso. The features were unrecognisable, but Joe remembered the dark wavy hair from the photograph Alise had shown him.

It was Kamila. She'd probably been dead for weeks, left to decompose in her underground tomb. The bones he had found must belong to a much earlier victim. He was too late. Now he had to get out of here before he froze—

A soft thud behind him, followed by a groan. Joe's body convulsed. The torch slipped from his grasp. Like a clumsy juggler he writhed and snatched at the air; caught the torch just before it hit the water. The light flickered, but stayed on.

He realised the sounds had come from the strongroom. The cell. He turned, careful not to slip, and reached for the padlock, holding it while he got his balance.

'Hello?' he called, his voice juddering from the cold.

The only response was another whimpering groan.

'Hold on. I'm going to get you out.' Fixing the position of the padlock in his mind, Joe eased the rucksack onto one shoulder, put the torch away and brought out the bolt cutters. He knew he'd need two hands for the job, which meant working without a light.

Groping for the padlock, which was now partially submerged, he sited the blades around the shank, held it steady and brought the bolt cutters together. The padlock twisted and the cutters slipped off, almost falling into the water.

Joe took a deep breath. He was rushing. He needed to be slow and methodical. Forget the

452

tunnel, the rising water . . .

On the second attempt there was a quiet snap and the padlock gave way. Joe dropped the cutters into the rucksack, retrieved the torch and eased the door open a fraction. Once he'd established that the cell was flooded to the same level as the tunnel, he opened the door further.

There was a girl: naked, freezing, barely conscious, and yet somehow still standing. As he stepped into the cell she toppled and slid into his arms. He grabbed her, and in doing so he lost his balance, jabbing his elbow on the door frame to stay upright.

Once he'd steadied himself, Joe managed to direct the torchlight onto her face. Her eyes were shut and her skin had a blueish tint. There was no living warmth in her body at all.

*   *   *

Leon's wrist was a constant, screaming agony, but he was damned if he was going to let it defeat him. After summoning Fenton, the two of them managed to haul Patrick Davy back into the house.

'What's going on?' Fenton gasped.

'Just broke my fucking wrist.'

Davy regained consciousness as they dragged him into the living room. Leon kicked him hard in the ribs.

'Settle down, or I'll stamp your head to mush.'

Once inside, Fenton pinned the Australian down while Leon fetched plasticuffs and a bottle of ibuprofen. Leon couldn't open the bottle with one hand so he had to get Fenton to do it. He crunched down four pills, then did his best to assist Fenton as he removed Davy's coat, tied the man's hands behind him and sat him up against one of the armchairs.

Fenton clucked like a mother hen. 'Leon, you're drenched. You need fresh clothes.'

'A towel will do. And get a knife,' he added, glaring at Davy. 'To make this fucker talk.'

The phone rang as Fenton left the room. Leon heard him pick it up in the hall.

Thank Christ, he thought. *That had to be either Glenn or Reece.*

*　　　　*　　　　*

Time had slowed to a crawl. The candles provided a cosy light, and thanks to the fire the room was deliciously warm, the wood popping and hissing while the rain beat down on the roof. It was an environment that normally guaranteed an afternoon doze, but sleep was the last thing on Diana's mind.

Glenn was constantly fidgeting, pacing up and down, looking at his watch. Diana was no less tense, though Ellie seemed remarkably laid-back, paying little attention to Glenn.

It was almost four o'clock when he made for the door with a more decisive stride. Diana snapped to attention. 'Where are you going?'

He glanced back, a wry smile barely concealing his irritation. 'I need a crap. Okay?'

Embarrassed, she looked away. Glenn shut the door behind him. Ellie put her magazine aside and stared at Diana. 'Go after him.'

'What?'

'He's up to something.' She nodded towards the door. 'He hasn't taken a torch.'

454

Diana felt ashamed that she hadn't noticed. She opened the door and crept out, tiptoeing along the hall like an intruder in her own home. She hadn't taken a torch, either. There was just enough light to see her way.

Even before she reached the toilet she could hear Glenn's voice, coming from the guests' lounge at the far end of the hall. He was finishing off a call when she got to the door.

'. . . let you know if that changes. Just get here as quick as you can.' His voice was gruff, as though he was trying hard to be taken seriously.

Diana was set to burst in, but some wise instinct made her pause. A second later Glenn was speaking again.

'Clive? Shut up and listen. Joe's still alive and he's on his way to you. He might be there already.'

Fenton must have responded with a question, but Glenn rode over it. 'Don't tell him anything. I've done my own deal. I'll cut you in, but you have to keep Joe there. Whatever it takes—kill Leon if need be, but keep Joe alive. Morton'll be here in an hour or so.'

Diana went cold. They knew who Joe was. They knew about the price on his head.

And Glenn had betrayed them all.

She turned and ran for the front door, not even considering the weather conditions or how she could reach Joe in time. She dimly heard footsteps behind her, then Glenn grabbed her hair and wrenched her to a halt, slamming her head against the wall.

CHAPTER EIGHTY-FIVE

Patrick Davy was starting to recover. He sat up straight, winced, and spat blood onto the floor. He even managed a grin when he saw how Leon was cradling his injured wrist.

Leon only held his temper in check by thinking of Cadwell: the expression on his face as he understood that he was going to die. Davy would know that feeling soon enough.

'Who sent you?' Leon asked.

'Nobody. Your thugs clobbered me. This is payback time.'

Leon didn't buy it. 'Why now?'

'Because you're about to be destroyed, and I want to play a part in that.'

It was such a bold statement that Leon was still grappling for a reply when Fenton strode in, holding the phone.

'Good news. Glenn'll be here any time.'

'Has he got Joe's stuff?'

Fenton looked blank for a second. 'Oh. Yes. Yes.'

'What about Reece and the others?'

Fenton pursed his lips. His face was bright red. 'Oh, Glenn spoke to Bruce. Just as we thought, the storm delayed them but they're on their way.'

Leon nodded. All very positive, on the face of it, but something didn't smell right.

'What's up with you?'

'Nothing.' Fenton shifted his weight from one foot to the other. 'I'll get that knife for you. And a bandage. Coming right up . . .'

He hurried out, shutting the door behind him. Almost immediately Leon heard a voice in the hall: not Fenton's.

The fat fuck was scheming with somebody else.

*　　　*　　　*

Joe's first plan failed. Bearing the woman's weight with one hand, he slipped the torch into the rucksack, then pushed the door open with his foot, holding it against the current while he tried to manoeuvre her alongside him.

As soon as he tried to move, her legs gave way and he nearly lost her to the swirling waters. Despite the occasional groan and murmur, she was effectively unconscious. The only option was to carry her.

Wedging his feet in the doorway, Joe leaned down as far as the confined space would allow and then lifted her over his shoulder. Her body was as cold and slippery as ice; his own muscles stiff and unresponsive. It took a monumental effort to support her and stay on his feet. He felt a tiny but growing conviction that they were both going to drown down here.

He backed out of the cell, standing as tall as he could to keep her head above the water. His own head touched the roof of the tunnel, where he could feel the terrifying force of the river vibrating through the rock and into his skull. A fireman's lift wasn't ideal in such a narrow tunnel, but at least this method left him a hand free to steady himself. Without that, he would almost certainly topple over.

By the time he reached the opening into the

basement he was exhausted; bruised and bleeding from where he'd bumped and scraped against the rock walls. His legs had lost virtually all sensation. His heart was beating fast and yet somehow felt sluggish; labouring against the cold as much as from the exertion.

And a constant prayer ran round and round in his head: *Don't let her die. Don't let her die. Don't let her die . . .*

Getting the woman through the hatch wasn't as difficult as he'd feared. He lifted her off his shoulder, held her with both hands and managed to set her down on the toilet cistern.

Then came a big problem. He'd have to let go of her while he squeezed through the gap—and there wasn't enough room.

Joe tried a compromise, shifting her gently to one side, all the while talking in a soft voice, urging her to wake up, to stand for a moment. He thought he saw her respond, her eyes flickering. Then she slid on the wet porcelain and dropped into the water.

Panic lanced through him. He kicked and fought his way out of the tunnel, slithered over the cistern, snatched a breath and fell head first into the filthy water. For one insane moment he was convinced he wouldn't find her: that somehow she had vanished.

Then he made contact. Her body was twisted beside the toilet. He grabbed her arms and hauled her upright, telling himself she'd be okay. Her head hadn't been under the water for more than a few seconds.

Back to the fireman's lift. The basement gave him more room to move, but it was now flooded to such a depth that none of the furniture was

458

visible. He had to tread carefully, negotiating a path between the drowned sofas.

Finally Joe reached the stairs, his fingers throbbing from the cold as they gripped the handrail. His legs like rubber, slowly emerging from the flood. Every step required an individual effort of will, but the reward was a few more inches of dry air.

Then he was at the top, soaked and shaking, close to passing out himself. But the ordeal was only just beginning: if he was to keep her alive, he'd need Davy's help.

He staggered into the hall just as Fenton emerged from the living room. There was no hope of hiding, so Joe didn't bother to try.

'Get some blankets,' he snarled.

Fenton just gaped at him. Then the door opened and Leon came out, shouting abuse at Fenton until the sight of Joe shocked him into silence.

CHAPTER EIGHTY-SIX

Leon gaped at him. 'You're dead.' It was a statement rather than a threat. Then his focus switched to Fenton: 'You fucking lied to me . . .'

Ignoring them both, Joe carefully lowered the woman to the floor. He stripped off his coat and laid it over her body—for modesty's sake as much as for any warmth it would provide.

'Were you part of this?'

Fenton blinked several times before mustering a profound indignation. 'Certainly not!'

'Then help me. If we don't get her warmed up,

she's going to die.'

Nodding that he understood, Fenton gave Leon an uneasy glance before scurrying upstairs.

'What's her name?' Joe asked. He noticed that Leon was cradling his right arm against his body. The wrist was hugely swollen. 'Did Patrick do that? Where is he?'

Leon found a spark of confidence. 'He'll be dead soon. Going the way of Derek Cadwell—and anyone else who wants to take me on.' But he wouldn't quite look Joe in the eye as he added: 'What happened to Reece?'

'He's not coming back. Neither are the others.' Joe let the information sink in, then he said, 'I found Kamila.'

'What?'

'I saw her body in the tunnel. When did you kill her?'

Leon winced, one eye closing involuntarily as though responding to pain inside his head. 'I've never set eyes on Kamila.' He gestured at the woman on the floor. 'Who the hell is she?'

'Don't pretend you don't know. I've just rescued her from your cell.'

'Cell? What cell?'

'In the tunnel beneath the house. You told Glenn it was a strongroom.'

Somehow Leon managed to look both agitated and mystified. Wincing again, he went to lift his right arm to his face, then realised it was too badly injured to move. 'I don't know what you're talking about. Why would I want to go crawling round a fucking tunnel?'

Fenton's heavy tread vibrated through the stairs as he came down, carrying towels and a duvet as

460

well as two hot-water bottles.

'I filled them from the hot tap. Not brilliant, but I thought that would be quicker.'

Joe laid the duvet on a dry patch of floor, lifted the woman onto it, placed the hot-water bottles under her arms and wrapped the duvet around her. He checked her pulse and her breathing, and decided she wasn't in immediate danger.

Leon watched from across the hall: not attacking, not retreating. Joe found his attitude confusing. What could he possibly hope to gain from lying at this stage?

A tiny voice in his head offered the answer, but Joe didn't want to hear it.

*   *   *

Leon's world wasn't just falling apart: it had gone apeshit fucking crazy. A dead man had walked into his home, carrying a naked, unconscious woman.

He couldn't deal with it. Couldn't think straight. The wrist was sending blasts of pain through his arm, and now he had the mother of all migraines brewing up.

'This is a set-up,' he cried. 'You couldn't find any evidence, so you brought her here to frame me.'

'Look at the state she's in,' Joe said with disgust. Fenton was tutting his agreement, staring at Leon as though he was some kind of monster.

'It's him you want to talk to.' Leon jabbed a finger at Fenton. 'Fucking pervs, him and his buddy Cadwell. Derek had this corpse in once. Fifteen-year-old girl, died of some heart defect no one knew about. Body of a porn star and not a mark on her. Derek couldn't resist. That's how he got his

461

kicks, and I bet you did too, eh, Clive?'

Fenton sighed. 'This is pure fantasy,' he said to Joe. 'In the past few days Leon has displayed signs of a serious mental collapse. He's prone to migraines, and regular psychotic episodes, hence the injuries inflicted upon your friend Alise.'

'You're lying,' Leon shouted. But the reality of his situation was hitting home. Fenton had switched sides. Leon was on his own. No Glenn riding to the rescue. No Reece or Todd or . . .

'Glenn!' he said, and grinned like a maniac. 'Glenn told you to lie.'

Fenton went pale, and despite everything Leon actually managed to laugh. Because now he understood why Clive had betrayed him.

He knew exactly what was going on.

*   *   *

Leon was desperately trying to shift the blame elsewhere, just as Ellie had predicted he would. But Joe didn't like the way Fenton reacted to this latest accusation.

'What did Glenn lie about?' he asked Leon.

'You. Fenton said you were dead. Glenn told him to say that.'

'When was this?'

'A few minutes ago.' Leon grinned. 'It's not looking good for you now.'

Logic told Joe this was a bluff, although he couldn't dismiss the idea completely. But why would Glenn break his promise not to contact Fenton or Leon, only to pass on a lie? Had it been a misguided attempt to help Joe?

'How much is he paying you?' Leon said to

462

Fenton, who gave an irritable shrug. It was a long way from a denial, and they all saw it. 'Your job's to protect the merchandise, I suppose. What a fucking joke.'

Fenton turned pompous. 'While we waste time, this young woman might be dying. Joe, I suggest we secure Leon until the police can take him away—'

'You're not going to call the cops,' Leon broke in. He gave Joe a scornful look. 'You haven't worked it out, have you?'

'Tell me.'

Leon inclined his head: Joe could see him weighing up the angles. 'Give me a route out of here and I might just save your life.'

*   *   *

Her first sensation was light, pouring through her eyelids, painful and yet pleasant in its normality. Her second sensation was warmth: of soft, clean bedding wrapped tightly around her. It had to be a dream, didn't it? A dream where she had regressed to infancy: a swaddled baby, safe from harm.

Jenny wanted to open her eyes, but she was scared. The dream might not withstand such a shock. To wake and find herself back in the cell . . .

But the cell was flooded. That hadn't been a dream, surely? The last thing she recalled was the water climbing above her waist, the terrible impulse to surrender to it.

There were voices, she realised. Two or three men arguing; the air charged with their negative emotions: fear, resentment, anger, jealousy, greed. Her mind was too confused to follow the conversation—until one word leapt out at her.

463

Leon.

They were talking about someone called Leon.

No. The man called Leon was one of them.

He was here.

Jenny remembered the friendly seduction. The drinks that might have been spiked. The glow of street lights sliding beneath the roof of the car.

She began to shake. Very cautiously, she opened her eyes, just a fraction. After so long in darkness, it hurt. She had to wait for her vision to adjust. Finally she was able to see a little of her immediate surroundings: she was in the spacious hallway of an old house. Lots of stone and timber.

And caves and tunnels beneath.

The man nearest to her was the one who had saved her life. How she knew this, Jenny had no idea, but she trusted him instinctively.

Another man, obese and unpleasant-looking, said, 'While we waste time, this young woman might be dying. Joe, I suggest we secure Leon until the police can take him away——'

He seemed to be talking about the third man, who was standing apart from the other two. Jenny peered at him for what seemed like a very long time, and then she drew on all the strength she could muster and said, 'That's not him.'

There was silence, but she couldn't be sure they had heard her. So she said it again.

'Please . . . That's not him.'

This time there was no doubt. The man she trusted—Joe?—knelt down and put a comforting hand on her shoulder. He gave her an encouraging smile. She managed a feeble grin in return.

'That isn't Leon,' she told him.

He looked sympathetic, as though this were an

464

acknowledged symptom of her madness. 'Yes, it is,' he said gently. 'His name is Leon Race.'

Jenny felt a rush of terror, as acute as anything she had suffered in captivity. Her mind must have gone. No one would trust her or believe what she said. There was no hope of living a normal life.

Then the confusion cleared from his eyes, and he said, 'The man who abducted you, did he call himself Leon?'

'Yes.' Jenny was absurdly grateful that he understood. 'But he's slimmer. Thick black hair. Much better looking.'

Now Joe's face had changed. Instead of expressing delight that they'd found a solution to the puzzle, he seemed to deflate before her eyes.

'Much better looking?' he repeated.

She nodded. 'And he knew it, too,' she said.

CHAPTER EIGHTY-SEVEN

Diana came round to a splitting headache, but no amnesia, no confusion. While she was still dazed, Glenn helped her back into the living room. She heard an exclamation from Ellie, then Glenn's blithe reassurance.

'She tripped over a shoe in the hall and went flying.'

'Oh God. Is she all right?' Ellie came to her side, but Diana shut her eyes for fear of what Ellie might see in them.

'Yeah. No real harm done.' Glenn set her down on the sofa, one hand trailing across her face. The touch made her squirm, but it must have convinced

Ellie of his devotion.

'I'll get her some painkillers. And water.'

'Sit down. She's fine.'

Diana let out a moan. Opened her eyes and found Ellie kneeling at her side, Glenn standing behind her. His face was cold, determined. Diana looked away, snatched a morsel of courage and held it tight.

'Just a couple of paracetamol, please . . .'

'Of course.' Ellie made a face. 'That's a nasty bump.'

'I know. Honestly, I swear I'm going senile!'

*   *   *

Glenn permitted Ellie to leave the room, apparently satisfied that Diana hadn't given him away. As soon as they were alone, Diana dropped the pretence.

'That was the only reason you saved Joe?' she hissed. 'To sell him to Danny Morton?'

'I had no choice. Leon wouldn't go through with it. I've agreed five hundred grand, Di. Cash and gold.' He puffed up, immensely pleased with himself.

'How long were you planning this?'

'Cadwell put the idea in my head this morning. Then I came here, and you begged me to get him back . . . It seemed too good an opportunity to miss.' A glance at the door. They could hear a tap running in the kitchen. 'Sorry about your head. I need you to stay calm, say nothing to Ellie till the deal's done. Then you won't see me for dust, okay?'

Diana nodded, as though she accepted his terms. 'Why didn't you keep Joe here?'

Glenn sniffed. 'I was gonna go with him, deal

466

with him on the way. It took me by surprise when he said I should stay here. One against three, there wasn't much I could do.' He shrugged, automatically giving her the kind of winsome look that she'd once found so disarming.

She sighed. 'You really can't think on your feet, can you?' Her tone was so loaded with regret that it gave no offence. 'And Morton's on his way?'

'He was near Bristol when I called. He'd been searching for Joe there.' Glenn checked his watch. 'Maybe an hour or so now, that's all.'

'And where will he find your money at such short notice?'

'I dunno, do I? That's his problem.'

'Oh, Glenn. You're being taken for a fool. Have you any idea of the kind of man you're dealing with?'

He sneered, but she could see the doubt in his eyes. 'I know what I'm doing.'

'No, you don't. You've thrown away everything you had for a few empty promises.'

'Half a million quid, that's not peanuts,' Glenn snarled. 'Either way, Joe was going to end up dead.'

*   *   *

Ellie returned with the paracetamol and a glass of water. Aside from her concern for Diana, she didn't seem to sense anything wrong. Kneeling once again, she took out two tablets and helped Diana sit up to swallow them.

Scowling, Glenn settled in the armchair that Ellie had vacated. It was the chair nearest the door: not the subtlest of moves.

Ellie snorted, said in a light-hearted voice: 'Hey!

467

You pinched my seat.'

Glenn just looked at her and grunted, and Diana had a sudden insight: he was psyching himself up for more brutality. He wouldn't allow either of them to leave until the handover was complete. Even then, would he be prepared to let Diana go when she knew what he'd done?

No. He's got to silence me, she thought. *And whatever he does to me, he has to do to Ellie.*

She sat up straight, took another sip of water and put the glass down. She could feel Glenn's gaze burning into her, but she wouldn't look at him. Wouldn't look at Ellie, either, who had picked up another magazine and sat in the other armchair. Diana felt overwhelmed by guilt. Ellie shouldn't have to suffer for Diana's misjudgements.

'I do believe the rain's easing off,' she said with brittle good cheer. When Ellie looked up, she added: 'Perhaps you should see if there's a clear route home?'

'It's pissing down,' Glenn said, glaring a warning at her.

Ellie nodded. 'I'm fine here. Better to wait till Joe gets back, at least.'

Tense silence for a minute or two, which Diana found all the more unbearable for her past cowardice. She had been weak for so long; clinging to a bad relationship because she was scared of being alone: so pathetically frightened that Glenn might abandon her for a newer model that she'd turned a blind eye to all his negative qualities.

'Will Joe find Kamila, do you think?' she asked him.

'Dunno. She's bound to be dead, though, after all these weeks.'

'I'm surprised you never mentioned this tunnel before. You must have been working on the strongroom when we . . .'

She faltered. Across the room, Ellie seemed to bury herself deeper in the magazine.

Glenn said, 'Maybe. Can't remember.'

'But didn't you ever wonder if there was a connection, once you heard about the missing women?'

'Never occurred to me. I haven't given it a thought in years.'

'I don't mean recently. What about the girl that Roy was trying to find? That was around the same time you were building it.'

Her voice changed, turning flat on the last couple of words. She prayed he wouldn't pick up on it. Another insight: this one had struck her like a punch in the chest. Ellie was staring at her as though she'd felt it too, a mental shock wave.

Aggrieved, Glenn said, 'Are you trying to say I knew what Leon was up to?'

'No.' Diana shook her head quite vehemently. 'Not at all.'

She met Ellie's gaze again, and just for a second she saw all the same doubt and fear that must have shone in her own eyes. Like an inadvertent glance in a mirror during some dreaded ordeal; a reflection to crush the spirit.

*   *   *

More silence. Diana listened to the rain on the window, knots exploding in the fire. Some of the candles would need replacing before long. Another unwanted thought began to worm its way into her

469

consciousness.

Maybe Joe's not coming back. Maybe Leon got the better of him . . .

Ellie sighed, slid the magazine half off her lap and contemplated Glenn with a strange, dreamy smile.

'What will you tell Alec?' she asked.

Glenn flinched. His son despised him for cheating on Ellie and, for all Diana knew, probably despised her, too. The subject wasn't raised often, but occasionally Glenn had bemoaned the fact that he couldn't have the sort of father–son relationship that he felt was his due.

'Tell Alec what?' he said, exasperated.

'About the women. How many were there, in all?'

Glenn regarded Ellie as though she'd let him down by raising such an indelicate subject in the presence of his current partner.

'You mean girlfriends? You want to talk about the women I've shagged?'

'Not girlfriends, no. Unless that's what you call them.'

Another disbelieving look, this time shared with Diana, inviting her to wonder just what his loopy ex-wife was getting at. But Diana didn't react: every muscle in her body might have been encased in stone, the way in a nightmare you watch a tragedy unfold, helpless to intervene.

'What I mean is,' Ellie said, 'how many women will Joe find in the tunnels?'

'How should I know?'

Ellie shook her head, her lips pursed with an inexpressible sadness. 'Because you killed them.'

470

CHAPTER EIGHTY-EIGHT

It wasn't Leon. It was Glenn. A crushing revelation; all the more so because Joe had suggested—practically *insisted*—that Glenn stay behind with Ellie and Diana.

Almost as shocking was the knowledge that Glenn had managed to conceal his true nature for so long. Joe knew that when a killer was unmasked, the women in his life were often tainted with the accusation that 'they must have known', when in fact they had no idea of the crimes their partner was committing.

We see what we want to see, he thought. And what they had seen was what Joe himself saw in Glenn: a good-looking ladies' man, a rough and ready charmer.

Joe hadn't wanted to exhaust the woman—she told him her name was Jenny—but he gave her a brief description of Glenn, and right away she confirmed it was the man who'd come on to her in a pub in Exeter, and possibly spiked her drink.

'He called himself Leon. He bragged a lot. How rich he was, how successful. I thought at the time it must be bullshit.'

Joe was aware of Leon edging closer to listen. He seemed genuinely appalled, particularly when she told Joe the date on which she believed it had happened.

'She's been down there for ten days?'

'Probably. And she's not the first.' Joe sighed. His anger with Leon was a reflection of the anger he felt with himself. 'How come no one else knew

471

about the tunnel? Surely you saw it when he was fitting out the basement?'

'I hardly ever went down there.'

'Weren't there other tradesmen?'

'Glenn did most of the work himself. He was in and out for months, and I was happy to leave him to it.'

'And since then? When he was bringing them food and water.' Joe shuddered. 'Visiting them.'

'You've seen how it is. There's always people coming and going. Some of 'em live here, more or less. If Glenn wanted to sneak down to the basement when it was quiet, nobody would be any the wiser.'

Leon was telling the truth, but he seemed rather too eager to talk about it, Joe thought. Which jogged his memory of the conversation before Jenny's disclosure.

'What haven't I worked out?'

Leon shrugged. 'You got anything to offer me?'

*   *   *

As Leon taunted him, another voice cried out: 'You murdering son of a bitch!'

Patrick Davy. Wild-eyed and soaking wet, his wrists slick with blood, coming in fast, swinging the cricket bat with fury and determination.

Joe shouted at him to stop, but it was useless. Davy didn't acknowledge it; probably didn't hear a thing. Too intent on his target.

And his target didn't stand a chance. Hampered by his injured wrist, Leon moved stiffly, trying to twist and duck at the same time. It made little difference to the end result. The bat connected with

472

his temple. The noise was astonishingly loud and vivid: a hard resounding crack that made Joe feel sick.

Leon was looking at Joe as the bat struck: a look of sad, imploring self-pity. His body hit the floor with a shuddering force. Davy was drawing back for another swing; this time he heard Joe's cry and hesitated.

'The bastard would have killed you today. You don't owe him any mercy.'

'It's not that simple,' Joe told him. 'I don't know how much you heard?'

'Not a lot. I managed to get the cuffs off, then I went out the window, retrieved the bat and climbed back in.' Davy was matter-of-fact about it. What he'd left unsaid was that he could simply have run away, abandoning Joe to his fate.

Joe started to thank him, then noticed Fenton edging towards the front door. He grabbed the fat man by the collar and hauled him back. 'Sit down,' he said. Davy emphasised the order by prodding Fenton in the gut with the cricket bat.

'Is the girl okay?' he asked. Jenny's eyes were closed once more, but her breathing was steady.

Joe described what he'd found in the tunnels, then explained that it was Glenn who had been responsible. Not Leon.

'Ah, shit. But he still deserves what he got. For Alise, if nothing else.' Davy gazed at Leon's prone form. 'I don't see what Glenn was playing at, letting you come here when he knew what you'd find.'

'I suppose it was because everything pointed to Leon. The location. The history of violence, the way he'd tortured Alise. And if Glenn was using Leon's name when he met these women, he must

473

have planned to frame Leon from the start.'

'Jesus. From what I saw of the guy, I never put him down as all that bright.'

'Me neither. He managed to fool us all.'

'So what now?'

Joe nudged Fenton with his foot. 'Tie this one up, for a start.'

While Davy fetched the plasticuffs Joe examined Leon. He was alive, despite a badly fractured skull, but it seemed far from certain that he would survive. Joe decided that he wasn't going to lose any sleep over the outcome, either way.

They cuffed Fenton's wrists and ankles, ignoring his repeated claims that he'd taken no part in any criminal activity, and was firmly on Joe's side.

'So tell us what Leon meant. You're "protecting the merchandise". What kind of merchandise?'

Fenton looked gravely at Joe, at Davy. At the cricket bat. He was not a brave man.

'You,' he said. 'It's the same deal that Leon had intended to make.' Fenton paused. Swallowed. 'Glenn's selling you to a man named Danny Morton.'

* * *

In a garbled rush of information, Fenton explained how Joe had been surreptitiously photographed on his first visit to the property. The picture had been circulated among Leon's acquaintances, and finally somebody who knew Joe's true identity had come forward and supplied the link to the Mortons.

As Joe listened, he was starkly aware that he had no one to blame but himself. 'When is Morton getting here?' he said.

'Soon. Less than an hour, according to Glenn.'

Davy's advice was simple. 'You've got to run for it, mate. Right away.'

'I can't. I left Glenn with Diana and Ellie.'

'He has no reason to hurt them, does he?'

'Would you want to guarantee that, knowing what he's capable of?' To Fenton, he said, 'So Glenn tipped you off, told you to watch me. What next?'

'He said he'd bring Morton here.'

Joe sighed. Not what he wanted to hear. If Ellie or Diana became suspicious—or if Glenn decided he couldn't risk leaving them behind—then he would have to kill them.

'We need to call an ambulance for Jenny. And for Leon.' Joe pointed to Fenton. 'Then I'm giving you an opportunity to redeem yourself.'

CHAPTER EIGHTY-NINE

It was Ellie who said it, but Diana had been thinking it, too. Somehow it was a greater shock to hear her own conclusion spoken aloud by someone else.

Glenn didn't deny the charge. Instead he acted as though it was beneath his contempt to respond.

'Diana didn't trip over a shoe,' Ellie said. 'You hit her, just as you hit me, once or twice. Do you remember that? When I was young and naive.'

'Bullshit. I never did,' Glenn whined, but Ellie went on as though she hadn't heard.

'I just wish I was more surprised, but I can't say I am.' She sighed. 'People usually picture sex attackers as creepy loners who can't speak to women, let alone form relationships. And some of them are. But of course there are others, like you—handsome, charming men who get so used to women saying yes that it becomes more than an assumption. It becomes a right. The idea that somebody *wouldn't* want to sleep with you is offensive. An insult.'

Ellie gave a sad laugh. 'It's ironic, isn't it?' she said to Diana. 'When I looked at you just then, I *knew*, and I think you were the same. All these years of mutual suspicion, but if we'd ever met up and talked, I wonder how much sooner we'd have worked out what a monster he is.'

Diana nodded. 'He poisoned us against each other to prevent that from happening.'

'Hey!' Glenn shouted, more riled by being ignored than by the accusations, it seemed to Diana. 'You've really screwed up now. Both of you.'

'I think we have an admission,' Ellie said, but the triumph in her voice was tinged with real fear.

'It didn't have to be like this,' Glenn said. 'But yeah, all right, I'm admitting it. And you'll have to take the consequences of that.' Still the whine of self-justification in his voice. 'It was an accident, how it started. I had this girl, really up for it, then she goes and changes her bloody mind when it's too late. She started threatening to go to the cops, get me put away. I couldn't let that happen, could I? We had bills coming in, Alec was only a little kid—'

'No!' Ellie roared at him. 'You will not use our son as an excuse.'

Glenn shrugged, sulky about the reprimand. 'I'm just saying how it was. Then I got the job at Leon's, found the tunnel and built the cell as a bit of a challenge. Like a secret camp. Could I get in and

476

out without anyone knowing? Then it just came to me: get a girl down here and I could do whatever I liked. It was mind-blowing.'

Into his stride now, he looked up and seemed disorientated when he registered that they didn't share his enthusiasm.

'I was worried someone would find the hatch, so I blocked the toilet up a couple of times, deterred people from using it.' He tapped his temple with a forefinger. 'Not just a pretty face, see.'

'How many victims?' Ellie asked.

'What does it matter to you?'

'How many?' Diana insisted.

'I don't know. Seven, maybe. Eight.'

'So we're nine and ten, are we?' Ellie said.

'You didn't have to be,' Glenn said regretfully, checking his watch. 'But that's how it's looking.'

He got up, moving towards Ellie. Then his phone rang.

*   *   *

Danny Morton. That was Diana's guess. Calling for directions. Perhaps moments away.

She could barely contemplate the slow, agonising death that Joe would face: Helen widowed without knowing it, the girls growing up sad and bitter, wondering why their father had failed to track them down . . .

The letter. At first it had slipped her mind; then she'd been waiting for the right moment to tell him. Now, watching Glenn answer his phone, she decided that it made little difference. What she knew couldn't really have helped Joe, and might just have added to his torment.

477

Glenn looked disappointed. 'Clive,' he said to the caller, instinctively turning away.

Ellie shifted position on the chair, wriggling her toes and flexing the muscles in her legs. By the time Glenn turned back she was completely still once more.

His demeanour changed as he listened to Fenton. He straightened up, smiled. 'Brilliant,' he said, and Diana's last hope crumbled to nothing. 'What about Leon?'

The line couldn't have been very clear, for Glenn had to hunch over. Again he turned his head towards the fireplace, missing another swift movement from Ellie. This time it was her hand, slipping inside her cardigan and emerging with something that she hid at her side.

Diana felt sick. She didn't dare look Ellie in the eye. She was sure that Glenn would sense her fear and quell the rebellion before it had begun.

But Glenn was saying cheerfully: 'Even better if he doesn't pull through.' Talking about Leon? A pause to listen, then: 'Yeah. Plenty for us both. I'll bring him over the minute he gets here. Won't be long now.'

Won't be long now. The phrase echoed in Diana's head. *Won't be long till Danny Morton gets his hands on Joe. Won't be long before Ellie and I are killed . . .*

Still having trouble hearing, Glenn covered his other ear with one hand. 'Say that again?'

And Ellie sprang up. She had a knife in her hand: a small paring knife from Diana's kitchen. Serious intent on her face: this wasn't a threat, a bluff. She was going to use it.

As Ellie launched herself at Glenn, the door burst open. A gust of wind extinguished all but

478

a couple of the candles—and that was the cue for everything to go horribly wrong.

CHAPTER NINETY

Joe was all too aware of the potential for disaster. It hadn't been much of a plan to start with, conceived in desperation and haste, with any number of risks that couldn't be properly assessed. For a start, he'd failed to factor in Ellie's resourcefulness.

As soon as he entered the room he knew he was too late—even if only by a fraction of a second. The vital element of surprise had been lost, but by then he was committed.

*　　　*　　　*

Back at Leon's, he'd outlined what he wanted from Fenton. Davy was staying to make sure Fenton did as he was told.

They decided to leave it ten minutes before making the call. Given the conditions, Joe would have preferred twice as long to reach Diana's, but he knew that even this delay could be fatal.

After retrieving his phone and his ID from Leon's office, he borrowed Davy's Land Rover and drove like a maniac. Half the town was in darkness. The top of the High Street was a blizzard of blue and red flashing lights. At the bridge a temporary barrier was being erected, overseen by a police officer. Joe hurtled past, sending one of the plastic barriers flying. He checked his mirror to see if the cop would give chase, but fortunately securing the bridge took priority.

To avoid alerting Glenn, he headed for the next street along and parked by a footpath that ran between a pair of stone cottages. He'd brought the rucksack with him, but decided he only needed the crowbar.

The rain didn't seem quite as intense as he followed the path, stamping through puddles that were ankle-deep in places. He climbed a wide slate wall that divided Diana's property from that of her neighbour and dropped into her garden. The lawn was a quagmire, wet mud splattering his jeans as he ran, but after the freezing cold waters of the tunnel Joe barely noticed it.

He let himself in the back door and crept through the kitchen, leaving a trail of water on the floor. In terms of weapons there were plenty of knives at his disposal, but he decided to stick with the crowbar. He didn't like fighting with knives: as with guns, they were just as liable to end up hurting the person who wielded them.

*　　　*　　　*

The house was eerily silent. Joe had a horrible premonition that he'd left it too late.

Then, as he eased the kitchen door open, he heard a phone ring. A moment later he made out Glenn's voice, acknowledging the caller: 'Clive.'

Joe saw a flickering light coming from the lounge. He could hear Glenn speaking again. So far, the plan was working: get Glenn on the phone, let him believe that Joe was being held captive at Leon's, then take him out while he was distracted.

Joe reached the door, and Glenn was saying '. . .

I'll bring him over the minute he gets here. Won't be long now.'

The door was open a few inches, but the angle was too narrow for Joe to see into the room. There was no sound apart from Glenn's voice and the crackle of a fire, but Joe felt sure that Diana and Ellie were in there with him. No other logical place for them to be, assuming they were still alive.

Glenn said, 'Say that again?'—and Joe kicked open the door, saw Glenn standing in front of the hearth, the phone in his left hand, the arm already falling in response to a blur of movement from Joe's right: someone rising from an armchair, throwing themselves towards Glenn, directly across Joe's path.

It was Ellie. Joe was coming in behind her, to her left: she probably had no idea he was there. And she had a knife.

Joe reared back, stumbling as he tried to avoid a collision. Glenn reacted fast, whirling away from Ellie's knife hand and registering Joe's presence. Somebody wailed: Diana, possibly, while Ellie kept on coming, the blade scything in on Glenn, but he dodged it, grabbed Ellie by the shoulders and shoved her into Joe. She overbalanced, gasped as she struck Joe side-on and tumbled past him, collapsing onto the sofa. A winded groan and more cries as she landed on Diana; Joe glimpsed a foot kicking up, a hand thrown out in panic.

The dim pulsating light made a slow strobe of their movements: Ellie writhing on the sofa, Diana helpless beneath her, Joe tripping and falling as Glenn swung his arm in a clubbing motion, catching Joe as he went down, the crowbar slipping from his grasp.

481

The survival instinct made Glenn a dirty fighter. He kicked out at Joe, caught his thigh, his belly. Joe was trapped between a low table and an armchair, his head almost on the hearth: no room to manoeuvre.

He tried to curl into a foetal position, drawing his legs up and then kicking back at Glenn. His foot connected with Glenn's shin but lacked the force to do real damage. Glenn roared with fury and threw himself down, his hands wrapping around Joe's throat.

'Tricked me, you fucking—' The words dissolved into an incoherent screech. He lifted Joe's head a couple of inches and tried to smash it down on the hearth. It only caught the edge, but even that was enough to stun Joe into submission: for a second everything went black.

*   *   *

A high, piercing scream brought Joe back. That and the pain.

The open fire was searing the top of his head. It felt like his hair was about to ignite. Every instinct urged him to propel himself away from it, but instead he extended his arm, reaching behind him until his fingers brushed against the edge of the fireguard. It was dome-shaped, made from steel mesh. Lightweight and easy to lift, but extremely hot.

Joe couldn't let himself dwell on that. He snatched it up and swung it at Glenn, letting go as soon as it made contact. In swatting the fireguard away, Glenn released his grip on Joe and fell sideways towards the armchair.

Knowing he had only one chance to gain control, Joe twisted round and managed to get onto his knees, facing the fireplace. He spotted a sturdy-looking log, the size of a man's forearm. One end was plunged into the fire, but the other end was untouched by the flames. Joe grabbed it and felt Glenn moving in again, panting and growling like a wild animal.

No room to swing it, so Joe had to settle for ramming the burning-hot timber at Glenn. It struck the side of his head with a heavy thud, a duller sound than the blow which Davy had inflicted on Leon, but no less sickening—and no less effective. It drove Glenn back a foot or more, and Joe saw his eyes roll up, the growl cut off mid-breath, and then he collapsed. Maybe not dead, but out of the game.

Joe threw the log back into the fire and blew on his hands, then realised that Ellie was still screaming.

CHAPTER NINETY-ONE

The first thing he registered was the blood, a black gleam in the wavering light. It was all over Ellie's arms, all over her dress, and yet she wasn't hurt. Joe could tell that straight away.

She was half-sitting on the sofa, leaning forward, one hand clamped on Diana's chest, the other seeking his attention, fluttering like a bird afraid to settle. Between the two, a shadow caught his attention, jutting out, unmoving.

'Oh no. No.' Joe got up, saw Diana's face turned towards his, her eyes open but barely seeing. The

483

knife had buried itself in her chest.

'I didn't take it out,' Ellie said. 'I read that you're not supposed to. And keep pressure on the wound—is that right?'

Joe nodded. Diana tried to speak, little pink bubbles frothing on her lips. Joe knelt in front of her, found her hand and grasped it gently.

'Kitchen,' she gasped. 'Cut . . . cutlery.'

Joe pretended it made sense. Diana still had the wherewithal to look cross with him for humouring her.

'Cutlery. Drawer.'

'She said that just now,' Ellie told him. 'We can't wait for an ambulance. We'll have to take her.'

Joe agreed, but he also feared that it might be futile. She'd lost a lot of blood, and would inevitably lose more while being carried to a car and transported to hospital.

As if she could read his mind, Diana drew him closer. 'I want to go.'

He nodded. 'We'll take you ourselves, right now.'

'No. I want . . .' Her eyes closed.

Joe frowned at Ellie. Futile or not, they had to try.

*   *   *

They needed to rig up a makeshift stretcher. A sudden itching in his throat made Joe cough: there was a foul taste in his mouth. He glanced over his shoulder, noting with relief that Glenn was still unconscious, and then he spotted a tiny swirl of smoke drifting up from Glenn's hair. Beyond him, the bright orange glow of embryonic fire, rapidly taking hold of the carpet.

484

'Oh Christ. Come on.'

Joe pushed his hands beneath Diana, braced his legs and lifted her into his arms while Ellie tried to maintain pressure on the chest wound. Diana didn't react to the movement, her limbs flopping under the weight of gravity. The sofa beneath her was drenched with blood.

Ellie had been protesting about the urgency until she saw the flames and understood. One of the armchairs was blistering and smouldering. She moved alongside Joe and they staggered and bumped out of the room, the smoke already irritating their lungs.

You want the house to burn, a malicious voice told him. *It destroys the evidence.*

*　　　*　　　*

They'd reached the kitchen before Ellie was able to grab his arm and twist round into his path.

'Don't stop. What are you doing?'

'Joe, I think she's dead.'

Crossly he shook his head, took another step as though he might blunder straight through her. Ellie held her ground. Joe looked down at the body in his arms. He didn't object when Ellie grasped Diana's arm and felt for a pulse.

'Nothing,' she said.

Joe carefully set Diana down on the floor. He'd known from the moment he saw her that it was probably hopeless: the kind of medical help she needed was simply too far away. There would be no helicopters available in a storm like this; no paramedics within easy reach.

They had lost her.

'What did she mean about the cutlery drawer?' Joe was thinking aloud, wondering if there was some sort of medicine, something that could save her.

He couldn't find a pulse at Diana's neck, couldn't detect a heartbeat or respiration. But he went on searching for signs of life, while Ellie groped in the darkness and located the drawer. The cutlery was stored in a plastic tray. She lifted it on to the counter and riffled through the contents, then checked the drawer again, and Joe heard a tiny exclamation: 'Oh.'

He didn't ask what she'd found. He didn't much care. It couldn't help Diana now.

Ellie returned to him as he stood up. There was a small white envelope in her hand. She was shaking violently as the adrenalin rush subsided and shock took hold.

'I don't know how it happened. Glenn pushed me and . . .'

'You did nothing wrong, Ellie.' Joe held her by the shoulders, bringing his face only an inch or two from hers, close enough to see the horror in her eyes. 'You were trying to save her. Glenn would have killed you both.'

Ellie nodded dumbly. Joe wasn't sure if she was really hearing him. But then she said, 'Kamila?'

'She's dead, I'm afraid. There was another woman in the tunnel. In a bad way, but I think she'll survive.'

'And Leon?'

'Seriously injured. If he does pull through he may have brain damage.'

486

Another blank nod. Then a wash of light cut across the window and dipped out of view. They heard the growl of a car engine.

At first Joe was confused, as though the trauma of the past few minutes had wiped his memory. Who would be coming here now?

Fortunately the amnesia didn't last. The answer was only too obvious.

'Danny Morton,' he whispered.

* * *

Joe took a look out of the back door. There was no one in sight. Around the corner of the house the engine died; above the sound of the rain he heard several doors open and close.

'We have to go over the back wall. Quickly.'

Ellie nodded. Taking her hand, Joe checked that the way was clear and hurried across the lawn. Trees and shrubs loomed out of the dark, forcing them to weave a zigzag path. The squelch of their feet on the grass seemed horrifically loud. Joe urged Ellie ahead of him, trying to shield her from any attack. He couldn't shake off the feeling there was someone breathing down his neck.

Reaching the wall, he glanced back. The garden was impenetrably dark, the house a dim outline, blurred by the thick grey smoke pouring from the chimney.

Ellie needed a boost to get onto the wall. Joe laced his hands together to make a step. She cut herself as she grabbed for the top, sucked in a breath but said nothing.

Joe hauled himself up after her, his foot slipping as he scrambled for purchase. He got one knee onto the top, and for a second he was lying flat, his other leg still dangling. *Almost safe*, he was thinking.

Almost—but not quite.

CHAPTER NINETY-TWO

The figure just materialised. A man in rain gear, with the hood up. He raced to the wall and grabbed Joe's foot, only then looking up to see who he'd caught. That was when Joe spotted the distinctive scar on his cheek.

Danny Morton. An incredulous smile crept onto his face: he'd struck the jackpot. For half a second, neither of them moved.

Then Danny roared, 'Over here,' and his hand went to his pocket for a weapon. Joe tried wrenching his foot free, but from his prone position on the wall he couldn't get enough force or leverage. Already there were answering shouts from across the garden: Morton's men coming in fast.

Joe thought about rolling onto Danny, taking him on hand to hand. An unwinnable fight, but at least it might enable Ellie to get away. Morton's gang had no dispute with her, after all.

He had to be quick. Danny's hand was already coming up, now holding a gun. Then he felt Ellie step past him on the wall. She kicked out with a savage whip-crack motion, like a cancan dancer, her foot striking Danny full in the face. He stumbled back, losing his grip on Joe, who drew his leg up and rolled over the wall.

Ellie jumped at the same time, and they landed almost on top of each other. They dashed along the footpath, stumbling and splashing in deep puddles. Once again Joe moved behind Ellie, encouraging her forward. A shot rang out. Both of them ducked instinctively; Ellie screamed but kept running. Just shock, Joe told himself. She hadn't been hit.

Another couple of shots, way off target: Morton firing blindly into the dark.

'Land Rover,' Joe muttered, thankful that he'd left it unlocked. He found the key, wrenched open the driver's door and had the engine running by the time Ellie had thrown herself into the passenger seat.

As he pulled away he saw movement on the footpath—Danny Morton and one of his men running towards them. Danny slowed, went into a crouch and took aim, but Joe floored the accelerator and steered the Land Rover away from his line of fire.

'Are you all right?'

Nothing from Ellie. She wasn't moving.

'Are you hurt? Ellie! Are you shot?'

'I'm okay. Winded.'

The promenade was directly ahead, a white sheen of spray bursting above the sea wall. Joe positioned the Land Rover for a right turn but Ellie gasped, 'Go left.'

He took her advice. She knew Trelennan much better than he did. Having come so close and failed a second time, Danny and his men would be scouring the town. Ellie and Joe weren't out of danger yet.

*   *   *

489

'How do we double back up the hill?' he asked. They were on Crabtree Lane, where he'd first encountered Alise and Derek Cadwell. He'd warned Ellie about the roadblock being set up on the main bridge, and now they needed an alternative route.

'We don't,' she said, leaning towards him to peer through the screen. 'Look for an opening on your right.'

He eased up on the accelerator as the headlights picked out the entrance to a farm track. Trusting that Ellie knew where it led, he swerved across the road. The rain had churned the track to mud, and the steep gradient was a challenge even for the Land Rover. Realising that stealth was preferable to speed, Joe dropped to ten miles an hour and turned off his lights, rendering them invisible to anybody on Crabtree Lane.

Eventually they crested the hill, heading south-west, and passed a collection of farm buildings. Another mile and they reached a minor road that would enable them to travel east again, bypassing Trelennan completely.

As they eased out of the junction, Joe switched the Land Rover's lights back on. Ellie slowly exhaled, inspecting the vehicle as if seeing it for the first time.

'Where did you get this?'

'Patrick Davy. He helped me up at Leon's.' Joe waited a second. 'I might need you to return it for me. In due course.'

'Okay. Fine.' Her turn to pause. 'Where are we going now?'

'Bristol. I know someone there who'll help us. We can clean up, get a change of clothes.'

490

Ellie looked down at herself. Like Joe she was wet and muddy. The rain had washed some of Diana's blood from her arms, but there was a huge dark stain on her cardigan.

'I suppose the longer we're away from Trelennan, the better.' A tiny gasp as a thought struck her. 'Will I go to jail?'

'It's unlikely. My advice is to say nothing. Danny Morton won't be putting the fire out. By the time anyone reaches the house I doubt there'll be much forensic evidence left.'

Then a sombre silence: both of them reflecting on Diana's fate. Joe sensed Ellie wrestling with the morality of not coming forward.

'What about Patrick Davy?'

'His version of events should be supported by Jenny, the girl we found. And I suspect Clive Fenton will be only too happy to blame Leon and Glenn for everything.'

Ellie nodded. The mention of her ex-husband's name made her shiver.

'I had no idea what he was doing,' she said. 'I want you to know that.'

'I believe you.'

'Not everyone will, though.' She sighed. 'Maybe I'll move back to Oxford.' A glance at Joe. 'Where will you go, after Bristol?'

'I have no idea.'

*   *   *

They stopped to refuel near Launceston, close to the Devon border. Used the restroom to clean up as best they could. Joe dug a couple of sodden ten-pound notes from his jeans and stretched them

491

out under the hand dryer for a couple of minutes.

Back in the Land Rover, Ellie brought out a small white envelope. It was the one that Diana had urged them to find. Inside was a sheet of thick, expensive notepaper, folded in half. Ellie opened it, frowned, then passed it to Joe.

He recognised the handwriting at once. The note was addressed to Diana, but the most important address—that of the note's author—was absent.

The message was brief: *So very sorry that we haven't been in touch for so long. I wish I could explain, but life has become unbearably complicated. Please don't show this to anyone, or tell anyone about it. I know how much you must miss Roy. We're all thinking of you today. With love, Helen, Joe and the girls.*

Joe read it again, and then a third time, before he could tear his gaze away. Then he remembered the envelope. He took it from Ellie and studied the postmark. It was smudged and faded, but it seemed to have been sent from the Gatwick mail centre in December 2008.

The anniversary of Roy's death, Joe realised. By that point he'd been living apart from Helen for more than two years. And yet she had chosen to include him in the message, creating the illusion that they were still together, still one happy family.

Had that been for Diana's sake, he wondered, or for Helen's?

*   *   *

Sensing Joe's excitement, Ellie gently took the letter from his hand and examined it carefully on both sides.

492

'Tunbridge Wells,' she said.

His head snapped up. 'What?'

'There's a watermark. Look.' She held the notepaper up, tilting it to catch the light. In the bottom right-hand corner Joe could make out a line drawing of an elegant colonnade. 'That's the Pantiles, in Tunbridge Wells.'

'Really?'

'I think so. Just the sort of area where you'd buy expensive stationery.'

He took the letter back, stared at it for a long time. Ellie smiled, enjoying his obvious delight. Finally she nudged him. 'Are you going to tell me what it means?'

Joe looked up. 'I don't know if it means anything. But it's a place to start.'

ACKNOWLEDGEMENTS

Many thanks to my editor, Rosie de Courcy, who helped immensely in improving my working practices and thus getting this book finished in record time! Thanks also to Nicola Taplin, Trevor Dolby, Nick Austin, Justine Taylor, Louise Campbell, Kate Elton, Rob Waddington, Jennifer Wilson and Andrew Sauerwine.

At Janklow & Nesbit, I'm indebted to my agent, Will Francis, as well as to the great team there: Rebecca, Kirsty, Tim, Claire and Jessie.

The usual thanks are due to family, friends and first readers: particularly Niki, Claire and Tracy, and not forgetting James and Emily. And a very special thank you to Andrea Best.

The town of Trelennan is entirely fictional, but one of its landmarks was inspired by the genuine and quite extraordinary Shell Grotto in Margate, Kent. For more information, visit www.shellgrotto. co.uk.